Nicely Out of Tune

Julia Florrie

First published 2024
by Rowanvale Books Ltd
The Gate
Keppoch Street
Roath
Cardiff
CF24 3JW
www.rowanvalebooks.com

A CIP catalogue record for this book is available from the British Library.

ISBN: 978-1-83584-001-6
Hardback ISBN: 978-1-83584-002-3
eBook ISBN: 978-1-83584-000-9

Nicely Out of Tune is the title of Lindisfarne's unbelievably good debut album.

This book is dedicated to my wonderful family.

Chapter 1

July 1970

"Why not?" Eirwen asked, her beautiful face distorted with annoyance.

"I don't like discos," I responded evenly, hoping not to fall out with her over something so trivial.

"You've only been to one."

"And?"

"You can't make a sweeping statement after one disco."

"Who says?"

"Be reasonable," Eirwen coaxed. *As if she ever was.* "It was just a school disco with silly boys and squash. But next week's disco is at the rugby club."

"So?"

"There'll be alcohol and men."

"As if that makes a difference."

"And women and girls," she said with a cheeky grin.

I huffed and gave her a glare. "It's quite simple. I don't like discos."

"But you like music and dancing," she said, unperturbed by my now obvious irritation. "How many times have I caught you in your bedroom having a *Top of the Pops* Pan's People moment to a Led Zeppelin or Rolling Stones track?"

"And?"

"Well, that's what discos are about, music and dancing."

"Discos are cattle markets."

Eirwen had to lean against the wall from laughing so much. I wanted to throttle her.

"Aw, M, you're such a fuddy-duddy," she managed to say, sounding more of one than me. I folded my arms, gritted my teeth and waited. I was unlikely to get off so lightly.

Eirwen stood away from the wall, hoisted her satchel back onto her shoulder and changed tack. "I'll speak to you tomorrow when you're in a better mood. And you'd better watch out in case the wind changes and your face gets stuck like that."

Before I had a chance to answer, Eirwen breezed off down the side street that led to her house. "Bye," she called with her back to me, wiggling her fingers.

I turned away and stomped up the main road to my house at the top of the hill.

She always manages to get the last word in, I thought and slammed the gate shut. At which point my father appeared from around the side of the house.

"What did that gate ever do to you?" he asked.

"Oh, sorry, Dad," I said, looking back at the gate dolefully.

He put an arm around me. "I was joking," he said. "Bad day at the office?"

I managed a small smile.

"School is one long break-time now that exams have finished. Noughts and crosses, hangman, boxes and cards in our form rooms and athletics outside. We're all just biding time till the end of term."

"There are worse things you could be doing."

"Very true," I said, with the makings of a proper grin. "You're home early," I added.

"I left work to post a pile of office mail, and despite the queues there, I still managed to get the earlier bus."

"Well done, Dad."

"Right, I'm off down the allotment," he said. "Your mother left a note. I'm to get some potatoes and lettuce to go with the boiled ham and beetroot for tea."

"Oh, yum," I said, alongside him in the scullery as he pulled on his wellingtons. "Where's Mam then?"

"Down the road. Jane Davies is doing her grade whatever tomorrow and wanted an extra lesson."

"Okay. I'll get the rest of the salad together and lay the table." Dad responded with a thumbs up and headed out.

I should have changed and got on with my tasks but I needed a moment or two in the parlour first. In the perpetually chilly room at the front of the house, I sat down at the piano. Although there to escape thoughts of Eirwen, seeing the piano prompted a memory of her lying on the top board, her glorious hair shimmering like silver against the dark wood of the cabinet… and her dropping down a leg to duet with me.

From the outset Eirwen had been intrigued by me learning to play the piano, asking endless questions about the keys, the pedals and the instrument's internal structure. Even the music books interested her. But she couldn't understand my need to practise because my mother was a piano teacher, as though the skill could be imbided or bestowed.

I shook off the memory and lay my cheek against the piano's closed lid, reaching round with my arms. It was an embrace of sorts. Savouring the scent of the polished wood, I contemplated what I'd play. A punch of Beethoven's fifth, a stab of *Carmina Burana* plus a couple of bars from Fleetwood Mac's "Oh Well" would certainly suit my mood. I raised the piano lid and played George Harrison's "Here Comes the Sun". It made me smile.

I loved my piano, my mother's piano, and whomever it had belonged to previously. I felt a connection with all those who had placed their fingertips on the cool ivory keys now beneath my own: a shared passion, pleasure, commitment. I was not alone when playing the piano.

***

By mid-morning the next day Eirwen was at the door suggesting an hour or two on the allotment.

"Changed your mind about the disco?" she asked as we passed on the pavement beneath the brooding bulk of the chapel.

"No. But it won't kill me to go with you. I grudge the money, though."

"Will you be wearing a hair shirt on the night, martyr Mari?" she asked while I undid the string on the allotment gates.

"Yeah, yeah," I said and pulled a face which prompted Eirwen to tug at my plait. I flipped a hand at her but she was already out of my reach and about to climb over the fixed gate.

She's for it, I thought, as Eirwen darted down the path to the lower half of the hillside. Climbing the gates was tantamount to a crime among the allotment stalwarts.

By the time I caught up with her, my father was dishing out penance tasks that somehow included me.

He handed us weeding and watering equipment. "Coffee in an hour," he said straight-faced and returned to the greenhouse.

"He does know that we don't mind helping out?" Eirwen said as she filled the watering can at the nearby standpipe.

"Of course he does. He's just making a show of reprimanding us for nosy Jones up there." I nodded towards the plot above and diagonally across from us, at the face gawping through a small gap in an impressive run of kidney bean plants.

"Yoo-hoo," Eirwen called and waved.

"Wen," I muttered through gritted teeth, sorely tempted to poke her with the hoe I was holding.

She grinned back at me. "What?" she said, all innocence.

An hour later we settled on an old rug with our backs pressed against the warm wood of the shed.

"Sunny summer days on the allotment always remind me of your *tad-cu*'s shop," Eirwen said.

"Really?"

"The air smells so sweet," she said.

"Yeah," I replied, still not getting the connection.

"Don't you remember the big jars of sweets on the high shelf?"

"Oh yes. Jars of sherbet lemons, pineapple chunks, pear drops, barley twists, mint imperials…" I could almost see the shop's dark wooden fixtures and fittings and my father's rotund parents behind the high counter.

"I still can't believe we got paid to help out in the shop," Eirwen responded. "All that weighing out of sweets and more gossip than you could remember. It was so much fun."

"Life was simpler then," I said with a smile.

"It was five years ago, not last century," Eirwen said. "You sound like an old woman."

Sadly, she was right. My *mam-gu* used to say I was old beyond my years. I'd been pleased at the time, thinking it was a compliment. Now I wasn't so sure.

"Right, I'm off home to help with Dad." Eirwen used my shoulder to lever herself up from the rug. "Bye," she called, and darted up the path.

It always amazed me how positive and upbeat Eirwen generally was. It was what I loved best and hated most about her. I looked and felt catatonic by comparison.

Eventually, I got up and made my way further down the hill to where my father was busy staking some leggy broad bean plants. On my approach, he paused in his task to stretch. "Shall we make a move and go home for dinner?" he asked.

"I fancy a walk down to the den, Dad. I'll catch you up."

"See you in a bit," he said.

I continued down the path that petered out at the boundary hedge, an almost impenetrable barrier of barbed and knotted branches of Disneyesque proportions. Given its proximity to the willow den, the hedge had loomed large in my and Eirwen's childhood games.

I ducked into the den. *Dad must love this place as much as we do,* I thought. *Ten years on and he's s still taking care of it.* Lying within the den's cool, leafy interior, I noted the familiar murmur of the nearby stream and the chatter of the sparrows busy in the hedge. Yet I kept returning to Eirwen's comments. *Fuddy-duddy, martyr, old woman…* Words delivered with humour, yet disparaging nonetheless.

However, Eirwen was wrong to even jokingly suggest that I didn't like boys. I genuinely fancied the pants off her elder twin brothers, as she knew only too well. I just didn't like discos and the way the boys stood around looking the girls over as though they were animals at a show.

Perhaps it would be best if I kept my fuddy-duddy opinions to myself, I considered, and ran up the path after my father.

Chapter 2

After another endless Monday at school largely spent outdoors with tennis, rounders, field events and lying around under the horse chestnut trees on offer, Eirwen and I were on our way home from the bus stop when she suddenly rounded on me.

"You know, that's a very irritating habit," she said accusingly, as if I was a blatant nose-picker.

"What do you mean?" I asked, quite affronted.

"If you're not singing, you're humming. If you're not humming, you're lah-lah-ing and/or tapping out a beat on something or other."

"Rubbish," I declared adamantly, convinced we'd just enjoyed a silent ten-minute interlude – and said as much.

"You don't even know you're doing it," she said in disbelief. "Not sure if that makes it better or worse."

"You've never mentioned it before," I replied, certain that the music – my own enjoyable tinnitus – remained in my head.

"I got used to it. Then I hoped you'd grow out of it. But you're eighteen now, and the tunes keep coming."

"I don't know why you bother with me at all," I said and huffed off up the road.

Eirwen increased her speed enough to grab the strap of my satchel and all but stopped me in my tracks.

"Ignore me, M. Just one of those days," she said, but I was already regretting my fit of pique.

I managed a silent moment or two with my hands deep in my blazer pockets.

"What?" she yelled, rattled by my lack of response.

"I'm trying to think of an appropriate tune," I replied, and laughed as she swung her arm to slap mine.

Eirwen rarely appeared upset. She was just more or less of herself. This could be a blessing and a curse.

"Have you asked your parents about the disco?" she said, changing the subject.

"Yes, I can go. Although why I agreed to in the first place, I don't know. Especially after all you said about the rugby club when you sneaked in there last year. What was it? Oh yeah, 'Packed to the rafters with beached whales and walruses.'"

"Well, I was in there at post-mortem time."

"What are you on about, Wen?"

She gave me a withering, long-suffering look. "I forget what deadbeats you Morgans are where rugby is concerned. Now, let me see. A post-mortem is a…" She paused, searching for an appropriate noun. "A discussion, i.e., who should have played and how they should have played. And it can last, intermittently, from one game to another. Years, in some cases. But the first stage usually takes place when the players are showering and the experts are pontificating at the bar."

"So?" I puffed, taking care not to stop or look her in the eye. I did not want to give her the opportunity of a frontal attack. Wen was easier to deal with from a distance. "Just old men talking," I added with what I hoped sounded like disdain.

She tried to overtake me, only too aware of the power of her gaze. "Not all old men," she said. "Mostly recently dropped thirds."

Eirwen was always skilled in the art of working me. I stopped and turned. She smiled.

"I'm not interested," I replied, despite an urge to ask what a "third" was, images of body parts lined up at the bar crossing my mind.

"They're the leery, beery has-beens who'd have a job bending down to pick up a ball, let alone run with one. A word of warning, M: never marry a rugby player. They tend to run to seed when they stop playing."

"I'll cross your Terry and Trefor from my list then."

"Ooh." She grabbed my arm. "Still lusting after my big brothers, eh?"

Her eyes danced as I coloured. Her six-foot-tall, dirty-blond-haired older twin brothers featured in my, and many others', fantasies.

Sadly, with the twins now working full-time shifts in the steel-works, I rarely had the chance to have one or other of them brush past me in the confined spaces of Eirwen's home, leaving me reeling in their wake – a heady mix of Old Spice and testosterone. I cherished their curt nods and grunts of "Mari" while imagining fevered kissing and caressing.

"Nothing they don't already know. They're used to silly schoolgirl crushes."

"Perhaps I need to spell out the depth of your affection," she crowed, her face alight with mischief. "Yeah, it might keep them at the table a bit longer than the ten minutes it usually takes them to bolt their food. She dropped her voice to a whisper and pulled me close, enjoying my now obvious panic. "You know, what you'd like to do to either one of them, being as you can't tell them apart."

"Look, I've said I'll go to the disco, so lay off with the threats."

"How dare you suggest such a thing!" She feigned a swoon. Then she slipped her arm through mine and outlined the arrangements for the following Friday as though my interest matched hers.

Chapter 3

"Smock top and jeans. You're joking. You must have something else to wear."

Before I had time to think, Eirwen was in my wardrobe, rattling coat hangers.

"I do and I've no intention of wasting it on Ponty Rugby Club."

"I'd forgotten about this." She waved a brown grandad-vest-style mini dress at me.

"I'm keeping that for a special occasion," I replied and snatched it from her. (I'd saved long and hard for a dress like that.)

"You got it last time we were in Cardiff," she said, unperturbed and rummaging again, her voice muffled. "C&A, wasn't it?"

"Yeah." I held the short-sleeved dress against my front and smoothed the soft fabric. "You bought me a lovely velvet choker to go with it."

"Oh, yeah, for your birthday. There's a pretty brooch thing on it." She emerged from the deeper recesses of the wardrobe, her hair wild with static. "Not much in there," she conceded.

"Yeah, well I don't have an older working sister lobbing cast-offs my way." I returned the dress to the wardrobe.

"Pity we're not exactly the same size." She looked down at her chest, then at mine. But I'd have sooner gone without altogether than be lugging that lot around in my bra.

"I'm glad of the jeans and trousers, Wen, even if I have to turn the hems up. But what are you going to wear?"

"My new tie-dye vest, cast-off midi skirt and boots."

"You'll never get past your mother in that outfit. The skirt's split up the front, and the vest is very skimpy," I said, sounding older than both our mothers.

"Let your hair down, Grandma," she teased and grabbed my plait. "I have a plan, don't you worry. Talking of hair…" She lifted my plait again. "I hope you're doing something different with yours."

"Yeah, thought I'd wear a bag over my head. Solve all my problems."

"That's the spirit," she said and caught me over the head with a discarded cardigan, wrestled me onto the bed and tickled a promise out of me to make an effort to enjoy the disco.

***

Trying to dry my hair without adding any further waves was generally a waste of time and involved too much looking in the mirror. Although, given my colouring, I had a lot to be grateful for. A girl in the upper-sixth science class at school, with the same sort of wavy auburn hair as me, burnt to a crisp in the sun whereas I tended to tan.

Perhaps it's because my eyes are brown and hers are blue, I considered, peering in the mirror. Then again, Eirwen – a blue-eyed natural blonde – was also inclined to tan. My dad reckoned it was because we'd spent so much time on the allotment. Claimed we'd weathered like fine timber.

With promises to be home on the last bus from Ponty, I hugged my parents and set off downhill to meet Eirwen. The weather was suddenly cold again for July, and I was wrapped up like a parcel, with a shirt on under my smock top and a second-hand, slightly-too-big velvet jacket over the lot. I expected laughter and derision from Eirwen – if she'd actually made it out of the door past her parents, that is.

However, visible on the corner of her street, Eirwen appeared to be as parcel-like as me, but only if you discounted the sheet of almost-white blonde hair that hung like silk around her shoulders. I anticipated news of parental intervention and an exasperated friend for company.

But her greeting smile was broad and she fairly buzzed with excitement. I noted the boots and the midi skirt (minus split) were in place but barely visible beneath a much-too-large raincoat, which was doubled across her chest and held in place by an equally large belt. Only Eirwen could pull off such an outfit. Still, it was a far cry from her planned apparel.

"Parental sabotage?" I asked as she threaded her arm through mine.

"Nope. Clever camouflage. Right, let's get going or we'll miss the early bus." Then she broke into a surprisingly brisk trot given the height of her platform boots and dragged me along like a small child.

On the way to Ponty, the split in Eirwen's skirt was reinstated with the removal of several small safety pins. She then tested the gap by crossing and uncrossing her long legs.

"That'll do," she said, suddenly aware of the attention she had attracted – not all of it positive.

"It's a good thing there's no one on the bus from Gwaun or news of that skirt would be home before you."

"Give over," she said with a poke to my ribs.

At the far end of town, we got off the bus to a chorus of wolf-whistles, applause and warnings regarding pneumonia and death of cold, none of which were aimed at me.

On the trek through the terraced backstreets of Ponty, we met some local girls from the year below us at school who were mightily impressed with Eirwen's skirt. As all three were wearing minis, they were exposing far more leg, but as one or other of them commented, Eirwen's skirt had the "now you see me, now you don't" factor. Whatever that was.

The access road and car park at the rugby club took some negotiating, pitted and pot-holed as it was and certainly no place for wearers of platform footwear.

With more noise and fuss than was necessary, we finally joined the small crowd gathered at the club entrance. The external double doors of the building opened into what was obviously a cloakroom area, where we were greeted by a lank-haired, middle-aged man in undersized trousers and a jumper, busy taking the tickets.

"Lovely to see you, girls," he shouted above the din audible through another set of double doors, his high colour as blatant as his beer belly.

The three younger girls and I removed our coats and had to search for hooks on which to hang them. In contrast, Eirwen slipped off her raincoat only to have it whisked away and secured on a suddenly available hook by a tall, handsome and unfamiliar young man.

"Well," said Angela, a plucky girl in white plastic platforms, mini skirt and peasant top. "Who was that? Houdini? And for my next trick…"

By which time the stranger was opening the next set of doors for us. Eirwen then quickly turned to mouth "Okay?" at me. I nodded but pulled what I hoped was a put-out face. Eirwen grinned in reply. There'd be no point complaining anyway.

Considering how early it was, the place was packed: evidence of how thin on the ground entertainment was in these parts. Dana warbled weakly from a dimly lit corner while Ponty's answer to Tony Blackburn, but with less shiny hair and teeth, endeavoured to adjust his disco lights.

"All kinds of everything remind me of you," Dana continued – The Eurovision Song Contest had a lot to answer for – while the largely disinterested occupants of the dance floor remained immobile.

"Ooh, I love this," said Susan. The three of us turned pitying eyes on her and she ceased moving to the music. Given the press of people around us, all seemingly intent on out-shouting each other, we'd progressed little from the doors.

"What is that smell?" Angela wrinkled her nose.

"I dunno," responded Pam, "but it sure as hell beats the stink of piss that greeted us at the entrance."

"Language, Pam," retorted Susan.

"Why don't you f—uh," Pam muttered as Angela's elbow connected with her ribs.

"That'll do, ladies," Angela said and sniffed again.

"Beer, BO, dirt and damp with undertones of Aqua Manda and Brut," I suggested.

"I think you may be spot on there, Mari," said Angela, "and it's certainly a pungent pong." She paused theatrically, certain of her audience, then added, "Alcohol is needed to take the edge off it."

"Words of wisdom, Ange," responded Susan, leading the push to the bar.

It's going to be a long night, I thought.

By the time I reached the girls, Angela was ordering drinks: a barley wine, a Babycham and a Pony... An eclectic mix worthy of note if not consumption.

"Mari?" Angela queried, as three pairs of eyes swivelled my way. I handed her two bob, or perhaps it was one of those new ten-pence pieces, and set my shoulders for scorn.

"Lemonade," I said defiantly.

Pam spluttered into her barley wine, while Susan's barely discernible eyebrows totally disappeared into her fringe.

"Heavy day on the allotment tomorrow, is it?" Angela responded, her mouth a mean line. "Or have you signed the pledge?"

The others sniggered.

"Spare me the sarcasm. I'll get my own drink." I held out my hand for the money.

"We're tolerant, aren't we, girls?" Angela plonked the coin in my hand. "Just don't start spouting the Bible at us." They all guffawed and grabbed at each other in an over-the-top display of amusement.

Well used to gibes relating to my former-chapel-minister maternal grandfather, I ignored them and set about trying to attract the barman's attention - not an easy task given the number of people all attempting to do the same. Shouting was essential, with the addition of swearing a fairly effective option, from what I could hear. But I couldn't be bothered and turned from the bar to scan the crowd for Eirwen and her magician friend.

By now the atmosphere in the club was tropical. The windows ran with condensation and the faded curtains, previously stiff with dirt and dust, had begun to wilt in the humidity. Attempting to move proved difficult on a floor as damp and sticky as the people pressed against me. Nevertheless, move I must, as not only was my shirt unnecessary, it was seriously compromising my *Mum* roll-on deodorant.

I'd told the others where I was going and headed for the cloakroom where I planned to remove my shirt and somehow get it into my jacket pocket.

By this time the DJ had found his groove. Lurid bubble-effect lights raked the room, and the volume of the music was set at somewhere between pound and perforate. The glass in the large picture windows that ensured an unobstructed daylight view of the pitch rattled in their frames as The Temptations belted out the lyrics to their latest charting single – which, ironically, was entitled "I Can't Get Next to You". With the surge to the dance floor, my exit was seriously hampered.

I pushed on but my path was blocked by a young man with unkempt, wavy hair and an engaging smile. I tried to sidestep around him, which was difficult, given the crowd and the fact that he mirrored my moves. Exasperated, I flapped my arms and leaned forward to shout in his ear.

"Excuse me. I'm trying to get past."

His smile broadened. It was the sort of smile a shark might sport prior to pursuit.

"You don' wanna leave." His smile slewed as he struggled to speak. "You wanna stay with me." Then he slid one hand around my waist and pulled me closer.

"Nice hair," he mumbled, en route to my mouth.

Engulfed in his beery, faggy breath, I levered him from me with both hands, which sent a ripple through the crowd as he lurched sideways. Unfortunately, he was propelled back towards me on a wave of profanity, his smile now a sneer.

"Frigid bitch," he called after me.

No stranger to such and similar terms of endearment, I had convinced myself that I was waiting for the right boy, the right mouth. Like the brown dress in my wardrobe, I was saving myself for the right moment.

I pushed through the first set of doors eager to shed some clothing. A blast of cooler air, regardless of whether or not it was urine-tainted, would have been welcome too. My hopes were dashed when faced with a snaking queue of sullen females, all bound for the facilities. Then I noticed Houdini loitering with intent near the exterior doors. Planning a quick getaway, no doubt.

"It's wrong there are only two toilets for us," said a disgruntled voice near the front of the line, "especially when I know there're five urinals for that lot."

An arm was extended in the general direction of the gents, where business was brisk – and more importantly, did not involve a queue.

"How do you know?" another disembodied voice queried.

"Know what?"

"How many urinals there are."

"Forms part of my extensive research into the male-biased provision of public conveniences," Disgruntled swiftly replied.

"I bet," said another voice, and the queue cackled.

Then Eirwen emerged from the door to the ladies, unsurprisingly turning heads as envious eyes noted her every detail. I was far from inured to her impact but I was familiar enough with it to notice that she was probably well on the way to being quite drunk. Knowing how little money she had brought, I had my first real misgiving about her companion.

We moved towards each other, Eirwen rolling like a galleon in a heavy sea while I extended my arms in case she floundered.

"Let's go home." I made to take hold of her arm, only to be intercepted by Houdini, who was really beginning to annoy me.

"She's with me." He slipped an arm around Eirwen's waist and hoisted her right arm over his shoulder. I tried to identify his accent. It wasn't local. Welsh, but only just. It was travelled Welsh. Army? Navy? Door-to-door salesman? Yes, I could imagine him menacing money out of vulnerable old people. What was Eirwen thinking?

"Ooh, you're so strong," my friend said and her head lolled against Houdini's shoulder.

I grabbed her left hand in both of mine and stood my ground.

"Wen, come home with me now. Please."

"Nah. Come with us, M. Glyn's got a van. You can go in the back." Eirwen sounded as though she was gargling with the individual letters of each word.

Her head rolled again as her captor prised my hands from hers, his fingers as hot as his eyes were cold.

"Leave 'em be," chipped in a raised voice from the queue.

"Yeah, piss off, you bully," braved another, and we were jostled as the queue became a crowd.

But Houdini (he wasn't a Glyn. Glyns were ordinary, nice and safe) was strong, sober and unencumbered by high heels, platforms and other fashion faux pas, and he swept Eirwen out of the doors as a wave of catcalls and abuse crashed around the entrance. But only I trickled out into the night in pursuit.

"Wen," I called, trailing behind them. "I'll wait at the bus stop. I won't go without you. We'll get a taxi. Wen, can you hear me?"

She raised an arm and wiggled her fingers as Houdini bundled her into the passenger seat of a dark-coloured van. I was trying to memorise the number plate when Houdini walked around the back of the van to the driver's side.

"Fuck off," he snarled.

"I'll call the police if she's not back for the last bus," I shouted, my voice as shaky as my body.

He glared at me for a moment, spat on the floor, then opened the door and got in.

As the van bounced and bobbed out of the pitted car park, I fleetingly considered following on foot. But like an animal caught in the glare of headlights, I was transfixed by the red glow of the solitary rear light. Perhaps I'd overreacted? I'd wait at the bus stop. It would be okay. But my mouth was dry, and despite my layered-on clothing I felt cold.

I returned to the clubhouse and rejoined the queue for the toilet. I checked my watch. It was quarter to ten… less than an hour till the last bus. Still, the time dragged.

Chapter 4

With Eirwen not amongst the raucous group at the bus stop, I leaned back against the wall and allowed myself the luxury of worrying whether or not she would be dropped here and whether or not I would see her on the bus when it eventually reached me.

A bus arrived, and all but one of the waiting crowd got on before it pulled away in a grind of gears and diesel fumes. The girl and I coughed and exchanged glances.

"Mari Morgan," she exclaimed.

"Hi, Karen."

"Been to the disco, have you? Where's your friend?" Her words came in a rush as she looked about for Eirwen.

"She'll be here for the last bus," I said with a conviction I didn't feel.

"Got off with someone, did she? No surprise there. That face, that hair, that body…" she continued, mimicking the size of Eirwen's chest with cupped hands. "And funny. God, the girl's got the lot."

Yes, and she's about to waste it on a stony-eyed sod called Glyn, I thought through my fixed smile.

Annoyingly, as though the events were unknown to me, Karen continued to reminisce about Eirwen and her "hilarious" exploits at school: the fake vomit and turds, the hairy rubber hand and the toy machine gun with the *uh-uh-uh* firing sound. I wanted to slap her into silence but on I smiled. Then she moved closer to me and checked over her shoulder and mine as though she were about to impart official secrets.

"Is it true?"

"Is what true?" I asked, worried that there might be even more to worry about.

"You know…" she said, digging me with her still-folded arms, "school, last year." She checked the area again, the soul of discretion. "I heard she nearly got expelled."

"Well, the truth is our whole year was nearly expelled," I said, which wasn't strictly true. I let out a sigh. Old sins, no new ones. Not yet, anyway. I took a sideways step away from her and hoped she'd take the hint.

No such luck. Karen moved in again with her smoke-laced whispers.

"Something to do with a condom, wasn't it?" she said, going all Frankie Howerd and mouthing the word "condom". Of course, she was right. And I'm certain our teachers (the majority of whom were elderly spinsters) had been traumatised by the sight of the used condom Eirwen had left hanging from the knob of the female staffroom door.

I nodded in reply, fairly sure Karen knew every last detail anyway. Eventually, she gave up quizzing me about Eirwen and we talked typing speeds, shorthand and her new job in a solicitors' office in Cardiff. Thankfully, her bus arrived, swiftly followed by mine – a single-decker minus Eirwen.

Fortunately, Karen had also talked of taxi ranks. Apparently, there was a number of a reliable firm written up on the information board in the telephone box around the corner. It was the number preceded by the letters *TR*. The other abbreviations were best avoided, by all accounts.

I decided to wait ten minutes. Then I'd ring Eirwen's house. Thankfully, my wait was curtailed when Eirwen appeared from around the corner. She was hunched over, her coat clutched to her like a life buoy. She seemed diminished.

I rushed forward and I gathered her to me. Momentarily, she was stiff in my arms. Then she relaxed and leaned against me. I whispered her name and finally she looked at me, silent tears tracking down her marked face.

***

The prompt arrival and speed of the taxi driver ensured we weren't far behind the bus when it deposited just two men at the bottom of the hill at Gwaun.

Eirwen and I pooled our money to cover the fare, and the taxi pulled away, leaving us huddled together on the pavement having said very little to each other. My father took in every detail but remained under the streetlamp, a hazy halo forming about him as a damp mist descended.

"Fighting again, Wen Watkins? Anything we need to inform the local constabulary about?" His tone was breezy, but he winced on turning Eirwen's marked cheek into the full glare of the lamplight. Eirwen managed a faint smile but did not reply.

"Wen," he urged, his voice sharper, probing the shutters Eirwen had dropped. "Do we need to do anything official about this?"

He looked at me. "Mari?" All manner of questions were contained therein, but I had no answers.

"*Ti'n iawn?*" (You're alright?) His voice softened as he spoke to Eirwen.

"*Iawn, diolch*, Mr Morgan." It was a barely audible whisper, but a response nonetheless.

My father and I relaxed. We were a curious tableau in the lamplight as the mist thickened to a heavy drizzle, our similarly themed thoughts holding us hostage.

"Stay at our house tonight, Wen. I'll call in and speak to your parents," Dad eventually said. Eirwen looked panic-stricken.

"I promise not to say anything about this," he continued, with a nod at her cheek, "if you promise to tell us the whole story tomorrow. *Iawn?*"

"*Iawn*," she replied sheepishly.

"Take her home, Mari."

Now it was my turn to panic. My mother would be over the phone box across the road before we got upstairs. My father chuckled.

"Mam is in bed. Billy Owen's efforts on the piano brought on one of her heads."

Phew, I thought. We didn't need my mother's pointed prying.

Eirwen was silent all the way home, and before long we were tucked in together in my room, despite there being a spare bed available in the room my *taid* and *nain* had shared.

I stared at Eirwen's shoulder, as steep and unassailable as any cliff face. On feigning sleep, I soon felt rather than heard her crying.

"Wen," I murmured, my grip on her shoulder conveying, I hoped, all the confidence of a seasoned climber. "Wen," I urged, making it clear I wasn't to be ignored. She sighed and turned towards me.

"I can't believe he hit you." I touched her cheek, which was just visible in the gloom of my room.

"He didn't."

"Come on, Wen, you'll have to do better than that."

"No, really. Cross my heart," she said, our proximity meaning that she crossed mine too.

"Like you used to cross your fingers behind your back to get out of a promise?"

Eirwen levered herself up onto an elbow. "*I* did this. Okay? I caught my cheek on the van door rushing to get out after I hit him."

"What? You hit him?"

"Yeah." She dropped back onto the bed. "I hit him hard, where it hurts, with a torch I found on the floor."

"In the…" I struggled with the word.

"Nuts, balls, goolies. Take your pick. That's where I hit him. Seemed to think being nice to me entitled him. As if he owned me. No one will ever treat me like that again."

Then she turned onto her side again and promptly fell asleep. But I struggled to relax, not sure that my friend had revealed exactly what had happened or how deeply she had been affected.

***

Thankfully, when Eirwen and I finally got up the next morning, my mother had already left for her first lesson of the day. So Mam wasn't present when a sanitised, pared-down version of the previous night's events was convincingly relayed to my father and, later on, Eirwen's parents. Apparently, we'd been offered and rejected a lift home, and Eirwen had knocked her cheek when shutting the car door. Scrutiny of her injury supported the story – there being a definite line across her cheek, from which now radiated a palette of purples along with the makings of a black eye.

However, the interrogative gaze my father directed at me suggested that he was not totally taken in by Eirwen's performance. His dilemma was evident, and I saw him waver before deciding not to rock this particular boat.

The smile of thanks I gave was tinged with guilt. Despite not having spoken a word about the event in question, my silence weighed as heavily as any uttered deceit. I was complicit, as usual.

Chapter 5

After dinner that afternoon, I was lying on my bed reading when a strange noise attracted my attention. At the window, I instinctively ducked down, and caught my knee on the ottoman in the process, as a second grass-and-mud missile made contact with the glass.

Then I spotted a purple-eyed Eirwen standing on the chapel wall as she prepared to lob a third projectile my way. I rapped on the window and glared down at her.

"Come on," she mouthed, gesticulating. Then she dropped down into the graveyard and headed for the gates. Luckily, I managed to escape the house unnoticed as my parents were busy in the parlour sifting through *Nain*'s old seventy-eight records.

"Well, that's a first," I said when I joined Eirwen outside the chapel. "I'm going to have a devil of a job getting the mud off the window."

"I couldn't face your mother with this." She made a stabbing gesture at her shiner. "You know what your mother's like," she continued, as though the whole pantomime was my fault.

"If your story's true, facing my mother shouldn't be a problem."

"Sermonising again. You know, I'm beginning to think that preaching runs in your family. On your mother's side, of course." Then she abruptly turned about and took off down the unmade track that led to the allotment gates.

"Get the coffee on," Eirwen said when I finally caught up with her, and she handed me the key she'd retrieved from the hook under the eaves of my dad's shed. I'd long since abandoned asking what her last servant had died of. Her retorts were always too sharp, and too close to the truth.

I opened the door and was enveloped by the shed's unique aroma: a blend of wood and earth and weather. Once I'd filled the small kettle at the nearby standpipe, I returned to the shed, lit the Primus stove and located the deep tin where the powdered milk and coffee were kept, by which time Eirwen was ambling further down the path to the den.

She reappeared as the kettle whistled its way to the boil.

"They've gone, then." Eirwen hooked a thumb at the empty space behind the door.

"To a good home," I said, referring to the now absent stack of comics. "A work colleague of Dad's has taken the lot. He has two daughters just the right age for the *Bunty* and its paper dolls."

"Do you mean we didn't cut up all those pages? Get them back, M," Eirwen said jokingly.

We grinned at the shared memory... the time we'd spent cutting and glueing, putting together the dolls and their hook-on clothing, matching paper outfits beyond our wildest dreams.

"You could spot the point in that pile of comics when we'd lost interest in the dolls and their dresses. When we were *Jackie*-ready," I said.

"You went through the pile."

"Yep, I'm ashamed to say."

"Always knew you were soft." She laughed. "I used to love those comics, mainly because your dad had gone against your mother to get them for us. It was such a thrill to sit at your dad's workbench with our contraband reading material."

"My mother has a real aversion to comics. No idea why, though."

"Goes to show how brave your dad is. Imagine actually daring to defy one of your mother's commandments."

"You do it all the time."

"Defy your mother? Me? Never," she said in mock horror.

Thinking Eirwen was now more amenable, I said, "So, who was the bloke at the disco?"

She huffed and moved away from me. "No one in particular." She folded her arms as though putting up a barrier to any further questions on the matter. But I asked anyway.

"Why do you keep doing that? Wasting your time on all and sundry."

"I think you'd be surprised," she said, suddenly subdued. "Possibly shocked."

"Tell me then, and you'll find out," I said, bothered by her shifting mood.

Eirwen quietly considered me for a moment, and I think she was on the point of telling me when she erupted.

"I manage to avoid a grilling by your mother to be subjected to one by you."

Then she yanked open the shed door and stormed off.

"You haven't drunk your coffee," I called pathetically after her.

"Stuff the coffee," she shouted, already halfway up the hill.

**

The next day I went to chapel for the first time in weeks, and I was glad to note that the minister's address continued to lack my *taid*'s memorable delivery, content and fervour. Eirwen reckoned the old biddies used to get off on my grandfather's North Walian accent and the fire and brimstone nature of his sermons. The girl had always been incorrigibly irreverent.

My attendance at chapel was mainly to please my mother. Yet it seemed fitting to make the effort – to properly say farewell to the place and all it had once meant to me. Nevertheless, I found being there strangely unsettling and imbued with a feeling of loss… of something gone forever. Was I troubled by the girl I'd been, or the woman I might become?

The parishioners were kind and wished me well with my course, as though my place at university was a foregone conclusion. I suppose I was fairly confident that I'd get the necessary grades, but I was also fearful of doing so. Contemplating the future filled me with a quiet dread that left me uncertain about the plans I'd made, and my part in them. I seemed to be hurtling uncontrollably towards a brick wall of my own making.

***

After dinner, I washed the dishes. Dad wiped and Mam set about making some Welsh cakes. When Dad finally bolted for the allotment, my mother said, "No Eirwen today?" and I hunched my shoulders noncommittedly.

"Perhaps she's poorly," Mam suggested with a look that made me wonder what exactly my father had divulged about Friday night. "I'll make extra cakes and you can take some down to her," she added kindly.

An hour later I knocked on Eirwen's door. Thomas, the youngest member of her household, let me in and relieved me of the tin I was holding.

"Wen," he called up the stairs before prising off the tin's lid. "It's Mari, bearing gifts." Then he popped a whole Welsh cake in his mouth and headed down to the kitchen, the tin tucked under his arm.

I stood awkwardly in the hall, unnerved by the quiet. The twins were probably at work, and Eirwen's mam like as not. That left Thomas, Eirwen and her dad at home. Three people, the same number as at my house. But my house was rarely quiet. There was always music playing somewhere. If it wasn't the piano, it was the radio, or me playing records or my guitar.

Eirwen and I had habitually spent more time at my house because it was bigger. Even when my *nain* and *taid* were alive, there had been more room. And in the eight or so years since Eirwen's dad had been diagnosed with muscular sclerosis, we'd tended to spend even less time at her house. I felt hollowed out just thinking how tall, strapping Phillip Watkins had been diminished by his illness. Goodness knows how his family felt.

The silence was eventually broken by Eirwen tiptoeing down the stairs. She didn't speak but propelled me on to the kitchen where Thomas was devouring butter and jam Welsh cake sandwiches.

"There'd better be some left, Tom." Eirwen relinquished her hold on me to peer into the tin.

"She's a right bossy-boots when Mam's at work," Tom directed at me. "Nice cakes," he added between bites. "Want one?" He held the tin out to me.

Eirwen grabbed the tin and almost dropped her own cake. "Don't waste one on her. She's got a constant supply at home."

"Which is true," I said, "but thanks for asking, Tom."

He smiled at me and then poked his tongue out at Eirwen.

"Clear off," Eirwen said.

"I was going anyway," Tom said with a parting grimace for his sister.

"Your dad okay?" I asked her, knowing he wasn't likely to be.

Eirwen ignored my inane question. "He likes a game of chess after dinner, and it always puts him to sleep. I stayed long enough to make sure he was comfortable and safe."

Her words brought home to me the weight of responsibility she carried, yet she had spoken without a shred of self-pity. This was everyday life for Eirwen and she embraced it without complaint.

"I'll give your house a miss until my eye improves," she added matter-of-factly and tentatively touched her cheek.

I tried to mirror her manner, to not become emotional, fighting an urge to hug her to me and howl.

"But you can come here if you like. Bite?" And she offered up her second Welsh cake to me.

***

I stayed longer than I had intended and helped Eirwen to prepare vegetables to accompany the casserole she was to reheat for the family if her mam wasn't back when the twins returned from work. I was no stranger to household tasks, but since her sister's move to Cardiff, Eirwen's duties had certainly escalated.

Dad was laying the table for tea when I returned in a sombre mood.

"*Iawn?*" he asked, and I merely nodded before lending a hand.

With Mam being the chapel organist, we usually ate our Sunday roast for dinner, between services, that is. Mealtimes for Eirwen and her siblings were as changeable as Megan Watkins' work was unpredictable.

She was the district midwife, which meant that the family home boasted not only a telephone but a car, something of a rarity at the time. Nevertheless, a chronically ill father meant financial constraints and a seize-the-day mentally, particularly with the younger two children, Eirwen and Thomas.

"Eirwen alright?" Dad ventured at my ongoing silence.

"You know Eirwen. Much as she always is."

"Mm," he said noncommittally, although he knew as well as I did that only a fraction of what was really going on with Eirwen was generally evident.

On my mother's return, I told her about Thomas and his Welsh cake sandwiches.

"And Eirwen is well?" she asked.

"Well enough to squabble with Tom over your cakes," I replied, and my mother smiled at the news, and the compliment, no doubt.

Chapter 6

We whooped when we got off the school bus for the last time. Then Eirwen tore off up the hill while I trailed behind, giddy with laughter as she gasped and spluttered through the age-old anthem of school children everywhere:

"Build a bonfire, build a bonfire. Put the teachers on the top. Put the prefects in the middle and burn the bloody lot."

Eirwen then swung her relatively empty satchel around her head and let it go. It was airborne a short while before hitting the pavement and belting downhill like a bobsleigh.

Then she surprised me by darting down to retrieve the now stationary bag herself, neglecting to order me to get it.

I watched her brush debris and dust from the satchel and check for damage, as though tending a small child. Once satisfied, she held it to her chest and returned to me.

"One of the only two leather satchels in our house," she said, which was unusual for her – explaining her actions, that is. "Dad was well and working when he bought two for the twins to start grammar school. The next three were cloth and plastic. Horrible things," she added, patting the satchel. Then she sped up and began singing again. "Build a bonfire, build a…"

She was misty-eyed and I knew better than to offer any support, verbal or physical. She didn't always respond well, so I waited. Eventually, she turned to me and smiled. It was like the sun breaking through heavy storm clouds. Warmed, I smiled back. She squeezed my arm, threaded hers through mine and pulled me to her.

"See you later, alligator," she sang, still off-key, and I duly returned with, "After a while, crocodile," the answering line from the Bill Haley and His Comets hit we'd loved so well, so long ago. I was surprised and touched that Eirwen remembered our once habitual way of parting company. It was a good note on which to end our school days.

***

Later, after tea, we were squashed together on my bed and Eirwen was chattering excitedly about leaving home and our new life in Cardiff. My heart sank.

"What's up?" she eventually asked. It had taken her long enough to notice my silence.

"I'm not sure I want to go."

"You are joking." She levered herself up onto an elbow and scowled down at me, still prostrate on the bed.

"Far from it."

"So, you're staying here. With your parents. Watching *Going for a Song* and *Noggin the Nog*. Until the kids you teach at Sunday school have kids of their own. And you are old and sick." Eirwen's words came out in heated, stilted phrases. You'd think I'd suggested that she should remain with me.

"The waste. The sheer waste of talent. Of life. You need to get out of this cosy nest of comfort. This backwater valley." She grabbed my upper arms and pulled me up from the bed.

Eirwen was quite breathless from her railing tirade when she eventually released her hold on me to get off the bed. She stood stiffly with her back to me, arms folded, and looked out at the graveyard below that stepped by the steep hillside.

"Aren't you just a little bit scared about it all?" I dropped my feet to the floor but remained perched on the edge of the bed like a reluctant swimmer at a poolside.

Eirwen turned away from the window and fixed me with a glacial glare. "What d'you think?"

Of course, she wasn't scared, of anything. Eirwen was a grabber – of attention, chances and life. She wouldn't stagnate here for anyone. And she wasn't about to let me do so either.

She sat down on the ottoman directly opposite me and took a deep breath.

"At the end of August, I'm going to the Isle of Wight Music Festival and I want you to come with me," she said evenly, as though suggesting a trip down to Ponty.

I laughed. "I'm scared about going to Cardiff. I'm hardly likely to agree to leave the country."

"It's just for the weekend. It'll be a trial run. A break from this place, and then perhaps you'll be happier about going to Cardiff." She moved to sit alongside me on the bed.

"We won't be allowed to go," I said, certain our parents would veto such an undertaking. My trump card, I thought.

"That's why we won't tell them. I've got it all worked out." And as she outlined her plan, I could see the hunger in her eyes, how much she wanted this and *all* its possibilities.

"We can't," I stammered, fearful of not just the consequences, but the whole idea.

"Oh, we can. We will. Imagine seeing The Doors, Jimi Hendrix, Free, The Who and loads more." She took hold of my hands and squeezed them tightly. "Live music, M. Not like on the telly. But in the flesh."

To feel the music, to witness the effort of endeavouring to recreate studio recordings of songs that were merely mimed to on *Top of the Pops*… I imagined it feverishly, suddenly engaging with the idea, swept up by Eirwen's enthusiasm. Live music. Live rock music. Eirwen's trump card, as it turned out to be.

"The end of August? We won't get tickets now," I said, downcast yet somehow relieved.

"Oh, ye of little faith. I got tickets months ago." She wiggled my arm and whooped with satisfaction at my stunned expression.

When Eirwen left, I paced around my room jittery with nerves. I should tell my parents, I reasoned, certain it was the right course of action. But I was reluctant to wreck Eirwen's plans, which confessing to my parents would surely do. So, I did the only thing I could do and wrote a morale-boosting memo in tiny letters on my wardrobe noticeboard.

Actually, the "noticeboard" was just a long sheet of wallpaper folded over the top of the door and secured on the inside with Sellotape. I used it to display timetables, notes, et cetera, without marking the external woodwork. My mother considered it to be quite innovative at the time, in that age before Blu-Tack. Eirwen thought it restrictive and retentive, much like my mother. Her bedroom walls, along with some of the furniture, were plastered with posters and photos.

"*Noli timere*," I said out loud to my empty bedroom, unnecessarily searching out the words as though they actually possessed the power to make me as fearless as Eirwen. *Don't be afraid*. Easier said than done.

The next day, Eirwen tapped the wardrobe door.

"What's this?" She pointed to my minute missive. "Isn't that Latin?" Then her face lit up as she recalled the meaning of the phrase. "I couldn't have put it better myself." She gave me a squeeze.

Chapter 7

So began the lies that allowed us to attend the festival, but the number of times I developed cold feet increased apace with our deepening deceit. The goody-two-shoes part of me (Eirwen's term, of course) continued to yearn to tell my parents, to ask for permission to go. But the desperate-to-go, previously unknown reckless part of me vetoed the idea. My parents would not allow me to go.

When I voiced my concerns, Eirwen said, "Forget it, then. Ifor Jones down in Ponty is pestering me to buy our tickets. Offered three pounds ten shillings each. Seven pounds, mind." As if I couldn't add up.

"Like he said, it would be worth it to see Hendrix, The Doors, The Who, Free, Jethro Tull, Family, The Moody Blues…" she continued, almost reeling off the entire weekend's line-up without a pause for breath. But her winning card was Desert Heat. I was desperate to see Brendan Bradshaw's band. By the time she said the name, I'd have denied knowing my parents rather than let Ifor Jones have my ticket. Even if he offered ten quid for it.

Eventually, our cover story was fairly watertight. We were to spend Friday and Saturday night in Cardiff with Eirwen's older sister, Rhian, who was a nurse at Cardiff Central Hospital. We were going on the pretext of getting to know a little of the city prior to us taking up our university places in September. We'd actually spoken to Rhian and gained her approval of such a visit. We just hadn't specified when we'd be going. Providing Rhian made her usual weekly phone call home on a Monday at eight-thirty (unless she was on nights, which she wasn't that week), we'd be alright. We'd also decided that we'd ring home on the Sunday to reveal our true whereabouts when it was evident that we weren't back from Cardiff.

The biggest concern for us was the possibility of anyone checking our story, which, beyond Eirwen's mother confirming with Rhian that she was happy for us to stay, no one did. In fairness to Megan Watkins, she had a lot more than most on her plate. But my parents? What was their excuse? That they trusted me, of course. Deceitful child that I'd become.

No one could know that during our lengthy phone calls to Rhian from the local phone box, Eirwen's mam's phone being for work only, we never once pressed button A. Had we done so, our money would have been retained and our call connected. No, button B was our choice, which returned our coins for further feigned calls to Rhian.

That Thursday I was supposed to be at Eirwen's with her, and she at mine with me. In reality, we were camped in our borrowed tent in Ifor Jones's back garden, so as to get the first train out of Ponty down to Cardiff. It was a very early start and the first of three different train rides to Southampton, where we'd get the ferry to Cowes.

I found it very difficult saying goodbye to my parents. Despite the many lies I'd already told them as we wove our obviously credible web of deceit, it didn't get any easier.

"Look after yourself and be careful," were my mother's final tearful words while my father pressed a five-pound note into my hand. Suddenly short of breath and my eyes full, I just managed to kiss them both.

"You'll be fine," said my father, thinking I needed reassurance. "Cardiff's just down the road."

I was about to tell them the truth when Eirwen breezed in through the gate to greet my parents in turn and drag me away.

"Wave and smile," she ordered through gritted teeth. I choked back my guilt and duly did as directed.

***

Given the level of planning and preparation we'd put into getting to the Isle of Wight, the lack of thought we'd given to what we'd eat, drink and wear once at the festival was staggering. But we weren't alone. Our fellow festivalgoers were equally ill-prepared. In fact, our collective lack of foresight was only outmatched by that of the organisers of the event.

I have an image of us trudging along the main road that connects Freshwater and Newport, newly flared jeans flapping around our bare ankles, thin-soled daps blistering our feet. The level of needlework we formerly reluctant seamstresses had indulged in prior to our departure should have rung alarm bells for our parents. The hours we'd spent cutting dark denim triangles from old jeans to insert into the partially opened seams of our recently purchased stonewashed versions should have raised more than just eyebrows in our respective homes.

The ferry journey to Cowes proved to be a real eye-opener, surprisingly as much for Eirwen as for me. And it had nothing to do with travelling on water; the sea was millpond calm. Suddenly, we were aware of how very far from home we were, and not just in miles.

Eirwen grasped my shoulders and steered me to the stairs.

On the top deck she spotted a bloke painted up like Arthur Brown at his craziest. "They can't all be freaks and weirdos, can they?" she asked.

"I wouldn't bet on it." I nudged Eirwen, but her gaze was still trained on Arthur. I nudged her again and hooked a thumb at a group of people wearing elaborate hats and feathers and very little else.

"Avert your gaze, M. Such sights are not intended for chapel-going girls." Eirwen giggled and attempted to cover my eyes.

We spent the rest of the crossing pressed against the upper deck rail taking in the sea air – which was a marked improvement on the *weed* air of below deck – while on the lookout for "normal" people. There were few. And we had thought our two-toned flared jeans were far out… about as far out as my outhouse.

Once we'd disembarked, all those festival-bound were rounded up, corralled and bussed out of town westwards. We walked the last mile or so, our meagre belongings bagged up and hanging about our necks like yokes, chafing our sunburnt skin.

We ate what was to be our last meal for nearly twenty hours at the chippy at Freshwater after a lengthy wait in the meandering queue. Generous portions of fish and chips were consumed, washed down with dandelion and burdock. What remained of the brown beverage was to be the following day's breakfast. We'd probably have exercised a little restraint in our liquid consumption had we been aware, that Friday, of the extortionate prices at the site on Afton Down.

During the run-up to the trip, Eirwen and I had been preoccupied with the logistics of the journey and the details of the necessary deception. We'd not discussed what we expected of the festival, other than seeing our musical heroes. I suppose we envisaged something akin to the National Eisteddfod: a full-on event on a grand scale, by Welsh standards. How wrong we were.

We stalled as we approached the entrance to the campsite, staggered by the evidence of occupation. A vast tapestry of canvas, cars, people, vans and litter spread out on either side of the road and up the hill behind us. But the biggest shock was the perimeter fence of metal sheets surrounding the arena, patrolled by men with dogs.

"Shit. It looks like a psychedelic concentration camp."

A nearby voice echoed our thoughts, but it was the accent that turned our heads.

"Ron! Brian!" Eirwen shouted in disbelief.

"Wen? Wen Watkins?" was the amazed response.

We gravitated together out of necessity as the growing crowd encroached.

As was proper, we shook hands – vigorously. I'm sure the boys thought, *Right, that's the catering sorted. Wonder if there's any chance of a snog, a grope or maybe more?* But their bewilderment at seeing us there overrode their baser instincts.

Although we had all attended the same grammar school in Ponty, we were on different sites. No mixing of the sexes in valley grammar schools.

"*Uffern dân,*" said Ron incredulously. "You're two of the last girls from Gwaun I'd have expected to see. How'd you get round your parents?"

"We didn't even try," Eirwen said.

"You're for it when you get home, then. Do they have any idea where you are? Or have they already got the plod out combing the countryside for your bodies?" said Brian.

The enormity of what we'd done suddenly hit me like a bag of bricks. I almost reeled.

"They'll not be concerned because we organised this trip so as not to worry them. It took courage, cunning and—"

"Balls," cried Ron and he slapped Eirwen on the back. "C'mon, let's get in and find a pitch before it gets dark." Then he hitched his rucksack high on his shoulder and picked a path through the melee to join the queue at the entrance.

With the tents pitched we relaxed and soaked up the scene, the sound, the squalor – and we starved as we drank in the monumental occasion. When the others considered it wasn't worth the effort of struggling to the stage, or if the resident DJ was playing T. Rex's "Ride a White Swan" *again*, we'd lie around outside the tent and talk, conserving our energy and limited supply of liquid. The acquisition of the latter required a trek of expeditionary standards, with little guarantee of success. Nevertheless, there was a plus side to dehydration: less need to use the foul facilities.

A kaleidoscope of human emotion and behaviour was on display at that festival – the full spectrum, ranging from compassion to gratuitous violence, from care and consideration to total disregard, and all points in between.

Much since has been made of the violent episodes that occurred, the disorganisation, the greed and poor performance of some of the stars. However, it's not how I remember it. But then I was there for the music, nothing more. And in that, I was not disappointed.

Obviously, recollections of youth involve rose-tinted glasses, but nothing can detract from the facts. There were no deaths, and in excess of half a million people cohabited under extremely primitive conditions and largely enjoyed themselves. It was described at the time as being "the biggest gathering of humankind". And it certainly felt like it.

***

That Friday night, when we finally settled down, we slept like logs, which was just as well as the next, almost endless day was packed with a plethora of surreal moments. Free were fabulous with Paul Rogers's voice as skin-tinglingly good as Paul Kossoff's guitar playing. In contrast, the imminent implosion of The Doors, and ultimately the death of Jim Morrison, was evident in the band's lacklustre performance.

Tiptoeing through the tulips, Tiny Tim's routine proved more memorable, I'll wager, than anticipated by anyone present that Saturday. He somehow managed in the unforgiving sunshine to get the best part of the audience swinging, swaying and singing their hearts out to "Land of Hope and Glory" and "There'll Always Be an England".

Yet a section of the same crowd behaved rather badly towards Joni Mitchell. All credit to the lady, she rose above the heckling and abuse and told a soothing story then soldiered on through her set.

What made for strange listening was the misplaced berating of the audience by one of the comperes. To the amazement of those present, the man took to the stage and harangued us about the ongoing intermittent attacks on the perimeter fence and the resulting clashes with the security force. All of which took place on the outside of the offending barrier, obviously. And at that stage of the festival all those present in the arena, and having to listen to Ricky Farr's tirade, had actually paid for their tickets.

By early Saturday evening, I could stand it no longer and made it known to my comatose companions that I was off in search of food and drink.

"I'll come with you," said the suddenly lucid Ron.

We'd heard that there was curry and salad on sale in the arena but faced with the extra trek, settled on the burgers and Coke available on the campsite.

"I'll be as quick as I can," I said and headed for the loo, as Ron joined the queue for the burger stall. The boys had not needed the facilities thus far.

The loos were easily located, the stench and the gathered crowd hard to miss.

"I'd sooner shit in a field," a girl with bare feet and rolled-up jeans announced as she pulled out of the queue some way ahead, all but gagging. "Me too," said another, also on the point of heaving. With the exodus from the queue continuing, the smell of urine, and worse, intensified and I too chickened out.

"You weren't long. Are the bogs as bad as everyone says?" Ron asked when I joined him in the queue for food.

I nodded and grimaced.

"You should try the field up on Desolation Row," he suggested.

"Desolation Row? Isn't that a Bob Dylan song?"

"Yeah." He pointed to the hill behind the festival site where huge numbers had set up camp. "That's what they call it. There's a golf course people are using as a latrine too. The view from there is fantastic." He started to laugh.

"Share a burger and Coke?" Eirwen said when we got back, her indignation only marginally exceeding Brian's, who slung "You tight git" at Ron.

"It's all we could afford for today," I chipped in, outraged at their total lack of appreciation.

"Some bloke almost pushed the burger stall over. He reckoned the prices have quadrupled since Wednesday," Ron said as he carefully divided his burger in two. Both Brian and Eirwen muttered inaudibly and accepted their portions.

We ate swiftly and shared a couple of bottles of Coke. Brian wiped his mouth and burped loudly. "Sorry," he said, although the grin on his face suggested otherwise.

"The sound is far better up on Desolation Row," Ron said. "The wind takes it there from the arena, apparently. They're selling fruit at reasonable prices there too. And you girls would be able to waz – sorry, pee – in the nearby field if we move there."

Ignoring the ongoing toilet humour, I said, "I want to *see* tonight's bands, whatever the sound is like."

"She'll hear it in her head anyway," Eirwen added.

Which was true. But my need to be close to the musicians was confirmed with every solitary struggle I now made to the stage. It wasn't just about who was playing, it had more to do with experiencing the music. Not just hearing it but feeling and smelling it too. I could almost taste the kick some players got out of performing. And I realised all that I had jeopardised to be at the festival, including my parents' trust and my safety, had been worth it.

But it was the thudding of the drums and bass guitars along my diaphragm which confirmed my genre of music. Suddenly, I knew that this was what I wanted from life – to be involved with real music making, *rock* music making. Not as a performer necessarily, but in some capacity or another. It was an epiphany, of sorts. A revelation, an unattainable dream probably. Nevertheless, to suddenly want something so badly was intoxicating.

Chapter 8

Despite having paid for our tickets – unlike many there – we didn't stay till Monday as we'd planned. We missed Jimi Hendrix, and the rain. Given the lack of sustenance and sleep we'd endured by the early hours of Sunday morning, we should have been bedding down for what remained of the night, and I had planned to, but Eirwen and the boys had opted for a joint so I took off rather than start one of my tirades on the dangers of drugs. Besides, I was already high, strung out on the performances of the last few bands, which included The Who and Desert Heat.

Not sure of where I was going, I began to cross the campsite's murmuring sea of canvas, tentatively picking a pathway illuminated by pinpricks of light from cigarettes, torches, candles, the odd Gaz lamp and the occasional illicit fire as smoke and laughter rose and marked the night sky. Every so often the welcome tang of salt wafted up from the bay below, a brief respite from the smog and smells of the site.

Now determined to get to the arena's mainstage, I had to zig-zag across the campsite, avoiding the sleeping, copulating, tripping and some still dancing bodies, along with the detritus that littered the ground between them.

I continued my trek with images of The Who dancing across my mind: John Entwistle, sedate in a skeleton outfit, boiler-suit-clad Pete Townsend wildly windmilling, and bonkers Keith Moon bouncing and bashing his drums as Roger Daltrey whipped the night sky with his vocals and fringed sleeves. But visions of Brendan Bradshaw on stage eclipsed everything else for me.

The fire of him…

He'd lit up the night, his hands flashing across piano keys or guitar strings, his body arched in exquisite pleasure, lost in the music. But we were with him, the hundreds and thousands of us there that warm August night, when his performance reached its earth-shuddering climax. We screamed and sighed when he left the stage, still wanting more.

The music and noise of the night had now hushed to a whisper punctuated by the odd shout, a stifled laugh, a scream or cry as the sky across the began to lighten, and I finally completed my pilgrimage to the now quiet arena and its mainstage.

Suddenly nervous, I quickly rounded the back of the stage and almost collided with a baby grand piano. I ran my fingers over its glossy surface then checked over my shoulder. In the distance I could hear male voices and vehicle doors slamming shut… People were evidently packing up, but they were some way off. It would be okay.

A total music junkie, I was unable to resist the lure of the trip this baby promised. Just to touch the keys that had previously felt the pressure of whose fingers?

I dragged a large prone speaker into position and sat at the keyboard running through the night's events, recollecting all the pianists. I glanced around again. *To hell with it*, I suddenly thought, and lifted the keyboard lid.

"Clair de Lune" seemed apt, with the morning light extending an arm across the sky as though reaching for the still-present moon. Oblivious now, I played, racing along, savouring the quality of the sound of the Bechstein piano, until I was suddenly reined in by urgent calling.

"Chrissie?" a hoarse voice queried. "Chrissie?"

Did I imagine the longing packed into the uttering of just a name?

Panicked, I stood up, not daring to look back but nevertheless taking care to close the lid of the piano. Keenly aware that I was being followed, I retraced my steps at speed only to be jolted to a halt as my pursuer grabbed my arm.

Normally a law-abiding person, I ran through the possible punitive consequences of my actions. But because I'd been swung around like a ragdoll, another more alarming scenario seemed likely. Anticipating hitting the ground hard, I held my breath, a range of violent outcomes flashing across my mind. Imagining rape, torture and possibly death, nothing readied me for the concerned face that peered into mine.

Brendan Bradshaw… Gorgeous Brendan Bradshaw, his eyes as blue as the chink in the expanse of grey sky behind his head. My mouth, which had been poised to emit a scream, remained agape as I exhaled loudly.

"Sorry, I must have given you quite a shock," he said with a smile.

A lot of what he said to me was lost in the burr of his accent, but I nodded and attempted to close my mouth, which seemed beyond my control and as large as a cave. He maintained his hold on my arm, albeit with a slackened grip, and steered me back to the piano.

He looked down at the prostrate speaker. "Not the best of seating arrangements but at least there's room for two."

Trembling, and still unable to speak, I watched as he sat down and extended his long legs under the piano. I tried not to think about how he had looked on stage earlier that night… those legs spread wide and his arms hugging his guitar, which had been slung around his groin like a tango partner.

"Now you." He patted the space beside him, a hint of a smile twitching the corners of his mouth.

Oh God, I prayed, hoping my thoughts weren't evident on my face. Eirwen maintains I can be read like a book. *Oh, and please may I not be humming Amen Corner's "Bend Me, Shape Me, Anyway You Want Me", however appropriate.*

I positioned myself gingerly on the speaker, my hands safely tucked out of the way, taking care not to touch him. He then took up the piece on the exact note I'd ended on but minutes before, his fingers moving deftly across the keys in front of me.

"You play well from the little I heard," he said, effortlessly drawing more out of the melody than I could even dream about. "You don't say much, do you?" He craned to look at my face, which was shrouded by my hair. Its restraining band had been lost in the struggle. "Come on. Say something."

I returned his stare but remained mute, taking in the sharp outline of his face, the darkening stubble, the equally dark lashes fringing the strangest blue eyes I have ever seen. Eirwen's eyes were a constant baby blue but this man's eyes were mercurial, changing colour like a sea pool. On the "Pinch me, I'm dreaming" scale, this was way out there, somewhere in the stratosphere.

Suddenly, I began to spout a passage from *Y Mabinogi*. In Welsh, of course.

I'm not sure who was the more surprised. Me or Mr Bradshaw. I blame our Welsh teacher, Mrs Miller – Miller the Killer to her victims. At school she put the fear of God into every girl she taught. When Mrs Miller said to learn such-and-such a passage or poem, you did. And woe betide the girl who failed to correctly enunciate every phoneme, to remember every nuance in the text. Hence in moments of genuine fear or panic, I'd catch myself silently mouthing one of the many dreaded tracts. Never aloud though, until that moment.

But Brendan Bradshaw didn't laugh. He didn't understand, either, but as a musician he recognised the rhythm and the rhyme and the sheer beauty of the passage. He had stopped playing, and when I had finished, he clapped. I flushed, feeling an even greater fool than before.

"What was that?"

"Welsh."

"Ah, Shirley Bassey, Tom Jones…" he responded, picking out "'It's Not Unusual" on the piano. I chuckled at the ease of his skill.

"You thought I was someone else, didn't you?" My sudden boldness surprised me, and I made to leave.

"No, don't go," he said, continuing to play. "And yes, you do remind me of someone I once knew. But what's your name?"

"Mari Morgan," I replied, marvelling at his repertoire. I had yet to learn that his ability had nothing to do with learning the music. If he'd heard a piece enough, he could play it.

"Mari Morgan… M.M." He made my name sound smooth, like cream. I felt I could touch the sounds he made.

His rendition changed in a heartbeat from Jones to Hendrix, and he began to play "The Wind Cries Mary", only the barely audible lyrics he sang were adjusted for me, as Mary became Mari. I blushed to the roots of my hair, fearful and yet hopeful. Of what, I was not sure. He ended abruptly on "Mari" and searched my face again. Then he extended a long, tanned hand to my hair.

"You know"—he dropped his hand before it made contact with my unruly mop—"alliteratively speaking, we are meant for each other." His eyes met mine again. I stared back uncomprehendingly.

"Alliteration," he continued, "like Bogart and Bacall, Benedick and Beatrice… uh… Louis Lane and Clark Kent, Peter Parker and Betty Brant. They're all I can think of at the moment, but I expect there are others."

My confusion increased apace with my embarrassment. What was he talking about? I moved off the speaker, thinking I'd leave with some measure of dignity before I got any further out of my depth.

"Mari Morgan: M.M. Brendan Bradshaw: B.B.," he said as he closed the piano lid.

I briefly shut my eyes, my colour deepening. "Dim and more than a little tired. I'd best get back." I waved an arm in the general direction of away from this strange scenario. No one would believe any of this. I'm not sure that I did.

I backed away from the piano, retaining eye contact, reluctant to relinquish the moment. Brendan Bradshaw was now leaning back against the piano, having swivelled around on the speaker to watch my reversing retreat. His shirt had slipped another button in the process to expose more golden-brown skin and chest hair than was good for me. I swallowed hard, still gesticulating ineffectually away.

"I should get back to my friends." I tried to drag my eyes from his flesh while imagining how it would feel under my fingers. I coloured again. An all-time record, even by my standards.

"I'll walk back with you." He re-buttoned his shirt. Had he read my hungry stare? I cringed at my predictability. Within half an hour I'd veered from speechless schoolgirl to mindless prospective lay.

"Really?"

"Of course." He pulled a bush hat from the back pocket of his jeans and, affecting a posh accent, added, "A gentleman always sees a lady home. Lead on, Mari Morgan."

He extended an arm away from the piano, out towards the mess, the tents and the bodies. Then he pulled his hat low over his eyes. It was a disguise of sorts. But to me he seemed to glow, an inner neon sign declaring his charisma. I stumbled forward, waiting to wake at any moment.

"What did your parents have to say about you coming here?" Brendan Bradshaw suddenly asked.

I looked away shamefaced and mute.

"Ah, that would depend on them knowing your plans, wouldn't it?"

Again, I felt a fleeting stab of guilt at my recent behaviour. Not enough to bring me down to earth, though. For goodness' sake, I was with Brendan Bradshaw, no less. It would be a crime not to make the most of this parallel universe moment. I had merely temporarily forsaken the life my parents were a part of… the life that would still be there when I eventually landed.

Yet my uncharacteristic reasoning shocked me. What was going on with me? What had the festival unleashed in me?

Chapter 9

By the time I caught sight of the vibrant red Welsh dragon, the sky around us was alight with the promise of another beautiful day. The flag, which was suspended between our tent and that of the boys, barely fluttered in the light breeze, but it was a beacon back to the others.

Eirwen and Ron were sitting back-to-back, silently passing a joint over their shoulders to one another. Eirwen had evidently noted my return as she faced me across the campsite's tented terrain.

"Ooh, Mari Morgan. Who's the old guy?"

Affronted, I turned to Brendan Bradshaw, about to declare him a rock god and her a fool, only to find he was hunched up into his hat and barely recognisable.

"Thanks," I aimed in his direction, searching for his eyes.

He nodded towards Eirwen as she blew smoke rings into the air.

"This your friend?" His voice was clipped and critical.

Without thought or hesitation, I rose to her defence. "She's not normally like this."

Brendan lifted his head, his now visible eyes intense and serious.

"No?" He held my gaze.

"Not all the time." *What sort of friend was I?*

"A brave if brief defence, but not entirely convincing." He looked back at the still-puffing pair. "And him?" He nodded at Ron.

"We just happened to meet him and his mate here. They live near us."

"I'll see you girls home, if you like." There was no arguing with his tone, but I was all confusion again.

"Home?" I was stupid enough to ask.

"Yeah. Home, as in Wales. Get your bags if you want a lift back with me."

He looked at me and waited on my decision. I barely hesitated. I didn't give a thought to not staying for the remainder of the festival, to missing Jimi Hendrix, nor to the consequences of accepting lifts from strange men, before nodding my assent. He smiled then moved towards Eirwen as she received the last of the joint from Ron. It never reached her lips, as Brendan snatched it from her fingers and stamped it out when it hit the ground.

"Hey," wailed Eirwen, a petulant child deprived of its treat. While planning her next move, the effort of which was evident on her face, she was yanked off the parched patch of ground and fleetingly onto her feet, then onto Brendan's left shoulder. Without Eirwen's support, Ron crashed backwards.

"Wow," he exclaimed, immobile where he'd fallen. "Some weed that."

I rushed forward with our meagre possessions crammed into our bags, fell into step behind Brendan Bradshaw and guiltily glanced back at the borrowed tent we were abandoning.

Throughout our meandering return to the arena's mainstage, Eirwen remained carcass-still over Brendan's shoulder, her hair swaying with his movements. Whether her stillness and silence could be attributed to the firmness of his grip or the joint was anyone's guess.

On nearing the stage, we became aware of a knot of men heatedly discussing the whereabouts of Mr Bradshaw.

"How the fuck should I know where he is? I was busy trying to get Denny on the copter," exclaimed a solid rectangle of a man, his broad back turned to us.

Smiles of recognition spread among the crew facing us as the stocky man continued to rant, until nudged by another, pointing in our direction.

The man spun around to confront Brendan. "Where the hell did you go? The rest of the band left nearly an hour ago." His spittle-laden words flew out and scattered like bats from a cave, but his angry frown turned to a smirk when his knowing eyes alighted upon Eirwen and me.

"Not like you to go out for takeaway," he commented.

I blushed, not sure of his words but certain of his expression.

"They're just travelling with us," Brendan replied as he passed the growing group of bemused crew enjoying the thinly disguised rebuke dished out to the boss.

"Didn't know you picked up strays, either," scoffed the roadie. A ripple of laughter ran through the group.

"And I don't pay you lot to stand around, so get your backsides in gear and let's get out of here."

He deposited Eirwen on the back bench seat of a flash Volkswagen campervan while another man got behind the wheel and my heart sank, only to soar again when Brendan climbed in alongside the driver at the front. I then checked on Eirwen, settled back and tried to relax.

"Okay?" Brendan said, his face barely visible despite the brightening sky. I nodded, incapable of speech, my thoughts confused and fragmented without the aid of any illicit substances.

Brendan Bradshaw then reached over to pat my arm. A concerned, older adult gesture. I smiled wanly but basked in the warmth of his eyes and willed our exodus from the island to last forever.

***

Unfortunately, our return to South Wales took a fraction of the time the outward journey had taken. I tried to stay awake so as not to miss a moment, but the minute we boarded the ferry I was lulled into a deep sleep. A sudden lurching of the van catapulted me into consciousness.

"Strewth, that was close," Brendan Bradshaw exclaimed as a heavy lorry thundered past. "You okay?" He peered over to where I lay on the floor, partially pinioned by Eirwen's upper half.

I started giggling at the ridiculousness of the situation. I had hoped at some point to impress the sophisticated older man now grinning down at me, but I hadn't foreseen being bombed by my blonde bombshell of a friend.

Mr Bradshaw leaned at an alarming angle over his seat and attempted to aid me in my efforts to lever my still oblivious friend back onto the seat. With Eirwen flopping about like a fish out of water, we were both laughing helplessly while the driver swore colourfully about the commotion we were making.

Eirwen finally surfaced just before our last stop for food at the Severn Bridge services.

"Hey," she muttered, as the van slowed to exit the motorway, her silky hair spilling around her shoulders.

The driver's eyes almost popped when Eirwen emerged from the back of the van. She exuded sensuality, her stained and crumpled T-shirt no drawback to her allure.

I placed a protective arm around her and scowled at the man. Then Brendan Bradshaw removed the denim jacket he had on over his white shirt and dropped it around Eirwen's shoulders. The gesture was warm, but his eyes were quite cold when Eirwen turned the heat of her beam his way. They remained so, despite his brief smile.

Once Brendan had established that there was a telephone at Eirwen's house, he suggested that we ring her mother at the services to report where we were and when we would be home. So, our hearts were heavy and our faces glum as we approached my house, sure of what awaited us.

The Watkins family member who had been dispatched to pass the message on to my parents probably informed all those unaware of our transgressions, together with the expected hour of our return. Consequently, the crawl to the top of the hill and my house was accompanied by as much net- and curtain-flapping as on a springtime washing line. And Brendan's van was as gaudy as a parrot on our grey hillside, its signature engine tone unknown on a road generally devoid of traffic.

My parents appeared as soon as the van pulled up. The relief that flooded their faces tore at my innards, but Eirwen rallied and bounced onto the pavement as buoyant as the bubble that Brendan's departure was about to burst. I felt rooted to the spot, weighed down by a psychiatrist's bag full of conflicting emotions. I recognised one or two of these on my mother's face.

She caught my eye and took a sharp intake of breath, only to almost choke on her tirade when Brendan stepped forward to shake her hand, and then my father's.

"Nice to meet you, Mr and Mrs Morgan," he said, his strong Northern English accent seeming to echo down our valley. "And your daughter is a charming girl. A credit to you.

"Well," he added to the growing number of open-mouthed onlookers. "Must be off. Long way home from here. Bye, Mari." He took my right hand in both of his.

I quickly closed my fingers over the piece of paper he had secreted in my palm, hoping that the joy that leaped within me did not register on my face.

He turned to Eirwen just as she began to remove his jacket with a movement that was a little too provocative given the circumstances.

"You can keep it," he said with a curt nod, and he moved away without a backward glance. He climbed into the van, which roared into life, its throaty throb demanding attention all the way down the hill.

I slipped the note into the back pocket of my jeans, tore my gaze from the road and turned back to the crowd. Then everyone started talking at once. By which time Megan Watkins and the remainder of her brood had arrived, along with several more neighbours.

I hugged my parents and mouthed a "sorry" at each of them. But in reality, I was oblivious to everything except that flimsy, folded piece of paper in my pocket, which seemed to have taken on a greater form that pressed into my flesh.

***

The seriousness of our deception was brought home to me when my mother did not attend the evening chapel service. As if that wasn't enough, when I appeared after a long-overdue bath, glowing inside as well as out and seemingly walking on air, I was brought back to earth with a bump when my dad turned off the television during *The Black and White Minstrel Show*.

My parents did not have a list of grievances, as I knew there to be. They merely voiced an obvious sadness that I had lied.

"And where would we have looked if something had happened to you?" was my father's final, heart-wrenching query.

But I offered no reply. What could I have said? Besides, I could not regret events that had ignited such a blaze within me.

Chapter 10

Things were never the same after that trip. *We* were never the same. The changes were barely perceptible, but they were nonetheless there.

The more stalwart chapelgoers of our village, predominantly middle-aged females, would cross the road or move seats in chapel rather than have to acknowledge us. Even our parents looked askant at us for a time, as though a part of our skin had peeled back to reveal an alien form, something that was nothing to do with them.

And Eirwen was like an unhooded bird of prey, tethered and fretful, desperate to soar into the sunlit sky. She worried and railed at me as though I was the bond holding her down.

"When will this bloody month end?" she directed at me on a regular basis, as though I had control of the passage of time.

"On the thirtieth, as well you know," I returned, as unsettled as she was, but for different reasons. "You ought to be glad September only has thirty days."

"Yeah, yeah. Very funny. But I can't wait to get to Cardiff. To get away from this shithole."

She huffed and flapped her arms against her sides and raised her face skywards, closing eyes as blue as borage flowers. Then she looked back at me questioningly, the "Well?" unspoken.

"You think being in Cardiff might be the answer?"

She studied me in a way that reminded me of my parents… a concerned and confused expression.

"What is it?" She peered into my eyes, a frown puckering her face. "What's wrong?"

I looked away, suddenly interested in kicking a stone from the pavement. We were on our way to the shop on an errand for my mother.

"Same as you. Bored."

"Hmph," she returned, sounding unconvinced. I could feel her gaze, hot as ash, on the side of my face. The girl could have penetrated rock, had she the mind to.

"Roll on." She looked away from me, letting it go. Thankfully. I wasn't up to any level of interrogation, unsure of what I was feeling, except that I didn't want to be there or in Cardiff.

The temperature in the shop dropped a degree or two when we walked through the door. The buttoned-up matrons present sniffed bad smells and turned away from us.

I immediately coloured – confirming my guilt in their eyes, I'm sure. In contrast, Eirwen walked right up to them, greeted them by name and wished them a "very good morning". They scuttled beetle-like from her brightness, exiting the shop to return to their mean, dark domains.

As quickly as possible, I located the icing sugar, sultanas and flour that my mother required. My eyes were lowered, while Eirwen's blazed a warning: ignore me at your peril.

At the till, the owner Mr Godfrey, a big fleshy man who looked as though he consumed most of the profits, guffawed as he tapped the keys and slid our items along the desk.

"Ah, the reprobates," he said as I stuffed our purchases into my mother's string bag. "I may have to ban you two. Bad for business, see."

I winced, wondering if my parents were also victims of the fallout of our escapade. Then I realised that everyone associated with us was likely to be.

"Do any of that skinny-dipping while you were away, girls?" he said with a leer as I handed him the money.

"Only in your mind, Mr Godfrey," said Eirwen as she swept out of the door, wiping the smile from his face and putting it on mine.

***

In bed that night, I unfolded the piece of paper that I'd not let out of my sight since receiving it from Brendan Bradshaw. I smoothed out the creases in the note as it lay on my turned-back blankets. I didn't need to read the message anymore. I had memorised every word and digit, but I had yet to act on the request.

Please ring me, Mari, it said.

It must be a joke. But I'd never find out if I didn't ring the number.

Reverse the charges.

Simple. No cost involved, even if it was a joke. So why hadn't I rung?

Fear. I ran my palms over the paper again. I was afraid that it might be a joke, and I was afraid it might *not* be a joke. My biggest fear was why I had not given Eirwen all the details of my encounter with Brendan Bradshaw – in particular, the existence of the note.

I refolded the sheet of paper, put it back in my purse, slid under the blankets and tried to sleep.

Chapter 11

Eirwen and I were assigned to the same hall of residence in Cardiff, with her flat two floors above mine. We'd achieved the necessary A level grades. We'd arrived. It should have been fantastic.

But I was not happy there. I annoyed Eirwen by not fully embracing student life. Everyone and everything else annoyed me. Most of the people I met seemed to be trying too hard to be trendy, or clever, or different, or funny, or just trying too hard. My only pleasure was playing the grand piano in the university's main hall. It was there that I met the only other person who didn't get on my nerves.

I should have recognised her from lectures but I was in some sort of unfocused daze most of the time and didn't register her until she took to joining me in the hall. Initially, I played on regardless of her presence until she eventually requested a chance to play.

"Sorry," I said, colouring, mistakenly thinking her a possible music fan or just a downright nuisance.

"Don't apologise, Mari. I've enjoyed your music. I'm Steph, by the way."

"How do you know my name?"

Steph explained that we shared not just classes but personal tutors. Never mind being in a daze, I must have been wearing blinkers too.

Steph and I didn't talk about the specifics of our individual emotional turmoil, we just shared a sadness and a feeling of not fitting in with university life. The music we played for each other seemed explanation enough.

***

Finally, after weeks of studying Brendan Bradshaw's note, I decided I was ready to make the requested call. I found a telephone box a very long way from our hall of residence and dialled. A woman answered. She sounded old… older. I gave my name and asked to speak to Mr Bradshaw. Curtly, she told me I could not, adding that I should not ring again.

Crestfallen, I waited for the clunk of a replaced receiver, but a silence followed. So I waited, sweaty pennies tight in my fist, ready to feed the phone, and prayed.

Then Brendan Bradshaw's voice echoed down the line. "Mari? Mari Morgan?"

The fact that Brendan Bradshaw had remembered my name and actually wanted to speak to me rendered me momentarily speechless.

"I know you're there," he said. "I can hear you breathing."

"Isn't that supposed to be my line?" I managed to say despite my dry mouth and pounding heart. He laughed and I tingled in response, certain I'd left the ground.

"Give me your number and I'll ring back."

Is this a polite, if devious brush-off? I considered, as the phone took an age to ring. In a panic to answer when it did eventually ring, I lost my grip on the handset and it swung away from me.

"Hello? Hello?" I bellowed.

"Stop shouting or put down the loudhailer."

My turn to laugh.

"So, congratulations are in order," he commented when I told him I'd made it to Cardiff University. "What do you plan to do with your degree?"

"You're assuming that I'll get a degree."

"Don't be so modest. You're an accomplished pianist. Of course you'll get a degree. Do you have a job in mind?"

"I've been told I'll never want for work as a teacher who can play the piano."

"You don't sound committed to the idea. Do you like children?"

"I've been a Sunday school teacher since my mid-teens but that's just for an hour a week. Imagine a class full of the blighters, day in, day out. And the music would be very prescriptive. Little of my choice, I would imagine."

"Mm. Well, don't be persuaded on a career path that doesn't motivate and excite you."

"I'll do my best."

Later that week, a leather music case and a food hamper arrived.

***

We talked on the telephone three times a week for almost a month. I'd ring him from a phone box and he'd ring me back, and we'd talk and talk. We'd talk about music, my course, family, friends, poetry, the news, anything really. Listening to his voice was enough; the content of the conversation was irrelevant. His laugh… well, that seemed to ripple up my spine. And judging by his reluctance to hang up, he felt the same.

I'd walk for miles to find a phone box that I would be able to occupy for at least an hour at a time. But with the shorter days as winter approached, Brendan expressed concerns about me wandering the backstreets of Cardiff after dark. Despite my efforts to allay his fears, he restricted our calls to once a week on a Sunday morning.

"Is that your teeth chattering?"

"Baby, it's cold outside, and in here," I sang with an attempt at a *femme fatale* rendition.

He chuckled.

"A phone box isn't the warmest of places, admittedly. I haven't used one for years, but they were cold even when packed."

"Packed?"

"With people."

"A phone box?"

"Me and my mates were always packing into small spaces. It passed the time."

"I'm glad it hasn't caught on here. It's hard enough trying to find one in working order," I replied.

"Are you wearing warm enough clothing if you're feeling the cold?"

"Silly me. I thought a bikini was fine all year round."

"Mm. I'll savour that notion for a moment or two."

I giggled. "Talking of temperatures, why is your band called Desert Heat? Not something the North is known for," I said cheekily.

He said something unfathomable in an exaggerated Geordie accent and I giggled again. "In English, please."

"Well, nay, pet, tis cold *t'up* 'ere," he began. "Which is why we fantasised about the heat of the desert while freezing *wor* boll… pardon my French, our extremities off in a Bedford van. And one of the reasons we headed to California as soon as we possibly could."

The following week, a fabulous hooded woollen coat arrived. The Sunday after, I said,

"Listen, Father Christmas, once a year is the tradition."

"You're such a spoilsport. Now please tell me you're wearing a bikini under that coat…"

When we next spoke, Brendan said he needed to see me and arranged to meet up the following Sunday outside the Angel Hotel, opposite Cardiff Castle.

By this time, I'd started skipping lectures. My mind was preoccupied, and I was uninterested in anything but Brendan. I'd also stopped playing the piano in the hall, doing my best to avoid Steph. Even Eirwen failed to engage me.

"What is it with you, M? You haven't listened to a word I've said. Is there something wrong? What are you not telling me?"

There was plenty I wasn't telling her. Yet I was fearful that if I voiced what I felt or hoped for, Eirwen's ridicule or disbelief would destroy whatever it was Brendan and I were enjoying.

Eventually, the Sunday of his visit arrived. I was early and stood looking at the hotel from across the road, shaking and shivering despite my woollen coat. To steady my nerves, I paced the pavement outside the castle walls, the stiff, almost sightless stare of a soldier on sentry duty fixed on my face.

Brendan emerged from the main doors bang on time and watched me cross the road. He seemed to be as awkward and agitated as I felt. He noticed that I was shivering and moved towards me, his hands hovering uncertainly in the air around me. Then he withdrew.

We both were as jittery and jumpy as an apprentice puppeteer's marionettes. Brendan settled for thrusting his hands deep into his pockets. But his gaze was as hungry as mine.

This was only our second meeting, yet the realisation suddenly struck me that I was irrevocably bound to this man. Not the rock star – certainly not the millionaire, not even the musician – but the very essence of him... the man who shared his ideas with me and valued my opinion; the man who could make me laugh and whose smile I could hear in his voice when we spoke on the phone.

I'd known him all my life, because he was a part of me – albeit a part I hadn't recognised until this moment. But from that moment on, nothing else mattered. I felt utterly selfish, and yet selfless in my need.

Although fairly sure he felt the same, I was just as sure that he was troubled by whatever had brought him to Cardiff.

"Come in and have a coffee," he said, his voice thin and flat.

He seemed to be roped to me, tied to my sternum, so that every movement he made away from me caused me pain. Despite listening carefully to every word he said, I still failed to process much of the speech he made. However, "for the best" and "end this" told me all I needed to know.

He moved from the table, his coffee untouched. I lurched to my feet, fearful of asphyxiation.

"Wait," I gasped as he strode off down the corridor.

"Go home, Mari." He didn't look back.

I caught his arm but he shook off my grasp. Not before I'd registered the jolt that seemed to surge between us, though. At this he stopped and backed against the wall.

What I did next was instinctive, basic. I knew that this was where everything could really begin or finally end. Encircling his waist, I pulled his hips towards me. But I was unprepared for the ferocity of his kiss, the taut power of his arms as he crushed me to his chest.

Alarmed, I struggled to free myself, staggering on release to wipe my face, his saliva warm in my mouth and the metallic tang of blood on my lip.

"There. You're not ready for this, and I'm old enough to know better."

Cursing myself for the innocent I was, I winced at the thought of never looking into those glorious eyes again. To never again hear his laugh or brave Geordie attempts at Welsh pronunciation. My chest constricted with pain.

So, throwing care, caution and all that my mother had taught me to the wind, I launched myself at him for the second time.

"Teach me," I begged, clutching at him. "I want to learn."

He shook his head with his gaze averted, but his jaw relaxed and his eyes softened as he looked down at me.

"I told you, Mari. I'm going on tour. Enjoy your time at university. Get on with your life. I'm an old man."

I let go of his arm and clenched my fists, my body stiff with agitation.

"I don't care about uni. I can't concentrate. All I think about is you. I'll follow you."

"You don't need to follow me. Stick with your course. We can write. I'll ring regularly, and we'll meet up when I come back."

But the thought of him leaving the country filled me with an empty dread.

"I've no interest in my course. I want to be with you, if you'll let me."

"Touring is hard work, not a holiday. You won't see a lot of me."

"Sounds as if you don't want me there."

"That's a long way from the truth. But I'm aware of what you'll be sacrificing even if you're not. And I don't want you to be under any illusion about how the tour would be."

"If things don't work out, I'll re-apply to university next year," I said brightening, sensing that he was yielding.

"An ultimatum with a sub-clause, eh?"

There was humour in the comment but a cloud crossed his face. So I waited and watched as he relaxed, and heard the sigh he emitted echo with resignation. Something had been set in motion, something that was beyond his control. But the upward curve of his mouth was more than the beginning of a smile; it was part of an inner glow that warmed me. Then he slowly bent down to gently brush my mouth with his. I closed my eyes as he folded me into his arms, savouring the warm, earthy smell of him as he kissed the top of my head.

Despite feeling safe and deliriously happy, a small knot of anxiety began to develop deep within me.

What if he doesn't like me after this? I know so little. What if it's not like I've imagined? What if I don't like any of this? Perhaps I am frigid. What if no woman really likes it? There's a definite reticence to seriously discuss sex once it's embarked upon. Even Eirwen has very little to say, other than in jest, on the matter.

Nevertheless, despite my mother's voice and her favourite saying echoing in my head, I decided not to heed her advice regarding familiarity and contempt. To hell with everything I'd ever been. I wasn't going to miss the chance to be with this incredible man for anyone. I wanted him, and the world he inhabited, above all that had previously defined me. Grinning broadly, I began to tremble in anticipation, suddenly abuzz with excitement and desire.

***

Needless to say, I never went back to university. We spent three days at the Angel. Well, we spent three days in a room at the Angel. We fed each other, bathed each other and, after a tentative start, loved each other. Again, and again.

My tutelage had begun. I was molten for three days and three nights, unsure where I ended and Brendan began. I was definitely not frigid. Unfortunately, when we did surface for air and a change of scenery and bed linen, Brendan insisted that we go back to Gwaun to speak to my parents.

I knew that he was right, but I baulked at the prospect of tainting my happiness with guilt… of facing their disappointment, their fears and disgust. Girls like me didn't do things like this, not in my valley. Not then.

Brendan wanted to reassure them that he would look after me. But there was no mention of the love or marriage prerequisite of their generation if a girl was to be properly looked after.

Besides, Brendan already had a wife, from whom he was separated, and there was a child. This was information he'd divulged to me, devoid of detail or emotion. Not that I cared about them, or the girl called Chrissie he'd mistaken me for at the festival. All that I cared about was being with him.

But I'm not sure my parents ever got over the shock. My father kept searching my eyes, his own bleak with fear, as my mother plucked at his sleeve, plaintively repeating his name. I've never known her so short on something to say.

"This is what you want, is it, Mari?" my father asked again, as though Brendan had cast some sort of spell over me.

"Yes," I replied, hand in hand with Brendan, alight with love and happiness.

My father looked at me intently and opted for a different tack.

"Excuse us a moment, Mr Bradshaw. My wife and I need to have a quiet word with our daughter." And he took hold of my elbow.

Brendan looked blankly back at my dad for a split second, momentarily fazed. But he got the drift as my father steered me towards the parlour, my mam trailing in our wake.

Panicked by the heavy-handed closing of the panelled parlour door and the clink of the metal rings as the curtains cut out the street light and probable prying eyes, I squared up to my parents, prepared for the first time in my life to do battle with them.

"You mean to do this, Mari? Leave university, after all your hard work?"

My mother nodded but remained silent, her eyes full of panic and tears. But I was unmoved. I was driven by a greater panic.

"I don't care about university. I've not been to lectures for weeks."

My father nodded and paused as if he'd lost his place on his list.

"Do you think you're the first young girl he's charmed?" He was angry, his voice strained, which rendered his antiquated vocabulary more stinging than any profanity.

"I know I'm not the first and I doubt I'll be the last, but I don't care."

"You'll be ruined." My mother had found her voice, her words as outdated as my father's.

"I am already. The Isle of Wight trip saw to that. It gave them licence to speculate." I spoke of the few mean-spirited *them* of our valley who could turn something innocent into something sordid, and with repetition make it as good as true.

"That's it, then." My father's voice no longer bristled. It was flat with resignation and acknowledgement.

"I know what I'm doing. I know I'm hurting you in so many ways, and I'm sorry for that. But I have to go with him or after him. I must."

My father sighed, momentarily closed his eyes, and then snatched me to him in a stricken embrace.

"This will always be your home," he said, his voice broken with emotion. "Whatever happens, you can come back to us."

He released me and looked to my mother, who seconded his sentiments with a tearful nod.

They weren't happy but all they wanted was my happiness, and for that they were prepared to accept all that was to follow.

My father's voice was edged with anger when he summoned Brendan through to the parlour... a Friday afternoon headmaster's voice for the school's serial offender.

Brendan was appropriately apologetic on all fronts – enough to appease my parents to a small degree. He reiterated promises of care and dared to put a protective arm about me, which probably carried more weight with my father – if not my mother – than any ingratiating statements.

Then, with a barely perceptible nod of his head, as though acknowledging a bid, my father brought his right fist down gavel-hard on his open left palm.

"Mind you do look after her, my boy. Mind you do," he said emphatically, his expression steely grey and hard.

The deal was done, but my father knew I was already Brendan's. He'd read as much from my face.

Chapter 12

Telling Eirwen proved harder in some respects. Brendan had left for London to finalise the arrangements for the forthcoming tour and would return in a fortnight to collect me. I didn't doubt for a second that he would do so.

It was Saturday morning. I climbed the two flights of stairs up to Eirwen's flat and found her alone in the kitchen she shared with her fellow flatmates. It was a twin of the one I'd just left but with racier posters, more rubbish and a pungent odour that was almost solid in places.

Eirwen was wearing a bloke's T-shirt, minuscule pants and the remnants of last night's make-up, and she looked fantastic. She was walking around the room, eating a bowl of cornflakes that I knew would be plastered with sugar. She seemed to be giving off sparks. In between crunches she relayed details of the previous night.

"I met some great girls." She dribbled milk in her haste to speak. "Girls like me."

She paused and looked intently at me.

I frowned uncertainly: Barbie doll lookalikes? A party of Scandinavian students? Or something quite different? Fortunately, I was too distracted to ask.

Eirwen dropped her gaze and wiped her chin. Then a dishevelled young man sauntered in, sidled up behind Eirwen and slid his arms around her waist. "Found you," he said. He was wearing the other half of the outfit Eirwen had on but was in danger of losing his un-belted and partially unzipped jeans as he squeezed Eirwen's breasts.

"I'll leave you two lovebirds to it," I said, grateful for an excuse to leave the room and my confession for another time.

"No, you don't," Eirwen said to me. She shook off the young man's embrace and levelled a searing look at him. Taken aback he quickly stepped away from the evident heat of her anger.

"Get lost," Eirwen flung at him and plonked her bowl down on the table.

He barely hesitated before scooting out the door. Eirwen slammed it behind him.

"So, I finally meet the right girls and yet I end up with a bloke like him. Why is that?" Eirwen dropped onto one of the eight dining chairs arranged around the large table in the centre of the room and looked at me expectantly. But I had no idea what she was talking about.

We both were distracted by the gusting wind, which rattled the large windowpanes while redirecting the sheets of rain angled across the treetops. The resulting torrent of water cascaded down the glass, briefly obliterating the view.

Eirwen was silent for a moment longer. Then she turned to me. "Where the hell have you been? You're skipping more lectures than me, and that takes some doing."

By which time I'd joined her at the table with a view of the closed door (and its poster of a naked woman with drawn-on underwear), through which I willed the young man to return.

"I've met someone," I began, which stopped her drumming on the tabletop with her green-painted nails.

"Hurrah. The Ice Maiden melts." But the humour of Eirwen's words did not reach her eyes as she looked at me across the table, which was littered with at least a week's worth of debris. Her detach-ment surprised me.

"Well?" she said, her voice icy. "Does this person have a name?"

"You've met him," I said, now seriously rattled, while thinking… *this person?*

Eirwen studied me for a moment. "Don't tell me you introduced him to me when I was stoned?"

"I didn't introduce him, but you *were* stoned when you first saw him. He gave us a lift home from the festival."

"Festival?" This she said while leaning back on the chair and frowning, as though it were a dim and distant memory. "Not the Isle of Wight Festival?"

Anyone would think we regularly attended festivals.

As briefly as possible, I divulged the details.

"I can't believe you didn't tell me any of this earlier. You're only telling me now because you have to."

Her eyes filled with unshed tears and she said no more. She seemed to wilt in the chair. I got up and stood at her side. I felt I had betrayed her yet was unable to provide any comfort or defence for my actions. I squeezed Eirwen's shoulder, promised to write, and left. A coward's exit.

Chapter 13

I'll never forget that first trip, that first flight. Like a young child on Christmas Eve, I was aquiver with anticipation and awe. In a fever of excitement about to board the plane, I stopped, convinced the aircraft steps reached up to the star-studded sky, not just to the doorway of a Boeing 747.

Me, on a jet, flying to America… unbelievable.

But Brendan had noted my hesitation. "Just one small step for a man, and a woman…" he said, with an attempt at an American accent.

But I didn't need any lunar landing quotes to heighten my excitement – or my nervousness. I tried to return his smile as he lowered his head to mine, but my face felt frozen.

"You don't have to do this. I can arrange a car to take you home. You can go back to university," he said reassuringly.

By which time, we'd moved out of the flow of people boarding the plane. But we had our satellites – people who needed Brendan on that plane, with or without me.

"Of course I want this," I said, not sure I could explain why I'd hesitated.

"Good." Then he lifted me off the ground and held me close to his chest. "Best to get going before you start spouting Welsh." And he made his way up the steps to the aircraft, humming the tune of "Come Fly with Me".

I hooked my arms around his neck, nestled into his shoulder and hummed along. A new life beckoned. Something beyond my wildest dreams.

When we disembarked at Los Angeles airport it was still daylight, and on clearing customs we were quickly ushered into an array of city-bound vehicles. As we sped eastwards along the four-lane free-way, Downtown LA (or Smell A, as it was aptly known) presented itself as an array of modern skyscrapers protruding from a vast lake of dense white smog. The older and, as they proved to be, more ar-chitecturally interesting buildings were completely obliterated by the swamp-like miasma.

Apparently, the topography and weather conditions together with emissions from refineries, traffic and local industries created near per-fect conditions for the production and containment of photochem-ical smog. Even though the smog season ran from May to October, if the conditions were right, smog could result whatever the time of year. All of which meant nothing to me. Later, I learnt that the smog could sting your eyes and burn your throat. It also contributed to some breathtaking sunsets.

LA seemed vast and fast. Bright and brash. I was staggered by the scale of everything, from the interlacing, heaving four-lane high-ways to the picture-perfect encircling hills and mountains, the noise, the light, the ridiculously tall palm trees, the billboards, the tightly packed buildings and the crowds. I was thrilled and frightened in equal measure and all but overwhelmed by a flood of conflicting emo-tions at being there. But above all else I was nervous of being around Brendan in such a totally alien environment in the company of so many unknown and obviously curious people. Everyone – the rest of the band, the road crew, their wives and girlfriends, the tour and venue management (to say nothing of the fans) – seemed to scrutinise me.

We had yet to unpack our luggage and I'd already been introduced to more people than I had previously met in my entire life. The only name that remained with me was that of the band's rhythm guitarist, Denny. I'd met him on the plane. He was a big, fair-haired bear of a man with a mild manner and a permanently bewildered look on his face. He was also Brendan's long-term friend, which was probably the reason I remembered him.

Sleep came in fitful, bludgeoning bursts that night. The next morning, I woke dazed and alone in a bed large enough to accommodate a small family. A note alongside a substantial pile of dollars explained Brendan's absence: *Find the girls. Ask for Sylvia or Ruth at reception. Go clothes shopping, visit a restaurant or Downtown LA.* He may as well of suggested I fly to Mars. *Out for best part of the day.* Well, he had warned me. But what would I do without him?

It then occurred to me that I was used to being directed – by my parents, my grandparents, my teachers and, of course, Eirwen. She certainly wouldn't be moping about bemoaning the absence of a guide. No, Eirwen would already be making her way to Rodeo Drive accompanied by a gaggle of new friends only too willing to help her spend the pile of cash in her possession. A sensible course of action would be to embrace my inner Eirwen (if only I possessed such an entity), or at least try to emulate her. I'd begin by exploring the hotel. After breakfast, though.

At the entrance to the restaurant, a waiter was directing people to tables. He wished me a good morning and asked for my room number. Of course, I had no idea what my room number was. But my awkward embarrassment turned to annoyance as he took in my tired C&A-best clothing. He was probably considering having me removed from the premises when I squared my shoulders.

"Whatever room Brendan Bradshaw's in is my room number." At this the man attempted a smile and checked his list before directing me to a table.

I quickly sat down, my gaze focused on the table while I fiddled with the napkin and cutlery, certain that everyone was staring at me.

"That took the wind out of his sails. There's nothing like a little name-dropping to unsettle the high and mighty. Mind if I join you? I'm Ruth."

A calmer, less high-looking version of Janis Joplin pulled out the chair opposite me.

"I'm with Jim," she added. He was the roadie who had chastised Brendan and made derogatory comments about me and Eirwen on the Isle of Wight. I was hardly likely to forget him. With Ruth proving to be as upfront and forthright as her man, I wondered if she was about to deliver a disparaging remark or two.

"You're from Wales, Mari," she said, not bothering with any pretence or social niceties. "Went there once when I was a kid. Never forgot the place: The Gower. Seemed to be all golden sand and real stone castles. Ever been there?"

"Ashamed to say I've not. But then I've seen almost as much of America as Wales."

"Spoken like a true band follower," she said, and the ice was broken. "If you're at a loose end, me and some of the girls will be at the hotel pool for most of the day."

"Swimming pool?" I said disbelievingly.

"On the roof."

"Wow. Isn't it cold up there?"

"It's about seventy-five degrees in the afternoon."

"Oh. Hot enough to swim and I don't have a bather."

"We'll go shopping then. You can't be without a cossie in California."

Her no-nonsense approach was just what I needed. I'd found another guide.

***

It was so exciting just to walk down the road from the hotel to the shops at the Sunset Plaza. With planted areas separating the lanes of the highway and a plethora of sidewalk cafés, boutiques and shops, it was a unique place in such an urban setting.

"This is fabulous," I gushed, my head spinning at the choice of shops, to say nothing of the views of LA.

"There's always so much going on along the Strip," Ruth said in what I was beginning to recognise as her signature, totally unimpressed delivery. "The music video for the Mamas and the Papas' video 'I Saw Her Again Last Night' was filmed here a few years ago at the De Voss boutique," she continued. "If you keep your eyes peeled when out and about, you're bound to see someone famous at some point or another."

"Oh good. I'm hoping to catch sight of Brendan Bradshaw before the day is out," I said jokingly.

"I wouldn't bank on it," Ruth replied with a grin.

We eventually arrived at the Hyatt's rooftop pool as the afternoon heat reached its zenith. After my unbelievable morning window shopping, trying on clothes, hats and shoes, followed by a meal at a roadside café, I was ready for a swim.

The roof terrace offered uninterrupted views for miles around the hotel, but the heat, the city's tainted tang and the decadence of the scene gave me the jitters. While I tried to steady my racing thoughts, the previously inert plethora of largely pubescent girls lolling by the pool suddenly erupted into life and surged towards me.

"Ooh, you've been to Holly's Harp," said a leggy slip of a girl who snatched away one of the bags I held. "And Belinda's," said another, making a grab for the remaining bag which, thankfully, I just managed to swing from her grasp. That bag held a gift for Eirwen, and no one was grubbing it away from me.

"Settle down, girls," said Ruth, retrieving my shopping. "Give Mari a chance."

The gorgeous gaggle fell back and stared sullenly at me. I didn't belong there, little me with my wavy auburn hair and dark eyes. Physically, they were in Eirwen's league, but I sensed nothing of the spark and individuality that made Eirwen such a character.

Suddenly, everything about where I was, and why I was there, seemed quite seedy. How could I have abandoned my parents, Eirwen, my hard-won university place and my piano to be *here*? And for a man I barely knew. But to return to all that I now craved meant leaving Brendan, a thought which caused me physical pain. I was no different from the girls around the pool: rudderless females gathered in surplus and waiting on the return of the men; harem hopefuls looking to snare a sultan.

"Thanks for this morning, Ruth," I said dolefully as the group about me began to return to their sunbeds, drinks and tedium. "I'll swim later, if that's okay?"

Ruth nodded, then said, "Not everyone sinks into the sleaze."

Was that a matter of choice or chance? I considered.

Later, in the relative sanctity of my room, I resolved to see some more of the city. But with no mention from Ruth of us meeting up again, I was quite anxious about doing so. Nevertheless, Brendan evidently had much to attend to and I should stop moping about.

I decided to begin with a swim and changed into the new bikini, immediately lamenting the absence of the exquisitely embroidered kaftan I'd seen, but could not afford, at one of the boutiques. Still, with a quick rummage through the laundry bin, I found a suitable coverall (a striped grandad shirt redolent with Brendan's musky earthiness), and the kaftan was forgotten.

An hour later, I was alone and dripping in the hotel lift, willing the doors to close when a tall, rather distinguished-looking man joined me. Seemingly oblivious to my appearance, he removed the pipe from his mouth, smiled and extended a hand to me. "Baz," he said. "Bassist. Good to see you again, Mari."

I shook his hand, noting his elaborately coiffed thinning hair and stylish three-piece suit with lapels wide enough to aid flight - an outfit more boardroom than rock band.

"Heard you're fresh out of university. Cardiff, I believe."

"Nothing as grand, I'm afraid. I dropped out after half a term."

"*C'est la vie,*" he said, puffing on his pipe again. "I'm a university man. Oxford," he managed to say despite the pipe still clenched between his teeth. He gave a little nod, gratified, no doubt, by my stunned silence. He ruined it by calling me "babes" when he exited the lift.

Back in the hotel room, I discovered Brendan prostrate and asleep on the sofa that dominated the far-from-large space. Used as I was to a subdued nineteen-fifties interior design palette, the hotel's clashing colour scheme fairly set my teeth on edge. The fabric adorning the offending piece of furniture resembled multiple overlaid graph printouts in an unsettling, "melted dolly mixtures" range of colours.

Although tempted to peel off my wet swimwear and set about my immobile lover, I decided on a shower. Chlorine-tainted skin left a lot to be desired. Half an hour later, fresh, fragrant and swathed in two fluffy towels, I stood alongside the still-sleeping Brendan. And my earlier poolside doubts dissipated. I tingled just looking at him.

He sighed and wrinkled his nose, reminding me of my *mam-gu's* cat, a creature perpetually asleep on the only chair alongside the kitchen range. It always looked so cute and content, lost in its dreams, and I could never resist petting and disturbing it. I received many a scratch for my trouble.

Brendan's nose twitched again, and with a deep sigh, he stretched a very cat-like stretch. I swiftly leaned forward and ran a hand up the inside of his trouser leg, gathering cotton material on the way. Flared trousers allowed quick and easy access to well above the knee, I discovered, by which time Brendan was weak and helpless with laughter. With one hand clamped about what he claimed were his crown jewels, he attempted to fend me off with the other, all the while laughing like a drain.

Eventually, he wrestled me onto the floor and I lost my hair towel. We were both quite breathless from laughing.

"Ah, you're such a tonic. You make me feel twenty again." Then he lowered his head to mine and kissed me, which was a marked improvement on the scratches *Mam-gu's* cat used to dish out.

"I met Baz in the lift," I said when we were settled on the lurid sofa, sated and relaxed.

"How did that go?"

"It was all very polite, I must say. Is Baz short for Basil? He's very posh. He went to Oxford."

Brendan started to laugh. "Baz is his take on Bernard, which he hates almost as much as Bernie. He went to Oxford *Technical* College. For a year." He laughed again.

I scowled at him and folded my arms.

"Hmph. A gullible backwater bumpkin, that's me."

He enveloped me in a bear hug. "A naïve and trusting soul. And lovely with it."

***

My next encounter with a band member took place in the corridor but yards from my and Brendan's room. A meeting that was anything but polite.

"My, my. If it isn't little Mari."

A voice that pawed at you.

Startled, I darted away and only looked round once I'd reached the relative safety of the doorway to my room.

Closer to me than I expected or wanted, a darkly handsome man grinned wickedly at me.

Who the blazes is this? I thought as he ran a hand scratchily around his jaw. He sported a heavy eight o'clock shadow at two in the afternoon along with an impressively long and sculpted set of sideburns which accentuated his angular features and sinister air. There was something fiendish about him, and more than a whiff of sulphur.

"So, you're H's new bit of skirt," he purred, his dark eyes glittering.

"I've not worn a skirt since I left school," I said as nonchalantly as I dared while hurriedly trying to unlock the door.

"When was that? Last week? By the way, when you're ready for a *real* man, let me know. I'm Jake." He leaned menacingly towards me just as I managed to unlock the door.

My heart racing, I dived into the room, my tormentor's devilish laugh still audible as I fumbled with the internal lock. I made for the bathroom. I needed a wash, preferably with carbolic soap.

That evening, I was quite agitated when I told Brendan I'd met Jake, whoever he was.

"Keyboard player. Did he make a pass at you?" Brendan seemed quite unconcerned.

"You didn't think to warn me that he might?"

"Jake would make a pass at a chair if there was a handbag over the back."

"What?"

"Men like Jake exist. Lots of women love him. I'm glad you weren't impressed."

"*Ach a fi*. He's slimy."

Brendan chuckled. "What was that you said?"

"It's an expression of distaste. He called you H. What does that stand for?"

"A number of things, none of them complimentary. Now say that Welsh phrase again. Please."

I loved that Brendan was enamoured with me being bilingual, but he wasn't going to distract me so easily.

"Was my meeting Jake some kind of test?"

Again, Brendan seemed unconcerned. In fact, he gave the impression of being ever so slightly amused.

"Well, people say we look alike but there the similarity ends. He's far edgier than me, and younger. Perhaps you would be better off with him." He was struggling to keep a straight face.

"I'm tempted," I replied, entering into the spirit of things. "But I like blue-eyed, older men who play keyboards, and guitar – on a long strap, of course." I pressed my lower half against his, at about guitar level.

"Mm," he said breathily, pulling me in closer. "If you're still interested, Jake does play the accordion too. Not on a long strap, though." We began to laugh.

Chapter 14

With Brendan and his manager busy dealing with requests for additional performance dates, I decided it was time to explore LA. But I only got as far as the hotel entrance porch, from where I glanced up and down Sunset Boulevard, my resolve leaching away with every passing car and parading person. LA presented as its usual benign, if over-the-top, self, but I was only too aware of some of the city's more recent dark moments.

Just over two years had elapsed since Senator Robert Kennedy was shot dead at the Ambassador Hotel, just six and a half miles from where I was standing. Only fifteen months ago, and but minutes away, the Manson Family murdered a number of people including the actress Sharon Tate at her home in Beverly Hills. And a mere two months ago, the most recent of the many demonstrations LA had witnessed ended in violence. Almost three hundred thousand participants had attended the National Chicano War Moratorium, an event which had been largely without incident until the arrival of the LA Sheriff's Department, whereupon three people were shot dead.

Come to think of it, surely there was something I could do without actually leaving the hotel. Perhaps I should look for Ruth? But I didn't want to pressure her into feeling she had to chaperone me everywhere. Briefly, I considered tracking down the younger girls but opted not to – they were such an intimidating bunch. Unsure of what to do, I continued to stare out at the sunlit road.

"You're not considering venturing out alone, are you?" The voice was cut-glass English, the speaker a tall, slim and immaculately dressed lady.

"I was, but I've lost my nerve," I said, returning to the hotel foyer just as Ruth exited the lift. I felt an unexpected rush of pleasure at seeing her again.

"I hope you two weren't planning a trip without me," Ruth said, her expression deadpan.

"As if we'd dare, darling." Then, on turning to me, the tall lady offered her hand. "Sylvia. Delighted to meet you, Mari."

"I'm beginning to think there's a name tag somewhere on me."

"You're new, darling. Everyone knows who you are. The Chateau for lunch?"

"Where else?" Ruth replied. And they led me out of the door, with Sylvia producing an elegant parasol from her capacious Mary Poppins-style bag the moment we exited the shade of the entrance canopy.

"Sylvia's a vampire," said Ruth at my surprised expression. "She'd shrivel up in direct sunlight."

"Don't tease Mari," Sylvia said, not in the least put out. And I grinned, pleased at the fortuitous turn of events.

We were an incongruous trio strolling the Strip: Sylvia in a tea-dance dress, sensible sandals and pearls while Ruth, beaded and bangled, was head-to-toe hippy chic with me her shabby shadow.

With little in way of architectural competition apart from the Sunset Tower, the Chateau Marmont stood out along that stretch of Sunset Boulevard. Modelled on a Loire Valley chateau, the hotel was unbelievably beautiful, with a plethora of arched windows, domed ceilings, cloister-like pillared passageways and quiet leafy terraces.

It was barely half a mile away from our unbelievably unattractive hotel, the Continental Hyatt House Hotel: a roadside multi-storey car park of a building, its only embellishment dark shallow balconies. Yet despite their many differences, both establishments had long been popular with the rich and famous. And their hangers-on too. Although Sylvia was wealthy in her own right and aristocratic to boot, I was to learn.

Sure the day couldn't get any better, on entering the Chateau's foyer (lobby in America, darling) I spotted a baby grand piano. I gazed longingly at the beautiful instrument, fearful of touching it yet itching to lift its gleaming lid, to sit before it and play. How long had it been since I'd last touched a keyboard?

"You're dribbling, darling," Sylvia said. I wiped a hand across my mouth. "Not literally, Mari."

Too preoccupied with contemplating the instrument, I failed to respond.

"Play the thing before you self-combust," Sylvia added. "Figuratively speaking, that is."

"Martini, Sylvia? Mari?" Ruth asked.

I looked up to see Sylvia produce a box from her bag, from which she removed what I assumed was a martini glass.

"Surely you're not expected to bring your own glass?" I said ingenuously. Sylvia gave me a withering look and made for the bar.

"Sylvia considers it her duty to play the eccentric upper-class lady, largely because she is one." I found Ruth's habit of explaining Sylvia's outlandish ways quite touching. She was quite protective of Sylvia in a laidback, unobtrusive way.

While my companions chatted at the bar, I remained with the piano, and the hotel's well-heeled clientele continued to come and go around me.

Eventually, Ruth and Sylvia returned with a tray of martinis, a platter of enormous sandwiches and, more importantly, leave for me to play the piano. Quite jittery with anticipation, I lifted the lid and lightly touched the keys.

"I hope you're not going to embarrass us," Sylvia commented.

"H says she's first class," said Ruth.

"Are you sure he was referring to her accomplishments on the pianoforte?"

"Sometimes, you go too far, Sylvia."

I ended the debate with the beautiful "*Ar Lan Y Mor*" – the words and music as distinctively crystal as Sylvia's glass. My toes curled in delight.

"You sing too. Bravo." Sylvia set down her glass and lightly touched her hands together. She'd already decanted my untouched drink into hers. Fortunately, there was also a glass of water on the tray, which I gulped down before setting about one of the sandwiches. Once crumb-free I returned to the piano, and a small audience began to gather around me as I played snatches of pieces I knew by heart. And the exquisite afternoon sped by.

On our return to the Hyatt, I was almost walking on air. Imagine a carte blanche to play the piano at lunchtime whenever there was no other function scheduled at the Chateau Marmont. *Magnifiqué*.

Much later, when Brendan finally returned to our room, I was all but bouncing off the wall as I relayed the afternoon's events.

"It doesn't take much to make you happy, does it? Just a grand piano and a martini or two."

"It was a baby grand, and I didn't touch a drop of alcohol."

"Just as well, you're high enough. Fancy sharing that?" Then he flipped my feet from under me, caught me and dropped me on to the ghastly sofa. "Mm. Still giving off sparks, I see," he said, suddenly close and staring into my startled eyes.

"You're a loss to the world of rugby," I said with a playful slap to his shoulder. He grinned and kissed me.

***

Unlike the greater part of the band's female contingent, I attended quite a few rehearsals, despite the often repetitive tedium of the sessions. It proved a revelation to observe Brendan interact with the other band members and support crew. He was harsher, more demanding and caustic, than I had expected, especially if they weren't as committed and focused as he always was. Which perhaps explained his being known as H. Sylvia had gleefully informed me that the moniker stood for Himself and/or Hitler, depending on Brendan's most recent transgression.

However, the first rehearsal session I attended could well have been my last had it not been for Denny. I hadn't told anyone I was going to be there – I didn't want to make a fuss or alter the dynamic. A mistake, as it turned out to be.

I was making myself comfortable on a chair some distance from the stage, out of the way and out of sight, I had thought, until an intimidating stranger bore down on me. I instinctively jumped up and backed away, genuinely petrified. The man was obviously enraged at my presence and raised a clenched fist as he neared me. I think my blood momentarily congealed in my veins as I waited for the blow.

Suddenly, Denny appeared between me and my would-be attacker.

"Whoa, Punchie," he said, grabbing the fist-wielding arm heading my way. "Friend," Denny added soothingly, not relinquishing his hold on the man… Punchie.

Punchie stared at Denny a moment like a disinterested customs officer checking out a tourist, then he unclenched his hand and nodded. Denny let go of Punchie's arm and waited until his bandmate swivelled around and returned to the stage. There, Punchie quietly positioned himself behind his drum kit, as docile as a lamb, while Brendan, Baz and Jake continued to harangue each other about Jake's proposed keyboard solo.

"You'll be alright now. I've introduced you."

I looked at Denny in disbelief, still shaking and trying to fathom out what had just happened, but I did manage to nod.

"Punchie's a bit unpredictable."

I nodded again.

"I'll get you some water," he added, obviously concerned at my ongoing distress.

"Please don't leave me," I rushed forward to grab his arm.

"You're okay," he said, giving me a reassuring hug. Then the hall echoed with a piercing whistle.

"H!" Jake bellowed from the stage. "Golden Balls has got a grip on your bird." He placed two fingers in his mouth and whistled again.

So, I'd finally met the drummer. I thought his nickname referred to his drumming style, but as I'd discovered, it was more straightforward than that. Anyone who unsettled Punchie was likely to be punched. Punchie only left his room to play drums, which was why I didn't encounter him until rehearsals began.

As Denny said, Punchie was unpredictable and generally only interacted with the band members, and then mainly Baz and Brendan. Communication between the three consisted of head nods of varying speeds and wide-eyed glares. Anyone else was likely to be ignored, punched or glowered at by Punchie from beneath a magnificent pair of eyebrows. But when Punchie did smile, which was seldom, it was completely transformative. It was the only time he looked human. Years later, with the first television screening of *The Muppet Show*, I was certain that Animal was based on Punchie.

***

When he returned from rehearsals Brendan was solicitous, but irked. "I hate to think what would have happened if Denny hadn't seen Punchie leave the stage."

"Yes, I'm very grateful to Golden Balls," I said lightly, hoping to convey that I didn't consider Brendan at fault. I'd unintentionally got myself into an unsafe situation and I'd been lucky. It was a lesson learnt. Besides, I wanted to know about Denny's nickname.

"I wished you'd stayed," Brendan said more calmly, referring to my hasty exit. "I should have introduced you and warned you that Punchie can be un—"

"Unpredictable. Yes, I've gathered that. I'll give him a wide berth from now on. But none of what happened was your fault."

Finally, Brendan enveloped me in a protective embrace.

"Better late than never," I teased. "But tell me, why did Jake refer to Denny as 'Golden Balls'? And don't say 'for obvious reasons'."

"There's a bit more to it than that."

"And Jake's involved."

"Jake's usually involved in one way or another."

"Why do you put up with him?"

"We're like a family. You take the rough with the smooth because of what binds you. Obviously not blood in a band. For all his faults,

Jake is a talented musician. He adds something to most tracks, generally attitude. But the minute Jake loses interest in the music, he's out."

"He's jealous of Denny? Sees him as the golden boy?"

"Jake just likes to stir things up. I'm tired of talking about him." Then he pulled me close and kissed me. End of conversation.

***

With rehearsals often intense and fractious, the gigs were emotionally and physically draining highs, and this was just my summation as an observer. I couldn't begin to imagine how the band felt. Although my choosing to be part of the audience rather than sitting side-stage probably explained how wiped out by a gig I generally felt.

Nevertheless, side-stage didn't offer the full innards-jangling musical high I preferred: the pushing and shoving, the sweat, the surges and the sheer exhilaration of singing as one with the thousands present, pressed together and yet oblivious of all but the band and the music.

The two biggest venues the band played in LA were the Hollywood Bowl and the Forum. The Forum, such a pretentious name, I scoffed. But I had to eat my words; it was impressive in a very modern way despite its design owing more than a passing nod to a Roman amphitheatre. It proved to be the better venue, as the Hollywood Bowl had issues with the acoustics that required massive use of electronic amplification (not always for the best) in order to reach its full audience of seventeen thousand.

But of all the LA gigs, my favourite was Brendan's solo night at the Troubadour, where he played in tribute to Jimi Hendrix, who'd died midway through September that year. Brendan's plan to play a range of the maestro's hits on guitar and piano left me more than a little apprehensive. It's a brave man (or woman) who takes on a Hendrix track. But Brendan was unperturbed.

"I'll do what I do. It won't suit everybody – uppity Englishman mangling an American legend's work – but it feels right to acknowledge the man's legacy in his own country." Which was ironic given

Hendrix was first lauded by the British public rather than his fellow countrymen.

I needn't have worried, Brendan was mesmerising. He took to what was barely a stage in long, easy strides and looked calmly around, taking in the sea of faces.

"This is for Jimi Hendrix and the gift of his incredible music" was all Brendan said, but little else was required.

The audience was close in that small, smoky club, packed as it was with many famous and up-and-coming musicians – not an easy crowd. Yet Brendan was unruffled, his husky voice powerful and affecting as he skilfully presented some of the many covers that Hendrix had made inimitably his own: "Hey Joe", "All Along the Watchtower", "Sergeant Pepper's Lonely Hearts Club Band" and "Wild Thing". And somehow Brendan managed to do what Hendrix did and make the tracks his own. He didn't better Hendrix. Who could? His pared-back performance evoked rather than mimicked Hendrix. The crowd gleefully lapped it up, their thunderous applause rattling glasses, bottles and window panes.

Brendan then followed with a selection of Hendrix's own works: "Purple Haze", "Voodoo Chile", "Angel", "Fire" and "The Wind Cries Mary". He sang the last to me, his gaze unwavering.

When Brendan finished and bowed his head, the crowd went wild. Men with sweaty faces banged the beer-stained tables; young men with cigarettes clamped between their teeth slapped their hands together and stamped on the floor; others whistled and clapped while many of the women cheered and brushed away their running mascara. By which time everyone was on their feet, and the chant went up. "One more. One more." After a minute or so Brendan motioned for quiet and said, "I'll give you two," and the crowd roared its approval.

"But before I do, I'd like you to listen to someone who is very special to me." The audience hollered again. "She plays like an angel, and two little birds told me that she also sings like one."

"She certainly does," came Sylvia's unmistakable voice, followed by a whoop – from Ruth, I suspect.

"So please, a big LA welcome for Mari Morgan!"

The crowd dutifully clapped.

What's he doing? I thought. *He has them eating out of his hand, and he ruins the momentum by inviting me to the stage.*

He held his hand out to me, and I gave a slight shake of my head. Undeterred, he jumped down into the crowd, which set them yelling again, and pushed on towards me. Resigned to my fate, I let him lead me to the piano.

I was no novice. I'd played at school concerts, county concerts and eisteddfods. I never sang – but I had at the Chateau, so why not here? For Brendan. What could I sing that wouldn't challenge my vocal range while also acknowledging Hendrix? Had Hendrix covered "Day Tripper" by The Beatles? I thought so. Well, that's all I had to offer. I'd put together a piano version of the song some years earlier, and the lyrics were straightforward enough. I just cheekily changed the pronoun.

The audience loved it, especially when Brendan came in on the second run of the chorus with the original lyrics, grinning at me like a Cheshire cat.

"A hard act to follow," Brendan said once the applause abated, and he blew me a kiss, which set the whoopers and whistlers off once again.

He then swapped his acoustic guitar for an electric one and thrashed out Chuck Berry's "Johnny B. Goode" (another hit Hendrix had covered) and Otis Reading's "Too Hard to Handle" and almost brought the house down. It was a fabulous finish, with people twisting and jiving and generally having a ball. I thought I might burst with love, pride and awe.

Chapter 15

With it being our last full day in LA, I envisaged a leisurely day packing while Brendan dealt with band stuff. So, I was surprised when he reappeared, having left some time earlier.

"I'll see you in the foyer in an hour. Breakfast is on its way," he said, popping his head around the door.

I leapt out of bed, quickly showered, and had just thrown on a clean pair of jeans and a T-shirt when there was a knock at the door... Breakfast had arrived.

I drank the unbelievably good orange juice and coffee and ate some fruit and rolls. Then I grabbed my denim jacket and dragged my hair into a low ponytail before plonking the floppy hat I'd recently purchased onto my head.

When I careered into the foyer less than ten minutes later, a frantic hotel employee was attempting to hold back a boisterous bunch of fans intent on meeting Brendan.

"This way." Brendan quickly steered me towards the back of the hotel. We left via the kitchen entrance having acquired a large, packed bag on the way. Once outside, Brendan donned a bush hat and a pair of sunglasses.

"Right, my lovelee," he said, mimicking my accent, "the rest of the day is ours. Fancy a picnic?"

"Fantastic," I gushed, and he grabbed my hand and headed for a car parked further along the hotel's rear access lane. Cars had never interested me, but this one was incredible – a sleek, streamlined, head-turning vehicle with an electric blue body and white soft top. A Ford Mustang convertible, Brendan told me.

"It looks as though it could fly. Definitely more Pegasus than Mustang."

"That would be handy. But I'm afraid we'll have to brave the roads."

With Brendan all mine for the best part of a day, everything else was small fry.

After a quick scan of a map from the glove compartment, Brendan took to the highway and headed east out of LA. Although it was a bright, sunny day, he did not drop the roof until we were well clear of the suburbs. Then, with FM blaring on the radio, the wind in my hair, and the San Gabriel Mountains drawing ever nearer, I wondered if I'd been beamed *Star Trek*-fashion into someone else's life: a film star, a minor royal, a pools winner. Anyone's really, other than my own.

We had been travelling for over an hour and a half when Brendan finally pulled off the road.

"The hotel manager reckons this is a good place to picnic," he said as we got out of the car. "How about a walk before we feast?"

"Good idea. I'm still full from breakfast." We set off along the path which, Brendan informed me, climbed to the summit of Mount Rubidoux. On the way I asked about the two unexpected structures ahead of us, just as Brendan fished a sheet of paper from his jeans pocket.

"They're known as the Peace Tower and Friendship Bridge, built in honour of a Riverside leader devoted to world peace, apparently."

"Flipping heck," I gasped, hoping to remember all the little details of the trip so as to savour them later, or perhaps on a cold, dark winter's day back home.

At the mountain top we sighted another landmark: a large cross marking the location of the annual non-denominational Easter Sunrise Service, that is.

"D'you know?" I said, quite excited to have something to relate that Brendan might not know about. "This place puts me in mind of the Evan Roberts Revival—"

"Oh yeah," he interjected. "A time of outdoor sermons, spontaneous singing, prayer and baptisms." I shouldn't have been surprised that he knew.

The spot also offered spectacular views of the surrounding countryside – a striking landscape, predominantly an arid terrain with low scrub and ungainly cacti.

"It looks like cowboy film country," I said excitedly.

"It does," Brendan agreed. "Worth the walk."

With the Santa Ana River below us and the San Antonio Mountain in the distance, it was hard to disagree.

Also visible from our viewpoint were the towns of Riverside and Rubidoux, but our attention was caught by a large bird circling in the air nearby, obviously intent upon an invisible (to us) but imminent lunch.

We stood comfortably silent and close, our breathing steadying after the climb as we took in the panorama. The sun began to drop in the sky, lengthening the shadows and igniting the landscape with a palette of tawny reds and golds. Awestruck, I marvelled at the moment, thrilled at our day and Brendan's efforts to organise it, to say nothing of all the previous stand-out moments of the past weeks.

"I've really enjoyed the tour so far," I said plainly, almost at a loss for words.

"I'm glad." He gave me a squeeze. "You've made quite an impression on everyone."

"Who exactly?"

"Well, me, for one."

"I thought I'd done that back at the Angel," I said with a grin.

"Maybe," he replied mischievously.

Then, with one last look at the stunning landscape, I said, "I don't know about you but I'm ready for that picnic," and I took off down the path. "Race you!" I called.

With the soft top covering us once more, we consumed most of the picnic settled on the back seat of the car. So far, the hotel food had been a mix of outrageously bad and incredibly good, but the quality and range of fruit and vegetables available was always a revelation.

More than a little distracted with trying to identify the filling of the roll I was enjoying, Brendan's words took me by surprise.

"Ruth's a fan."

"Of what?" I asked, thinking he might be referring to the roll's contents.

"You, of course," he replied, with an exasperated grin. "By the way, it's avocado and halloumi."

I coloured and grinned, chuffed on both counts to be so enlightened. "I'm a fan of both Ruth and Sylvia. It wouldn't have been the same without them. And I love this filling, especially the spicy chutney."

"Ruth says you're quietly spirited."

I blushed with pleasure. "Sylvia's not so keen on me then?" I had to ask, suddenly fearful of how that might affect the next leg of the tour.

"On the contrary. She's currently reserving judgement on you."

"That sounds like anything but approval."

"That's because you've not known Sylvia as long as I have. She's not one to hold back on the criticism front, yet is quite sparing with praise."

"I'll hold on to that," I said, brightening.

On the way back to LA, we stopped at a small café on the outskirts of the city where we ordered strong black coffee and cake. We ended up sharing the cakes, each swapping between bites of one choice and the other.

It was late by the time we accessed the rear of the hotel and the kitchen, where we left the now relatively empty picnic bag, along with our thanks. Then we took off for our room, where we indulged in sex that tasted, unsurprisingly, of sweat and cake.

***

It was strange to leave the Continental Hyatt after the weeks we'd spent there. Jim Morrison had also been a resident during our stay, though I never saw him. Such was my curiosity about Morrison that when I heard he hung out at Barnie's Beanery on Santa Monica Boulevard, I suggested the diner as a lunch venue, but Sylvia rejected the idea.

"A surfeit of beer and beans is not to be recommended," she declared disdainfully. "Besides, Morrison is such a conflicted individual. I fear for his future," she added, sounding like a Roman augury.

"There you go," Ruth said with eyebrows raised and a barely perceptible grin. "The Chateau for lunch?"

Jake considered himself as having much in common with the Lizard King and often used Morrison's lyrics as chat-up lines: "Hello, I love you, won't you tell me your name?" being an unsurprising favourite. Fortunately, Jake had yet to take up hanging from hotel balconies, an act of folly on Morrison's part (ongoing, as it proved to be) that resulted in his eviction from the Hyatt.

Morrison's ill-fated stay, along with subsequent visits by The Who, The Rolling Stones, and ultimately Led Zeppelin, contributed much to the legend of the Riot House or Riot Hyatt, as it became known. We never stayed there again. A Harley Davidson in the corridors… Punchie would have killed someone.

Chapter 16

We left LA before noon the next day, the bulk of our party travelling by coach. The kit followed in a couple of trucks, with the road crew sharing the driving. Our small convoy was on the road again, cruising the Pacific Coast Highway, Santa Barbara bound.

"The American Riviera, darling," Sylvia replied when I questioned her about our destination. "Although the oil spill last year may have tarnished the moniker."

I had difficulty understanding Sylvia on occasion.

"There was a blow-out on an off-shore platform, apparently. Four million tons of crude oil, darling. Can you imagine?" She returned her gaze to the view beyond the window and a cigarette holder to her lips. My brief audience with Sylvia had been terminated.

I wandered up the aisle to the rear of the bus (trying not to think about a crude-oil-coated coastline) to where Brendan and Baz were playing acoustic guitars. Punchie, not the best of travellers, could be settled to play his bongos when so prompted. Eventually, the trio set up a rhythmic, somnambulant sound that sent a few to sleep, including Punchie, which was largely the point of the exercise.

"Is he okay?"

"He hasn't been okay for a long time," Brendan replied, tentatively removing the bongos from Punchie's lap and then packing his own guitar into its case.

"What happened to him?"

"We're not really sure. But rumour has it he suffered a really bad acid trip."

I gasped.

"He's been with us four years. No one has done acid in that time. Punchie's not the best advert for the practice. We tried to get him medical help back home but they wanted to section him. Drumming keeps him sane. Being with us keeps him clean."

"What's his real name?"

"No idea. Believe me, we've tried to dig up something on him."

I glanced across at Punchie. "But he must have a passport?"

"He has two. The one we acquired for him, no questions asked, just cough up the cash. And a legally obtained British passport, providing you overlook the false name, that is."

My eyes opened wide. They'd practically abducted him.

"Don't look so shocked. At the end of Punchie's first tour with us, Baz and I spent the remaining time on our work permit trawling the coast, trying to jog his memory, to find people who knew him or places he recognised. Still no one has shown up to claim him. The only written record of him is with the LA police, identifying him as Punchie, along with a litany of his many offences including breaking the peace, vagrancy, assault and drug abuse. If we hadn't got him out when we did, he would be dead by now. And others with him, possibly."

"That's incredible. The man's a liability and you took him on regardless." I clutched at his arm.

Brendan opened his briefly closed eyes. "Don't make it sound heroic, cos it's not. Our drummer upped and buggered off home, leaving us with the best part of the tour to do. Good drummers are rarer than hens' teeth, and then Punchie showed up. We'd have been stuffed without him. You've heard him play; he's a perfect fit. We look out for him." He hunched his shoulders and closed his eyes again.

But I was buzzing, astonished that four men, Brendan and Baz in particular, made the effort to "look out for" the human equivalent of an unexploded bomb. Even Jake went up in my estimation, to say nothing of Denny, who appeared to be grappling with a number of his own demons. I was in awe of each and every one of them.

My dizzying disbelief precluded napping, and with almost everyone else aboard the coach asleep, I had no option but to stare out of the window at the breathtaking scenery. And I decided to buy a good camera. The postcards I'd sent home to my parents and Eirwen were all very well, but imagine capturing moments like this; Brendan leaning towards me, his face unlined and relaxed; Punchie, wedged up against the window and anything but relaxed; Jake entwined with a couple of girls; Baz, his pipe in his lap and his usually neat hair in disarray as he slowly slipped to the floor... The possibilities were endless.

If I saved every dollar that came my way, it shouldn't take too long, I figured. I felt the usual twinge of guilt regarding the money I never asked for, but nevertheless took, from Brendan and assuaged my conscience as best I could. Brendan's need to have me out of his hair, and safely occupied, came at a price. It was a job of sorts.

The next day, I was at the beach, taking pictures. Brendan had overheard me asking the hotel's receptionist for directions to the nearest camera shop and followed me. Some streets away, at a window displaying cameras, lenses, bags, tripod stands, et cetera, he sidled up alongside me.

"I'll get a camera for your birthday." Engrossed in jotting down prices, I almost jumped out of my skin at the sound of his voice.

"I planned on saving for one, and I've not mentioned my birthday," I replied tetchily, all too aware of the irony of my self-righteous indignation.

"A detail I needed to obtain your passport. Either way, I'll be paying for the camera." He grinned mischievously.

"Birthday and Christmas then," I said, already opening the shop door.

***

If I hadn't witnessed the event with my own eyes, I would never have believed it. Streamlined in a dark wetsuit, and as sleek and shiny as a seal, Punchie rose from the water and began to wade towards his bobbing board, his expression one of pure joy. Click – my very first photograph. Brendan, Denny and Jake splashing each other in the shallows. Click. Baz puffing on his pipe, a watchful eye on Punchie. Click. Then I turned away from the sea and walked purposely towards the palm-tree-lined road.

"Don't point that contraption at me," Sylvia exclaimed, dipping her parasol and spoiling the shot. How did anyone sitting beneath a large beach umbrella also have need of a parasol? Although I was beginning to think that titanium-plated Sylvia needed her props to maintain her idea of herself, whatever that was. And I loved her all the more for it. We all have our props.

"Does 'kid with a new toy' spring to mind?" Ruth said, invitingly spread-eagled on a towel, and pouting provocatively for the camera. Click.

"You're safe for the moment, ladies," I replied, poised to pack the camera into its case.

Then Jake emerged from the sea to be quickly encircled by a gaggle of girls eager to towel him down. Click.

"There'll be a market for some of your photographs, darling," Sylvia said, her unguarded gaze trained on the frolicking group. Click.

***

Rehearsals started the next day and fortunately did not preclude trips down to the sea. Punchie surfed daily, and although obviously capable of doing so without assistance or supervision, no one was prepared to let him. Punchie walking the streets alone and carrying a large fibre-glass weapon. Perish the thought.

I continued to attend some of the rehearsals, mainly because it allowed me to chat with Denny. He always was so solicitous, making sure that I was comfortable, and offered some of the food and drink laid out for the band. He was certainly more attentive than Brendan, who was always preoccupied with the music. I warmed to the gentle blond giant, who had more about him than I had first thought. We also shared an interest in photography.

"I remember trying to make a pinhole camera when I was a kid. The biggest problem was getting a shoebox. My shoes were always second-hand and tied together with string," he said matter-of-factly. Then he offered me a stick of gum.

I'd never been a fan of chewing gum, even less so after Eirwen's brief dalliance with smoking cigarettes as I too was obliged to chew gum. Denny was amused by my tales of Eirwen and would often ask about her. It was a thoughtful thing to do; it made her absence seem less obvious.

I found his quiet, unassuming manner difficult to resist, and I was clearly not the only one – as demonstrated by Sylvia who, when asked by Denny, agreed to be photographed (prop-less) with me and Ruth.

Santa Barbara is blessed with a plethora of photogenic sites, apart from its impressive beaches. There's Stearn's Wharf, The Old Mission, the Santa Ynez mountains and foothills, and the oak trees and vineyards of the Santa Barbara Valley. A budding photographer's dream.

The band had two consecutive early evening performances booked at the Santa Barbara Bowl – an outdoor amphitheatre capable of seating over four-and-a-half thousand people, set amidst lush grounds on the edge of town. The venue's acoustics were fab and the weather was kind, which together with a great set, impeccably performed, made for two incredibly good shows.

Our next major stop was at Big Sur, then we were on to Monterey, followed by Carmel, and after that Santa Cruz. By the time we reached San Francisco, I'd had a surfeit of sightseeing, to say nothing of sun, sea and sand. Or so I thought.

With its ocean-side location and rolling hills, San Francisco is such a beautiful city. It was difficult to be indifferent to its many charms, even with an out-of-season episode of its legendary fog. On the downside, we were booked into one of the city's less than inspiring hotels, whose architecture brought to mind a clichéd motel. Luxurious it was not. Fleetingly, I craved to be back at the Hyatt, until, that is, I discovered how convenient the Phoenix Hotel was for San Francisco's many delightful tourist attractions.

"The lobby tomorrow morning, ten sharp," Sylvia instructed as she and Baz stopped outside their room.

"Aye, aye, Captain," I said with a brief salute, which made Baz, if not Sylvia, smile. There was no arguing with Sylvia. I didn't have the vocabulary, never mind the nerve.

The following morning, I swung into the lobby with a minute to spare. Brendan and I should not have indulged in last-minute shower sex. On my arrival, Sylvia checked her watch and headed for the hotel entrance. "Come along, we've a cable car to catch."

I stopped, momentarily tickled by the idea of catching a cable car (was a large net required?) until Ruth grabbed my arm. "You heard her ladyship." She propelled me forward in pursuit of Sylvia, who was already striding purposefully down Eddy Street.

"That's a tram," I said upon sighting one of San Francisco's famous cable cars pootling along, packed to the gunnels with people. Sylvia silenced me with a look from beneath her parasol as we joined the queue at the stop.

After a bit of a wait, we boarded a car, and what a treat the ride proved to be, quite thrilling, in a clanging, clattering sort of way, and scenic too.

We alighted at Fisherman's Wharf, our destination Frank Crivello's Oyster Bar located in the Cannery Courtyard, his stellar crab sandwiches a must, according to Sylvia. I'm not sure my stomach agreed. However, as we ate our lunch, and Frank sang for the diners his signature tune "Come Back to Sorrento", I had to agree. Freshly caught crab *was* delicious.

It struck me, not for the first time, what I would have missed had it not been for Ruth and Sylvia. I left my sandwich a moment to consider the younger girls – a tightly knit group, as I knew to my cost, having tried but failed to breach their borders. Still, a little camaraderie on an outing or two wouldn't have hurt them.

"Why do none of the other girls come on our trips?" I asked.

"Cos we're too old and not with it enough," Ruth replied.

"I'm about their age. I don't think that."

"But you're different, darling. More discerning."

"We always welcome new girls but few hang out with us once they find their feet," Ruth added.

"I can't imagine how grim this tour would have been without you." I placed a hand on Ruth's arm and reached out to touch Sylvia.

She flicked at my hand with a napkin. "Crab fingers, darling," she said, mortified.

Over the next few days, we climbed to the top of Coit Tower for its panoramic views of the city, sampled the varied delights of China-town, took a boat trip across to Alcatraz Island, and strolled around Ghirardelli Square – where we later ate ice cream sundaes with hot fudge sauce. Not to forget visiting, but not crossing, the Golden Gate and Oakland Bay Bridges.

It was a shame the band's gigs would curtail our sightseeing, I jokingly said to Brendan, who made no attempt to conceal his annoyance.

"Don't put yourself out. Attendance isn't compulsory." He huffily stalked around our room in a towel, snatching up clothing.

"Got you," I said with a grin. "Just try and keep me away."

I reached up to tweak his cheek as he brushed past me.

"Got *you*," he retorted, catching me off guard and wrestling me onto the bed, losing his towel in the process. Ah, good times.

***

The last few gigs of the tour included three nights at the New Old Fillmore (formally the Fillmore Auditorium) and a couple of small shows at the Matrix. The latter was basically a bar with a small stage and room for one hundred and twenty people. Undaunted, the band put on a pared-back set, and the fans went away happy, given the intimacy of the show. But the Fillmore... the Fillmore was something else.

Dressed like a debutante and already on her second martini, Sylvia pointed to the venue's elaborately corniced ceiling.

"Crystal chandeliers, darling. So elegant," she commented, seemingly oblivious of the very inelegant throng beneath our curtained eyrie (one of the smaller boxes at the back of the hall, that is).

"Desert Heat. Desert Heat," the crowd chanted, clapping a deafening rhythm in time to the thud of thousands of Cuban heels, platforms and plimsolls that pounded the hardwood floor beneath our box. Busy on stage, the roadies scuttled crab-like hither and thither, checking the last of the cables and speakers. Then the main lights dimmed, and the crowd roared its approval as multicoloured spotlights began to rake the stage.

Punchie was the first to appear, pummelling the air, sticks in hand, until seated at his drums where he set up a thundering drumbeat. Then the remainder of the band bounded onto the stage and the audience surged forward, baying like banshees. My breath caught at the intensity of the sound and movement, despite my distance from the action. The band, pumped up on the power of the crowd's reaction, tore through some of their faster, rockier tracks, which proved absolutely electrifying. Meanwhile, Sylvia inserted plugs in her ears and headed for the bar, which freed up more space in the box for me and Ruth to dance.

The following two concerts at the Fillmore mirrored the first and heralded the end of a very successful tour. The celebration that followed was hedonistic. Well, for some it was. Brendan's weariness was tangible as he leaned against the bar, his drink untouched. And Denny, a bottle of Coke in his hand, watched and inhaled greedily as glasses of beer and spirits skirted by him. I worried for him and his obvious struggle with alcohol.

One of the road crew had already taken Punchie back to the hotel, and after an hour or so of polite chit-chat, Brendan, Denny and I also adjourned to the Phoenix. En route, Denny fell asleep, and soon Brendan also slumped down on the seat with his head on my shoulder. With him so still and quiet, I thought he too was sleeping, until he whispered into my ear.

"Thank you for making this such a great tour." He gave me a squeeze.

I looked at him in surprise. "But we've hardly seen each other. Or is that the point?" I shifted away from him.

"Tours are like that. To be honest, I didn't think you'd last the trip." He smiled wanly and began to narrow the gap between us.

"You didn't expect much of me then."

"No one is prepared for life on the road. But you… you've been incredible. A real boon."

"A good thing that sounds like the least desirable part of a baboon."

He burst out laughing and pulled me close. "Ah, you crack me up. I can't remember when I last enjoyed a tour as much."

"So, I've got the job, Mr Bradshaw?"

"You bet your sweet ass, Miss Morgan," he said in a much-improved American accent.

The next day, I was unsurprised to learn that Sylvia had been the last person still standing when the party finally ended.

Chapter 17

We returned to Britain and Brendan's home, a sprawling Tudor house on the banks of the river near Henley-on-Thames, just before Christmas.

We were travelling in a chauffeur-driven hire car, both asleep after the long flight, when I woke up just in time to see an impressively solid pair of gates closing totally unaided behind us.

Wow, I thought as the vehicle inched up the gravel driveway. Along the approach, intermittent lamps illuminated tall trees and dense shrubs. Suddenly, the house loomed ahead as brightly lit as the tall Christmas tree that stood adjacent to the large front porch.

I got out of the car and rushed towards the old oak door as the driver began to offload the luggage. Such was my incredulity at the prospect of living in this beautiful building, I all but did a jig. Then Brendan dropped my coat around my shoulders, Punchie loped off to his cottage in the grounds, and the large door opened into the house.

"Welcome home, sir," said the thin, grey-haired woman at the entrance as we entered the double-height hall beyond the porch. I sensed her disapproval of me despite Brendan being positioned between us.

Across the hall, opposite the entrance, a staircase rose up and divided into two, extending in either direction along the back wall of the huge space. Another Christmas tree, jewelled with dried, translucent slices of citrus fruits, stood to one side of the staircase, vying with the flickering log fire at the far end of the hall to scent the warm air. And there was so much wood on view, apart from the furniture. Beautiful carved, curved and polished wood gleaming in the lamp-light… banisters, balustrades, beams, panels and flooring… woods of varied grains and colours that somehow made for a harmonious, welcoming whole.

The house seemed to embrace and envelop me. I felt as though I'd stepped back in time, and said as much to Brendan.

"It's wonderful," I added, taking in Brendan's obvious pleasure in the praise. This was something unusual for him, someone constantly showered with compliments, which he generally ignored or rebuffed with glib retorts.

"I hope you'll be happy here," he said, and he made to kiss me only to be halted by a sharply emitted "Sir", which caused us to turn, and Brendan to apologise.

"Sorry, Mrs Parsons. I was somewhat distracted then." He turned to me and smiled wickedly, making me blush as he knew I would.

Mrs Parsons cleared her throat and narrowed her eyes at me before returning her attention to Brendan.

"Will sir take food in the dining hall or the kitchen?" she said in a voice as stiff as her stance.

Images of Miller the Killer came to mind, and I had to fight back an urge to quote. Mrs Parsons would not have been amused.

"Not for me, thanks. Mari?"

"No, thank you."

"By the way, Mrs Parsons, this is Mari Morgan."

I attempted a little wave and a smile, to no avail.

"Good night, sir," she said, ignoring me and striding out of view.

"Oh dear. I don't think she's fussed about me. Perhaps she prefers your wife," I said and immediately wished I hadn't.

"Don't waste the worry. Especially not on Maureen. I know she once lived here but it was years ago. Maureen's my wife in name only."

Nevertheless, she was still his wife, if only on paper. As I already knew. And yet it was only then, on entering her former home, that

Maureen Bradshaw's status suddenly veered from barely considered fairy-tale villainess to a living, breathing person… with a child.

Brendan and I climbed the stairs in silence. And I found it difficult to cross the threshold of what was obviously our bedroom – the large bed seemed to mock my audacity, daring me to proceed further.

"It's not the same bed."

I started as if surprised to hear his voice and looked at Brendan questioningly.

"Maureen took the bed we'd shared with her. Hideous white metal attempt at a four poster." He raised his eyebrows and smiled faintly.

"I'm sorry to have been so obviously squeamish." I hoped I didn't sound as unsettled as I felt.

"We're both very tired. Let's get some sleep."

I reached up and kissed his cheek, grateful that he'd understood.

***

The Christmas break flew by. I managed a trip back to Gwaun to visit my parents and had hoped to see Eirwen too, but my letters, cards and phone calls had all gone unanswered.

"She's stayed on in Cardiff," said her mother, as she closed the door behind me. She eyed the large, gift-wrapped package I placed on the table in the kitchen.

"That's not for us, is it?" she asked, as to the point as ever. "You've not dragged that all the way from America, have you?"

"No," I said, trying to hide my disappointment at not finding Eirwen at home. "I got it in Cardiff."

"Well, that's very kind of you, Mari."

"Has Eirwen been home at all over the holiday?"

"Only for Christmas Day. She's been working in some pub in Cardiff," she replied, engrossed in the label and suddenly remembering her reading glasses pushed up onto her head. "All our favourites are here, Mari. Phil is particularly fond of those Italian almond biscuits. He's having a nap at the moment, but thanks again."

We chatted amiably for another half an hour or so, neither of us letting on how conscious we were of Eirwen's absence. It was akin to sitting beside a large, dark hole without acknowledging it was there.

About to leave, I put another gift onto the table: the beautiful, blue-enamelled, silver cuff bangle I'd bought in Los Angeles.

"I'm sure she'll love it. Mind you, goodness knows when she'll get it, when we'll see her next," Megan said, suddenly as sombre as I felt.

On the way to my house, I readied myself for the battle I was certain would ensue with regard to the gift organised for my parents. Brendan had suggested it and, of course, would be financing the arrangement. This was "Operation Keeping the Parents Sweet", as he referred to his idea of installing and covering bills for a telephone. This was indicative of his limited knowledge of my parents. They were more likely to be scandalised than sweetened.

Familiar, forgotten smells washed over me as I clattered into the back porch. And I was struck for the second time since the taxi had dropped me off at Eirwen's how claustrophobic our valley felt, never mind our threadbare homes. It unnerved me how distanced I felt from all that I'd been reluctant to relinquish for Cardiff just five months previously. However, I instantly brightened when my dad appeared. He clung to me like a man drowning then stepped away and studied my face, following with a nod and another hug.

"Any chance of getting in by the Rayburn?" I asked, hoping that my embrace had conveyed all the love and longing I felt, and how happy I was, despite dearly missing my parents.

"Of course." He grinned broadly and bundled me and my baggage through the scullery and into the kitchen.

"Who is it, Dai?" my mother asked, her back to us as she placed a large casserole dish on the table.

My parents hadn't known I was coming home. In my letters I'd mentioned the possibility of a visit sometime after Christmas. As expected, my father had greeted me with an accepting, calm pleasure. But I knew that my mother would not be as calm or accepting of my sudden appearance. Visits should be planned, visitors planned for.

"Mari," she exclaimed. Only my mother was capable of arranging the syllables of a word in such a way, making it both a greeting and a rebuke. I hugged her and she patted my back. Then, running a hand down her crossover apron, as though suddenly aware that it was faded and worn in places, she started.

"Well, if I'd known you were coming, I'd have cooked more vegetables."

I smiled. She had provided me with the means to win this particular battle.

Check, I thought, saying, "How could I have done that? It was only this morning that Brendan and I decided on visits home to parents."

My mother glanced around at the mention of Brendan's name but would not be distracted.

"You could have left a message at Eirwen's."

"Eirwen's still in Cardiff, and you know what the boys are like – never there, except to eat. And I didn't want to trouble Megan. It's time you had a telephone, then I could ring home and let you know about visits."

Whether or not this was checkmate depended on her knight. I looked across at my father, who was now seated at the table, covetously eyeing the casserole dish. Our eyes met as my mother moved up a gear, her folded arms tightening across her chest.

"Do you think we're made of money or what?"

"No," interrupted my father, "but she's well acquainted with someone who is."

Momentarily bewildered, my mother looked across at my father and then the penny dropped.

"I hope you're not suggesting what I think you're suggesting."

"Well, I think it's a very good proposition. I like the idea of being able to speak to my daughter on a regular basis."

There was no arguing with that. I smiled at Dad and handed the letter with the details of the installation to my mother. I had other small gifts I'd purchased in America, but they could wait, whereas the casserole on the table could not. My father echoed my thoughts.

"Leave that till later, Mor. Sit down, so that we can eat," Dad urged, as Mam scanned the letter, already making plans.

Chapter 18

Although I'd enjoyed my trip home, I was glad to get back to Brendan. But Mrs Parsons was proving a real pain in the backside.

The fact I was in *her* house and still breathing added to my catalogue of offences, in Mrs Parsons' opinion – the details of which I'd hear her outlining to the part-time employees, including the cleaner, the kitchen assistant and the groundsman. Mrs Parsons invariably referred to me as "that Welsh girl", leading me to ponder on which was my greater crime: being Welsh or being a girl.

In truth, at that time, Brendan was my only ally at The Elms, although Joe, the gardener proved good company, matching my father in age and in his dedication to gardening. Joe was also very much his own man and not under Mrs Parsons' jurisdiction, as he shared the subdivided cottage in the grounds with Punchie. Added to this, he seemed to revel in going against the tide, which embracing me as a gardening protégé was bound to do.

Even so, it was fortunate, as far as I was concerned, that the greater part of my first year with Brendan involved touring rather than avoiding Mrs Parsons at The Elms. Initially, I made an effort to be friendly, but the wretched woman seemed to delight in mentioning Maureen Bradshaw whenever in my company.

"This is fab," I remarked to Mrs Parsons, genuinely taken by the lamp with a doughnut-shaped ceramic base and tall braided shade which stood on the floor in the hall alongside the teak and metal Decca radiogram.

"Danish. Mrs Bradshaw's choice." Wince.

Then there was the box of scarves. I was in search of the source of the overwhelming fragrance in my unnecessarily capacious wardrobe, given my meagre collection of clothing, when I discovered them. The scarves were silky, sinuous creations that could have graced Salome's seductive form.

"I'll post them on to Mrs Bradshaw" was Mrs Parsons' clipped reply to my query. But I'm sure there were the makings of a smile on her generally impassive face. Had she left them there deliberately?

On my arrival at The Elms, I had no idea of Maureen Bradshaw's appearance. However, aided and abetted by Mrs Parsons, my imagination was beginning to put together a fairly overwhelming photo-fit image. The chair incident all but completed the picture.

I can't believe it took me so long to discover the chair, especially as it resided in the music room. However, the beautiful grand piano and a wall rack packed with guitars proved major distractions within that space and probably explained my managing to overlook the stunning jukebox also housed there: a gleaming glass and chrome Wurlitzer 2000 Centennial (so Brendan told me), which was as much a treat to view loading a 45rpm single as listening to it play.

On first sighting the chair (and its matching white tulip side table), I thought it totally out of place – a cold plastic folly set amid a palace of warm-hued bricks and wood. But ultimately, I couldn't resist it… a Ball Chair, just like the one in *The Prisoner*.

Barely three years earlier, Eirwen and I had devoured the series starring Patrick McGoohan, as much for the fact that it was set in Wales as anything else. Portmeirion, and the estuary it overlooked, had never been more photogenic despite the intimidating presence of a giant white bouncing balloon. We admired Number Six's dark-coloured, braided rowing blazer and quoted lines from different episodes including the legendary "I am not a number…", but we didn't have a clue what the show was about.

Undoubtedly, I was initially drawn to the chair by its celebrity status, but I returned to it again and again because it was so comfortable. With its interior padded sections fitting together like the segments of an orange, the Ball Chair proved cocooning and such a great place to curl up with a book. Until Mrs Parsons discovered me there, that is. I was engrossed in a camera book from the local library at the time and didn't hear her approach.

"Mrs Bradshaw's favourite spot," she said accusingly, as though the aforementioned had only just vacated the room.

Startled from my study, I left the chair as if ejected from a fighter jet, hitting my head in the process. A small grin briefly flickered across Mrs Parson's face.

From then on, when not with Brendan, being out of the house became my priority. I spent an inordinate amount of time at the library in Henley, where the librarian proved most helpful. She ordered extra books to supplement the few on offer on site and also suggested that I join the local camera club. It was an appealing notion, but I decided to wait until after the next leg of the tour, when I hoped to be ready to try my driving test.

In the meantime, I settled on putting into practice what I'd gleaned from my recent reading along with getting the reels of film I'd taken in America processed. All credit to the camera, my first prints more than exceeded my expectations. The shots of Punchie surfing were surprisingly good – touching even, his enjoyment quite affecting, prompting me to buy frames for my favourite two.

Brendan was practising a Welsh hymn in the music room when I turned up with the framed photographs. Quite entranced, I remained by the door, savouring the rich tones of the piece, when Brendan suddenly stopped playing.

"Am I getting to grips with it?"

"No false modesty, Mr Bradshaw. You know how good that was."

"Always nice to hear, though. Are those some of your photographs?"

"What do you think?" I asked, as he took hold of the frames.

"What you said about my playing."

"They are good, aren't they?"

"Beginner's luck, perhaps?" He grinned and I gave him a playful poke to the ribs.

"Do you think Punchie would like them?"

"Anyone's guess."

Punchie had three daytime hangouts along with appropriate activities: in the cottage playing the bongos, in the garden working with Joe or in the games room playing his drum kit. The latter location was actually half of the building and had been the former stables. Given its open door and the sound of voices from within, I made my way there.

Joe and another man were chatting as Punchie worked at a long section of wood with sandpaper. No surprise then that the twelve-foot-long, eight-legged Thurston snooker table was swathed in protective sheets, as was the table tennis set and the table football game. Even the dartboard was dressed for dust.

My puzzled expression was enough to prompt Joe to explain, albeit in very simple terms. "The bowling alley needs sanding."

"I didn't know there was one."

My response prompted the stranger to speak. "The currently disassembled Polaris indoor bowling alley is an Amusement Company of Texas piece. At the moment the metal panels and rails are being re-chromed and the graphics, mechanical parts and electronic scoreboard restored. It will be set to vend free and run off a British power supply, and comes with a fully automated ball return," the man rattled off as though reading a manual. He then looked at me expectantly.

"Great," I said, barely any the wiser.

"Right, I'd best be off. I'll return when the parts are ready," said the expert man, making for the door.

Once he'd left, I held out the prints to Joe.

"Well, well," Joe said delightedly. "Punchie," he called out to his multi-talented assistant.

Punchie's lumbering gait gave no indication of his agility as a surfer. He stood directly in front of Joe, solemn and silent. "Mari wants to speak to you." Joe indicated to me. Punchie then turned himself rather than just his eyes towards me, eyes which were as dark and fathomless as cave pools.

I slowly raised the frames in front of him. "Santa Barbara, Punchie. Santa Barbara." I spoke softly, hoping not to spook him.

Suddenly, something flashed in his eyes and a spasm of fear ran through me. But his face was transformed by the widest of grins, his eyes alight with joyous recognition. "Santa Barbara." He grasped the frames. "Santa Barbara. Queen of the coast." He walked briskly away, still studying the photographs.

"Like an echo of his old self. As far as any of us would know." Joe patted my shoulder and followed after Punchie.

It wasn't the first time I'd heard Punchie speak, but it was certainly the most memorable.

On the way back to the house I began to sing. Not Leonard Cohen's celebratory track, though. I opted for George Fredric Handel's masterpiece. "Hallelujah, hallelujah. Hallelujah!"

That night in bed, Brendan said:

"Once I realised that you'd gone in search of Punchie, I thought it best to make sure you were alright. On the way I bumped into Joe." He then pulled me to him. "Seems Punchie was quite pleased with your gift." He kissed me. Just a thank-you kiss, nice but unnecessary. Punchie's response had been thanks enough.

***

I was looking forward to leaving The Elms, to escaping Mrs. Parsons, however temporarily. Fortunately, a tour of Europe meant everything was scaled down - the flight duration, the distance between venues, even the crowd reaction. Europeans made for a more reserved audience generally. There was a different vibe altogether on the continent. It felt like more of a holiday than the previous trip. Of the countries we visited, Italy proved to be my favourite for its beauty, architecture, antiquities, food and most of all, its people. And time spent with Ruth and Sylvia was always a major plus, with the added bonus of being able to quiz them about Maureen Bradshaw.

"How many tours did Maureen actually complete?" Sylvia asked Ruth. Her tone was clipped, military even, as though she sought information about an errant squaddie.

"Mo wasn't keen on touring. She only managed one and a half. You're not troubling yourself about Mo, are you?" Ruth lowered her sunglasses to look at me.

It was surprisingly cold for March as we briskly walked the Champs-Élysées, but the light was searing.

"I'm just curious," I lied – unconvincingly, given Ruth's ongoing scrutiny.

"She was immense fun. Larger than life. Quite a character." Sylvia drew on her cigarette holder as she considered further phrases with which to flay me.

"Loud, demanding and fond of the spotlight," Ruth volunteered.

"H was quite besotted."

Thank you, Sylvia. Her words were piledriving me into the ground.

"We all were for a while," said Ruth, taking my arm. "Apart from Baz. He seemed to have the measure of her from the start. Referred to her as the Mo of Babylon."

At this, Sylvia laughed out loud, something she rarely did. "Goodness. How could I have forgotten that?" She tittered more politely.

My mind was buzzing as I reflected on what had been said. First and foremost, it was apparent to me how very different I was from Maureen. Was this the basis of my appeal for Brendan? If so, it was a weak and worrying foundation on which to build a relationship.

Then there was Baz's summation of Maureen. If Maureen had behaved as Baz implied, it was unsurprising that the marriage failed. But with possible grounds for a divorce, why remained legally bound to an unfaithful spouse? Just more unanswered questions.

***

On our return to The Elms, Brendan and I were greeted by Mrs Johnson, the lady who worked in the kitchen on a part-time basis, on what was generally one of her days off. She imparted, with an excessive level of glee, I thought, given her former apparent friendship with Mrs Parsons, that the aforementioned had given and already worked notice.

I resisted the urge to link hands with Mrs Johnson and dance around the hall and thanked Providence and all known deities for this momentous news and did not give a second thought as to the reason or reasons behind the sudden departure of my nemesis.

It was a struggle not to hum.

Brendan's response to the news was unsurprising, given that he considered Mrs Parsons to be efficient and professional, if a little brusque. Brusque? The woman could pare back skin with a glance.

"What's happened?" Brendan asked, suddenly turning from Mrs Johnson to look at me, an eyebrow cocked. Was I grinning? Probably. Humming? More than likely. As long as lah-lah-ing wasn't involved, I reasoned, I might just get away with it.

"She's left a letter for you, Mr Bradshaw," said Mrs Johnson, doing her utmost to appear solemn but not before glancing at me, a conspiratorial gleam in her eyes, "in the music room. But the gist of it is she's gone to take care of her old dad."

Bless him, I thought, until that moment certain that Mrs Parsons had been hatched or conjured up in a cauldron.

"It's good of you to hold the fort, Mrs Johnson." Brendan patted her shoulder. "And I'd be grateful if you'd continue to do so until I find a new housekeeper."

"Happy to be of help, Mr Bradshaw."

"Let's take a look at this letter," he said to Mrs Johnson.

And I watched him walk away. I never tired of this. His was the languorous, graceful gait of a tall person. Relaxed, feline, sexy and good to look at from the front or the rear.

Stop that, I thought, suppressing the urge to follow and fondle him.

***

Despite Mrs Johnson's best efforts, I came to realise just how efficient Mrs Parsons had been. The Elms no longer ran on the proverbial oiled wheels. On occasions there appeared to be at least one with a wobble.

Not that I mourned her absence. Sure that she had possessed powers that rendered me incapable of the simplest of tasks in her presence, I heaved a sigh of relief at her departure. Brendan found it all highly amusing. Nevertheless, he suggested that I meet her prospective replacement.

"Paul knows someone," he said, two weeks into the post-Parsons hiatus. "Need to snap her up sharpish, apparently."

Paul Maunders was Brendan's manager. Business had brought them together, but their personalities and principles bound them. In the cutthroat world of the music business, Paul was a rarity – a man of his word and a real gentleman.

True to form, Paul was not wrong. Enter Mrs Booker, whose arrival heralded an end to all my household nightmares. From the outset she was warm and friendly, and her physical appearance was also the polar opposite of Mrs Parsons. She was, as Brendan graphically put it, "an armful or two of a woman". Fortunately for us, her ability as a housekeeper equalled that of Mrs Parsons, her prowess as a cook and manager evident from the beginning.

I loved everything about her, particularly her lemon meringue pie and the fact that she'd hug you if she thought it was appropriate and/or necessary. Best of all, I loved that she referred to me as "lamb".

Brendan almost choked as he struggled to keep a straight face on first hearing Mrs Booker use the endearment.

"How appropriate," he laughed on her exit, what with me being Welsh, and Wales being famous for its lamb. "Like a lamb to the slaughter," he added, in what he considered was a Welsh accent. Then he baaed as he sidled up to me, a wolfish grin on his face.

With Mrs Parsons gone, I attempted to push Brendan's wife to the back of my mind, an ongoing challenge as it proved to be. But there was no point in badgering Brendan about her when he obviously wasn't prepared to discuss his estranged wife.

Then, with my clothing collection growing and no further room available in the large chest of drawers in the corner of our bedroom, I decided it was time to deal with the wardrobe I had actively avoided since the box of scarves incident. It must have been Maureen Bradshaw's parting gift to drench the interior of the wardrobe with the perfume equivalent of paint stripper.

Just as I opened the wardrobe door, Brendan entered the bedroom, and suddenly stopped and sniffed – unnecessarily, I'd say.

"A penny for them."

"I'll ask Mrs Booker to sort that for you."

"You didn't think about your wife then?"

"Hard not to, really. That perfume is as unsubtle as Maureen always was." He seemed puzzled.

"You don't miss her?" I felt I had to spell it out for him.

"Why would I?" He smiled and slid his arms around my waist.

Although somewhat appeased, I couldn't stop myself from asking, "Then why don't you divorce her?"

His hands fell away from me and his expression hardened slightly.

"I will when the time is right," he said shortly and walked away. At which point I resolved not to mention Maureen to him again. It wasn't worth the aggravation.

Still, with the tour over and the school summer break a mere month away, and Brendan yet to mention a prospective visit by "the child", I took it upon myself to suggest the possibility of a stay.

We were drying off after a dip in the pool, the sun on our backs, the flagstones warm beneath our feet and the air fragrant with the scent of summer blooms, when I tentatively broached the subject.

"Is your child a boy or a girl?"

"I don't have a child." He continued to rub at his chest with a towel.

"But... You told me you had a wife and there was a child."

"Doesn't make the child mine."

He still hadn't looked at me. Stunned into silence, I shelved the idea of a visit along with the countless questions his response evoked. With my limited experience, I couldn't be sure whether it was just Brendan who could so effectively close a door on such emotive issues, or men in general.

***

As July progressed, the weather continued to be hot, dry and sunny. Things were also heating up in Northern Ireland, but not, sadly, in any meteorological sense.

Brendan and I were lounging on the sun terrace and consuming vast quantities of Mrs Booker's delightful lemon barley water when the sound from the groundsman's portable radio filtered across to us with news of the seven explosions that had taken place in Belfast's city centre. I sat upright and looked across at Brendan aghast. I was no stranger to horror; there were televised images of the many atrocities committed in Vietnam that I would never forget. But Belfast was part of Britain, and it was difficult to reconcile the idea that such things could happen here.

"Hard not to be affected by such events," Brendan said, touching my hand. "No matter how near or far away."

Though not much of a swimmer, I loved the pool. But as a confident, strong swimmer, Brendan also liked to take to the dark, weedy depths of the Thames while I would hover anxiously on the riverbank, clutching a buoyancy aid, or pursue him in the rowing boat when he went over its side. He chuckled at my concern, maintaining that I was in greater danger, given my shambolic rowing style and fear of the river.

I preferred to observe the river from the safety of the boathouse. Despite loving the kitchen garden, the formal areas and the wider grounds of The Elms, my favourite place was the boathouse. A seemingly organic structure that grew out of the riverbank, its shallow pentagonal roof space was a furnished studio apartment with a glazed front that projected over the water.

On sunny days, we'd fold back the glass doors and secure the billowing gauze curtains so as to observe the creatures and birds that inhabited the watery world below. And on starry nights we'd lie on the bed and stare out of the roof window, listening to the nocturnal noises of the night-shift occupants of that same watery world and the bumping of the small boats on the river shallows beneath us.

The boathouse was our special place. Only Brendan and I stayed at the boathouse. It was a grown-up equivalent of the willow den Eirwen and I had enjoyed since childhood. As I lay or sat beside Brendan within our hideaway haven, I often pondered on whether or not I'd share this space with Eirwen if she ever appeared on my horizon.

I thought of her daily and continued to make regular phone calls to her parents' home and to send written updates to Cardiff Uni in the hope of hearing from or about her... all to no avail. Eirwen had gone to ground.

To her credit, she regularly sent brief letters home, all from Cardiff, saying that she was fine. So, everyone had to be satisfied with the hand they'd been dealt, while Eirwen currently held all the cards.

Chapter 19

As the days passed, we settled into a comfortable routine. Brendan was often busy with the business of making music, be it writing, jamming or recording. He regularly disappeared into the music room or down to Denny's, along with Punchie and his latest riff or line of lyrics. But we still managed to spend a lot of time together.

Denny visited The Elms as often as Brendan went downriver to Denny's house at Richmond. Sadly, Denny was currently experiencing what Brendan termed "woman trouble" – something Denny was no stranger to, apparently.

"I don't know where he finds them," Brendan briefly commented when news first reached us of the escalating animosity between the starcrossed lovers. "Nothing but gold diggers, every last one of them."

We knew things were really serious when Denny appeared in our bedroom the following Monday at three o'clock in the morning, pacing the width of the room at the foot of the bed.

"What the fuck do you think you're doing?" Brendan demanded as he flicked on the bedside lamp and glared at Denny.

"Christ, I need a drink, Bren."

"You did the right thing. We'll have some tea." He looked back at me as I sat up in bed, no longer quivering and now slightly bemused.

"What's the matter?"

"I'll explain later." He stepped into his jeans. "Try and get some sleep."

And somehow, I did, only to be jolted awake for a second time that night, although now it was almost light when Brendan pressed his cold, hard body against mine.

"Laying claim to my half of the bed, eh?" he said, shunting me across to my side while I twitched and gasped at his icy touch.

"You should share the bed and your body heat," he whispered hoarsely before clamping his mouth to mine, his arms and legs around me.

Better than an alarm clock, I considered, matching Brendan's fervour.

Less than an hour later we were devouring bacon and eggs in the dining room with the French doors spread wide. The sun was already warming the flagstone terrace.

"I'll get him up once we've eaten," said Brendan in between mouthfuls.

By the end of the pre-Christmas part of the tour, I was aware that Denny didn't drink. However, alcohol wasn't Denny's only problem.

"I think he has an addictive personality, if there is such a thing. Drink, drugs, gambling… all the usual. You name it, he's tried it." Brendan stopped eating and speaking at this point, as if contemplating the past and its problems.

"You've never been tempted by drugs?"

He seemed distracted. Then he looked at me as if deliberating on a reply. He went to speak, hesitated momentarily and then ploughed on.

"Oh, I've done drugs. Heavy drugs. In my teens. Before I met Denny. I'm lucky to be here. I owe it to… myself to stay clean. Which is just as well for Denny. He's okay now, but it was rough at times when we were younger. That's why he has a key and just turns up. I'm his safety valve."

I put down my cup and my fork and touched his arm.

"You're so… so…" I searched for the right word.

"Hungry," he said, deflecting my attempt at praise. "Now finish your food. We need to keep our strength up," he added with a wink.

Nevertheless, I wanted to voice how I felt, but a tune kept getting in the way. Meanwhile, Brendan dragged the remnants of his last piece of toast around his plate.

"I'm taking Denny home to get his locks changed. Shouldn't be long, my love. And what's that you're humming? Sounds familiar." He pecked my cheek and left the room just as I identified the chorus of the song I'd been struggling with.

"You've made me so very happy," I sang as the brass and keyboards built to the chorus crescendo. "I'm so glad you came into my life…" Blood, Sweat & Tears and their fabulous song.

Then his words echoed above the sounds in my head.

"My love… my love."

He'd called me his love.

***

Denny's bank balance and homestead were now secure from any further attempted access by the former girlfriend and part-time pilferer. I'd never met her, as she and Denny weren't together long before she did a bunk with the gardener. Nevertheless, she'd regularly been returning to Denny's house to remove small items of value.

"So, what do you think?" Brendan asked on his return.

I gazed blankly at him. "I fail to understand how anyone could treat Denny so badly. He's such a nice man."

"That's his trouble. He needs to toughen up and treat 'em mean now and again." Then he suddenly nipped my ear.

"Hey!" I raised my hand to slap his face, but he responded swiftly and caught my wrist.

"Have to be quicker than that," he drawled and moved in to kiss me. I bit his nose.

"Ow!"

"I thought you were quicker than that."

"Touché." He rubbed his nose. "But what about this party?"

"Party?"

"Yes. To celebrate." A bit of a smile played around his mouth.

"What exactly?"

"Almost a year since we first met."

"Aw," I mumbled, welling up. How could I have forgotten? Too concerned with Brendan's wife, I'd say.

I leaned across to kiss him while thinking that a party might just lure Eirwen back.

***

A sense of urgency rather than panic descended upon the normally tranquil environs of The Elms. Seldom-used rooms were scrubbed, spruced up and aired. Windows and doors were polished, gutters – high and low – cleared. Around the grounds, bushes, hedges and ornamental trees were pruned and new pots and plants appeared. Garlands of lantern lights bedecked the terraces and grounds. Machines whined and whirred in every corner of the house and gardens. It was a giddy merry-go-round of activity without, as far as I was aware, any fairground attendant.

Brendan had taken to the music room, so I assumed either Mrs Booker was in control or there was some kind of manual that everyone consulted. Meanwhile, I focused on how to inform and invite Eirwen to the forthcoming extravaganza.

Knowing that she would have quit halls at Cardiff, my only option was to try and make contact via her parents. I decided against phoning. I wasn't ready to lock emotional horns with Eirwen. A very public reunion at the party might be safer, perhaps.

Satisfied this was the best course of action, I took one of the two bicycles from the old stable block and set off for Henley. My first stop was at Woolworths in Bell Street where I purchased an invitation. Then I picked up a postal order to cover all of Eirwen's costs should she decide to attend the party. I also enclosed a list of local inns and small hotels if she preferred not to stay at The Elms.

Despite the morning's financial outlay, it was not a problem, as Brendan had ensured that money was not an issue for me. Although merely formalising the on-tour set-up, Brendan's suggestion of a monthly income had annoyed me.

"Really?" I commented irritably.

"How do you plan to manage when I'm not around? We won't be living in each other's pockets, in any sense of the phrase."

"And how will your accountant itemise me? Expenses? Services rendered?"

"Calm down, Mari." He attempted to grab my arm, but I shook him off.

"I can't take money for nothing. Give me some sort of job." I huffed and folded my arms out of his way.

"My, but you're a feisty little thing." He encircled me with both his arms and drew me close. "I can think of a job you can do right now." His mouth twitched with the effort of not grinning.

Still annoyed, I disentangled myself.

"I'm serious, Brendan." Although it was a struggle not to return his grin given the gleam in his eyes.

"Obviously, my little firecracker." He thought for a moment. "Okay, how about this? You deal with any fan mail that manages to make it here instead of the office and ah, um… you can do any notation copies of new works that are needed at short notice. Mari?"

"You have a deal, Mr Bradshaw." I extended my right hand for him to shake.

He pulled me close and whispered in my ear. "Now, Miss Morgan, about that other job I had in mind…"

Chapter 20

The great hall at The Elms was probably designed for parties – well, gatherings, anyway. In the soft August light, the space seemed to glow. The warm weather had continued, although it had become a heavy, sultry heat that suggested rain. Possibly a storm would soon follow.

Getting ready had taken longer than usual. I straightened my hair and applied make-up with shaky fingers and dressed in the black satin trousers and gauzy, strappy top I'd bought in Los Angeles along with Eirwen's present. *Will she turn up?* I wondered, as nervous about seeing her after so long apart as I was about meeting Brendan's guests.

Having convinced myself I didn't need to rush down from my vantage point on the minstrel gallery landing, I remained screened from view by the balustrade, watching and listening, enthralled by the antics of some of the guests. Brendan had said that Jack and Jeff had been invited, Messiers Bruce and Beck no less… and I'd thought he was referring to some obscure European duo.

Baz was there minus a poorly Sylvia, and Ruth and Jim were also absent with a sudden death in the family. Jake always gave Brendan's parties a miss, apparently, as he considered them boring. Unidentifiable music burbled in the background, but no one as of yet was dancing.

Paul Maunders and Brendan were talking and I had to shuffle around almost to the top of the staircase to hear the details of their conversation above the now louder music.

"Someone I know at the *Melody Maker* saw David Bowie at Glastonbury. He's not given to gushing, well not in print anyway, but he described Bowie's set as groundbreaking," Paul commented. I recalled how I knew Bowie's name – he had received the Ivor Novello Award for his hit single "Space Oddity" the previous year.

"I've heard much the same about his musical arrangements," Brendan enthused. "But with Mick Ronson on board, I'm not surprised. Classically trained and a truly innovative arranger and guitar player. A fellow Northerner, no less. Bowie's lucky to have him."

"You Geordies are taking over," Paul joked. "We'll have to build another wall."

"I never said Ronson was a Geordie," Brendan said in mock horror. "He's from Hull."

"Hull's a northern city, isn't it?" Paul said with a wry smile.

"Whey aye, man," Brendan replied, exaggerating his accent. "Nevertheless, Geordies are from Newcastle upon Tyne, bonny lad." They both started laughing.

I stopped listening to the conversation just taking in how good Brendan looked in his new close-fitting cheesecloth shirt. He was standing close to the left-hand newel post of the staircase, facing my way.

Freshly shaved, Brendan's sharply shaped features were animated as he and Paul talked and laughed together. Then he looked at his watch and turned to scan the crowd before looking up the stairs.

My cue, I thought, gathering my courage to join the party, when some disturbance at the door to the front porch caught my attention. There was only one person I knew capable of making such an entrance.

Eirwen was wearing a turquoise column of skin-tight, silky material that left little to the imagination. It was a dress of sorts, which perfectly complemented the silver and enamel cuff bangle on her bare arm and her heavily made-up blue eyes.

On her entry the atmosphere in the hall altered perceptibly, as though suddenly charged by an electric current. After a cursory glance around her, Eirwen sashayed across the hall in a haze of heady perfume. She knew where she was going and reached Brendan just as he turned to follow Paul's open-mouthed gaze.

She snaked brown arms around his neck and pressed every possible inch of her silk-clad body against Brendan's. Given her extra
height on mine and a spectacular pair of high heels, her mouth was
level with his, and their lips met. Did he have time to back away? Did
he want to? I stayed long enough to see Brendan unhitch her arms
and step back. How long did that take? A second? A minute? Longer?

Already on my feet, I ran back to our bedroom. But suddenly
I had to get out. Using the old servants' stairway at the back of the
house, I reached the kitchen.

"Mari," Mrs Booker called, initially surprised to see me. "What's
the matter?" she continued, obviously aware of my distress to the extent that she followed me out into the garden. But I couldn't face her
comforting ways and sound logic. I needed to get away, to clear my
head, to make sense of what I'd just witnessed. The air was damp and
cloying, tinged with the smell of warm earth and the intense floral
fragrances from the heavily planted grounds.

Constantly rerunning images of Eirwen and Brendan's clinch, I
began to wander aimlessly around the grounds, starting at every random couple, shadowed shrub, solitary smoker and bulky bush that
seemed to materialise menacingly out of the darkness.

Suddenly, the wind picked up, whipping through the trees and
hedges and adding to my confusion until I registered the familiar
swish and swirl of the willows, noisy on the riverbank. Then I heard
the first roll of thunder.

A breathless shout nearby alerted me to Brendan's approach as the
sky was lit up and split by lightning. "Where were you?"

The thunder rolled again, closer this time, swiftly followed by a
shaft of lightning that sparked the air just before the first fat drops of
rain began to fall.

"Come on," he urged and propelled me towards the boathouse
as a deafening crack of sound and light caused the sky to upend and
drop a month's worth of rain onto us. By the time we got into the
boathouse flat, we were soaked to the skin.

Brendan didn't bother to put on the light. He just set about removing my clothing – and none too carefully, at that. The air in

the flat seemed fetid and dank, a little like my mind. I felt strangely removed as the rain beat down and the wind became wild while Brendan, thwarted by damp, clinging material and fiddly fastenings, began to tear my clothing from me.

Then the boathouse rocked as another crack of thunder rumbled directly above us, abruptly followed by a bolt of lightning that flashed through the roof window, throwing the flat's interior into a stark focus.

Suddenly jolted back to cognisance, I slapped at Brendan's hands. "Don't you dare!" I screamed, now pummelling him.

He stepped away, suddenly subdued and shamefaced, his sodden hair clinging to his scalp and dripping down his face. I began to shiver and shake, my hair crinkling into wet waves around my shoulders.

"We ought to get out of these clothes," Brendan said, regaining some of his usual composure and unbuttoning his shirt.

"I'm barely in my mine," I replied acidly, holding up my torn top and damaged trousers.

"I'm sorry." He stepped forward and reached out to me, but I backed away and darted out through the door, ignoring his angry calls and the raging storm as I raced back to the house.

Glad to find the kitchen unoccupied, I hurried up to our bedroom and bolted the door. Still shivering, I eventually got out of my clothes, put on a dressing gown and gratefully crawled under the bedclothes.

If I'd stayed in the boathouse, I don't doubt that raw, rough sex would have followed – and not for the first time. But previously I had been an eager, equal partner, matching and returning every ragged thrust, each clawed caress and biting kiss. Had I stayed in the flat, passive and unresponsive as initially I'd been, how might we have been affected?

It was difficult not to think that Eirwen's provocative behaviour had contributed to Brendan's anger-driven actions. I pushed the thoughts away, trying to focus on all that was positive about our deepening relationship. But it wasn't easy.

Gradually the storm moved on, and with the rain lessening to a soothing patter, once warm I drifted off into a deep, dreamless sleep.

Chapter 21

A party's success can generally be determined by the level of damage caused. No mess indicates a dismally short affair. Total devastation means much the same type of failed event that went on far too long. A good party, I would say, mostly results in a medium amount of mayhem. Such was the disarray that greeted me the next morning when I eventually showed up for breakfast.

Mrs Booker was in full control of the clean-up operation, and ever the professional, she did not bat an eyelid when I finally appeared downstairs on Brendan's second attempt to lure me out of the bedroom. Nor did she comment on my hasty exit from the house the previous night.

"I'll take those from you," she said, relieving me of my damaged and still-damp clothing, by which time I was beginning to feel rather silly. Although my reaction to Brendan's behaviour in the boat-house flat and his subsequent banishment from our bedroom had seemed justified at the time. On the other hand, who had kicked off the whole demonic debacle? Who else but my friend and guest, the Mistress of Misrule?

Brendan and I were subdued during breakfast. I was aware that he kept glancing at me but I avoided his gaze as I tried to untangle my confused emotions.

Mrs Booker had informed us that no one had stayed over, which prompted Brendan to suggest a trip to Denny's.

"He did say he might not turn up. I'd like to see how he's doing, anyway."

"I'll stay here, if you don't mind." I had hoped he'd have mentioned Eirwen by now. The omission was damning, I felt.

"You're sure you won't come with me?"

I shook my head listlessly. He made to move, then stopped.

"Eirwen was here last night."

I looked at him properly for the first time that morning.

"I know. I saw her arrive. I was on the landing."

He held my gaze, went to speak but changed his mind and left for Denny's.

Mrs Booker bustled in to clear up soon after Brendan's departure.

"Oops, sorry, lamb. I thought you'd left with Mr Bradshaw. Oh, and by the way, your friend left this for you."

She presented me with a sealed envelope and a look that informed me that she'd heard all about Eirwen's entrance.

***

I was surprised to find her still at the café when I finally deigned to show up. She was as bright as a button and free of stale make-up – unusual, by Eirwen's post-party standards.

"You took your time," she complained, an array of crockery stacked in front of her.

For almost a year I had imagined this moment, yearned for it even, and how it would be. Not once had I considered the possibility of wanting to punch her.

She leaned back on her chair to look me in the eye. "Standing to grow, eh?"

Immediately an image of her mouth level with Brendan's flashed up in my mind. I tried but failed to unclench my hands and teeth.

"Sit down, Mari," she ordered. "You're making my neck ache."

Not sure whether I was likely to break or combust, I did what I'd always done where Eirwen was concerned and obeyed. But I couldn't speak.

"Where were you last night?" Her tone was accusatory.

"I was there." I all but spat out the words seemingly stuck in my throat.

"Well, I didn't see you. I expected you to be at the door, at the very least, after that fancy invite and the money."

My hands curled into fists in my lap.

"Yeah, I had to make do with your boyfriend."

"He's thirty-three." I banged my hands on the table like a child.

"And don't hit me until you've heard how he did in the test."

Hit her? I was likely to kill her. "What are you talking about?"

Heads swivelled in our direction. There was a split-second hush, then the murmur of voices and the clink of cutlery and cups continued.

"He passed. He's okay. He's yours." She looked around at our seemingly disinterested audience and waved.

"I can't handle your nonsense at the moment," I said and made to leave.

"Let me explain," she said. "Man Golf. He passed with flying colours."

"That's it. I'm off." I headed for the door.

In the street outside, I briefly looked through the café window as Eirwen rummaged in her bag at the till. I quickly walked away and turned into the side street where I'd left my bicycle chained to a one-way signpost.

"Which one's yours?" Eirwen said, suddenly at my side eyeing the swanky cars lined up the street.

"I haven't passed my test yet."

"Okay. Which one is the chauffeur sitting in?" She strained to look for an occupied vehicle.

"Brendan doesn't have a chauffeur. I came on my bike," I replied wearily.

She almost choked. She held herself, then held on to me as she crowed and spluttered. "Ah, M, that's so like you. Shacked up with a millionaire and getting about on a bike." She laughed some more, then dabbed her eyes with a hankie she found in her bag.

"Finished?"

"Yep. Right. The Man Golf test. He passed with full marks."

"You've said that several times now, and I still don't know what you're talking about."

"You remember, I started it at uni. Came in handy when any of the girls needed to test their boyfriends."

"I was at uni very little."

"I was stoned most of the time. More so after you left. Then you seemed to be with me all the time."

She looked at me dejectedly and I almost hugged her, but an image of her pressed against Brendan stopped me.

"Tell me about the test," I said shortly, thinking that maybe she was just working me like she always did.

She seemed to shrink at my coldness.

"Yes, well, there are different levels of failure." She sounded businesslike, as though discussing a new product. "Such as, does he touch your hair, return your embrace or kiss? Does he pull you in closer?"

He'd have had a job to do that, I thought.

"But a full fail is the 'Hard in One'."

"What?"

"Golfing term: *hole in one*. Man Golf: *hard in one*. Does he get a hard-on with one kiss? Simple."

"Oh God," I gasped.

"But he passed, M," she said, suddenly solicitous. "You've nothing to worry about. Walk back with me. I'm staying at a pub just up the road near the market square."

"You wouldn't lie to me about this test, would you, Eirwen?" I pleaded. *As if it mattered*. What man wouldn't respond with Eirwen all over him?

I was shaking by the time we got to the pub. Eirwen put me in a quiet corner of the lounge and then went to the bar. She returned with two whiskeys. I hate whiskey, but I knocked mine straight back. Its warming glow calmed me.

"The only hard thing about your man was the look in his eyes. And what eyes. Almost worth abandoning me for. Mind you, the rest of him isn't bad as far as I could tell." She looked at me with just a hint of a smile around her mouth.

I stared stonily back.

She cleared her throat and lost the smile. "He removed me from him as though I were dirt. It's a wonder he didn't hit me. He looked as though he might. I did not arouse him. In fact, I think I disgusted him. Okay?"

I nodded and sighed, struggling not to cry.

She touched my hand. "It was a mean thing to do. I hadn't planned to. It was just a laugh."

I believed her. I had to.

"How long are you planning on staying?" I asked, changing the subject.

"I'm off home tomorrow. I'm going out for a meal this evening with someone I met last night. He seems nice, quiet, though. He didn't say much, but his eyes said plenty," she said with surprisingly little enthusiasm.

"You didn't test him, then?" I said scathingly, reluctant to name the game.

"Oh, I'm playing it cool for a change as he's old school," she replied, unperturbed by my manner. "Fortunately, he arrived a long time after your man had left. He's a guitarist. Big man with fair hair."

A trickle of fear ran through me.

"His name's Denny. Denny Clarke."

Poor Denny, I thought guiltily. As if he didn't have enough to deal with, I'd invited in – and whetted his appetite for – trouble with a capital T.

Chapter 22

I consoled myself with the idea that Eirwen couldn't be worse than Denny's last companion. Then again, she'd only dented his bank balance, whereas Eirwen was capable of wrecking hearts and minds.

There were fewer cars and pedestrians as I pedalled back to the bridge at the bottom of Hart Street, which is flanked on one side by a pub and by a church on the other. The church of St Mary the Virgin, to give it its full title, a flint cob edifice whose tower dominates the skyline of Henley. There have been places of worship on the site since the early thirteenth century. It seemed like a good time to visit, with the doors invitingly open.

Churches, chapels, cathedrals – places of worship generally – always soothe me; the last vestige of the faith I'd briefly shared with my mother, no doubt. The beauty of such places, whether it's solemn, stark or sumptuous, I've found, distracts the mind, erasing all but the glory of God and the effort taken to manifest it on earth.

Peach-tinged columns soared heavenward supporting arches and a vaulted ceiling. A kaleidoscope of stained glass was arranged around me, and polished wood and floral arrangements scented the air. My muddled mind gradually emptied as my ears filled with the sound of a small choir practising in the stalls.

Half an hour or so later, I arrived back at The Elms. When I pushed the bike around to the back of the house, I was confronted by Brendan, who had obviously just returned from Denny's. He took the bike from me, wheeled it into the garage section of the old stable block and locked the doors.

Calmer than I'd been all day, I thought I was ready and steady enough to deal with whatever he had to say. But his tone, like Eirwen's, was accusatory, which rankled.

"You went out."

Briefly, I told him about Eirwen's letter.

"So you know about Denny?"

"Yes."

"And?"

"And what?" I matched his tone.

"Come on, Mari, I've told you about Denny, and you know what she's like. The woman's dangerous."

"She may have felt like a woman to you, Brendan, but she's just a girl, and anything but dangerous."

He sighed and looked away from me. "I admit I don't know her as you do, but I've not been impressed so far."

He had a point. Two encounters: stoned for the first, sexually provocative for the second.

"Denny's track record leaves a lot to be desired," I lobbed back at him.

"This is pointless." He turned away from me and headed for the walled kitchen garden and access to the back of the house.

I ran after him, ready to fire the question that was burning a hole in me.

"If we're discussing bad behaviour an explanation wouldn't go amiss as to why a kiss from Eirwen provoked a near assault on me."

He stopped dead and whirled around, his face unusually pale.

"I'm ashamed of how I behaved. I've apologised, and I swear it will never happen again. If that's not enough, there's nothing more I can do or say."

He looked abject. But he had not answered my question, and I said as much.

"You saw what happened, Mari. Eirwen didn't just kiss me. Whatever I felt, above all else I was angry at her disloyalty to you."

"So she did arouse you!" I exclaimed triumphantly.

"Eirwen's built to arouse, and ten years ago I'd have been happy to accept whatever was on offer. But not anymore. You've no worries on that score."

"I'm more worried about how you behaved towards me last night."

He took hold of my hands in his and looked me in the eye.

"I was as angry with you as I was with Eirwen."

"Oh, so it's my fault." On the verge of tears again I struggled to free myself.

"Please listen. I'm trying to explain."

I nodded, and he let go of my hands.

"I suggested a party thinking it would give you a chance to make up with Eirwen. I knew you missed her."

"You knew that?"

"Just as I'd miss Denny." I nodded. "But it was your reluctance to join the party which allowed Eirwen to do what she did," he continued. "Then Mrs Booker said you were upset, which suggested that you'd seen everything."

"Were you surprised that I was upset?"

"Of course not. But I'd done nothing wrong."

"Not at that point," I said.

He sighed. "You were so sad when I found you. I thought I could show you how much I wanted you. But I was angry, and I'd been drinking. And you were so unresponsive, so cold. Not that I'm blaming you. But…"

He paused.

"You know the rest."

He looked like a naughty schoolboy with his head bent, his eyes lost in his long, dark hair. I reached up to push it back from his face and he grasped my hands, his eyes intense.

"I don't just desire you. I need you in my life. I love you."

I buckled against him, overwhelmed by his declaration yet over-wrought by last night, at the sudden shift in our relationship – the Eirwen-related turn of events. But he held me close and kissed me, and I was comforted.

We were alright, weren't we?

Chapter 23

It was the Wednesday after the party. I'd promised to ring Eirwen, but I was reluctant to do so. She was a mischievous genie, released from the bottle of my past. Another of my mother's sayings – *Be careful what you wish for* – was ringing in my ears.

I'm not sure I'd given much thought as to how Eirwen was going to fit into my new life. I'd missed and worried about her, despite being very happy and content. I'd just wanted to see her again. I certainly hadn't bargained for how things had turned out. And where were they going? I wasn't sure I wanted to know.

Nevertheless, I'd promised to ring, and I was making my way to the study to do just that when I was halted in the hall by the crunch of gravel and the slamming of a car door. Denny burst in, beaming like a twenty-one-year-old with the key to every door. Until that moment I'd never noticed his eyes. They shone a brilliant blue, as though lit by a bright new bulb.

"Just the person I want to see," he said, enveloping me in one of his bear hugs. His beam did not waver. The man was ecstatic, and I did not want to know why. He held me from him, broadened his grin, and then drew me in again for a repeat performance. People have asphyxiated after less.

"Seems I owe you a debt of gratitude. I haven't felt this good in years," he said when he finally released me. I backed away to avoid further hugging. My ribs weren't up to it. Besides, I was beginning to panic about his level of involvement with Eirwen.

The sudden appearance of Brendan from the music room took both Denny and me by surprise.

"Yah reet, man?" queried Brendan, going all Geordie – something he was prone to do around Denny. "Got the volume cranked up a bit, or is it something else?" He looked intently at Denny, concerned.

"No, I'm feeling great. Everything's great."

"And this without the aid of drink and/or drugs?" Brendan said bluntly.

"Totally substance-free." Denny held his hands in the air as if waiting to be frisked. "Just high on love – or the possibility of it, anyway."

He lowered his hands and beamed again.

"I take it the date went well," Brendan said without enthusiasm.

"Ah…" Denny sighed ecstatically. "Beautiful, interesting and so nice."

I'd known Eirwen most of my life. I loved the girl, but *nice* was not an adjective that came to mind in connection with her. Nice implied ordinary, and Eirwen had never been that. Eirwen was the *extra* part of *extraordinary,* as in "more than is usual, expected or needed".

"Oh yeah?" Brendan said flatly, sliding a steely sideways glance at me.

"Didn't you know? We're all nice people from Wales," I aimed at Brendan. Then I patted Denny's arm. "I'm glad for you. I need to make a phone call. I'll see you again."

"You can bet on that. I may need to pick your brains about a certain young lady."

He beamed at me but I struggled to return his smile. What my brain harboured about Eirwen was best left undisturbed, especially by a prospective suitor.

***

"Hello, M," Eirwen quickly responded when I dialled.

"Standing by the phone, were you?"

"You said you'd ring about eight, and it's only just gone."

"I'm that predictable, eh?"

"I prefer *reliable*," she said, yet there was an edge to her voice.

"What's the matter, Wen?"

"Aw, come on, M, you're the one with the bee in her bonnet."

"We haven't properly spoken in ten months and you're behaving as though it's my fault."

"That's because it is."

"Why—" I began, but Eirwen cut in.

"I'll have to go. Mam needs the phone for work."

And she was gone.

I continued to hold the receiver, the disconnected tone barely audible above the buzz of questions in my head.

Eventually, I sat down on the leather wing chair. I loved being in the study – being cocooned by books and the smell of leather, wood and beeswax polish pervading the air. Brendan did all his research regarding the places we visited in the study. I pictured him sitting at the desk across the room from me, head bent over a book and jotting down notes. I closed my eyes on the image and made my own plans.

Brendan appeared soon after I heard Denny leave. I jumped to my feet, my thoughts guilty spurs. Brendan stood just over the threshold as though barred further entry. Why was that?

"You're leaving," he said flatly.

I looked at him and realised how little I knew him. I believed it when he said that he loved me, and I certainly loved him. But what did I know, beyond the idyllic ten months we'd shared? The past few days had proved I had a lot more to learn, a prospect that unnerved me.

"I need to go home for a few days. I want to speak to Eirwen."

"When you do, ask her what her game is," he said, his voice sharp.

"Do you think I haven't tried? Eirwen will only tell me what she wants to."

"I'm sorry. I just can't believe how she treats you." He moved towards me. "She properly sets my teeth on edge."

"Which is probably her aim," I said with the makings of a grin.

Encouraged, Brendan reached out and drew me to him.

"I'll just have to view her as a female equivalent of Jake. He's always trying to provoke someone or other, usually me. Mind you, that doesn't stop me from reacting every now and then."

"I should apologise for inviting her here but…"

"She's your friend. I understand. But it doesn't mean I have to like her."

I sighed. "Eirwen isn't everyone's cup of tea."

Brendan laughed.

***

My father worked in the administration department at the local mine just outside Ponty and had done so ever since he'd stopped working underground, not long after the war. Dad had actually preferred working underground; the physical effort and the camaraderie were part of what made him tick. But with the working conditions impacting his health, he'd retrained to make the move upstairs, as he referred to the admin building.

Of course, Dad was just as happy in the office, because he was that sort of person. He maintained that if you have your health, you have all you need in life to be happy. Everything else can be managed if you're well.

The bus station was thick with people, vehicles and diesel fumes. The noise was just as pressing, as bus engines roared and brakes and passengers screeched. Going home from work on a Thursday evening with the weekend around the corner encouraged high spirits and laughter. But what would I know of the pressures and possible pleasures of a working week?

Fortunately, the number forty bus for Gwaun pulled into the station and I was saved any further self-analysis. Then I saw my father, deep in conversation with another man.

I recognised the man as Mr Jenkins, Eirwen's next-door neighbour, just as he spotted and pointed me out to my father.

My father turned as I neared and gathered me to his chest in a warm embrace. Despite my smile, his brow puckered as he scanned my face.

"*Iawn, cariad?*"

"*Wedi blino*, Dad." Thankfully, movement within the queue for the bus prevented any further discussion, which was just as well. I didn't need to be airing my dirty linen on the bus back to Gwaun.

"Really nice to see you after all this time, Mari," Mr Jenkins said genially on the walk up from the bus stop. Then a sly look slipped into his eyes. "Been a week of unexpected returns."

He paused theatrically, waiting for a response. My father and I did not oblige him.

"What d'you think?" said Mr Jenkins, undeterred. "Eirwen came home earlier this week with a long-haired hippy."

"Eirwen recently visited me, Mr Jenkins. As for the gentleman with the long hair, he is a talented, hard-working musician, a very nice man and a good friend." I wanted to add *So stick that in your pipe and smoke it*, but as my father's eyebrows had almost disappeared up his forehead, I thought better of it.

Then he prompted mine to reach similar shocked heights. "Consider yourself told, Bert Jenkins." Then he about-turned, threaded his arm through mine, and hauled me homewards.

"Eirwen's visit wouldn't have any bearing on your long face, would it?"

"As I said earlier, Dad, I'm tired."

"Hmph." His expression suggested he wasn't entirely convinced. But he didn't pursue the matter, and we walked arm in arm up the hill to our house.

In the back porch, we swapped our shoes for slippers and Dad led the way into the kitchen, where my mother was busy preparing tea. The radio burbled and my mother, absorbed in her preparations, almost jumped when my father spoke.

"Look who I found at the bus station, Mor. One more for tea. Will I peel extra veg? Oh, and she wants some Welsh cakes. Have you got sultanas?"

My mother was all confusion, as my dad had planned, I'm sure. Surprised by a barrage of information and questions, my mother was momentarily distracted. Then I moved in to hug her, and the awkward moment passed.

"Lovely to be home, Mam, if only for a few days."

"Lovely to have you." She patted my arm. "Dai, get some more veg from the pantry. I've already started the Welsh cakes," she said, displaying her floury hands. "Must have had a premonition about a homecoming, as I certainly didn't have a phone call."

We all started laughing. There was no pulling any wool over my mother's eyes.

***

The next morning, I walked down to Eirwen's. She answered the door with the bag she'd just packed for her return to Cardiff in her hand.

"When do you leave?" I asked when we were settled at the table in the kitchen.

"After dinner."

"You're still working at that pub, then?"

"For the time being." She lounged back on her chair and studied me through narrowed eyes.

"Until you go back to university?"

"I'm not going back to university. Why are you really here? To lecture me on my behaviour at the party?"

Which made me want to do just that, but I bit back my annoyance.

"The party's over, literally. It wasn't the reunion I was hoping for, I admit, but I'm here now so that we can talk. Like friends."

"Missed me, did you?" Eirwen said, her expression still harsh and angry.

"I wrote incessantly, rang your mam, called at your house when I could, and invited you to the party… Of course I missed you." This was panning out no better than the party.

"And I turned up and didn't play by the rules, which puts me in the wrong as usual." Her eyes flashed with a barely controlled fury.

"When did you ever play by the rules, Wen?" I responded with a tentative smile. She burst out laughing.

"Aw, M. I've missed you," she said, grinning broadly.

Then she got up from the table and I thought she was going to hug me, but she didn't. Saddened, I looked at her forlornly.

"Cup of tea?" she asked, avoiding eye contact.

"Yes, please," I said despondently, getting up to help.

Then Eirwen suddenly caught hold of me and held me close. "I really missed you," she said, her voice breaking up a little.

"I missed you more," I replied, equally as emotional.

"When you were busy gadding about the world with a rock star? I don't think so," she replied emphatically, moving away.

I grinned in reply, determined to keep the peace. Then I selected two mugs from the motley collection on the draining board as Eirwen filled the kettle. With the tea made we sat across the table from each other.

"Denny was all fired up when I saw him yesterday." I tried not to make it sound like an accusation. There'd been enough of those over the past few days.

"He's a nice bloke. Much better company than I was expecting. I like him," she said flatly. *Nice, company* and *like* weren't the usual benchmark terms of Eirwen's encounters.

"You're right, Wen. He's a very nice bloke, but—"

"He's an alcoholic," she cut in. "Or an addict in general, as he put it."

"So…" I said, mentally crossing everything in the hope that Denny's moment as a novelty had passed.

"He's coming back in a fortnight."

"Back?"

"Back here," she said, as though I should have known that. "He brought me home on Monday. Met my parents. Put on a tie." She scoffed. "But I made him take that off. They like him. He stayed somewhere in Ponty on Monday night. All very proper." She laughed.

Had I imagined a slightly hysterical edge to her voice?

"Right," I said calmly, while a klaxon went off in my head. "Your mam and dad okay?" I added, changing the subject.

"As they'll ever be," she said, her expression suddenly closed. Then she glanced at her watch. "I'd better get a move on and have some food or I'll miss the bus."

"I'll see you soon. I promise," I said, hugging her.

"One of your promises, remember, not one of mine," she said with a grin, crossing her fingers.

It was such a relief to have cleared the tension between us. I all but floated up the hill to my house, thrilled that we'd made up. Which proved that I was still more or less the same gullible girl I'd always been.

Chapter 24

The following Monday I was back outside the gates to The Elms, rested and resolute but a little nervous. So much had happened since the party. Nevertheless, I'd enjoyed my weekend at home, seemed to have patched up things with Eirwen and had managed to call in on her parents too. And despite their efforts to make light of Eirwen having flown the coop yet again, leaving few details of her precise whereabouts or life beyond Gwaun, Megan and Phillip Watkins's anxiety regarding their elusive, evasive daughter was evident. The only certainty known to them was that she'd be home when Denny was due to return, as I already knew.

It had been colder of late. The storm of just over a fortnight ago on the night of the party had heralded in a period of changeable, unsettled weather.

I pulled my thin coat closer and buzzed the house, but the gates opened without me having to give my name. Buoyed by this, I picked up my bag and began to walk briskly up the drive.

Alarmed at first by the fast, rhythmic crunch of gravel up ahead, I realised that someone was running towards me. Certain it was Brendan, I dropped my bag and sprinted up the drive.

We almost collided on the bend, scattering gravel as I leapt into his arms and smothered his face with kisses. He trembled as he rocked me back and forth, holding me close.

Eventually, we released each other, and Brendan set me back on my feet. Then he stooped and took my face in his hands and kissed me very gently on the mouth.

"Welcome home, my love," he whispered, his breath fluttering my escaping hair. I covered his hands with mine and returned his kiss.

"I'd better get my bag," I said as we moved apart.

"We'll send somebody to get it." He wrapped an arm around my waist and pulled me close. I leaned in and we ambled towards the house. It felt as natural as breathing.

Outside the house, Brendan turned to me and brushed a tendril of hair from my face. "It was as though the sound had been turned off. You're such a noisy little thing." He ran a finger down the side of my face.

I felt such joy bubbling up within me.

"There," he said, cupping my chin. "You're full of laughter and song. Always humming a tune and tapping a tempo. I thought I'd gone deaf. Even when I was playing the piano or the guitar, all I could hear was your absence."

We kissed again, pressed hard against each other, our mouths increasingly hungry.

Suddenly, Brendan broke away from me and grabbed my hand. "Come on," he urged, and we dashed into the house.

Just then Mrs Booker appeared to check on what had caused the commotion at the door.

"Send someone down the drive to get Mari's bag, please," Brendan said without looking back, but I turned and wiggled my fingers at Mrs Booker, whose smile was as wide as mine.

***

More than a year was to pass before Eirwen next crossed the threshold of The Elms, but, although she was rarely spoken of between Brendan and me, she was an almost constant presence. Denny made sure of that. If he wasn't pestering me for the minutiae of her life to date, he was ensconced in the music room with Brendan, working on his latest Eirwen-inspired lyrics, music or sometimes whole songs. Brendan was staggered by his creative output and its quality. Denny hadn't contributed much of any value for some time, apparently.

Meanwhile, Eirwen remained in South Wales, boomeranging between Gwaun and Cardiff every fortnight, and orchestrating a courtship a Victorian maiden aunt would have approved of.

Once a month I accompanied Denny back to Gwaun, not just to visit my parents but Eirwen also. The post-party horrors on both our parts seemed not just forgotten but erased. Yet there were fleeting moments of strangeness between us, a pulse of something that eluded me… something that would eventually surface, perhaps.

During one of my morning visits to Eirwen's, prior to Denny's arrival from Ponty, I said to her, "I can't believe you haven't had sex with him after all this time. Certainly not your usual MO."

"I'm not playing my usual game," Eirwen replied, unperturbed by my sarcasm.

"Game? Eirwen…?"

"Life's one big game, Mari. Largely a game of chance."

"What does that make people? Pawns to be played and lost?"

"Don't worry, M. There are few special pieces on my board, but you are one of them."

"It's not me that I'm worried about, Wen." I searched her face. But Eirwen was skilled at maintaining eye contact yet somehow looking around or through you.

"A year should be enough, do you think?" she said, turning her attention to making a cup of tea.

The house was unoccupied apart from us. Eirwen's parents were staying with Rhian in Cardiff, and her brothers were at work.

"Why bother to wait if it's just a game?"

"There's more at stake this time."

"In what way?"

"I'm not sure. It just feels like an opportunity."

"Oh God, Wen. Don't tell me it's about the money. You sound just like a bank manager."

"No, although it's definitely a plus point. It's more about how he makes me feel…" She hesitated a moment. "Precious and special, I suppose. He's put me on some sort of pedestal. Unfortunately, I know I'm bound to fall off."

I was totally perplexed. From my point of view, she'd always been on a pedestal that she regularly attempted to throw herself from, unconcerned as to the outcome either way.

Chapter 25

1972 began much as the preceding year, with a late, not really necessary, breakfast (given the gastronomical excesses of the festive period)
followed by a period of reflection – another year older, barely any the
wiser, and just as disbelieving of my incredible life.

Two days later, Brendan passed on information that I delighted
in.

"When?" I gasped excitedly.

"You've seen us perform at a number of iconic venues across the
world and you're ecstatic about the BBC Maida Vale studios?"

"Touring is jam-packed with fantastic, unexpected unknowns.
On the other hand, I've been listening to recordings made at Maida
Vale since… forever. I feel I know the place. It's the home of the BBC
Symphony Orchestra, and I'm going there. I can't believe it. When?"

"Not until the beginning of March," he said, evidently amused by
my enthrallment.

"Imagine, me on Pete Drummond's *Sounds of the Seventies* show,
if only in a listening capacity," I enthused.

"And I was going to suggest that you spend the time with Ruth
and Sylvia."

"Oh, I'm sure I'll manage to see them as well," I said determined-
ly, already making plans.

"I don't doubt it," he said with a knowing smile.

***

"I'm… I'm not sure I'm the right person to ask," I replied hesitantly, taken aback by Brendan's proposal.

"Why would that be?"

"Because it will be a recording of a new track."

"What difference does that make? You can sing. You do it incessantly," he teased.

"But I have a limited range."

"I would disagree. But what do I know? Okay." Suddenly, he was on his feet and making his way to my side of the kitchen table. "Let's settle this now." He pulled me up from my chair and began to tow me towards the music room.

Seated at the piano, Brendan played a simple melody that resonated with yearning, but the chorus – a slap in the face riveting rebuttal – turned the song into something more memorable.

"I wasn't expecting that. And it's Denny's song. I hope the lyrics live up to the music."

"He's got most of the verses together, and I've rearranged the chorus music. But neither of us is happy with the chorus lyrics." He looked at me expectantly.

"Are you suggesting that I might come up with something where you two professionals have failed? I thought we were here to prove I have a limited range as a singer."

"You know Eirwen. How would she react to the imploring opening of the song?"

"In the way you've written the chorus."

"So give me the words to go with the music," he said with a grin.

"Let's have the verses then," I said, suddenly keen to see if I could actually do this.

His angst-driven, hungry vocals on the pleading verse lines totally floored me.

"Well?" He looked across at me all aquiver on the sofa near the piano.

There was such a contrasting vibe to the chorus, I considered. Was it possible to adequately convey that juxtaposition in a few short lines? Then, suddenly, I had an idea.

"How about echoing some of the verse lyrics but in the negative? And not as politely."

"Good idea," he said his eyes gleaming. I studied the written verse lines for a few minutes.

Then I quickly recited my proposed lyrics aloud, tapping out the chorus beat: "Don't look at me. Don't question me. I won't play your way. Don't touch me. Don't love me. You know I won't stay."

"Fabulous. Simple yet so effective. Right over here. I need my lyricist by me." He patted the piano stool. All aglow, I crossed the room and sat down beside him.

He then sang the first two verses, nodding me into the chorus, which I fluffed on my first attempt, improved upon with my second and took off with on the third.

"Oh my God!" I screamed when we finished, buzzing with elation. "That was incredible." I bounced excitedly up and down, my hands in the air like a convert at a revival meeting before repeatedly hugging and kissing Brendan.

"A limited range, eh?" he said with a grin, returning my enthusiastic embrace.

Then Mrs Booker burst in unannounced, evidently concerned.

"Sorry, sir," she said, unusually flustered and belatedly knocking on the door. "I thought someone was being murdered."

Brendan and I almost fell about laughing.

***

It was strange to be a part of the rehearsals. I'd attended so many as an observer, it was unsettling to be amid all the banter and bluster associated with so many male egos. And what Denny thought of my involvement on his track continued to worry me. He seemed as affable as ever, which told me nothing.

"Were you annoyed by my lyrics?" I asked, thinking it best to be forthright – for me, that is, or I'd continue to fret.

Denny gave a slight nod of his head and grinned. "Bren said you'd ask. I was definitely put out by his reworking of the chorus and how it changed the track, but along with your lyrics it's now a bigger and better song. So, thanks." He smiled warmly and patted my shoulder.

After a brief discussion about the playlist for the Maida Vale session, everyone completed their final tunings, followed by a few warm-ups, and then we were away. Nevertheless, I was a bundle of nerves, but with Brendan and Denny smiling encouragingly every time I faltered, we eventually completed the first full run-through of "Please…" when Jake said, "Excelled yourself with that one, Golden Balls," his tone suggesting quite the contrary.

I noted Denny's sudden tension as he studied Jake.

"Your new bird must be quite something to spawn such a song," Jake added, more appreciatively. "I can't wait to meet her." He gave one of his characteristically devilish grins.

"Fuck you," Denny shouted menacingly, which set Punchie off on one of his profane diatribes.

"I hope so," Jake exclaimed emphatically, darting off the stage as Denny lunged his way.

"Pack it in, Jake." Brendan placed a restraining hand on Denny's shoulder as Baz attempted to calm Punchie with a soothing chant.

"Peace, man," Jake said with a Churchill two-finger gesture for Denny, yet he took the long route back to his keyboards.

"It's like being back in the playground," Brendan said in exasperation, to no one in particular.

***

The BBC Maida Vale studios on Delaware Road proved surprising. I hadn't expected anything quite so long and low.

"It was built as a roller-skating rink," Brendan said as I stared down the street on our arrival.

"Well, that explains it," I replied, continuing to study the distinctive white edifice.

"The largest indoor skating rink in Europe at the time. It even had its own orchestra balcony," he enthused.

"You put me in mind of the speaking clock," I said teasingly.

"I'm far more informative than the speaking clock. Besides, I'm a man," he said in mock annoyance.

"I had noticed that. My very own speaking encyclopaedia. Further education at a personal level." I wrapped my arms around him.

"I do my best," he replied with a playful squeeze.

The Maida Vale complex continued to surprise, its elaborately embellished Edwardian façade affording no indication of the building's unique and unnavigable interior.

I glimpsed the studio's control room through a glass window and was as transfixed as ever by the array of equipment arranged around the small space. I was beginning to catalogue quite a range of mixing desks, all of which I found quite fascinating, though goodness knows why.

The band and I ran through the set playlist while the engineer and technicians behind the window worked their mixing magic. And despite the calls for repeats or changes, I enjoyed my part in the session, particularly the band's unanimous thumbs-up approval of my performance. The three tracks recorded would feature later that month when Pete Drummond's show was aired, we were informed. An exciting prospect as far as I was concerned.

Much later that day, I dined with Ruth and Sylvia at the hotel where Denny, Brendan and I were staying on Warrington Crescent. Not having attended the recording session, my friends made the mistake of asking about the event. I waxed lyrical and long about everything.

"Well," said Sylvia when I eventually stopped for breath. "I feel almost parental in my tolerance of a favoured child to have endured such an unnecessarily detailed account." Then she rose from her chair and headed for the bar, leaving Ruth and me chuckling together.

Chapter 26

Within a year of their meeting, Eirwen moved to Richmond to live with Denny. So I regularly took to the A40 in my new red Volkswagen Beetle on visits to see Eirwen, which prompted her to get driving lessons. This led to lengthy discussions between us regarding the finer points of a hill start, an emergency stop and a three-point turn – details of which I'd bore Brendan with on my return to The Elms. But the stalemate on possible time spent as a foursome continued.

Then Brendan divulged news of his mother's plan to visit us. A prospect that unnerved me.

"There's nothing to worry about," he responded to my suddenly glum expression. "Just be yourself and Ma'll love you as much as I do." Which was heartwarming to hear but didn't lessen my anxiety.

After some thought, I settled on the idea of inviting others to stay the weekend of Mrs Bradshaw Senior's visit. As Brendan had suggested that my parents should come to stay with us sometime soon, I decided to extend the invitation to include Eirwen's parents as well. And if a dinner party was scheduled for that weekend, it would be reason enough to invite Eirwen and Denny too. A number of major attention-diverting events, I thought.

Now all I had to do was convince Brendan. I tracked his musical trail to the music room. This might seem the most obvious location but, given Brendan's penchant for a good vibe and the layout of the old house, sounds often carried to unexpected corners of the building. It was not unusual to find him strumming on the minstrel gallery or in the large walk-in pantry off the kitchen because of their individual echo qualities, or sitting next to the Aga just because he liked the spot. Of course, this only applied to guitar playing. He had yet to start dragging the grand piano around the house.

As I stood outside the music room door, I wondered if it was the right moment to broach the subject of additional guests during his mother's proposed visit. The sounds emanating from within were harsh and almost discordant, as though there were two instruments playing the same music – but in different keys, which did not quite sit well together. The resulting sound was unsettling but intriguing.

I pushed open the door. Brendan was standing in front of the French doors, half-turned towards me, his head bent in concentration as he worked on the intricate finger placement involved in the piece. As usual his guitar was on a long strap, slung low and pressing against his right hip. I was insanely jealous of all his guitars, but not of the piano. Piano playing never seemed as intimate.

He stopped playing abruptly and looked up at me and smiled. I blushed, caught mid-lascivious thought.

"What do you think?"

I blushed again, then realised he meant the music.

As I crossed the room towards him, he slid the guitar around to his back. I then pressed myself against him and encircled his waist with my arms.

Have that, guitar, I thought. *I take precedence.*

"Sounds like two people arguing," I said, now forgetful of why I was there. I was more concerned with relaying a message via the lower half of my body to Brendan's groin.

"Spot on," he said breathily and removed the guitar. "It's called 'Crossed Lines'. And what are you up to?"

"Fairly obvious," I replied, now certain that my message had been received and understood. I unzipped his jeans and quickly removed my own pair.

We coupled on the floor rug with an urgency that belied our flippant conversation.

"No," he said with a groan as I gripped him tightly, "you were humming purposefully when you opened the door."

I stopped moving, which made Brendan sigh and relax slightly.

"How do you know this wasn't my sole purpose?" I giggled, contracting my nether regions and making him groan once more.

"Because, my love, you purr when looking for sex."

***

"Is the new song our row?" I asked, pulling my T-shirt over my head. We'd indulged in seconds, which had necessitated the removal of all our clothing, so now we were cold as well as hungry.

Brendan looked momentarily confused. "You and your grasshopper mind. Of course, it's our row."

He got up from the floor, extended a hand, and hauled me up onto my feet. I wrapped my arms around him again.

"Strewth, woman," he said in mock alarm. "I can't go again for at least another five minutes."

I wiggled my arms and leaned my chin on his chest, looking up at him. "So 'Crossed Lines' is two people saying the same thing but from their own viewpoint, hence the discordant sound. Very clever."

"I have my moments. Now let's get some food. Or I'll have to eat you all over again."

"Promises, promises."

***

"You still haven't told me why you came looking for me," Brendan said, in between bites of sandwich.

We were sitting opposite each other at the scrubbed pine table, the debris of our preparations pushed to one side. Now it was my turn to be confused. Then the penny dropped.

"How on earth could you hear me 'humming purposefully' when you seemed so engrossed in your music? And it was very loud."

"I can hear you in my sleep."

"Oh, don't tell me I snore."

"No. I'm aware of you, that's all."

"I keep you awake?"

"Quite the opposite. You're like rain on a windowsill, the beat of a heart… my white noise of comfort, which I miss when it's not there."

He shrugged his shoulders and smiled again, while I struggled not to cry.

"None of that." He waved a finger at me. "You still haven't answered my question."

I rummaged in the pocket of my jeans, found a hankie and blew my nose. Then I launched into my plan.

"Sounds like a good idea," he said, brushing crumbs from his shirt front. "We'll run it by Mrs Booker later, okay?"

"Great," I replied, more than a little surprised.

"Oh, and I approve of your methods," he said with a grin. "Tea?" he added, making his way to the kettle.

"Yes, please. What methods?"

"Well." His grin widened. "Ravishing me will always get you what you want."

He laughed and ducked as I lobbed a coaster at him.

Chapter 27

The visit was arranged for the end of September. Mrs Booker drew up a menu based on our guests' preferences; a hire car was arranged for my and Eirwen's parents, whereas Brendan's mother, Dorothy, apparently always came by train and rarely stayed longer than three days.

"Well, fancy that" was Eirwen's response to the invitation. We were strolling in the garden at Denny's at the time.

"Your idea?" Eirwen said with a grin.

"If that's your attitude we'll bin it right now."

"Calm down," she said and gave my ponytail a tug. "But seriously, thanks for making the effort. Now what about the dress code? Formal or casual? What if I wear that blue silk dress I had on for the party last year?"

She had started running away before she'd completed her sentence, with me close behind. Given that she had longer legs and a head start, I should not have been able to catch up with her, but it's difficult to run at any speed when convulsed with laughter. I gave her a good thumping for her cheek.

***

Despite my machinations, I still had to spend the best part of a day alone with Brendan and his mother. Thankfully, Mrs Booker proved a major diversion and managed to push out the culinary boat farther than I had thought humanly possible.

"I may have to visit more frequently," Dot (as she insisted I address her) enthused after our impressive lunch. "Good food and good company would make the journey worthwhile," she added, kindly.

I quickly warmed to Dot's effortless ease and lack of pretension to the extent that I became quite worried that not only was the dinner party unnecessary, but likely to be a disaster.

When I mentioned the dinner party to Dot she said, "I'm looking forward to meeting your friend. You girls have made quite an impression on my two favourite men. I understand you've known each other a long time."

"We've been friends since we were five years old. We started school together. I thought she was an angel." I smiled at the memory.

"Hilarious," Brendan commented, earning himself a bit of a glare from me.

Dot raised an eyebrow in what was a disturbingly familiar manner. "Now *that* comment demands an explanation." And she leaned in closer to me.

The fear of an only child on the first day at school must have struck a chord with Dot, as the mother of an only son. She nodded knowingly as I related the subterfuge our school had employed that involved the older children luring us into a classroom – where a surprise awaited, we were told. The surprise was that our mothers were no longer with us – and as far as many of us were concerned, we might never see them again.

"There was quite a panic with some children attempting to break free in pursuit of their mams. But for the likes of Eirwen, with three older siblings who boomeranged back and forth largely unscathed, school held no such threat."

Dot nodded again, caught up in a bygone drama – the like of which Brendan had probably endured and not spoken of.

"Even when the teacher managed to coax the rest of the children to the piano, I couldn't move. I felt frozen with fear. Then a warm hand took mine and Eirwen smiled at me just as the September sunshine sparkled through the window, illuminating her blue eyes and making a halo of her bobbed blonde hair. An angel."

"Well," said Dot, "I'm looking forward to meeting this angel of yours."

Flipping heck, I considered dolefully. *What was I thinking? How could I share such a notion?* At which point Brendan started laughing.

***

After brief introductions upon arriving at the Elms, my father spent most of the time talking to Joe in the kitchen garden. Conversely, my mother was enamoured with the house and had asked more questions of Brendan and his mother than a curious five-year-old as to its history and provenance. She reverently and indiscriminately touched doors, walls, furniture and furnishings, her expression one of rapt awe. Meanwhile, Eirwen's parents had left to visit Eirwen and Denny.

Despite the earlier quiet ease between my parents and Brendan's mother, once the other guests began to arrive, the atmosphere altered slightly, with almost everyone seemingly unsettled, as though presented with the wrong script for their part in a very amateur production of a Brian Rix farce.

Only Denny seemed totally unaffected. He was oblivious to everyone except Eirwen – who, for her part, was playing the femme fatale to Denny's amiable hero. Despite being demurely dressed in swathes of a dun-coloured fabric, Eirwen still exuded sensuality. She pulsed with it, like a neon sign.

The first course arrived: prawn cocktail for everyone except Denny, who professed a lifelong aversion to any food that had lived in or near the sea. His salad was accompanied by pâté and toast.

"How can you not like prawn cocktail?" Eirwen declared.

"Prawns and cocktails shouldn't share a sentence, never mind a glass," responded Denny, as he spread pâté thickly across a slice of toast.

"Have you ever tried prawn cocktail?" Eirwen continued.

"No," replied Denny, his pâté-laden toast level with his mouth, "and I've no plans to, either."

"Really?" Eirwen's voice was silky but I saw the flash in her eyes and recognised a gauntlet moment.

"She's very persistent," Dot whispered to me, drawing my attention away from the developing drama.

"You could say that," I murmured back, still observing Eirwen, who had stopped eating her cocktail to watch Denny munching on his toast.

"Not been easy, eh pet?" Dot quietly replied.

"It's been lots of things. Mostly a privilege," I countered.

"That says more about you than it does your friend, Mari."

I smiled at Dot but was drawn to look at Eirwen again. With her dramatic fall of blonde hair rippling around her shoulders, Eirwen's dark-lashed blue eyes glittered with mischief as she watched Denny and hatched a plan. Her full lips were pursed in concentration, accentuating her high cheekbones and aquiline nose. Eirwen was beautiful: ethereally, classically, remarkably beautiful. *And as angelic looking as she's ever been*, I thought wryly. Returning my attention to Dot, I was about to ask a distracting question about her home in Northumberland when…

"For fuck's sake, he doesn't like seafood," Brendan exclaimed. At this my mother gasped and others coughed and spluttered. He then scraped away from the table, hurled his napkin down and stalked out of the room. I was surprised he didn't slam the door.

My and Dot's gaze snapped back to Eirwen, who was using her fingers to force-feed Denny with prawns.

"Excuse me." Dot folded her napkin and quietly followed in her son's footsteps.

By now, Denny was licking Marie Rose sauce from a girlishly giggling Eirwen's fingers while her parents stared at her in open-mouthed disbelief. My mother was almost rigid.

"Right, my girl, that's enough of that. There's a time and a place," my father said, his voice sharp and as effective as a slap. Eirwen seemed to shrink. Then he rose from the table and also left the room. At which point Denny lost his glazed expression, dragged his napkin across his mouth and followed the others from the room.

"Sorry." I looked towards Eirwen's parents, uncertain as to whether or not I should remain.

"What have you got to apologise about?" Phil responded, before glaring at Eirwen, who was wiping her fingers on a napkin. She avoided his gaze and gulped from her glass. Her grimace indicated that she had forgotten this was an alcohol-free occasion.

"Bit of fuss over nothing," I said with a forced laugh. On the surface it *was* a fuss over very little. But we were all aware, I believe, that the outburst was just the tip of the iceberg. There was a lot more going on underneath. What, exactly, I was reluctant to contemplate, except that an iceberg probably wasn't the right analogy.

"As Dai said, 'a time and a place'," Phil replied, while Megan narrowed her eyes at Eirwen as though seeing her daughter for the first time. Eirwen sighed but continued to avoid eye contact. I marvelled at my mother's ongoing stillness. She must have won every game of Statues as a girl.

The ensuing silence screamed as loud as any child.

Thankfully, the door opened and Mrs Booker bustled in. "Second course in five minutes," she blithely announced to a half-empty room. Then she stood aside to allow the remaining diners to return to their places.

Tension now had a dining partner: suppressed anger. Oh joy.

Brendan was the last to take his seat. Apart from the scraping of chairs and the flapping of napkins, the room was silent. Then Mrs Booker reappeared with a food-laden trolley in her wake. Brendan jumped to his feet to hold the door for her, suddenly the thoughtful host.

For a second, I wanted to laugh at the silliness of the situation, but a brief look at all the stern faces stopped me. Then I caught Eirwen's eye and saw that she was struggling to keep a straight face too. Were we too young or too inured for this?

I closed my eyes and shut Eirwen out while Mrs Booker and Brendan offloaded the trolley.

"Bon appétit," said Mrs Booker, about to exit the room.

"Thank you," I called. "Smells absolutely delicious." I only hoped that we could summon some sort of appetite to do the remainder of the meal the justice it deserved.

"I'd like to apologise to everyone for my outburst and bad language," announced Brendan as he stared at the ceiling above my head.

"Please finish your meal, if only for Mrs Booker." He dropped his gaze to mine, raised his shoulders and smiled.

I raised my eyebrows and returned some sort of a smile. *A time and place*, I thought.

The main course was delicious: tender chicken in a blue cheese and leek sauce. It was eaten but I doubt it was enjoyed, given the stilted attempts at conversation. Everyone wanted to be out of that room, the sooner the better. Further courses were declined across the board.

We exited the dining room as sullenly as a crowd of football fans after a bad home game. Megan declined all offers of help with Phil's wheelchair, then struggled to negotiate the doorway. Brendan came to the rescue as Denny and Eirwen retrieved their coats. As the only ones not staying at The Elms, they then made ready to say their goodbyes. Understandably, they began with Eirwen's parents, which caused Brendan to back away.

Eirwen then moved on to embrace my parents, to shake hands with Dot, and finally to hug and kiss me as Denny grasped Brendan's shoulder. Relief washed over me as Eirwen made to move to the door with Denny at her side, rummaging in his coat pocket for the car keys. Suddenly, she spun around, planted a kiss on her fingers and made to press them to Brendan's mouth – only to be intercepted as he grasped her wrist and twisted it away from his face.

I saw his nostrils flare and his jaw clench, but it was the momentary flash in his eyes that disturbed me. Had it been dislike or desire?

Eirwen rubbed her wrist on release, but her eyes were triumphant. A reaction was a victory, whatever she'd identified in Brendan's eyes.

It all happened very quickly, and then they were gone. No one followed them out to the car, but I stood and stared out of the window until the car lights disappeared.

Good, I thought, exhaling heavily.

I turned around to be confronted by four pairs of concerned eyes. Brendan and his mother were nowhere in sight.

My father went to speak then shook his head and hugged me, as did my mother.

"Good night, God bless." Mam smiled and patted my arm before moving away to follow my father up the stairs to their room.

"We'll speak to her tomorrow," said Phil, his voice strong and steady, in marked contrast to his fragile frame.

"Whatever for?" I asked, determined to make light of it.

"Well—"

"Phil…" Megan interrupted. "Good night, Mari." Then she set off with her husband for their ground-floor room.

Dot reappeared in time to wish Megan and Phil a good night and inform me that Brendan was walking in the grounds and not to wait up for him. She smiled reassuringly, embraced me and then made her way upstairs.

I stood in the hall until I got cold. The best-laid plans of mice and men and naïve friends, eh, Eirwen?

***

Upstairs in our unlit bedroom, I was able to make my way to the window as the landing light illuminated a slice of the room like a cinema usherette's torch. I opened the window and the decay-tinged autumn air seeped in. I shivered.

Then, beyond the kitchen garden, near Joe's potting shed, a dark shape appeared and crunched across the gravel towards the edge of the terrace. There Brendan leaned back against the trunk of a tree and, to my surprise, lit a cigarette. From his outline, and the movement of the glowing cigarette end, I knew he was looking out across the black lawns to the distant orange glow of the London-lit sky.

Suddenly, he turned and looked up at our window. I stepped back. Then, as he stubbed out the cigarette, I reached forward again to close the window and watched as he made his way back to the kitchen garden and the rear access to the house.

I was still shivering under the blankets when Brendan came into the now dimly lit room. By the light of a single bedside lamp, he unselfconsciously removed his clothing and dropped each item onto the chair near the door.

I savoured each moment of the softly lit tableau as though it were my last chance as a voyeur of this particular scenario. His long, lean limbs rippled as different muscles tensed and relaxed. Then he strode across to the bed and slid under the bedclothes.

His body was cool, as was his demeanour. He knew I was awake but remained flat on his back, silently staring at the ceiling. I longed to wrap myself around him, to taste his smoky mouth, but was uncertain of how he'd react. Suddenly, he flipped onto his side to face me, causing me to jump in alarm.

"Sorry," he said, his voice flat, "about everything."

I edged closer to him and ran a hand down the side of his face. He closed his eyes and sighed. The frown creasing his forehead disappeared, but he remained immobile. Braver now, I edged closer. His eyes flicked open, a shadowed black in the gloom. Still, he did not move, but his tobacco-tinged breath brushed across my face.

"I didn't know that you smoked," I said, struggling not to press myself against him.

"I haven't smoked since I was seventeen, which was the last time I felt this bad… If you discount the party."

Eirwen wasn't mentioned, but the inference was there.

"You've got a secret stash of fags, then?" I asked, avoiding the obvious Eirwen-related questions.

"No, but Joe has."

"Joe?"

"Yeah. He gave up over twenty years ago but he still keeps and regularly renews a packet of ten."

"Surely he wouldn't start again after twenty years?" I asked, aghast, having never fully understood the nature of tobacco dependency.

"He keeps them as a deterrent. Opens them when the need arises, inhales, and then coughs – and it's enough, apparently. I caught him mid-sniff once, so his secret stash is known to me. But I won't do it again." Then he finally put his arms around me. "Nor will I behave in a 'Now I need a fag' way."

"Never again? Promise?"

"Well…" he said, grinning.

Chapter 28

After breakfast the next morning, Eirwen's parents set off in the hired chauffeur-driven car for Richmond. Phil's face was as steely grey as the grim autumnal sky. Heavy rain had been forecast, and it started as soon as the car pulled away from the house. Phil and Megan had decided to curtail their visit and were merely calling in on Eirwen and Denny before heading back home to Wales.

I stood in the porch waving, long after everyone else had returned to the hall.

Who am I trying to kid? I thought, and closed the porch door on the bouncing raindrops, my feet already damp from the deluge. Things had not turned out as I'd hoped or planned. The meal had been nothing more than a masterclass of the stiff upper lip and good manners attitude that the British do so well. I'm not sure that I wouldn't have preferred a good slanging match.

By the time I closed the inner door, the hall was empty apart from me. My father, given the weather, was probably ensconced in the greenhouse with Joe. As for my mother, was she, I wondered, continuing her touchy-feely tour of the house?

Voices and the fulsome sound of Mozart led me to the music room. My mother and Brendan were sharing the long stool at the keyboard of the grand piano, while Dot sat adjacent to them with her back to me on the even longer leather sofa. The muted light from the French doors was reflected in the glossy surface of the piano and all the guitars lined along the end wall, providing a soft, stage-like lighting. I joined the audience of one as the performance ended and Dot began to clap.

My mother blushed like a girl and made to move from the piano.

"Stay where you are, Mam. I don't get to hear you play these days."

"You're by far the better pianist, Mari," she argued, but she had sat back down on the stool. "She could have been a concert pianist, you know. Mind you, you're no mean player, Mr Bradshaw," she gushed.

"Brendan, please," he said softly.

My mother nodded and smiled, although obviously on edge and nervous.

"What a talented pair they are," she said to Dot, her voice strained. "Imagine the musical child prodigies they'll produce."

I could have died had I not been distracted by the reactions of both Brendan and his mother. I'd have expected a joke or laughter from Brendan, and something positive regarding prospective grandchildren from his mother – certainly not the comment-less void that followed.

Sensing disapproval, my mother clasped her hand to her mouth as though she'd spouted flames or belched rather loudly.

"Play a rousing Welsh hymn, Mrs Morgan," coaxed Brendan, attempting to restore the equilibrium.

"Morfydd, please," she replied, regaining her composure, but not before glancing questioningly at me.

But I had no answer. The more I learnt about Brendan the less I knew him.

My mother's strong opening of "Rachie", the wonderful piece by Carodog Roberts, stirred everyone, and I struggled not to take up the lyrics, "*I bob un sydd ffyddlon*". After all, this was my mother's moment.

But I should have guessed that Brendan could not resist the temptation of trying to impress my mother. Or was it just another distraction?

Either way, Brendan began to duet with my mam, causing her to stop while he continued to play on alone. He regularly listened to my records and my playing and absorbed the music like a sponge.

"*Rhagorol*," my mother gushed again.

"*Diolch yn fawr*," returned Brendan, which startled both our mothers.

He looked at me, and I smiled with pride despite my misgivings.

***

As expected, Dot was packed and ready to leave on the morning of her fourth day at The Elms.

After embracing my parents in turn, she then hugged Brendan and me, lingering to kiss and hug her son once more.

"Well," she said as Brendan helped her on with her coat, "despite a shaky start, it's been a pleasure."

Turning to my parents, she patted my mother's arm. "She's a credit to you. And I don't doubt we'll see a lot more of each other over time, but all the best for now."

Brendan wrapped an arm around me and smiled. It unnerved me how reassuring I found his actions and Dot's comment after yesterday's strangeness. Previously I'd not given a thought to having children, but having the idea greeted with such indifference was unsettling.

Outside the porch, a taxi stood idling, exhaust fumes billowing into the now much colder and drier air.

Brendan opened the car door for his mother and she climbed in. Then the taxi pulled away and Brendan and I waved as his mother set off on the first leg of her journey back to Northumberland.

***

We had decided to take my parents to Henley to visit St Mary's and a few other places of interest in the town. We would possibly stop for tea and cakes depending on how much attention we (or should I say Brendan?) attracted.

Obviously, Brendan was known in the town. But depending on the time of day and whether or not the schools were on holiday, he could, if appropriately dressed, usually get away with a short visit. He was happy to interact with fans but preferred to do so by prearrangement – such as opening a fete, visiting schools or hospitals or by providing items to raise funds for charities. As Eirwen had once commented, everything was on his terms.

The following morning, the same taxi driver arrived to take my parents to the train station. There were more goodbyes, but this time with the addition of tears, largely shed by my mother.

On the surface, all was as it had been. But I wasn't. I was unsettled, disturbed and anxious to speak to Eirwen. Not that I expected any answers or explanations from her. Loosely speaking, Eirwen fought and flirted with everyone. It was how she functioned. She was engagingly confrontational. Still, I was keen to find out what she was up to, if anything, apart from being Eirwen.

Chapter 29

"Goes to show he's as much of a shit as the rest of us."

Eirwen was sprawled out on one of the two sofas in the room, her hair lost on the blonde leather except where it flicked up onto a huddle of dark cushions the colour of oxblood. Denny referred to the stark white space as the living room. For me, it conjured up hospitals and dentists and interrogations: a clinical space associated with discomfort and pain, rather than something as ordinary as living. Apart from the cushions, the only other colour in the room was an abstract painting that could have been entitled *Bloodbath at the Butchers*. I tried not to look at it.

"What are you on about? I ask a simple question and you start screaming at me."

Denny and Brendan were at the recording studio in London with the rest of the band, laying down the foundations, as Brendan put it, on the new album they'd take on tour sometime next year.

Eirwen sat up, put her forearms on her thighs and leaned across the gap between the two sofas. Her blonde hair swished forward, framing her face. She looked like a fairy perched on a toadstool. But the look in her eyes was predatory, and it made me her prey and her stance more pounce than perch.

I sat back and waited a moment.

She sat up and relaxed back against the soft leather, but her eyes flashed and I could hear the anger in her voice as she spoke. "Everyone goes on about how marvellous he is. Denny thinks he walks on water. But we know, don't we, M? He's human, just like the rest of us. Nothing special."

The "he" she referred to was Brendan, of course. She looked across at me and dared me to disagree. A year ago, prior to the party, I would have. But not now. He was human and fallible – and I loved him all the more for that, I now realised, even if I understood him less.

"Glad you agree," Eirwen said at my continued silence. "You can be sure of one thing, M. I enjoy reminding him that he's not always in full control of everyone and everything and often not even himself."

Her smile was one of self-satisfaction. It was then that I realised they'd never get on and that I should be glad. If they ever did, they might get on too well, and that was far too painful to contemplate.

***

In the run-up to Christmas 1972, Eirwen and I spent a lot of time together because the band was recording, and Brendan and Denny tended to stay on at a London hotel. Thankfully, Baz put Punchie up and, as another Londoner, Jake also had no need of a hotel. With the men busy, Eirwen and I filled our days visiting art galleries, museums and generally taking in the sights and sounds of the city. At which point I decided it was time to introduce Eirwen to Ruth and Sylvia.

A part of me was thrilled at the prospect of showing off Eirwen. Conversely, I feared the consequences of a possible clash of such titans.

Two weeks before Christmas, Eirwen and I were returning to the hotel to change before heading out to see *Jesus Christ Superstar* at the Palace Theatre where we were to meet Ruth and Sylvia.

"A musical about Jesus? As ridiculous a notion as a Cod War" was Sylvia's comment when I telephoned Ruth to suggest the trip. Eirwen said much the same (minus the reference to the ongoing war between Britain and Iceland, which began when the latter extended its exclusive fishing zone). The whole trip seemed destined for disaster.

The show surpassed not just my expectations but also those of Ruth and Eirwen. Sylvia slept up to the last twenty minutes of the performance, whereupon she woke and inserted ear plugs.

"Far too much music" was her summation of the production once the standing ovation finally ended. Then she sliced her way up the aisle to the exit.

"Is there something wrong with her?" Eirwen asked as we struggled through the crowd to keep up.

"Shh," I replied, glancing back at Ruth who was actually laughing.

"She puts me in mind of that stupid song from school. Remember? 'Who is Sylvia? What is she?'" Eirwen said.

"I can tell you exactly what Sylvia is," Ruth eventually managed to say. "She's the daughter of a duke, ousted from her home in her mid-teens on her father's death when the title passed to her uncle."

I was stunned by the revelation, but Eirwen merely sniffed and said, "Well, that explains her irritating autocratic manner," which made me and Ruth snort.

"The Cambridge," Sylvia said on our approach outside the theatre, then she was off again.

Within a stone's throw of the Palace Theatre, the Cambridge was packed to the rafters.

"The Crown," Sylvia announced as we neared, already moving away.

"Is she a tour guide in her spare time?" Eirwen asked, evidently unimpressed. "Or does she just know the whereabouts of quite a few pubs?"

Ruth and I exchanged glances but didn't comment.

We caught up with Sylvia at the bar of the Crown just as she produced her martini glass box from her bag.

"How pretentious," Eirwen commented as Sylvia handed the glass across to the barman.

"Style is necessary to successfully affect ostentation." Sylvia considered Eirwen for a moment. "Drink?" she added.

"A pint of bitter, please," Eirwen said, in an exaggerated Welsh accent.

"Here we go." I shook my head and sighed.

"Only the brave take on Sylvia in a game of dare," said Ruth, avidly studying the combatants as the crowd around us grew.

Eirwen did not fare well in the competition. I tried to stop her, as did Ruth. She and Sylvia were not in the same league on many levels, let alone where alcohol consumption was concerned.

"The girl has stamina" was Sylvia's comment when she finally packed away her glass, by which point Eirwen was hanging from me and Ruth like a sodden blanket.

"I can't take her back to Denny like this," I muttered as we packed Eirwen limb by limb into a taxi.

"It'll cost you if she makes a mess," the driver announced irritably.

"I'm prepared in the event of such an occurrence," Sylvia said shaking open a thick plastic bag as Eirwen slid down the seat beside her.

"What?" the driver demanded, glaring at Sylvia. At this, Ruth gave a distracting cough, quickly following with an address, and the man turned his attention back to the road. Meanwhile, I attempted to haul Eirwen back into a sitting position.

"Don't concern yourself, darling. Your friend is not troubled."

***

Ruth had to summon Jim to help us get Eirwen into the house. She seemed to have doubled in weight and developed extra limbs during the journey, and the taxi fare and the driver's ire were mounting by the minute.

The next morning, Eirwen was definitely troubled. An inglorious night of vomiting had been superseded by a range of less obvious but no less painful symptoms. By the time we'd returned to the hotel, she just wanted to lie down and die.

"A grave mistake to take on Sylvia." Brendan laughed when I related the events of the previous night. I nodded in agreement, somewhat distracted by the excerpts of the many outstanding songs from *Jesus Christ Superstar* whirling around my head.

"Show sounds quite impressive," he added.

I looked at him blankly, wondering if I'd missed a chunk of conversation during a musical flashback: one minute a mournful Mary Magdalene, the next an accusing Judas.

"In fact, I may have to take a break from recording to see it," he continued, increasing my confusion. "That is, if the snippets I've heard from you are anything to go by." He grinned.

"Of course. I've been burbling through the tracks. Sorry about that."

"On the contrary. Your musical morsels are a great plug for the show."

"A walkabout singing advert. Could be lucrative." I giggled.

"A great idea – we'll save it for a rainy day. Right, I'm off to the studio after breakfast. Do you have any plans?"

"I'll stay with Eirwen, which will hopefully reassure Denny."

"That'll save me a job. We don't need to be a man down at this stage of the recording." He kissed me and left.

I tapped on the door of the adjacent room, and Denny answered in record time.

"I was about to call round to speak to Bren." He looked slightly frazzled.

"He's gone down to breakfast. Don't worry about Wen. I'll stay with her today."

"She's sleeping at the moment," he whispered, looking back into the darkened room where Eirwen lay, an indistinct shape amongst the mound of bedding.

"I'm not surprised, given the night she's had."

"Are you sure you'll be alright?"

"I'll probably join her, if that's okay with you?"

"Of course," he replied, with a friendly squeeze of my arm. "And thanks."

I quickly removed my jeans and jumper and slid under the blankets as near Eirwen as I could get without disturbing her. Once warm, I drifted off to sleep, only to wake with a start, unsure of where I was.

"Hi, M," Eirwen said, unnervingly close, her breath sour from the night's ordeal.

"You sound better than when we last spoke," I said, surprised by her nakedness as she drew nearer.

"I feel much better. Thanks for looking after me." She briefly pressed her lips to mine.

I backed away slightly, not sure what to do with my hands.

"It was a joint effort. I couldn't have managed without Ruth," I replied awkwardly. Then I sat up and put on the bedside lamp, breaking the vaguely erotic atmosphere to be taken aback by Eirwen's restored appearance. She looked positively blooming.

"Ruth? Oh, the hippy. That was kind of her," she said, stretching under the bedclothes. "Or is she used to having to deal with her ladyship?"

"Sylvia is largely unaffected by alcohol. You want to remember that," I said, annoyed by her thinly disguised criticism of my friends.

"Keep your hair on," she said and tugged on a hank of mine like a bell rope. Then she jumped up and out of my reach. "Come on, I need to eat and, more importantly, drink. A bucket of tea, preferably," she added, sweeping the blankets from me. I crumpled with laughter.

Chapter 30

The next day at breakfast, Eirwen declared herself recording-studio-ready. Nevertheless, her meeting the rest of the band was not a prospect I relished: akin to tossing a burning ember into an arsenal of weapons, I considered. I'd tried to prepare her for the moment, identifying not just the unpredictable drummer and the male near-counterpart of Sylvia but also the Neanderthal lothario.

"Just blokes being blokes then" was her unconcerned response.

Fortunately, Eirwen and I arrived at the studio just behind Sylvia and Ruth. Another plus was finding the band busy with the engineer at the mixing desk – so we adjourned to the lounge area, temporarily delaying the inevitable. About half an hour or so later the sweaty, bickering men filled the room.

"You're so wrong, H," Jake opined, jabbing a finger menacingly at Brendan.

"Okay, we'll check the keyboard track again," Brendan said equably, despite Jake's aggressive stance.

"I say we vote on it now," Jake demanded, looking around at the others for support. Then he spotted Eirwen at the kettle, busy topping up a mug. With a slight turn of her head at the commotion, she felled him. I saw his stunned expression and momentarily pitied his likely enslavement to an unrequited love. But within a flash he was flexing his fingers – shark grin in place – and advancing on Eirwen.

It all happened so fast. Jake placed his hands on Eirwen's waist, for which he received a vicious elbow blow to the solar plexus followed by a swift punch to the nose when Eirwen swung round to hit him as he doubled up from the first strike.

The lounge seemed to upend as people lurched from different corners of the room. Brendan managed to restrain Denny, who lunged at Jake, prostrate on the floor and bleeding profusely, a protective knot of howling girls around him as Eirwen kicked out. And fair play to Baz, he quickly incepted Punchie, whose eruption from his quiet corner put me in mind of the leaping women drawings from the Playtex Living Girdle newspaper adverts.

Ruth and I bundled the still incandescent Eirwen into the corridor as Denny attempted to shake off Brendan's hold.

"Leave him," Brendan urged as Denny strained towards Jake, all but spitting.

"Try anything like that again and I'll kill you," Denny growled at his injured bandmate.

***

In the badly lit, mould-pocked toilet Ruth turned on the sink tap. "Hold your hand under the water. It'll help with the swelling."

"Could it be broken?" I placed a tentative hand on Eirwen's arm.

"Possibly," said Ruth, "as could Jake's nose." At this, Sylvia stifled a small snort of laughter.

"It feels fine," Eirwen said, now quite calm, and with a reassuring smile for me as she flexed her fingers under the flow of water.

Suddenly, a skinny girl pushed past Sylvia.

"Get back, you old cow," she hissed, pressing into the crowded dank space and elbowing Eirwen away to rinse a bloodied cloth at the sink.

"Bitch," she spat at Eirwen as she made to leave.

"Bye," Eirwen chirpily replied, wiggling the fingers of her good hand.

"Manners cost nothing, dear," Sylvia commented as the girl bowled past her.

"Fuck off," the girl spat back.

Totally unruffled, Sylvia turned her attention to Eirwen. "Box for your school did you, darling?"

Eirwen rotated her hand under the stream of water once again before looking up at Sylvia.

"Do you want a further display of my skills?" she asked icily.

"My dear girl, I meant no offence. I've waited a long time in the hope of witnessing a dressing down of that man," Sylvia managed to say despite her evident mirth. "I just hadn't envisaged anything as spectacular," which set the rest of us off.

***

The album, when released, was hailed as a long-overdue return to the band's glory days. Reviews were positive almost across the board, with many lauding the new bluesy-rock sound of the band. "A coming-of-age concept album" was a popular phrase bandied about by many critics – a ridiculous notion, given the average age of the band members. Brendan thought it all very amusing.

However, the forthcoming tour now carried the added pressure of faithfully reproducing the songs and the new sound, which upped the ante for everyone in and around the band. Eirwen was far from pleased. She was already beginning to tire of many of the pressures associated with the band and had not visited the recording studio or attended a rehearsal since the fight with Jake. Not that Eirwen was bothered by him, but why waste a *carte blanche* not to be around him and the rest of the band? I didn't mind occasionally skipping out with her but had no intention of missing, as she was to suggest, the tour planned for early spring.

On New Year's Day 1973, Brendan got quite excited with news of the non-event of the year, as far as I was concerned.

"But can't you see how much easier this will make touring on the continent?" he asked.

"Britain joining the Common Market?" I said, nonplussed.

"Well, with no border controls, travelling times will drop, and with less bureaucratic hoops to jump through, I would imagine touring costs generally will be reduced," he said, searching my face.

I clapped.

"Is that a clap of scorn or ridicule?"

"An I'm-out-of-my-depth one."

"I doubt that," he said with a grin.

Then, with the tour just weeks away, Eirwen surprised me with her sudden eagerness to go.

"What's changed your mind?" I asked.

"The IRA are blowing up London again," she said irritably.

I found the randomness of the attacks unsettling (this time the Old Bailey was targeted) whereas Eirwen was affronted by the audacity of the perpetrators. Either way, we were both keen to escape car-bombed Britain for a month or two.

Her first tour was much as mine had been almost three years previously, although there were far fewer of Jake's camp followers this time round, suggesting either he was growing up or doing his best to impress Eirwen. Certainly, Jake was in awe, bordering on polite wariness, of Eirwen, almost as if she were a wild and uncaged animal – beautiful to behold, but best viewed at a safe distance.

For me, it was so much fun to have Eirwen along, like all my Christmases rolled into one. Ruth and Sylvia were great company but Eirwen, well, Eirwen was Eirwen... a one-off.

The tour flew by, back-lit with golden sunshine, littered with laughter and the constant click of my camera. But there were some disconcerting moments. As the weeks passed and her confidence and curiosity grew, Eirwen would sometimes disappear during the day. Just for an hour or so, but too long nevertheless. I'm not sure which of us was the more worried, me or Denny.

"Don't concern yourself," Sylvia said. "She's a wily one, your friend."

And secretive too, I thought, with Eirwen never letting on where she'd been or if anyone went with her.

I followed her once, and she led me around and around in circles and back to the hotel, where she waited for me in the foyer.

"Enjoy that, did you?" she asked scathingly.

I never bothered again. And by the time we reached San Francisco, I was less inclined to ask about her absences despite my ongoing anxiety.

So it came as a surprise one afternoon when she returned from one of her disappearances demanding that we take Punchie to a near-by pizza parlour.

"Who exactly do you mean by 'we'?"

"You and me." She pulled on my arm.

"Punchie isn't safe without a male escort, Wen."

"Okay, cissy. Will Denny and H do?"

I nodded, and pointed in the direction of the outdoor pool, and away she sped. I decided to wait in the foyer, comfortably ensconced in a chair with a magazine, certain that Brendan would have nothing to do with Eirwen's plan, whatever it was.

With their dripping hair and cowed demeanour, Brendan and Denny looked as though they'd been press-ganged into service. Eirwen followed behind, shepherding a skittish Punchie.

"Ready, M," she said, gesturing for me to join her motley crew as they headed out into the street and the glaring sunshine.

Less than half an hour later we were standing outside a packed pizza parlour.

"I thought you said pizzas were pointless."

"Okay, I admit an open cheese and tomato sauce sandwich can be improved with heating. But that's not why we're here," Eirwen said, and my triumphant grin faded.

"What's going on in there?" Brendan peered in at the crowd gathered in the corner of the parlour.

"They're playing an arcade game."

"A pinball machine in a pizza parlour. And this is something Punchie should try?" Brendan's annoyance was almost parental.

"It has no flashing lights, no naked ladies and no explosions," Eirwen said, undeterred.

Brendan dropped his steering hold on Punchie's arm but he didn't move. Nor did Punchie.

"We're here now. Let's just give it a go," Eirwen coaxed.

"Okay. Five minutes," Brendan grudgingly replied. We stepped into the parlour just as the crowd around the machine momentarily thinned, enabling us to fill the brief void.

"Pong?" said Denny in disbelief. "It looks like a bloody telly." And it did – a telly screen with two dials set in a tall, brown and orange, homemade-looking cabinet. Then Eirwen tutted us out of the way, dropped a coin into the attached side slot and gave a demonstration of the game, which was basically a black-and-white, two-dimensional, bats-only representation of a game of ping-pong. More boring you couldn't get. But Punchie's face swayed everyone – he was utterly enthralled.

"Told you," Eirwen crowed when Brendan enquired at the desk about obtaining a Pong arcade game – one of the first ever video games, as it turned out to be.

Chapter 31

We'd barely been back in Britain a month when Eirwen began a campaign to wangle her way out of the European tour. We were listening to Elton John's fabulous *Madman Across the Water* album on the radiogram when she first mentioned opting out.

"Not a chance."

"Ah, come on, M. You know you'd rather be somewhere else with me than on a damn tour bus." She wiggled my arm.

"I could do without all the travelling. But as it's where Brendan is then it's where I have to be."

"Oh, don't make me sick." She mimicked vomiting on the floor.

I folded my arms and sighed. "It's their work. It pays the bills. We should support them."

She turned to study my face as though I'd said something outrageous.

"Are you sure it has nothing to do with the groupies? Are you afraid of what he might get up to if you aren't there to keep a beady eye on him?"

Eirwen knew when she was beaten, when it was pointless to continue a battle. But she was also well versed in the striking of a painful final blow. She may not have got her way, but she certainly left me with a festering sore of a suggestion that I picked at for some time.

Having read some of Brendan's fan mail, I was all too aware of the effect he had on other women. The lustful declarations and the depth of emotion expressed unsettled me. It was bad enough running the gauntlet of the very physical presence of the groupies on a regular basis without having some of their baser desires graphically described on paper.

The groupies – well the female ones, anyway – usually fell into one of two camps: those who'd expose their ample breasts while uttering profanities at me and offers of lewd acts to Brendan, and the more subtle, seductive types who undressed him with their eyes, a ready quip or smile on their provocative, pouting and generally glossy lips.

As the antithesis of these sexual veterans, I couldn't help but wonder whether Brendan would tire of my naïvety, my lack of presence. He assured me his groupie days were long gone, but I couldn't help but note any interaction he had with the women who littered every corner of any concert venue.

Then there was the girl who impacted our lives. We first saw her at the Crystal Palace Garden Festival in September 1973. It was a strange venue. A small lake directly in front of the stage distanced the audience from the bands and hampered the establishment of any sort of rapport. However, the hard-core berserkers, as they were known, overcame this obstacle by wading into the shallow sludge of the lake to be nearer the stage and, ultimately, the performers.

However, the girl in question did not stand at the front with the others. A veritable Arthurian lady, she stood alone in the centre of the lake throughout Desert Heat's performance, ostensibly unaffected by the music, the mud, her sodden clothing or the increasing humidity.

By the time the band had finished their performance, the sky had darkened as night and a storm approached. The stage was cleared in record time with everyone keen to get packed up and on the road before the rain started.

James Taylor's roadies moaned and muttered around ours as they set the stage for his performance. His was to be an impressive show, given the torrential rain and the heavenly pyrotechnics, which had seemingly synchronised to start with the opening bars of his heart-wrenching ballad, "Fire and Rain".

With the equipment and instruments loaded onto the trucks, we were about to board the tour bus – glad that, despite the thunder and lightning, the rain had held off – when the forgotten girl from the lake swooped out of the darkness as silent as a nocturnal bird of prey.

Her pale, naked body was luminescent against the black cloak she wore tied at her throat and spread wide like wings about her. She was spectacularly beautiful, but there was a look in her eyes that spoke of the madness which followed.

The girl's black hair mimicked the flowing movement of the cloak as she lunged at Brendan, clamping herself to him, her lips hard on his mouth. Then she collapsed, and Brendan reeled on release as though injured. I remember screaming at the sight of the blood on his T-shirt, which previously had been as white as the girl's body. Just as distraught, Punchie was howling uncontrollably, certain that H was wounded.

A frenzy of activity followed as several stewards sprang into action. The on-site medical team was alerted while Brendan shrugged off assistance from Jim and another roadie as he tried to stem the flow of blood from the girl's wrist.

She wasn't much older than me – in her mid-twenties, perhaps. Yet she'd risked her life to attain the attention she now received from her idol. Brendan held her and maintained pressure on her bleeding wrist. He spoke in soothing whispers, asking her name and generally comforting her until an ambulance arrived and a medical team took over her care.

Brendan was visibly shaken by the encounter and despite our attempts to assuage his concerns regarding the girl, he was reluctant to leave her side. Eventually, Baz persuaded him to board the bus, as opposed to riding in the ambulance with the girl. Later on, Paul Maunders advised Brendan not to contact her personally, and he had to be satisfied with ensuring that the girl's parents were informed about the incident and their daughter's worrying state of mind.

From then on security was improved at concerts, with access backstage denied to all except those with passes, which was a major plus really. Then, with a break from touring, the girl slipped from our minds. Besides, there was much else to distract us in the run-up to Christmas.

***

"A punch-up in the Middle East and fuel prices here rocket," Jim complained to his largely female audience that included me and Eirwen, there because we'd spent the day shopping with Ruth and Sylvia.

"The original nomenclature is more indicative of the gravity of the situation in the Middle East," Sylvia commented with Baz nodding and puffing in agreement.

"The Yom Kippur War means sweet FA to me," Jim said brusquely. "Apart from what it costs to fill up a truck." He had a point.

Then Baz surprised us with his remark. "An oil embargo, striking miners and power workers, and a government-declared state of emergency. Britain looks to be going to hell in a handcart."

"The IRA will blow us all up long before that happens," Eirwen countered.

I was about to say that Eirwen was developing an obsession with the IRA when Ruth cut in.

"This conversation sounds like the episode from *I'm Sorry I'll Read That Again* when a bunch of old duffers at a gentlemen's club were trying to outdo each other on the hardship and misery front."

"Quite so," said Sylvia. "With a recent royal wedding, not all is lost. We should toast the happy couple." She advanced on the drinks cabinet.

"A partially royal wedding," Jim said. "The groom was plain old Mark Phillips,"

"*Captain* Mark Phillips," Ruth corrected, handing him a glass of beer and a stern look.

Nonetheless, with 1974 heralding the beginning of the three-day working week, and reduced television broadcasting, Baz's words resonated. Not all bad though, according to Jim, Ruth was amused to report when we spoke on the phone. Apparently, with the ongoing power shortage, professional football matches were, for the first time in Britain, scheduled on Sundays.

"Jim's quite taken with the idea of spending a spotlight-free Sunday afternoon at Craven Cottage," Ruth said. Whatever that was. Something Fulham-related, no doubt.

Chapter 32

Then something of a major distraction came our way.

"No, we did one in the rush of our breakthrough into mainstream popular music. Not our finest moment though," Brendan said in answer to my question.

I looked at him incredulously. "You've made a music film and I've not seen it?"

"Like I said, we weren't proud of the track, never mind the 'pop promo'."

"But why another after such a long break?"

"There may be money in it. Our record label figure that with the right marketing, the next album, like the last one, could go platinum," Brendan said wryly. "If you're interested, the producer has requested that we bring along as many female hangers-on and girlfriends as we can muster."

"I'm sure Jake can rustle up enough girls from both categories," I said with a grin.

Midway through March that year, not long after the return to a five-day working week, the whole band adjourned to the Capital Hotel in Knightsbridge, chosen purely on the basis of its proximity to the filming location, so the producer informed us. And this despite the hotel having gained a Michelin star the previous year, one of the first hotels in London to do so, apparently.

The hotel's interior public areas were ultra-modern, light-filled spaces with high ceilings and long windows. The bar room was quite striking with shiny textured walls and ceilings, lots of chrome, leather buttoned chairs and backless bar stools. Jim was not impressed. He described the décor as hangover-inducing… that is, if you survived the fall from a backless stool after a skinful. He was hoping for a short shoot.

"You don't have to stay," Brendan said, once he'd stopped laughing. "We can always wheel in your second-in-command. Ruth stays, though. We need all the women we can get."

"Is there going to be an orgy scene?" Jim countered with a leer, rubbing his hands together, for which he received a clout from Ruth with her bag.

"I'm glad you don't carry a martini glass box in that thing," he muttered.

I don't think any of us were expecting the level of intensity that set in from the moment we left the hotel the next morning. The cameras were rolling from the off. We were filmed leaving the hotel, entering the vehicles, travelling down Chelsea Bridge Road and so on. There was no sign of the producer but the cameramen seemed to be drawing up a love letter to that part of London. Then we pulled up in the three Rolls Royces at a turnstile entrance to Battersea Fun Fair.

Brendan had said the producer was reluctant to provide any details about the shoot, claiming that the record label had given him *carte blanche* to do his own thing. We just hoped his vision for the promo wasn't as highfalutin as his attitude.

I've never been keen on fun fairs. Eirwen and I had been on a miners' annual trip to Porthcawl when we were young, and they had to stop the big wheel to take me off because I'd been sick. In fact, a few people had to get off (I won't go into the gory details), including Eirwen. She was not pleased.

In the full glare of daylight, the closed fun fair in Battersea Park was quite sad and depressing. The many varied rides, sideshows, galleries and food stalls had been constructed to tempt, thrill and please but the place stank of oil and mould and was worn and grimy. It resembled a grotesque manmade Grand Canyon of garishly painted steel and wood-board, I thought – a hanging ledge here, a tapered column there; a tiered gorge, a steep drop down to water.

The place put me in mind of the music hall scene from *Oh What a Lovely War* when the new enlistees go up on stage to discover that the beautiful girl promising "to make a man" of them is caked in make-up and far from alluring.

"What a shit-hole," Eirwen declared as we all huddled together, already fed up. At which point the producer, gesticulating like a policeman directing traffic, spun away from the two cameramen he'd been talking to, intent on berating the speaker. Until, that is, he clocked Eirwen wreathed in an ethereal cloud of cigarette smoke, Sylvia's second since our arrival.

"Merciful heavens," he sighed, evidently overcome. "Our angel."

Our party exchanged puzzled glances. With the track's repeated reference in the chorus to "Life's Wild Ride", we all understood a fun fair as the designated filming location, but as for a higher being, we were at a loss.

"What has an angel got to do with this?" Brendan said, advancing on the producer, a tall, bulky man with a pouchy face.

"There's a line with mention of an unwanted angel," the man explained in a condescending tone.

"I know. I wrote it. But it's not the focus of the track," Brendan said in exasperation.

"I say we go back to the hotel," Jake chipped in, a girl on each arm, his eyes alight with the promise of discord.

"Are you aware of the cost per day of the hire of such a venue?" the producer asked irritably.

"I heard the place is shutting down permanently. Not been the same since the Big Dipper disaster a couple years back," Jake countered. "You know, five kids died."

"We're wasting time. The costume department has set up behind The Rotor. Make your way there," the producer said dismissively. He waved at some distant point and turned back to the cameramen.

"Christ, it's like being back at school," Jake complained. At which point Punchie started swearing, which was often a prelude to violence in one form or another. Fortunately, Baz quickly stepped in to take Punchie's arm and set about calming his bandmate.

"Let's get this over and done with," Brendan commented, looking across to where the producer had indicated. "Come on, The Rotor's this way." Then he took hold of Punchie's free arm.

"This could be fun after all," Eirwen declared as we fell into step behind Brendan and the others.

From the outset I hadn't wanted to be involved with the piece. I just wanted to watch the proceedings from a safe distance, but the producer was having none of that. You were either in or out.

With the fun fair every bit as ghastly as I had envisaged, I certainly hadn't expected much from the wardrobe ladies, imagining they'd take an age to kit us out, which couldn't have been further from the truth. They had been furnished with the details necessary to dress us as the characters specified by the producer and we were quickly issued with our respective costumes before being directed to the changing area.

Eirwen was still laughing when we entered the curtained female section.

"You'll look like Looby-Loo in that get-up," she managed to say before dissolving into fits of laughter again.

"Yeah, yeah." I pulled a face and yanked my *Andy Pandy & Co.* costume from its hanger.

Unsurprisingly, Eirwen was a vision in her outfit which comprised a shimmering white full-length shift with a pair of wings perfect enough to turn Gabriel's head. A halo completed the illusion that she had stepped from an illuminated medieval manuscript. It was quite unnerving to behold her.

When we all reconvened from make-up, the consensus was that I did look like Looby-Loo and that the producer was some kind of pervert. Ruth and Jim were cast as my parents, which set me and Ruth off but properly irked Jim. Then the band appeared dressed as a bunch of roughs in dark trousers and white collarless shirts with the sleeves rolled up, along with different coloured waistcoats and matching neckties.

Jake, initially bolshie about his outfit, put aside his protest on sighting his two female friends dressed as schoolgirls, despite the intimidating presence of Sylvia as their teacher. In fact, Sylvia was there as herself, although she was quite taken with the offered academic gown which she was eventually persuaded to wear over her dress. She refused to relinquish her cigarette and holder, though, and the producer, realising he'd met his match, finally conceded defeat and filming began.

Brendan, Baz and Denny mimed singing and playing a motley array of guitars, with Punchie on bongos and Jake at a battered white piano, while the rest of us followed marked paths around the site. I had to spend some time after the ramble removing candy floss from my hair.

Meanwhile, Eirwen was filmed observing the band from nearby high spots including the top of the Ferris wheel, a stationary car above the Cyclone drop, a carousel horse and descending the water chute. At which point I began to look forward to seeing the finished piece.

The day remained fairly sunny but quite cold, especially for me in my overly short, spotted red skirt and white *broderie anglaise* top. Of course, Eirwen couldn't resist undoing the red ribbons on my pigtails, with a resulting call to "Cut!" from the producer and a subsequent ear-bashing for me.

The next morning began with a shock at a transport downgrade to a minibus for the mile-and-a-half journey to Battersea Park. The weather was largely unchanged though, which pleased the producer. It would help with continuity, apparently.

The bulk of the morning was taken up filming the band (minus Punchie) riding the Cyclone, with Eirwen in pursuit. The remaining crowd scene and finale were to be filmed after lunch. Lunch? The previous day we'd been thrown sandwiches between takes like performing seals at a zoo.

With the pleasant change in pace and mood came quite the converse on the weather front. Throughout the morning, the cloud had been building, and after lunch – at tables in the fun house – we emerged to discover that the site was now shrouded in a drifting mist.

Very atmospheric, the producer maintained, as he informed us that the angel was to be cast from the fun fair by the band members and a now angry crowd.

I'm not sure who was first to notice the new cast member amid the increasingly featureless fun fair, but it may well have been Ruth.

"That was creepy," she said, knocking my candyfloss-bearing arm as she veered my way.

"What was?" I asked, busily checking my hair for floss, regardless of my cold hands.

"Someone done up all in black is skulking about the place." She looked nervously around. "And where's Jim?"

"It's probably Jim you've seen," I said, pleased to discover that I was floss-free.

"The producer told him to shadow Punchie. And whoever I saw was too tall to be Jim," Ruth said uneasily.

"It's probably part of an elaborate surprise ending," I said, more concerned with getting into some warm clothing.

"You're probably right." Ruth sounded far from convinced.

On the designated signal, when Eirwen approached the now open gate alongside the entrance turnstiles, the band and the crowd were to rush forward from some distance away. At which point all those still on site became aware of the person Ruth had mentioned, running up the park steps beyond the entrance, in pursuit of Eirwen.

"What the…?" the producer shouted, following with, "Keep rolling," as Eirwen's pursuer lowered her hood.

"It's that girl from the lake!" Ruth shouted, breaking into a run. And a tremor of fear swept everyone on through the gate to shout warnings to Eirwen who, in her winged efforts to run, was evidently oblivious of the stalker gaining on her, armed with a child's cricket bat.

Then Punchie broke free of the clamouring crowd at the gate, bounded up the steps as if possessed and leapt forward just as Eirwen finally responded to the cacophony of calls and warnings all but lost in the muffling mist and the city's hum and hiss.

Eirwen's face froze in horror and she stumbled and fell backwards as the grappling pair advanced on her. During his struggle with Eirwen's would-be attacker, Punchie managed to wrest the bat away but lost his grip on the girl when she shed her cloak to speed away down the park's main thoroughfare. But he doggedly followed her for some distance while the rest of us formed a protective knot around Denny and his crumpled angel.

"I've had worse fights with Mari," Eirwen said, dismissive of our concern when Denny scooped her from the ground. She looked to me to confirm her comment, and although now shaking with fear as opposed to cold, I dutifully nodded.

"Gone. Gone." Punchie was still clutching the bat when he returned.

Eirwen then stepped away from Denny to greet Punchie. "Thank you, my hero," she exclaimed. But it was the kiss she planted on his cheek that evoked Punchie's wide, surfer's smile.

On our return to the hotel, Brendan reported the incident to the police and then contacted Paul Maunders for details of the girl's home address. Even so, we were quite subdued, despite a reassuring visit from two constables who, furnished with our further information, were intent on tracking down Eirwen's stalker.

Our sombre mood led us to eat at the hotel rather than venturing out to a restaurant as planned. Most surprising was Jake's decision not to visit a nightclub, much to the disgust of his two companions, who promptly packed and left.

After our meal, we hunkered down in the bar like teenagers around a campfire to share stories and opinions about the events of the last couple of days.

Denny kept glancing anxiously at Eirwen, who appeared to be as unaffected by her ordeal as she had earlier claimed to be. But we were all concerned in one way or another.

The consensus was that the girl had targeted Eirwen because she was alone. We just hoped the police would be able to make contact with her so as to prevent any further incidents.

However, the police never did manage to track the girl down. And although we never encountered her face-to-face again, she became a part of the landscape of our lives. She attended every concert, and always wore a white T-shirt emblazoned with Brendan's name in red, dripping letters... only his name, but a veiled threat or warning seemed evident to everyone who'd witnessed our encounters with her. But it also confirmed her ongoing obsession with Brendan, which was better than it being Eirwen, he maintained. However, to me, the girl was not just unstable but an opportunist, which I believed made potential targets of us all.

Brendan thought it best to ignore her, but it was difficult with her seemingly everywhere – outside hotels and the recording studio, or on a balcony at an airport. She tailed us for almost a year in total, a year of madness on many levels. For me, that poor girl embodied the dark, oppressive mood of the time.

Then she was gone. We hoped – almost prayed – that she'd got over her delusions and was now embarrassed by her obsession. Unfortunately, we were denied such solace. On the twentieth of July 1974 at the Knebworth Park Music Festival, she cut both her wrists, climbed a sound tower and jumped. To be honest, I was relieved that no one else was hurt and that she was finally at peace and out of our lives.

However, Brendan thought himself somehow responsible for her death. He cancelled the remaining tour dates and retired to his music room. For over two months he all but lived there, eating and sleeping very little. The album resulting from this period was, understandably, a dark gloomy affair and an accurate reflection of his state of mind.

Brendan had obviously wrestled his demons and categorically refused to rework a single note of *Dark Dream,* which was panned by the critics of the day. But years later it became a classic, often used as background music during desperate situations in film and television work.

Unable to provide comfort or consolation for Brendan, I became quite wretched. This was new territory for me and I had no idea how to deal with the situation. Eventually, I decided to occupy myself and sought out the girl's family and friends, certain there was more to her than the lurid tales and speculation that appeared in the press.

The parallels between her life and mine were initially disturbing. Like me she was a product of a stable, financially secure home and had attained a grammar school education with the promise of academic excellence. However, when she'd left home aged eighteen, her parents had been relieved. It shocked me to hear her spoken of in such disparaging terms.

She had obviously not matched the precedent set by her older brother. She had fallen short of the exacting standards laid down by her cold and distant parents and had ended up in London, living rough in dilapidated squats, developing a drug habit and acquiring an abusive boyfriend.

Brendan's well-documented, clean-cut image ensured that he stood apart from most mainstream rock and rollers, and that beautiful, sad and unloved girl appeared to have focused all her hopes and dreams on him.

Her parents spoke of her as being sick and deluded. So why hadn't they sought help for her or at least located her when Brendan and the police had contacted them? Why had they not provided some sort of emotional support, if nothing else? I laid the blame for the whole sorry saga with them. But Brendan was grappling with the knowledge that as a musician he touched people's lives and what happened next was beyond his control. Keith Richards of the Rolling Stones is reputed to have said that as a musician it was your duty to *pass it on*: the passion, the pleasure, the pain, the skill. It's all you can do.

Chapter 33

June 1975

"Say that again," I croaked, aghast.

"You heard me the first time," she said, a lazy drawl to her voice.

I stared at Eirwen in astonishment but she ignored me and took a leisurely sip of her drink – an impressively tall glass of gin, tonic and vermouth – before closing her eyes and tipping her head back to follow the sun's rays like a flower. We'd taken to meeting on neutral territory of late. Well, since our last bust-up really.

Given the surprisingly warm weather for early June, The Angel on the Bridge at Henley, with its beer garden on the bank of the Thames, was an ideal rendezvous. We were having one alcoholic drink each then a coffee or two, depending on how long I could bear to talk to her.

"Well?" she said, obviously expecting a verbal response to her lobbed stone of a statement, although she had yet to open her eyes.

"Look at me, Eirwen, and repeat what you said or I'm going home." I wanted to shake her out of reverie, to rile her as easily as she did me.

"You're still mad at me, aren't you?" She opened one eye and squinted at me, which provoked me further. She had not repeated her statement and had also reminded me of our falling out. As if I could forget.

"If you're referring to Rome, what do you think?"

"You take everything far too seriously," she said, still almost prone on the seat, her eyes closed and her face trained on the sun. Although very tempted to toss Eirwen's tall tipple over her, I took a slug of my white wine and counted to ten.

My silence opened her eyes. She stared at me so I stared back.

"Only sex," she goaded, needing a response.

As I struggled with my emotions, determined not to give her the satisfaction she craved, I carefully placed my wine glass on the table and tried to calm down. She watched me like a cat waiting to strike a playful pat, to continue the game.

"I thought we'd agreed not to talk about it anymore," I said as levelly as I could manage given how my heart and head were pounding.

"Yeah, but you're still angry about it," she responded logically, bringing the conversation full circle again. She was like that Harry Belafonte and Odetta ditty from our childhood featuring a bucket with a hole.

It was my turn to shut my eyes. I folded my arms tightly across my chest and tried to keep it all in, all I wanted to say. I shuddered with the effort. Then she touched my arm.

I opened my eyes and looked into her untroubled face.

"I'm sorry. I go too far sometimes. It's mostly for effect," she said softly, maintaining contact with my arm.

"I know. But what you seem to forget is that it does affect people." I felt my anger dissipate as quickly as it had ignited.

She withdrew her hand and sat back on her chair. "I'm trying to make amends, though. You've seen that, surely?"

"Oh my God, Eirwen. Tell me that this talk of weddings is not about making amends."

"It's definitely not talk. We've already booked the registry office."

"But you don't love Denny."

"He knows that. Reckons he's got enough love for the both of us." She shook her head and laughed a sad, hollow laugh.

"But why get married? You're young. What's the rush? You might meet someone you can love."

"I'm not like you. I don't believe in all that happily-ever-after stuff."

"It's not about belief. I feel it." I thumped my chest harder than I had intended.

"Yes, without a doubt. But does he?"

She may as well have struck me. All the way back to Rome.

***

We went to Rome to avoid the last leg of the European tour. Well, I agreed to go so Eirwen could do so. More fool me.

We were relaxing by the pool after a busy morning with a tour guide at the Vatican Museum, very tired but mightily impressed with all we'd seen. Barely aware of the bougainvillea-scented breeze that brushed our lightly tanned limbs, we were enjoying a salad lunch and discussing plans for the last full day of our break. Then, out of the blue, Eirwen blithely spewed out the filth that made me want to vomit. To spill my guts onto the pristine poolside marble.

"You know, we should just fuck each other's brains out, your Brendan and me. Get it over with. Then we'd be fine around each other. No more atmosphere or tension."

While looking at her, a living version of the marble and alabaster beauties we'd admired earlier that day, I realised that she was probably right. Most likely Brendan could have fucked her brains out and still have loved me... if he did love me, as I thought he did. But what if he didn't? What if?

I carefully stowed my belongings in my bag and turned my back on her without a sound, comment or look. Then I made my way to the hotel reception desk, where I ordered a taxi to take me to the airport.

Eirwen made no attempt to follow me – neither to intercept me when I returned to our room to pack my suitcase nor while I waited outside the hotel for the taxi. Which was just as well, as I felt quite unhinged. Just like her.

Yet here I was with her again. Why was that? What was I hoping to prove? That he did love me or that he didn't? In reality, all I was proving was that I was a fool, a doormat to be stamped on by my friend. How could she have said those things to me? After all her promises and lengthy indifference to Brendan. How could she?

For a few numbed hours after my return from Rome, I sat in my parents' kitchen as the sun rose over the hill behind the house, waiting for them to wake. I was still wearing the poolside sundress from the previous day, which was as pocked with olive oil stains as my mind was marked by her words: "I should fuck your Brendan."

Her making amends had been a masterclass in manipulation. I could see that now. She didn't seek me out or apologise. Far too obvious. No, she fawned over Denny instead. But it was so subtle, so low-key and so seemingly genuine that I had been convinced, as had Denny. Hence the proposal of marriage. But I knew Denny was willing to take Eirwen on any terms. He probably saw the change in her as an opportunity, a chance that she might accept.

Now there was to be a wedding. A late August wedding, with me as bridesmaid and Eirwen's aptly named niece, Lily, as flower girl. They'd arranged a civil service at a nearby registry office and a marquee reception in the grounds of Denny's house. The perfect day. I wanted to laugh. Or was it to cry? Possibly both.

"Of course he loves me," I wanted to scream at her while pummelling her flawless face. But I did neither. Instead, I made my way to the riverside edge of the terrace, feigning interest in all the pre-regatta activity going on up and down the Thames.

The river at Henley is rarely quiet, but with less than three weeks until the Royal Regatta, the water below the town was as busy as the thoroughfares within its centre. The regatta installations, erected on both land and in the river, were nearing completion. Soon the visiting crews and spectators from across the world would begin to arrive for the great sporting occasion and social event.

As I observed the pleasingly distracting activity up and down the Thames, a warm breeze waved the bankside bushes and trees, wafting the scent of meadowsweet, elderflower and flag iris my way. The river's sounds and smells always transported me to the boathouse and, ultimately, to Brendan. At the thought of him a tremor passed through me as though I'd been touched.

Could I walk away from here, from this moment, from her? Could I walk away from our friendship, from the bonds that bound us so tightly together? Could I?

Looking back at Eirwen, I was surprised to see that she was perched on the edge of her chair, stiff-backed and staring intently at me. Had she read my thoughts? Was she as alarmed as me when contemplating life without the other? Our eyes locked and she smiled.

Go, a small corner of my consciousness urged. *Run. Don't look back.*

Did she intend to drive a wedge between Brendan and me? Was she jealous of what we had? I didn't think so. Then what drove her to meddle, to try to mend but ultimately break all that mattered to her? She was a conundrum, and I had had a surfeit of riddles of late.

Pausing only to collect my bag, I made my way up the steps to the rear bar and then on through the pub to the main entrance. As I made my way to the carpark, I contemplated how often of late I'd curtailed a rendezvous with Eirwen to leave in a hurried fit of pique.

Once the car windows were open, I started up the engine and its signature roar made me smile, sweeping the maelstrom of doubts and negative emotions away. In fact, I felt positively upbeat as I pulled onto Hart Street, and hoped to find Brendan in the boathouse when I got home.

Chapter 34

Almost a month elapsed before I next saw Eirwen. But, like an addiction, thoughts of her crept into my mind on a daily basis. I did my best to limit her occupation of my consciousness, to keep it minimal. Strangely, I savoured the sanity of this period of cold turkey.

Roughly four weeks after the altercation at the Angel, I'm sure there was an audible pop at breakfast when the bubble of peace and tranquillity I'd been enjoying was burst by Brendan's announcement.

"What d'you think? I've been summoned to Richmond. Alone, mark you."

My blood ran cold. Had Eirwen engineered a fucking-brains-out opportunity? I coughed messily on my toast, crumbs falling like confetti onto the pristine white tablecloth.

Brendan handed me a glass of water. "Denny said to leave within the hour as Eirwen is coming here to see you. Such a shame I'll miss her." He winked.

Flooded with the seesaw emotions of relief and panic, I sipped water while mentally treading it. Brendan had yet to mention the wedding, which suggested he didn't know about it, whereas I had failed to share the little I knew for almost a month. But then I had hoped it was a case of no news is good news and that the whole proposed debacle had been called off. No such luck, it would seem.

***

The crunch of gravel marking Brendan's departure for Richmond was repeated less than twenty minutes later on Eirwen's arrival, but with considerably more door slamming. Perhaps she'd brought reinforcements. Not wanting to appear too keen to see her again, I waited a while before making my way outside.

Whenever I revisit my memories of this moment it is always redolent with the fragrance of roses... sweetly perfumed, blousy old garden roses, Joe's favourites. The packed lavender-bordered rose beds flanked the front porch of the house with both species in full fragrant bloom that dull July morning.

Eirwen's face was a flushed pink and as beautiful as the best of Joe's thorny blooms. She was intent on retrieving and stacking an array of boxes scattered about the rear of her two-toned copper-coloured Mini Cooper, so she was oblivious to my approach.

"You'd never get a job with Royal Mail if that was anything to go by."

Startled by my voice, Eirwen again dropped the growing stack.

"I hope I'll never need one," she returned, surveying the scattered collection of cardboard, hand on hip, her left foot tapping an angry tempo. "Oh, and less of the sarcasm, and give me a hand."

"I'm surprised there wasn't a direct order for me to unload the vehicle on your arrival."

"You're pushing your luck now. Just as well I'm still making amends." Then she checked the labels on the boxes, selected two and handed them to me.

"I'm starting to enjoy this making amends." I peered down at the boxes in my outstretched arms.

"Make the most of it. It won't last," Eirwen said, which made me laugh. "Do you want to go first?" she added, setting her much taller tower alongside mine on the large oak coffee table in the hall.

"Go where?"

"Are you being deliberately perverse, or still enjoying the moment?"

"A bit of both, I think. Wedding outfits?"

"Gowns, darling," she drawled, affecting a posh accent.

"How about a simultaneous change?" I said, suddenly excited. "You use the second bedroom and join me when you're ready."

Neither of the boxes I placed on my and Brendan's bed was heavy. The smaller of the two was obviously a shoebox so I put it to one side and turned my attention to the second, larger one.

I ran my hand down the length of the box and suddenly I was six or so years old again and swinging on the chapel gates with Eirwen, impatiently waiting on the departure of one the many brides we'd viewed over the years, along with her groom and attendant maids. Oh, how we'd longed for a bride to attend to and be upstaged by.

I was now inured to being upstaged. With Eirwen as a friend it was inevitable, with or without fancy clothing. So my expectations with regard to the content of the larger box were very low.

Removing the tightly fitting lid caused the delicate tissue paper shroud within to flutter, revealing a tantalising glimpse of the glorious garment beneath its protective folds. I peeled back the translucent paper to reveal a gossamer beauty worthy of a midsummer night's dream.

I took hold of the shoulders and gently removed the gauzy confection from its cardboard casket, at which the garment took on a life of its own in a rustle of silk and a flutter of tulle. The opaque top layer of the dress was traced with the merest hint of tiny daisy shapes in warm, faint shades of amber. The underskirt was a silky-soft, pale, pale peach, and at the waist a wide glossy ribbon the colour of my hair spiralled in long tendrils to the mid-calf hem. I gasped at its beauty and shook it just to see and hear it move.

I had yet to change when Eirwen burst into the room. Every bit the proud Titania, she was resplendent in ivory from the beribboned ballet pumps on her feet to the circle of tiny flowers that crowned her blonde head. And her dress was a thing of magic, its fabric so fine it hid yet revealed the seductive contours of her body. Her loveliness caught my breath.

"Wen," I said, my voice thick with emotion. "You look wonderful."

"But what about your dress? Do you like it?"

I dragged my eyes from Eirwen and held my dress at the shoulder seams and pressed it against my body.

"I knew the colour was right as soon as I saw it. Put it on, M." She settled on the chair near the bedroom door, her dress billowing about her like a parachute.

Suddenly self-conscious, I struggled to do up the dress.

"Let me," she said and deftly secured the zip and tied the sash with a neat bow. Then, taking hold of my shoulders, she steered me to the large free-standing mirror near the window. "There. How fabulous do you look?"

I looked up from my reflected form, and our eyes met in the glass.

"It's beautiful, Wen. Thank you."

"No, you're beautiful, and the dress is… well, just it's you." Then she hugged me. I was too choked to speak.

***

As Eirwen and her precious cargo disappeared down the driveway, I marvelled that Brendan had yet to return. How could two men take longer to get suited and booted than two women took to ready themselves? Perhaps there'd been problems with the outfits, or possibly about there being a wedding at all. There was no point in speculating. I'd know soon enough.

Mrs Booker and I were enjoying coffee, lemon drizzle cake and wedding gossip when the kitchen door was angled open by Brendan.

"A private party, or can anyone have cake?" he asked, beating Mrs B to the coffee pot to pour himself a cup.

We chatted amiably for a further twenty minutes or so, during which time Brendan divulged that the groom and his best man were to wear light brown three-piece suits and dark brown ties for the forthcoming nuptials. Then he laughed, causing Mrs Booker and me to exchange glances.

"Don't look so worried, ladies. It tickles me that it's a first for both of us. We've somehow managed to get to our late thirties before needing to wear a suit. Not sure if that's a good or bad thing." He chuckled again.

After dinner that evening, we adjourned to the music room, where Brendan set about what he termed post-troughing tinkling. Pieces new and old merged and blurred, as though an overture for something quite wonderful, making me hopeful of happiness on his part regarding news of Denny and Eirwen's marriage.

"I'm sorry I'd not mentioned the wedding," I said, prone on the sofa and enjoying the view, one I'd never tire of: Brendan lost in the music, his beautiful hands creating beautiful sounds that touched my very core.

"You're not obliged to tell me anything you don't want to," he said matter-of-factly.

"I wanted to, felt that I should, but at the same time hoped that the wedding wouldn't happen and, if I ignored it, it definitely wouldn't. Does that make sense?"

"Of course. After nearly five years together I'm fluent in Mari-speak."

I threw a cushion at him, which he managed to deflect back at me without missing a beat in his playing. After quickly performing a double-handed ta-dah on the keyboard, he lunged my way, to drop onto the sofa and tickle me.

"You're not annoyed about the wedding?" I eventually asked.

We were no longer wrestling and laughing, but our proximity was leading to a different kind of intimacy as Brendan brushed hair from my face and gently kissed me.

"Don't think you'll deter me with wedding talk."

"Seriously, though, what do you think?"

He lifted his head from mine. "I think it'll end in tears, as my granny used to say. But for the moment Denny's a happy man. Who am I to argue with that? Now, is there any chance of you giving me your full attention?" I pulled his head to mine and kissed back my reply.

Chapter 35

With just twenty-four hours until the wedding, everything at The Elms was surprisingly calm. Considering that Mrs Booker was at the helm it was to be expected, surely. But then factor in Eirwen and her family and a sizeable Welsh crowd having taken up residency, and concerns regarding calm were understandable.

Brendan had decamped to Denny's to join the predominantly Northern contingent – or north-eastern, as Brendan corrected. There are very fine lines regarding boundaries and territories *t'up north*, apparently. It was going to be a heady mix, this wedding. Best we enjoyed the current calm while it prevailed.

The North-South divide had been ongoing since the hen and stag dos the previous weekend, when the men plus Denny's sister had undertaken an alcohol-free nostalgia tour of Newcastle upon Tyne. This had been harder than it sounded, Brendan maintained, given that Sandra, Denny's sister, was difficult to be around unless you were at least three parts pissed.

Sandra had been both mother and father to Denny in the wake of the loss of their father during the final year of the war, and their mother just two years later. Aged thirteen and eight respectively, Sandra and Denny were then passed around the extended family and accommodated with varying degrees of charity and charm for a number of years. Hence Sandra was able to present a very sound argument as to why she should be Denny's best man at the wedding.

"I was quite happy to defer to her better judgement and heftier punch," Brendan said, "but Denny convinced her that she was needed to supervise the Clarke clan at the forthcoming nuptials."

In contrast, Eirwen's hen do was an alcohol-soaked, power-struggle-free event that began in an Italian restaurant and ended in a dance hall within staggering distance of the former. But I sobered up the minute we hit the dance floor. Needs must. I'd forgotten what it was like to be out after dark with Eirwen in such places. She's like catnip, and without an attendant male, she had every tomcat in Cardiff circling her and watching her every move. It was a long night.

Moreover, here we were: Lily, Trefor and me, outside the ornate red-brick registry office at Kingston upon Thames, waiting on the bride, who was more than a little late. It was just as well the weather was kinder than it had been the previous Thursday, when a thunderstorm centred on Hampstead resulted in six and a half inches of rain in less than three hours.

Perhaps she's bolted, I thought, en route to the toilet with Lily for at least the third time since our arrival. At this stage in the proceedings, I'm not sure how I'd have received such news. Thankfully, my musings were curtailed by an urgent call to get a move on. The bride was on her way.

Lily and I swished down the corridor in a flurry of rustling fabric, arriving at the main entrance as Eirwen alighted from the side door of a beribboned VW campervan very much like the one we had travelled home in from the Isle of Wight almost five years previously. Terry opened the rear door of the van, and he and Trefor carefully lowered their dad and his wheelchair to the ground.

Illuminated by a sudden shaft of sunlight, Eirwen – a vision in ivory, and as fragrant as the flowers in her hair and hands – approached Lily and me, seemingly without making contact with the ground.

"Like a fairy," whispered Lily, evidently impressed.

Eirwen squeezed my arm and lightly touched Lily's cheek. She then positioned herself at her father's side and arranged her bouquet of ivory roses and gypsophila comfortably in her right hand so as to hold her father's hand with her left. Phil beamed across at me and

Lily, wiggling his fingers at his granddaughter, but his eyes were wet and full and his usually pale skin flushed.

Trefor dashed in through the large double doors to return to his spouse while Terry, his still single (and surprisingly unattached) twin brother pushed their dad's wheelchair towards the gathered throng waiting beyond the dark doors.

The marriage service was brief and conducted in a clipped if cultured tone of voice by a palpably irritated registrar. The lady was evidently unused to any sort of delay. Then, seemingly too soon to be legal, the ceremony ended and we were boarding an array of vehicles bound for Richmond.

I'd never really warmed to Denny's Art-Deco-style property at Richmond. It was too square and regular, despite some stunning feature windows. Denny loved its clean lines and uncluttered openness, characteristics that were mirrored in the layout of the garden. The garden's design was fortuitous, given the circus-size marquee spread-eagled on the lawn beyond the house and terrace that sun-kissed afternoon.

Guests gathered in drifts around the grounds while the bride and groom were photographed in and about the house. Lily and I were also summoned to be snapped with Eirwen, the most memorable being a pose on the hall's staircase, a striking sweep of metal and marble.

Once I'd reunited Lily with her parents, I returned to the terrace and picked out some canapés and a drink on offer from the wandering waiting staff. I was quietly enjoying a moment crowd-watching when Ruth and Sylvia accosted me. Well, Sylvia did, actually. I almost choked on a canapé.

"A penny for them?" Sylvia asked, a several-martinis-in gleam in her eyes. She probably had an optic of vodka in her bag. I looked blankly back at her.

"Did you think she'd actually go through with it?" she added. I was none the wiser, although Ruth's suddenly alert expression suggested that she knew exactly what Sylvia was talking about.

"She doesn't even like men," Sylvia added. I'm sure my mouth opened but my brain failed to provide an appropriate response. Fortunately, Ruth saved the moment.

"This isn't the time or place." She glared at Sylvia as she took her glass. "Have something to eat," Ruth added, relieving me of my plate and thrusting it at Sylvia.

"I'll get more food," I said and darted away as Ruth emptied Sylvia's glass into a nearby plant pot. I didn't re-join them. I already had enough concerns about Eirwen's motives in marrying Denny.

Yet the celebration of their marriage proved to be the polar opposite of the earlier barren, perfunctory service. It was a warm, emotional, joyous and, incredibly, alcohol-free occasion.

Information regarding the latter had been issued with the invites and received – more than likely – with much scorn and derision north and south of all the borders. Nevertheless, the toasts were made with elderflower cordial and soda water, and only soft and hot drinks were available to guests. Smuggled alcohol was consumed but subtly so. And almost everyone, I would say, enjoyed what was probably the best party of their lives.

"Why is Aunty Wen sad?"

Little Lily, her hair now wild, had hold of my dress and gave it another tug. She stared up at me with more than a hint of her aunt about her eyes.

"She's not sad." I glanced around in search of Eirwen. "Look, she's smiling." I stooped beside Lily to point out her aunt.

Lily gave me a glare that was well beyond her years and said, "She still *looks* sad." And off she flounced.

However astute, Lily was wrong. Eirwen wasn't sad; she just wasn't with us. It grieved me to think of where she'd rather be than here – here in this joyous moment of celebration with the people who loved her most. How could she?

Conversely, Denny was like a man possessed. Hyped up on joy and disbelief. He kept hugging Eirwen and searching her face. But the love that registered in his eyes and in everything he did was evidently not reciprocated by his wife. Most people were probably unaware of this, as Eirwen smiled on cue and nodded in agreement with everything Denny said. But I recognised that faraway look.

Then Phil rolled up beside me and took hold of my hand.

"Right, Mari. What do you think? Can he make my little lion happy?"

I smiled at his endearment, one I'd not heard him use for a long time, and covered his hand with my free hand.

"I know this much, Phil: Denny will certainly give it his best shot. He loves Eirwen unconditionally."

He completed the hand hold between us. "But will that do?"

Our continued silence was answer enough. We dropped our hands.

"Your speech was…" I struggled to steady my emotions as much at the memory of Phil's speech as our current conversation.

"That bad, eh?"

"It was marvellous, as well you know. Eirwen was genuinely moved," I replied, certain she had been fully attentive and responsive during her father's speech. It was one of the few moments when she *had* been that I was to witness that day.

"Aye, she was," he conceded with a smile.

"When you made to give her hand to Denny, what was that little poem?"

"Now hold this hand that I once held in lifetimes long ago,

"And take it forward, safely mind,

"As your lives together grow," Phil recited, a little shakily.

"Lovely." I was quite moved by the sentiment.

"Not quite worthy of the bardic crown, but not bad for an old has-been."

"Has-been? Hardly that. Fancy you of Viking stock saying such a thing."

"Me and my stories." He chuckled.

"More of a credible hypothesis, I'd say, considering the abundance of long legs and blonde hair among the Watkins tribe."

"Almost had to give up on my claims when our Trefor and Terry started digging up the garden in search of the longship and horned helmets I maintained were buried there."

We laughed together as we revisited the moment the twins were found – red-faced, mud-caked and breathless – knee-deep in a large hole, worthy of an archaeological dig.

"We'll just have to hope for the best," Phil said.

"Yes, it's in the lap of the gods now."

"Would that be Odin and Thor?" Phil said, setting us laughing again.

We were still chuckling when Megan sidled up beside Phil.

"In between making her laugh, have you told Mari how lovely she looks?"

"No. But you heard that, Mari. And Meg is never wrong. But, joking aside, you do look wonderful."

Flushed and flustered, I hugged them in turn.

Given the crowds at The Elms over the past two days, I had barely spoken to my own parents when I spotted them chatting amiably with Brendan and his mother. My spirits soared to see those I loved most so comfortable together.

My dad saw me before anyone else, and his face lit up as I slid an arm around Brendan's waist. Brendan briefly kissed me before I moved on to embrace my parents and then Dot.

"Never thought I'd see the day," Dad said through his grin. "My tomboy daughter comfortable in frills."

"More floaty than frilly, Dad," I corrected with a smile, enjoying his evident approval.

"Lovely, whatever you care to call it."

Embarrassed at all the attention, I was glad of the timely arrival of another tray of canapés. Momentarily silent, and busy with our food, we became aware of someone calling and beckoning to Brendan.

"See you later, my frilly little firecracker." He gave me a quick squeeze and made for the still gesticulating guest. As he walked away, I was suddenly aware of humming "I Get a Kick Out of You", much to the amusement of my father and Brendan's mother, whereas my mother was as mortified as I was.

"Seems like you and Eirwen are about to lose your men." Dot pointed out the young band I'd vaguely been aware of during my conversation with Phil. Evidently, they were now tuned up and intent on coercing Denny, Brendan, Baz, Punchie and Jake to perform a track or two. The youngsters were obviously in awe, and all but salivated as their heroes acquiesced and donned the proffered guitars.

Then a gathering giddy crowd began to call out requests for tracks from Desert Heat's extensive back catalogue.

Brendan was mesmeric. His voice had that quality that stirs hidden places, a husky throatiness that implied the breathlessness of desire. As he began to sing, head and spine arched back, the bulk of the audience - well, all the females, anyway - drew in an involuntary yet synchronised gasp as if touched suddenly. He was totally uninhibited behind the guitar or at the keyboard – with any instrument, really. The music took control and his movements were instinctive.

Strangely, without an instrument Brendan seemed to lack rhythm – well, with regard to dancing he did, or claimed to. I'd never seen him dance, nor danced with him, prior to Eirwen and Denny's wedding.

"I prefer to watch you," he'd argue whenever I attempted to cajole him onto the dance floor. And I'd dance without him because I loved to dance.

So I was unprepared for the tap on my shoulder an hour or two into the DJ's session later that evening, on the opening bars of a song I did not recognise.

"Dance with me," he softly sang, in unison with the record, as he turned me around. "I want to be your partner. Can't you see the music is just starting? Night is calling and I am falling. Dance with me. Let it lift you off the ground. Starry eyes and love is all around us. I can take you where you want to go."

Ridiculously, it became our tune. The irony was that it wasn't Brendan's or even British. It was a track by an American band called Orleans. But, as Brendan maintained, the song captured what he wanted to say at that moment in time, and it remained the only record to get him onto the dance floor.

"Dance with Me" had ended, and everyone around us moved apart at the start of a record with a more upbeat tempo. But Brendan and I remained entwined, our eyes locked. It was a surreal moment, as though the crowded dance floor had suddenly emptied. And there was no sound, apart from our breathing. Yet we remained immobile... unembarrassed and unaware of anything but each other.

Suddenly, Brendan released me, and I felt cast drift in an unreal sea until he caught my hand again and spoke.

"Madam, you have bereft me of all words. Only my blood speaks to you in my veins."

"Shakespeare. Not sure which play it is, though."

"Not the response I'd hoped for," he said with a sigh drawing me close once again. "And the words are Bassanio's to—"

"Portia. Merchant of Venice."

"You didn't think they were my words? Not for a second?"

"Not direct enough to be yours."

"True." He tightened his hold on me. "I'd have identified the particular vein that speaks to you the most." Then he buried his face in my hair as he made to bite my neck and swung me around until we were both giddy and helpless with laughter.

Chapter 36

March 1978

Two and a half years on from Eirwen and Denny's wedding, and how things had changed. Oh, so now everything in the garden was lovely – another of my mother's sayings – or perhaps Brendan's summation of it ending in tears was nearer the mark. A balanced bit of both, in fact.

Eirwen and Denny's metaphorical garden wasn't just lovely, it was positively blooming. And the tears? Well, they were never going to be Eirwen's and, surprisingly, they weren't Denny's either. They were mine.

Eirwen and I had been into Henley wandering around the shops. It had been her idea to meet up there. But she had seemed subdued, definitely not herself. I waited nervously, trying not to guess what was wrong. Then, as we were about to go our separate ways, and my "What's the matter?" was on the tip of my tongue, she told me.

"I'm pregnant."

"That's fantastic," I gushed, aware that her excitement did not match mine.

"Is it?"

"Of course it is. Congratulations."

Then I noticed how pale she was and how her eyes lacked their usual brightness and were smudged with purple hollows.

"Morning sickness and things?" I asked vaguely, unsettled by her continued apathy.

"All of it. Not sure I'm ready for this."

"Not planned, then?"

She shook her head.

I was about to ask what Denny thought, certain that he'd be over the moon, when Eirwen cut in.

"Look, I have to go. See you soon." And she was gone.

I watched her leave trying to remain magnanimous. But given how negative she had been about her condition, I found it difficult. I longed to be pregnant, yearned to hold a child of my own… a child that was mine and Brendan's.

I had stopped taking the pill over a year ago, to no avail. Just as well. Brendan hadn't greeted my suggestion – trying for a baby, that is – with any degree of enthusiasm. In fact, he managed to avoid any sort of discussion on the subject.

Everything was on his terms, as Eirwen had once commented. Stopping the pill without telling Brendan was an act of defiance on my part. I was sure he'd be thrilled once I was expecting. I know now that would not have been the case.

Perhaps that's why I've not yet conceived, I thought. My way of punishing myself for my duplicity – or some such psychobabble. Or perhaps I couldn't have children. Either way, I planned to tell him everything when I got home.

We never had that conversation.

***

Brendan was playing the grand piano when I arrived home, playing something wonderful that had hints of Grieg about it. Perhaps it *was* Grieg and he hadn't quite mastered it yet. But it was still wonderful. I rushed in and blurted out the news about Eirwen, at which his welcoming smile vanished. He seemed to become rigid, and his face registered at least three different emotions. Fear, sadness and anger… How strange. And I had yet to mention my deceit.

"What about Denny? Does he even know?"

"I assume he does."

"You of all people should know not to assume anything where Eirwen is concerned."

"What is wrong with you? Eirwen's pregnant. She's not committed a crime."

"Do you suppose I wouldn't have known if Denny knew?"

"Does that matter?"

"I'm going out." And he left.

Stunned and angry, I paced the length of the music room. Mrs Booker knocked and entered sometime after Brendan had left. If she was surprised by my request to dine later, and alone, in the small living room, she didn't show it.

Mrs Booker banked up a hearty fire and served a meal to match on a tray in the cosy room situated off the corridor to the left of the main staircase, along with Mrs Booker's own living quarters. Sadly, I lacked any sort of appetite, and picked at and pushed around her culinary endeavours while considering Brendan's reaction.

Had news of Eirwen's pregnancy reminded him of my tentative appeal of over a year ago? Was the idea of a child of our own so abhorrent to him? Or did it remind him of his wife, and the child he maintained wasn't his? Responsibilities he had abandoned physically and emotionally, if not financially. Or did Chrissie (whoever she was) figure somewhere in the mire of silence and secrets of Brendan's making?

But what bothered me the most was that both Eirwen and Brendan reacted adversely to her pregnancy. Why?

At eleven o'clock I rang Denny. Brendan still wasn't home.

"Hi, Mari. What do you think of our news?"

I could hear his joy and all but see his smile and lightbulb-lit eyes.

"Fantastic, Denny. Really thrilled for you both. Is Wen okay?"

"She went to bed early. Feeling a bit ropey. I've been worried about her. Knew something was bothering her. Didn't expect this, though. Still hasn't sunk in yet."

"Have you seen Brendan?"

"Yeah. He called in on the way to London not long after Wen had gone to bed. Said he had to sort something out with Paul. He was really thrilled when I told him about the baby."

"Of course. Congratulations and goodnight, Denny. Love to Wen. Tell her to get in touch when she's feeling up to it. Bye."

I stood by the phone for some time, totally bewildered.

***

Brendan was away for nearly a week, by which time I'd reached headless chicken mode. I paced up and down whatever room I currently occupied, was incapable of coherent thought let alone speech, and had probably lost a few pounds in weight. There was a loud hum where my head should have been.

Mrs Booker was doing her best to keep me fed, watered and washed, but she too was unsettled by the turn of events. Sometimes she'd join me in the small living room of an evening when I'd collapsed onto the sofa – exhausted by my empty day – and hold my hand. Occasionally she even tried to engage me in meaningful conversation.

"Isn't it wonderful?" she enthused during the news one night as if I had any idea what she was talking about. "President Jimmy Carter," she said, offering me a clue. I hunched my shoulders. "Well, he's decided to postpone the production of the neutron bomb," she added, excitedly pointing at the telly.

"Mm," I replied, not registering the reprieve humankind had been granted.

When Brendan returned, I launched myself at him much as I had at the Angel Hotel in Cardiff almost eight years previously. But there was no shared kiss. I hung from him like an unnecessary artwork. And him? He was as unyielding and impenetrable as a wall.

He'd returned to inform me that he was going to his mother's for a break.

"But we need to discuss this," I screamed at him.

"Discuss what?"

"Whatever has happened to us!" I was still screaming.

"Nothing has happened. We just need a break."

It was an Eirwen-like conclusion. I began to sing.

"There's a hole in my bucket, dear Liza, dear Liza. There's a hole in my bucket, dear Liza, a hole."

He slammed the door as he left.

***

Almost a month elapsed before Brendan returned. Mrs Booker had lost weight, never mind me. Brendan was cold and distant. Nevertheless, I swear he trembled when I clutched at him, before he batted me away with a wad of details from estate agents of houses for sale in South Wales.

"But I live here," I said, my voice wavering.

"For the time being… until you find a suitable property." He avoided eye contact and offered up the bundle of papers to me. I hit the sheets from his hand and they fluttered about us like a heavy fall of snow.

"Why are you doing this? Does it have anything to do with your wife and her son, or Chrissie?"

He winced, and his voice softened when he spoke, but he did not look at me.

"There are many reasons why it has to be this way, Mari."

"Is Eirwen having your baby?"

Finally, he looked at me, and when he spoke his voice was clipped and cold, but his eyes gleamed with a white-hot fury.

"That you can suggest such a thing says how little you know me. Pick out some houses to view, Mari."

And that was it. We'd had our break and he'd enjoyed it so much – not that you'd have known, for he was as thin as me – it was to continue… indefinitely. How had that happened? What went wrong? Nothing, as far as I was concerned, or had been aware of. It would appear that Eirwen's pregnancy flicked a switch that shut the door on our relationship. But why, I could not say.

***

I was alone again in a house busy with people. Brendan hadn't divulged where he was going this time so all those remaining at The Elms fretted and fussed, in their different ways, at his continued absence. Meanwhile, envelopes from estate agents accumulated in the hall. At which point Mrs Booker and I began our games of "Hunt the Bottle" – she'd search for whatever bottle I was currently swigging from while I ransacked the house for replacements. It was a costly exercise.

"Does Brendan know you're tipping that down the sink?" The air in the kitchen was heady with the acrid tang of alcohol.

"I have Mr Bradshaw's permission to do whatever is necessary to bring you to your senses."

"Oh, so you're on his side now."

"I couldn't be more shocked by the turn of events. But nothing will get better until you try to make it better." She shook the last few drops of soapy water from a bottle marked "Remy Martin" and placed it on the draining board alongside three other empty bottles.

"Do you think he'll change his mind if I make an effort?" I clutched at her arm.

Mrs Booker dried her hands and steered me to the table, where we sat down. She studied me for a moment, sighed and hooked a tendril of lank hair behind my left ear.

"This isn't a test, lamb." She smoothed more stray hair from my face. "Mr Bradshaw means to do this for reasons best known to himself alone. We have to accept that and carry on." She patted my hand, her voice and eyes heavy. I just sat there mutely, aimless and empty.

"We have to start somewhere." She got up and left the room.

On her return, Mrs Booker placed two handfuls of large, predominantly white, envelopes on the table.

"Sort them into locations and decide where you want to live then pick out three to view."

I looked at her in disbelief, stunned and hostile, and far too sober.

"There's no more alcohol in the house and the car and bicycle are locked away until you're fit to use them. I'll open the envelopes and you can arrange the properties by area to begin with." She grasped my hand. "Please, lamb."

Put like that, how could I refuse? It proved to be my most productive afternoon for some time, but only if my expeditions on foot into Henley to acquire more alcohol were overlooked.

***

I settled on Newport, a town familiar to most Welsh people as the last big landmark town before the Severn Bridge. The M4 passes through two tunnels high above the town. Ranged around the River Usk, Newport also boasts an eclectic mix of bridges, including a transporter bridge and one of the last remaining working bridges of its type in the world. However, Newport is largely only glimpsed in passing, bordered and overshadowed, as it is by the M4.

I divulged my three choices of prospective homes to Mrs Booker. I assume that she passed on this information, as the following week Eirwen and Denny turned up at The Elms to take me to view the earmarked properties. By which time I had discovered that travel sickness tablets and/or painkillers, plus a minimal amount of alcohol, induced a comfortably numb state of being. I slept most of the way to Newport despite Eirwen's attempts to talk to me.

We viewed the properties, all within easy reach of the M4 and the railway station, but a decision was beyond me. Eirwen held up the three sheets with the details of each house. We were eating at the Red Lion pub on Stow Hill at the time, but I had little appetite for my meal and scowled at it, and then at the sheets, which Eirwen continued to wave at me.

"Did you like any of these?"

I grabbed the nearest sheet. "I'll have this one."

Denny scanned the sheet.

"Are you sure? It's the one that needs the most work."

"Good. I hope it costs him a fortune."

Then I ate what was on my fork... Mushroom, my compromised taste buds suggested.

***

The weeks passed in a blur of inactivity and misery. Then a solicitor arrived with documents that needed my signature, and suddenly I was a house owner. News of my imminent departure for Newport was divulged in person by my generous benefactor.

The small living room had become my bolthole of choice. I slept, sat and ate there. Never having spent time with him there, it was my miniature Brendan-free world: a space without any memories of how things used to be. It was where he found me on his unannounced return.

I was, unusually, relatively sober and sensible. And just as importantly, clean. Mrs Booker had taken to removing clothing that had lingered too long about my person. She'd remove the grimy garments and leave a neat pile of fresh clothing along with a towel and toiletries. Very subtle, eh?

Brendan walked into the room and closed the door. I jumped to my feet, trembling.

"You need to sort out your belongings," he said without preamble. "I've arranged a removal van for next week. I've tripled your allowance and deposited a lump sum in your bank account to cover the cost of furnishing your house. Contact the solicitor if you need more money." The words spilled from him as though he'd learnt the text for a test.

I burst into tears.

Brendan crossed the room, caught me by the shoulders and gently shook me. Then he temporarily released his grip to wipe a shirtsleeve across my sodden face and leaned towards me.

It was the closest he'd been to me in weeks. I felt sick with disgust at the desire that uncoiled like a snake deep within me. His fingers seemed to burn into me as I moved achingly towards him, trying to decipher what blazed behind his eyes. But he kept me an arm's length away – much longer arms than mine – and held me there, like a badly worn outfit.

Unsurprisingly, there was no kiss, no reconciliation. He straightened my limp body with a jolt and spoke to me through gritted teeth.

"Mari." His voice was strained, not angry, despite his clenched jaw and fierce eyes.

He moved a little closer to me. "You've got to stop this nonsense and get on with your life. But"—he paused—"promise me, please…" He seemed to weaken again, which allowed me to narrow the gap between us while we traded air in laboured gasps.

"Promise me that you'll never lose your drive, your passion, your fire. Just go channel it into a more deserving cause."

Then he left. Not my life, but *me*. And along with my loss, it wounded me to think that I might never know why.

Chapter 37

"What are you doing?" Mrs Booker seemed uncharacteristically angry. I'd never known her to raise her voice, and it upset me to think I could have such an effect on her.

"I'm packing, as instructed by Mr Bradshaw. I don't want to be in his bedroom any more than either of you want me to be."

"You're putting your clothes into shopping bags," she said, as though I was unaware of my actions.

"As I said, I'm packing."

"But there's a set of suitcases that's yours."

"I don't have much to pack. Besides, the suitcases were bought by Mr Bradshaw. They're his."

"Stop doing that," she said.

"I have."

"I don't mean the packing." She gathered an armful of clothing from the wardrobe and deposited it on the bed. "Stop calling Mr Bradshaw Mr Bradshaw."

This, of course, made me laugh.

"Oh, Mrs Booker, how will I manage without you?"

Mrs Booker dabbed at her nose with a handkerchief and then indicated with a sweep of her arm the remaining clothing in the wardrobe and on the bed. "Where do you propose to put these?"

"Those were bought for me. They're his."

It was petty of me to suddenly acquire principles given I'd already decided to take the car, the bicycle and the piano. But they had been birthday gifts, I'd reasoned. And the house? Well, what could an evicted person do?

"Oh, for goodness' sake." Mrs Booker bustled out of the room to return less than fifteen minutes later with the matching set of luggage.

She hoisted the largest of the cases onto the bed. "Go and make coffee. Bring up some lemon meringue too."

I watched her neat, swift movements and the growing stacks of folded clothing in the largest of the cases.

"Well, what are you waiting for? Off you go."

I knew when I was beaten. Mrs Booker's lemon meringue pie could sway any argument.

***

By the time I made my way to the front of the house, my bicycle and piano were already on the removal van, their outlines still recognisable despite their blanket shrouds. Given the available space, my luggage was also loaded onto the van. Mrs Booker returned indoors just as Joe rounded the side of the house. He was pulling a small, wheeled cart packed with potted plants.

"Right, my girl." He took hold of my arm and indicated to his contraband. "I know these are some of your favourites. And this should do well." He pointed at a small Brown Turkey fig tree. "I hear you have a south-facing garden. Everything here is easy enough to come by, but I thought it would be fitting if you took a piece of *this* garden with you."

I welled up, just managing to plant a kiss on Joe's leathery brown cheek.

"There now," he said and patted my arm.

Mrs Booker reappeared just as Joe and I finished handing the boxes of plants to the removal men.

"Joe, there are more boxes and packages in the kitchen, if you could show the gentlemen the way."

"Will do, Mrs B," Joe said with a salute for her and a wink for me.

"And Mari, you'll want these tonight."

I opened the boot of my car. Mrs Booker was depositing the two packages inside when we were alerted to the sound of approaching vehicles.

Denny and Eirwen pulled up alongside the van with Ruth and Sylvia behind them. I looked at everyone expectantly, touched that they'd turned up to see me off.

"All set then?" Eirwen's tone of voice implied an expedition, not the painful exodus I felt the occasion to be.

"As I'll ever be." I was dreading the journey but more so, arriving at a house I couldn't even remember.

"Room in the boot for these, Mari?" Denny held a small case in one hand and a large box in the other.

"I think so," I said, distracted by Eirwen who had opened the driver's side door of my car.

"Keys?" She held out her hand to me.

By this time, the removal men were in the process of closing the tailgate of the van.

"What's going on?"

"Well, given your current drinking habit I'm hardly likely to travel as your passenger. Keys, please."

"How will you get home?"

"We can take her home," said Ruth.

"But—" A loud toot and gestures of exasperation from the cab of the removal van curtailed further discussion. I handed the keys to Eirwen and hugged Mrs Booker and Joe in turn.

"I'm glad you'll have company. Stay sober, lamb, and you'll find your way." Mrs Booker squeezed me tightly.

"Until next we meet," Joe said, which both rattled and reassured me.

"Come on," Eirwen called and started the car engine just seconds before the removal van roared into life. I got in beside her, and our small convoy started off down the drive.

Suddenly panicked, I turned to kneel on my seat, desperate for one last look at The Elms, and a slideshow of images clicked into my mind's eye: the willow-shrouded boathouse, the herb-scented kitchen garden, the sun-soaked pool terrace, the majestic hall, the music room… our bedroom. Brendan.

The house, and Joe, and Mrs Booker slipped from sight. I slumped back into a forward position, tears spilling from my eyes as the car seemed to fill with the scents and sounds of all the wonderful spaces and people I'd never again know.

Chapter 38

I studied my new house without a flicker of recognition. Eirwen took the house keys from me and told me to unload the car before opening the front door for the removal men. I dutifully ferried items in from my car until the removal men began to offload my piano from the van – a show-stopping sight that involved some impressive lifting gear.

Meanwhile, Ruth shifted boxes around the house as Eirwen rooted through labelled boxes in the kitchen. Then, when our paths briefly crossed in the hall, Eirwen suddenly asked, "Where's Sylvia?"

"She's sitting in my car. Sylvia doesn't do manual labour," Ruth said matter-of-factly.

"What *does* she do, apart from drinking and stirring?"

"Stirring?"

"Stirring up trouble."

"No, she doesn't. She's just blisteringly honest. And very entertaining," Ruth said, which made Eirwen laugh.

But I was too distracted by the dusty dado rail, and the bare wood of the stairs with its ghostly shadow of an absent carpet runner, to be touched by their words. Then, as the noisy removal van pulled away, a sudden clatter at the letterbox alerted us to Sylvia.

"I'd like to gain entry at your earliest convenience," she called.

***

"Wise to knock through, a dual aspect provides such light," Sylvia said of the lounge. A large kitchen-diner had been fashioned from the jumble of small rooms I vaguely remembered at the very back of the house. Alongside the remaining window, a set of French doors offered a view of the garden beyond.

"A lovely space" was Sylvia's assessment.

"Nice units and appliances," Ruth said, running a hand along a worktop. "Any chance of a cup of tea?"

"Good idea. Mrs Booker has sent the necessaries." Eirwen pointed out a box. "I'll continue with the tour while you play hostess, M."

I looked at her blankly, struggling to process what had been said.

"Make some tea, M." Eirwen touched my arm, obviously aware of my disengagement.

***

Sylvia was incredulous at the lack of furniture and the fact that Eirwen and I intended to sleep on an inflatable mattress as opposed to spending the night at the nearby Celtic Manor with her and Ruth.

"It is beyond my comprehension that you have actually used such items," said Sylvia, aghast at the notion that Brendan and I had occasionally camped in a rather small tent with very basic equipment.

"It was good fun," I said, remembering Brendan hunched over the small Calor gas stove, smiling at me. Brendan singing songs at daybreak to wake me, and then love me. Brendan...

"If you're certain." Sylvia cut in on my self-indulgent daydreams and bolted for the front door.

We had baked beans for tea, and never has such simple fare tasted so good. It was the first time in an age that food didn't seem like ashes in my mouth. Eirwen also devoured her food, laying claim to the remaining slice of toast as she spoke.

"A month ago, I would only have been able to eat the toast, without any butter, though. I couldn't even drink tea or coffee. Does weird things to your taste buds, being pregnant. Not to mention feeling nauseous for the best part of three months. Okay now, thankfully."

"You're certainly looking less peaky," I said.

"Which is more than I can say for you."

I ignored her. Despite feeling slightly more alive and less emotional than I had for weeks, I still wasn't in any way ready for Eirwen's often hard-nosed logic.

"I suppose we have Mrs Booker to thank for the food, dishes, toilet roll and all other sundries?"

"Who else?" We were only able to sit down to eat because Mrs Booker had also provided, bless her, a pair of padded garden chairs. It would have been a pretty grim start in my new home if it had been left to me. "Any ideas as to baby names?" I asked, changing the subject.

"Denny has loads in mind but I've not liked any of them. I reckon we'll know its name when we see it."

"Be handy if they came already labelled. No arguing with or offending anyone then."

"Mm." Eirwen stretched and yawned. "I don't know about you but I'm tired enough to sleep on an inflatable mattress." I took the hint and began to ferry the mattress, pillows and sleeping bags upstairs, while Eirwen cleared up in the kitchen.

In the smallest bedroom at the back of the house, Eirwen questioned my choice.

"Well, it's closer to the bathroom for a start. Plus, there are no street lights, and with a smaller window, there was just enough cardboard to screen off part of it."

"Fair enough," said Eirwen as she sat down on the low window sill to take off her shoes.

"I'll have a look for the cases," I said.

The first thing I noticed in the spacious, high-ceilinged main bedroom was the fitted cupboards flanking the chimney breast. Then I turned around and gasped as though punched on recognising the tall capacious mahogany chest of drawers from our bedroom at The Elms.

"Oh, my God," I gasped and burst into tears.

Eirwen rushed into the room. "What is it, M?"

I pointed at the chest of drawers as if identifying an attacker.

"And?"

"It's from our bedroom. Brendan must have sent it."

"So why are you crying? It's ideal for this room."

I cried all the more, sobbing wetly into my hands. Eirwen put an arm around me.

"Let's get out of here." She made to pick up one of the cases lined up beside the chest.

"I'll do that," I said, wiping my damp palms down the front of my shirt.

"Remind me not to hug you again until that shirt is in the wash," Eirwen said with a grimace.

We prepared for bed in silence. Well, relative silence. I was still snuffling, and Eirwen was huffing and puffing in annoyance.

I got into my sleeping bag and lay down on the mattress. Eirwen followed suit.

"Okay?"

"My bum's skimming the floor but at least I'm off my feet."

"I'm sorry, Wen," I said, about to blub again.

She patted my arm. "It's fine. Let's get some sleep."

Eirwen was asleep in minutes, her breathing relaxed and regular. But I was stiff and immobile alongside her, trying not to think of the last time I'd shared a bed. The fact that I could still smell the chest of drawers didn't help, fragranced as it was with Mrs Booker's signature polish.

And the memories flooded back – an olfactory record of the scents of a bedroom that was no longer mine. The odour of sweat and sex and aftershave and perfume and love... and I began to cry again. Strangled, suppressed sobs, but still enough to wake Eirwen.

She got off the mattress and I thumped to the floor, snivelling.

"Get up." She switched on the light.

I slid out of my sleeping bag and stood under the glare of the bare bulb, shivering.

"What's wrong now?" In spite of her exasperation her flushed and now fuller face was as beautiful as ever.

"Oh, I miss him, Wen. I miss him so much."

"He's just a man, M. There'll be other men." She reached out to take my hand but I shook off her touch.

"No there won't. I'll never love another man."

Spurred by my words Eirwen closed in on me. She grasped my upper arms and skewered me with a stare, her face close to mine.

"Come away with me. We'll sell this place. I'll get some money. We can buy a place of our own and bring up the baby together." She tightened her hold on my arms, her face alight with expectation.

"You'd do that, would you?"

Eirwen's stare intensified as she leaned closer to me. I felt quite light-headed – sure, yet unsure, of what she was really suggesting.

"Of course."

It was as though I'd tipped forward and looked into a hidden corner of her... a small, secret part unknown to me. A notion that disturbed me.

"You'd actually take Denny's baby away from him?"

Eirwen's hands fell from my arms as though they'd burned her. She turned away from me and moved to the corner of the room like a pupil isolated for bad behaviour. There she picked up the mattress pump.

"We need to get some more air into that thing then perhaps both our backsides will be off the floor." She avoided my gaze, handed me the pump and left for the bathroom.

When Eirwen returned I was prostrate on the now quite firm mattress. She turned off the light and settled alongside me once more.

"Goodnight, M," she said, and I wished her the same.

Again, Eirwen was quickly asleep. However, I remained awake long into the night, repeatedly turning over her strange proposal until I finally fell asleep.

Chapter 39

The next morning, we skirted around each other, polite and watchful – like lovers after a tiff. I felt that Eirwen wanted me to ask about her proposition but I didn't want to go where the obvious questions might lead. Besides, if it was bothering her enough, I'd know, sooner or later.

Breakfast was a choice of toast with eggs or toast with jam. Of course, the latter was no shop-bought, sugary concoction, but Mrs Booker's own mixed-fruit jam. I removed the lid and was immediately engulfed by the scents of summer. Hurriedly, I peeled off the circle of cooking parchment that covered the jam, struggling not to eat the jewelled contents straight from the jar.

"I hope you're going to leave some of that for me." This, surprisingly, was Eirwen's first full sentence of the morning. She'd barely responded earlier when I'd asked how she was.

"I'll do my best." I spread the fruity conserve across my toast.

"It smells divine. Like the fruit cage on the allotment." She was right. Although, for me, Mrs B's jam stirred more recent memories. Like a couple of big kids, Brendan and I inevitably ate as much fruit as we gathered. Then...

"You're alright with what I said last night?"

I was jarred back to the present, from Brendan's berry-stained mouth so close to mine.

"What?" I plonked the remains of my toast down onto the plate.

Eirwen repeated her question.

"You're not leaving Denny?"

"No."

"Well, that's fine by me. More tea?"

"Please. So I haven't spoilt things between us?"

I spun around from the sink, the kettle still in my hand. Pregnancy had evidently affected more than Eirwen's taste buds. When had she ever been concerned by something she'd said to me?

"Are you feeling alright, Wen?"

"Yeah, of course. But given what I'd suggested…"

There was patently more to what Eirwen had said last night. What exactly, I was still not sure. Nevertheless, I would not be seeking clarification. Life was complicated enough. I just hoped Eirwen didn't plan on spelling it out for me.

"We're friends, Wen. We love each other. We take the rough with the smooth."

Eirwen stood up and wrapped her arms around me. I could feel the small mound of her belly between us as I returned her embrace. Thankfully, she said no more.

***

The days passed in a blur of shopping and snatched meals. Nevertheless, it proved productive. We had already taken delivery of a number of ex-display shop items, including a sofa and a dining table and six chairs. After two nights at the hotel, Sylvia and Ruth made one last visit before their return to London. Basically, they'd called in to say goodbye. About to leave, Sylvia stopped in the hallway and turned to me.

"Mari, it concerns me that you'll be reduced to menial tasks." I thought she was joking but her expression suggested otherwise.

"And she'll be answerable to no one," Eirwen declared.

"You've been liberated, Mari. Of a sort," Ruth said with a chuckle.

"Great. Thanks for the company and the motivational chat. Safe journey home."

They grinned broadly at my sarky tone.

***

"That only leaves a bed," Eirwen said as we exited the carpet shop.

"I'll get a bed later on."

"But we're on a roll."

"Thanks, Wen, but I don't fancy an ex-display model bed."

"You've got a point there." Eirwen giggled.

On the way back to the car, Eirwen suddenly stopped. "We've forgotten about a TV."

"Least of my worries."

"It'll give you something to do until you sort yourself out."

"Really?"

"You need to join something, then. A choir, or an orchestra. Get a job, volunteer. There's loads you could do." She made it sound so easy.

"Yeah."

We stood either side of my car and eyed each other across its roof.

"You're not going to be stupid again, are you?"

"You've got the keys, Wen. Let's go home."

"Home, eh? Now that's progress."

***

The next morning, we were sitting at the table eating the last of the bread.

"I think we need to fill the fridge. We'll go to the supermarket in town, and afterwards, you can drop me at the train station."

Eirwen had been with me for five days. I knew she was leaving. She'd rung Denny from the phone box near the post office the previous day. But I was panicked by the mere idea of her absence. She'd kept me grounded in the mundane until the house seemed like somewhere I *could* be.

I contemplated her departure as apprehensively as a child lifting a mossy stone. What lurked in such a dark place? Then Eirwen's sudden exclamation shook me from my gloomy thoughts.

"Food! Where's your mother? And your father, for that matter?"

"What brought that on?"

"Well, your mother and food go together. She's always trying to feed people."

"True. She likes to nurture folk."

"I said feed, M, not nurture."

"Hey, that's my mother you're maligning."

Eirwen ignored my attempt to sidetrack her. "Why haven't your parents been here?"

I looked sheepishly at her.

"You haven't told them you've moved?"

I shook my head.

"What have you told them?"

"Nothing."

"You've not told them about you and Brendan?"

Again, I shook my head.

"Well, you'd better tell them soon or I will."

***

The train thrummed alongside us, making conversation difficult. I clutched at Eirwen as she returned my embrace.

"Thank you for everything," I said, reluctant to release her.

"You know what a bully I am. It's been fun." Despite her attempt at humour, Eirwen did not relinquish her hold on me either. We both were on the verge of tears.

A sudden blast of a whistle and the slamming of doors galvanised us into action and we boarded the train and I stowed her bag.

"Remember," Eirwen said, "no more drinking on your own. Let me know when your phone is installed. Look after yourself." She sounded like my mother.

Tearfully, I kissed and hugged her again. Then a polite cough alerted us to the guard on the platform alongside the still-open door. I stepped down from the carriage and the door was duly closed. More clanging followed as I stared sadly at Eirwen. Another whistle blast set the train in motion.

I walked alongside the train as it slowly gathered speed and eased eastwards down the track. Eirwen, oddly distant through the reflection on the train window, continued to smile and wave until I ran out of platform and she disappeared from sight. I felt as though I had reached the edge of the world… Another step would see me hurtling into the abyss.

Chapter 40

Later, I convinced myself I was going to the chip shop but ended up in the off-licence. I hadn't planned to buy a weekend's worth of alcohol yet I did. Saturday and Sunday passed swiftly, lost in a protracted alcoholic haze.

I woke with a jolt on Monday morning, certain that I'd missed the carpet fitter. The small alarm clock on the floor alongside the mattress reassured me that I hadn't. Time enough for breakfast once I'd dealt with my headache. In the same vein, I muddled through the week achieving far more than I'd thought possible.

However, in spite of my repeated attempts to conjure up the feelings I'd experienced on the Isle of Wight – the certainty, the desire for a role within the music industry – I failed. I also flunked contacting my parents. Before leaving The Elms, I'd managed to wangle myself a fortnight's grace, which was up on Friday when my mother would be expecting a call. Eirwen's threat was another imperative to ringing home sooner rather than later.

Further up the hill from me, the telephone box loomed on its corner promontory, as unassailable as a castle keep. When I eventually opened the door to the small, fouled place, I prayed that my father was holding the fort. After four rings my mother answered. I was glad to be short of change.

"Mam."

"Mari, are you ringing from a payphone?" my mother asked, already in detective mode.

"I don't have much time to explain, Mam. Please write down my new address."

"New address?" Her voice had started to scale the stave.

"Yes. I'm living in Newport now."

"Newport?" I was conversing with a shrill echo.

"Mam." I hoped that I did not sound as exasperated as I felt. "Please write down the address. I can explain when I see you. I'm busy with the house at the moment."

I quickly reeled off the address and repeated it as requested.

"Your father is working tomorrow. Perhaps we'll call in on Sunday between services. Could you ring again later tonight and I'll let you know?"

"You're busy on Sunday, Mam. I'll come to you next Saturday."

The extra-coins-needed beeps sounded in our ears and my mother's voice piped a harmonious near scream. "Mari…"

***

Unlike the previous Friday, I actually made it to, and ordered at, the chip shop. Unfortunately, I also made it to the off-licence, where they were quite happy to accept payment by cheque.

I trudged back to my house with a fish supper literally under my nose – on top of a box packed with wine bottles, to be precise. By the time I reached my front door, food was the last thing on my mind.

The best part of a bottle of wine and two aspirins later, an insistent tapping at the newly curtained living room window brought me to my senses.

I heaved myself off the sofa, stumbled into the hall and flung open the front door without a thought as to who might be on the other side. My parents (who had arrived by taxi) gasped in unison, too shocked by my appearance to be offended by my churlish "What are you doing here?" welcome.

"Pack a bag for the weekend," my father ordered.

"I'm fine," I said, sober enough to realise I was slurring my words.

"If I have to manhandle you into your car, Mari, I will. You're coming home for the weekend and that's final."

I knew when I was beaten. You didn't continue to argue with my father once his jaw was that clenched. I reached the foot of the stairs just as my mother was descending with the small suitcase from the matching set.

"David, Mari, are we ready to leave?"

The whole of my mother was as clenched as my father's jaw. And she only ever addressed my father as David in dire circumstances. I picked up my handbag, located the keys, passed them to my father and sheepishly followed my parents out to the car.

My hangover and the up-hill-down-dale drive home meant I was sick on arrival. Once clean I was packed off to bed. A glass and jug of water were laid out on the chest of drawers in the alcove and a bowl placed on an old towel on the floor. Instructions were issued to drink sparingly and to call if I needed anything. Then the light was extinguished and the door closed. I felt about six years old – roughly the age I'd been acting of late. I turned onto my side, the bowl within reach, and cried myself to sleep.

***

My parents were dumbfounded by the events that had brought me to Newport, yet they did not criticise nor condemn Brendan. It was as though they were silently sifting through the wreckage of my explanation for the answer. I only hoped that they found it soon because I was none the wiser after months of searching.

The consensus was that I should get a job. An objective I'd already given much thought. How to do so was the next step.

"Visit the employment office," my father suggested.

"You could go back to university."

"I'm going on twenty-seven, Mam. I don't think I can."

"Well, find out," Dad urged me. "Or try the Open University."

"Distance learning for a music degree?"

"Find out," chimed my parents.

"I will." Their faces ignited with joy at my sudden resolve, which made me all the more determined not to let them down. Perhaps I should settle on a more mainstream job for the time being rather than trying to break into the music industry, I considered.

Then out of the blue, a job came my way. Or to be precise, the person with the contacts that resulted in a job rang me.

Stephanie Laine and I had gravitated towards each other from the common desire to be somewhere else during our first (and, in my case, last) term at university. And despite my disappearing without telling her, Steph had managed to get hold of my home address and visited my parents to enquire about me. Since then we'd kept in touch, generally meeting up at least once a year. Steph still made contact via my mother so as to confirm my phone number before ringing me to chat or to arrange a reunion. We hadn't spoken since Christmas but with the recent phone installation at my new address, my mother was able to pass my number on to Steph.

"Hello, Mari. Steph here."

"Steph, how are you? I didn't expect to hear from you so soon."

"I won't be able to meet up for a while, but I'm hoping you can do something for me."

"Glad to." It was a thrill to be considered of use.

"Someone I know needs a pianist at short notice. I can't step in at the moment but I know how well you play. Would you be interested?"

"That would be great." I grabbed a pen to jot down the necessary details. I was amazed to feel an unexpected flicker of pleasure, an emotion I'd thought had been cut from my being. There was hope for me yet.

Chapter 41

It was July 1978 when I started as a session musician at City Circle Records in Bristol. The same day that the first test tube baby, Louise Brown, was born, to be precise. Funny the things you remember. Although I initially crossed the studio's threshold as a favour to Steph, it proved an event that ultimately resulted in a job that saved me from myself. Steph knew of my piano playing but was unaware that I could also pass muster on the violin. Nevertheless, it was my competence on the guitar that initially got me regular work.

And I had needed a job, a purpose. Although I'd acknowledged that there ought to be more to my life than Brendan Bradshaw, I hadn't made a move to find work. But I was lucky, very lucky, and grateful for the opportunity Steph put my way. To be gainfully employed and financially independent felt so good.

My job and its demands brought a new focus into my world, and things rolled on. Every task I attempted no longer seemed like running a marathon or climbing a mountain. I could do this, *my* life.

But the icing on the cake was Eirwen. Despite her increasing girth and other pregnancy-related issues, she chose to board a train and come to Wales, for which I was very grateful. I had no desire to visit Richmond, where there were so many reminders of my past life. Opposed to onward and upward, life became onward and onward – away from all that was no longer mine. Apart from Eirwen, that is.

"What's the plan?" she asked as we left the train station car park.

"A picnic in the grounds of Tredegar House."

"Not too much of a drive, I hope."

"Just a couple of miles."

"Perfect. I'm starving."

***

Eirwen made herself comfortable on the low retaining wall surrounding the southern end of the lake adjacent to the beautiful brick house at Tredegar Park. Within snatching distance of her perch, a plethora of alert and ready waterfowl gathered in the hope of some scraps.

"Your mother been round?"

"Why do you ask?"

"This." She waved a sausage roll at me and ignited a cacophony of cries and a frenzied wing flapping at the water's edge.

"I made those. And the quiche." I grinned at her disbelief as the birds squabbled on.

"The pastry?" Eirwen asked, genuinely surprised, as I would have been in her position. I nodded.

"I'm impressed." She popped the last of the roll in her mouth and swept the crumbs from her lap which set the birds off again.

My mission to feed Eirwen nutritious homemade meals was an attempt to assuage my guilt at her journeying to Wales. I'm not sure who was the more pleased at my sudden interest in acquiring basic culinary skills, Eirwen or my mother.

So, the somnambulant warmth and threadbare grass of summer and picnic fare gave way to flasks of homemade soup and brisk walks across Newport's now autumn-tinted park landscapes. Then, as shed leaves began to pirouette and pile in gutters and drains, Eirwen announced the curtailment of her visits. She was huffing about on my sofa like a nesting hen trying to make a suitable hollow at the time.

"I think this child is trying to punch its way out. Feel, M." She took my hand and placed it on her bump. It was an odd sensation, the undulating rise and fall of her belly, along with an acknowledging poke or kick from within.

Eleven days later, Eirwen and Denny's baby was born. On hearing Denny's ecstatic declaration but hours after the safe arrival of Philippa Joan, my instinct was to jump in the car and get to Eirwen's bedside. Yet I resisted the urge for a number of reasons, the least of which being I had work the next day.

Instead, I sent a card and a parcel of items for the baby. And I wrote letters to Eirwen when I wasn't talking to her on the phone. I revisited all the lullabies I knew as well as ordering sheet music for a few more at a music shop in Cardiff. Then the invite arrived. Three whole days (work had agreed to my having the Monday off) in Richmond with just Eirwen, the baby and the household staff. Denny and the rest of the band were busy recording in London. I was beside myself. I couldn't remember when I'd last been so excited and dug out my camera in readiness.

***

"Don't disturb her." I stared down at the tiny creature squirming in a carrycot.

"She's due a feed, M. She's waking up." I looked on in horror as Eirwen picked Philippa up mid-stretch and told me to sit down before depositing the lively bundle in my unready arms. I felt quite awkward, nervously watching as the baby stretched again.

Evidently unfazed by my incompetence, Philippa gave an enormous yawn, opened familiar blue eyes and studied me.

"Pippa, meet your Aunty M."

Immediately, Pippa turned in the direction of her mother's voice and began to complain about her Aunty M. It was a relief to hand her over to Eirwen for her feed.

I found it strange that I felt no envy of Eirwen. Had my desire for a child dissipated? Or had I just wanted a piece of Brendan that was utterly my own?

"It's great to have the place so quiet," Eirwen said at my ongoing silence.

"Sorry, Wen. I can't believe she doesn't suffocate in there. And the big gulps. Sounds like she's downing a pint."

Eirwen laughed. "Feels like it too."

"You're so good at this." I was amazed by Eirwen's relaxed confidence.

"Mam's been here a fortnight and imparted all she knows of the art of motherhood."

"A fortnight?"

Eirwen raised her eyebrows and grinned.

"She was at the hospital for the birth. What with the gas and air and, 'Breathe, breathe. Pant, pant. PUSH.' I didn't know whether I was on a slave galley or at the vets." I exploded with laughter, suddenly feeling less awkward, when Pippa emerged from beneath an enormous breast to glare at me.

My weekend of innumerable firsts sped by. On Monday morning my visit was topped off when Ruth and Sylvia turned up. I'd seen them twice since the move to Newport, and not one to hold back, Sylvia was quick to comment on the change in me.

"Marvellous, darling." She looked my way, unlike Ruth, who was cooing over Pippa. "Good to see you on form again. Alcohol dependency is not something I'd recommend," which left me speechless but keen to hug her. "Not while you're sporting baby vomit, darling." She pointed at my shirt, her face crumpling in a moue of distaste.

Within the hour they were leaving, Sylvia evidently eager to be gone. Perhaps she was fearful that motherhood might be contagious, or maybe she just needed a drink. At the door, she stopped and spoke to Eirwen.

"I hadn't envisaged you as the maternal type. I was wrong." Then she thrust a small box at Eirwen. "It was my mother's. I'd like your little one to have it." Then she bolted for the car.

"She's bound to outdo me on the gift front," Ruth said.

"Of course she is," I responded as Eirwen passed Pippa to me.

"Oh, it's beautiful." Eirwen turned the box to me. Secured within, on a pad of worn satin, a neat chain bearing a small cross of gold inlaid with tiny rubies and emeralds sparkled in the watery sunshine.

From the safety of the car with Ruth at the wheel, Sylvia acknowledged Eirwen's blown kisses with a little wave.

With Pippa asleep, we enjoyed a leisurely lunch with Eirwen still marvelling at Sylvia's generosity.

"Unbelievable," she said with a shake of her head. "She seemed to dislike Pippa almost as much as she hates me and then she gives her a family heirloom."

"She doesn't hate anyone, Wen."

"Well, she likes some more than others. She certainly likes you. You should have heard what she said to Brendan about his breaking up with you. It was a proper tirade. He just stood there and took it all. I was about to wade in too. But my own track record where you're concerned leaves a lot to be desired."

"We're still friends. And who's keeping score anyway? Not me, that's for sure."

"One of the many things I love about you." Eirwen leaned over to kiss me on the cheek. "Sylvia's not the only one to have a go at Brendan. Almost everyone has apparently. Even Jake. Something succinct and sweary, Denny reckoned." She chuckled. Suddenly, she slapped a hand to her cheek. "Oh, I nearly forgot about Punchie."

"Punchie?"

"Yeah. Brendan brought him here to see Pippa." For a split second my blood ran cold, but Eirwen's manner was too upbeat for there to have been any trouble. "He asked first, of course, and we were all primed for any sort of problem. It turned out to be surprisingly touching. Not just how taken Punchie was with Pippa but how good Brendan is with Punchie." She didn't elaborate further and I didn't need to ask.

***

Although contemplating my first Christmas without Brendan – December 1978, that is – and despite often bleak times over the last eight months, I counted my blessings. I had a comfortable home, the love and support of family and friends and, unbelievably, a job in the music industry.

I was looking out at my relatively neat back garden and mentally planting runner beans, strawberries, lettuce and various other plants and herbs when the phone broke in on my daydreams.

"Hi M. Fancy an outing tomorr— Ow, that hurt."

"What is it, Wen?"

"Only this little madam. She doesn't like me doing anything else while feeding her. Likes my full attention. Almost took my nipple off." I could hear the love and laughter in her voice as she repositioned Pippa.

"Ring me when you're free."

At three months old, Pippa exuded all the smells, charm and promise inherent in a small baby. I could almost feel her halo of white, down-like hair upon my cheek as I heard her gurgling over the phone.

"Hang on, M. I'm with Mam and Dad for the week. Meet me at Cardiff train station tomorrow. Bring your car. We'll go to St Fagans."

"St Fagans?"

"I'll explain tomorrow. See you at Cardiff Central at twelve-thirty. Bye." And she was gone, leaving me speechless but smiling.

Chapter 42

Saturday dawned relatively bright and clear with the promise of a cold but dry December day. Definitely a day for layered-on clothing – or so my mother would say. *Better safe than sorry* had never featured in Eirwen's vocabulary, much less her life. Nonetheless, she met all my mother's exacting standards where Pippa was concerned.

My spirits soared when I spotted Eirwen on the platform, Pippa in her arms and a gaggle of appreciative males vying to assist her with the trappings of parenthood. As ever, Eirwen looked glorious. Always picture perfect, she now looked and carried herself like a masterpiece – Botticelli at his best.

We were prompted to move by Pippa wailing. Eirwen shushed her daughter and strapped her into her pushchair. Lulled by the movement, as we walked into the city centre, Pippa was soon asleep. On the way, Eirwen and I talked about St Fagans, a former large country estate now billed as a living museum. We hadn't been there in years.

To this day, St Fagans continues to expand with the addition of buildings of historical, architectural or social importance that have outlived their purpose within their communities yet are considered too important or unique to be lost and are resurrected there. They are uprooted brick by numbered brick (or stone) to embark on a new existence within the confines of the Earl of Plymouth's former estate. Thank goodness they survive to be enjoyed by future generations.

Over lunch in one of the city's many Italian restaurants, Eirwen explained that she'd been to St Fagans with Trefor and his family earlier in the week. A smile twitched at my mouth, but I said nothing.

"Yes, I know," she responded, obviously aware of my amusement. "Hardly rock and roll, is it? St Fagans twice in a week. But I tell you, M, you'll be amazed by what's there."

She regaled me with tales of homemade toffee dished out by Santa Claus as he sat beside a smoky log fire in Kennixton Farmhouse, of carols and *bara brith* outside the small brick-fronted bakery, and the menace of the *Mari Lwyd* at the tiny tollgate house.

While we enjoyed a coffee, Eirwen draped a shawl about her shoulders and discreetly fed her daughter. I felt a lump in my throat as she chatted, overawed by her poise, her calmness, her contentment.

Back in the car, after a leisurely mooch around town, we left the city and headed westwards to arrive at St Fagans as the fading grey of the winter's day became the darker grey of evening. The carpark was surprisingly busy, with family groups, many of three generations, huddled in animated clusters organising prams, bags and cavorting children.

"C'mon, M. You must see this."

The dimly lit path was daunting after the glee, glitter and glare of the shop and reception area. But we were drawn on by the distant din and glow of illuminations away to our left. Soon larger buildings emerged from the darkness, resplendent with Christmas lights, and tailed by something even bigger… a brass band belting out "O Come All Ye Faithful".

Then Eirwen stopped abruptly and demanded that I close my eyes.

"You're joking."

"Please," she coaxed.

"Alright," I said and placed my hands alongside hers on the pushchair handle.

I dutifully closed my eyes, curious as to how this was going to pan out.

We moved tentatively forward, slowing down apace with the crowd so I became aware of familiar aromas even before we'd entered the building.

"Where are we?" Eirwen demanded.

Suddenly, I knew why the scents had struck a chord. "*Tad-cu*'s shop," I said, in a rush to open my eyes.

"Yes," she said excitedly.

Visually it didn't disappoint either. From the bare wooden floorboards, the smooth scrubbed counters, the barrels, the jars, to the equipment – it was all there, my grandfather's shop, as it had been before the owners saw fit to modernise.

Eirwen and I tucked ourselves into a corner (with Pippa asleep in her pushchair) and shared memories of our own long-gone Aladdin's cave. Dark it had been, with its precipitous shelves packed with sweet jars, biscuit and cracker barrels, packets of tea and plasters and bottles of disinfectant and squash. All, in fact, that the discerning householder would require.

I envisaged *Tad-cu* atop a set of foldaway steps, his grocer's coat snug about his ample frame. He'd be regaling a captive audience below with some snippet of gossip while those generally awaiting more mundane items (unlike the corn plasters and fuse wire which necessitated the climb) would be wondering whether today would be the day that Dai-the-shop fell off his perch. *Tad-cu*, as much showman as salesman.

A couple of hours later we left the brightly lit festivities and began to transfer our purchases – hanging from Pippa's pushchair like Christmas tree decorations – to the car. Then we headed back to Gwaun. I'd planned a visit, and now was as good as any time.

"Shame your dad never took over the shop," said Eirwen as we continued to reminisce during the journey across Cardiff.

"Dad hated the shop and all it entailed. It was no surprise to me that he didn't."

"Me neither, if I'm honest. But I loved that shop," Eirwen said.

Suddenly, my own thoughts of that time were interrupted by Eirwen humming. I checked the mirror, noting her gaze trained on Pippa, her mouth upturned in a satisfied smile. But humming? Surely not.

"Never realised it was catching." I flicked a glance in her direction and our eyes met in the mirror.

"Aw, don't tell me I'm doing it again. Our Trefor told me to either put a sock in it or get some lessons from you. Apparently, you hum and lah-lah in tune whereas I…"

"Don't," I said, barely able to contain my mirth.

"Am I that bad?"

"You're generally out of tune but nicely so."

And so she was. How could Eirwen be otherwise when humming and lah-lah-ing for her adored baby?

"Nicely out of tune. I'll have to tell our Trefor that if I do it again. Hang on, isn't that a song? 'Nicely Out of Tune', I mean?"

"It's the title of Lindisfarne's fabulous first album," I replied.

"Oh, yeah. The 'Lady Eleanor' album."

"And 'The Fog on the Tyne' and 'Winter Song' and—"

"Okay, show-off," Eirwen interrupted with a grin.

The chat and the tunes continued as we were gradually enveloped by the velvet blackness of our surroundings that deepened apace with the increasing gradient of the land. Dark mounds of mountains closed in around us to be momentarily illuminated by the car's headlights. Curves, corners, outcrops of rock, the occasional tree and the scattered lights of farmsteads veered past us on the pitch-black road to Gwaun. Home.

Chapter 43

At the front door of her parents' house, the still-sleeping Pippa nestled in the crook of her left arm, Eirwen, key-in-hand, turned the lock with the other. Motherhood necessitates taking dexterity to another level, I observed.

"Will you be going to chapel tomorrow?" Eirwen asked.

"C'mon, Wen, you know my mother. Course I'll be there for the morning service."

"Good. We'll come too." She nodded down at Pippa.

I dropped the pushchair onto the path in surprise. "You what?"

"Chapel will complete the trip down memory lane." She retrieved the pushchair and glanced back at me. "You're going to be alright, M."

Then she pushed open the door with her foot and disappeared into the dark hallway.

***

The joy with which my parents greeted me was palpable. There was no fuss at my unscheduled visit – those days were gone.

"Such a beautiful baby. Eirwen brought her here last week."

"Image of Eirwen. I've never seen that girl so content," said Dad.

On that happy note, we headed upstairs to our respective bedrooms. But despite feeling bone-tired, sleep eluded me. I felt cold too, so I pressed my feet against the warm chimney breast. Yet I still couldn't settle, restlessly churning up the seemingly corrugated cotton sheets beneath me.

As I became accustomed to the dark, I marvelled that my meticulously tidy mother continued to retain the detritus of my earlier occupation. In the wardrobe there were once-prized clothes, a decade out of fashion and now forgotten. School books, a few prized paperbacks and childish chalk ornaments still lined the shelves. My room was a shrine to the girl I had been, lost to my parents that summer.

Chiding myself for the futility of my thoughts, I got out of bed, straightened the bedding and added an extra blanket from the ottoman beneath the window. Pinned to the mattress by the bulky bedclothes, I listened to the house complaining at the wintery assault.

The roof tiles rattled as a cheeky wind sought gaps with furtive fingers and hurled heavy hail at the windows. Soon the drumming at the panes lessened as the hail turned to rain. Lulled by the rhythm of the raindrops, I eventually slipped away into sleep.

***

Eirwen arrived in time for breakfast. She removed Pippa's coat and plonked her on my father's lap. Then she relieved him of his toast and marmalade.

"Toast alright, Wen?" he queried, before blowing noisily onto Pippa's plump cheek.

"A little cold but it'll do."

She finished the filched piece, accepted a fresh round from my mother and leaned back against the Rayburn, munching, as her eyes followed her daughter's every move.

"Wen Watkins and daughter in chapel. Wonders will never cease."

"Hush, Dai," said my mother. She patted Pippa's chubby little hand, and added, "But won't it be a little long for Pippa?"

"It will, Mrs M. She's my get out of gaol card. Only going for a look."

"That's our Wen," roared Dad. "As irreverent as ever." My mother looked aghast.

Dad held Pippa on the top of his head and turned from side to side so as to tickle her tummy. Pippa gurgled in delight and clutched at Dad's curls that splayed out from his head like a ballerina's tutu.

With sound effects worthy of wartime radio, Dad swivelled and rotated Pippa until I feared an eruption of the vomit variety, and I ached with love for my funny father.

***

As ever, our chapel stood as solid and steadfast as a sentry on guard over our valley, its lidless window eyes focused downhill, scanning for the faithful. These were now fewer in number, but my mother's generation remained loyal and usually turned out in force.

Eirwen took up an end-of-pew spot near the door with me beside her. The congregation grew as Mam played gentle, soothing hymns aimed at keeping Pippa asleep, I should think.

Nervously I looked around and was greeted with smiles and nods, some warmer than others. I was particularly touched by an enthusiastic greeting from a previously grim-faced youngster of about eleven.

A quick glance at the child's mother and I recalled little Anne Griffiths… a tiny scrap of a girl who'd spent most Sunday school sessions straddling my hip with her head on my shoulder and a thumb firmly planted in her mouth. She had been too young for the group but her mother was grateful that I took both her children. Besides, I had enjoyed Anne's clinging company, her trust, and acceptance.

Anne's presence resurrected images of other young faces, together with a mountain of crayons and a drift of paper, criss-crossed with emergent handwriting and wax-crayon masterpieces: Moses, resplendent in a wizard's cape, parting the Red Sea; the Passover angel, dripping with blood and hovering above unmarked doors; and the empty cave tomb, its dark entrance flanked on one side by a huge boulder and on the other by a jolly Easter bunny.

Where were they now, all those eager, innocent souls, wide-eyed and wondrous at the religious tales of daring and devotion? Probably down in Ponty Park, hiding in the rhododendron bushes taking their first forbidden sip of alcohol, their first throat-singeing drag on a fag.

Nudged from my daydreams by the minister's nasal monotone, I considered how uninspiring he was. At which point Pippa erupted from sleep and, on contact with Eirwen, attempted to burrow through her mother's clothing.

Despite being the mistress of decorous breast-feeding, Eirwen obviously considered chapel not to be the place for a demonstration. She smiled apologetically at the curious congregation and opened the door. Once outside, Eirwen ignored Pippa's protests, strapped her into the pushchair and turned towards the allotment gates.

"Have you forgotten how grim the allotment is in winter?" I was jogging alongside the pushchair in an attempt to distract the now red-faced Pippa.

"A coffee and a bickie will more than compensate. Like old times."

***

With Eirwen installed on my father's folding chair and Pippa emitting contented gulping sounds from the depths of her clothing, I set about making a brew.

The coffee, powdered milk and biscuits were all in their allotted places, just as the spare key had been on its hook under the eaves of the shed roof. A creature of habit, my dad.

As the heat from the primus stove took the chill off the air, Eirwen and I talked. And talked, of times gone by... the shop and contraband *Bunties* and *Jackies*; Rowdy Yates in *Rawhide* and us riding our chair-arm horses across the parlour plains; laughing at the football results and the shipping forecast; school, music, *Mam-gu's* fragrant potions and lotions, and her syrup- and tincture-packed pantry. The willow den at the bottom of the allotment.

"It's still there, you know."

"I should hope so. Family heirloom, that. We'll be down there in the summer with this one." She withdrew a limp, rather drunk-looking Pippa from beneath her top.

"You'd recommend motherhood, then?" I said as Eirwen gently lifted Pippa to her shoulder to wind her.

"Ask me again in fifteen years' time when we're arguing about clothes and homework." Suddenly serious, she added, "In chapel they were always going on about faith, but I didn't get it. I do now. Pippa's put my life into perspective. She's the reason I'm alive. She's given me faith in life, in myself." Her face softened as she looked at her sated, sleeping child.

But I was staggered by her remarks. This was confident, ebullient, beautiful Eirwen talking. The girl who took life by the throat and shook it. The one who shot the rapids in a barrel and popped up with an "I'm alright" smile on her face.

Yet I'd known. Hadn't I always known she'd been searching? Fervently, feverishly searching. But I was just as certain she did everything with courage, conviction and confidence.

"But you've always seemed so sure of everything. Ever since our first day at school when you grabbed my hand."

"Yeah. But I chose you, M, because you're strong. Not like me."

"Strong? Me? I was terrified. Everyone was crying and—"

"You've got inner strength, M. It just shines out of you. You're stable and safe, like a rock, whereas I'm just something that drifted by and saw my chance. I've clung to you ever since. You keep me sane, M. I've been so near the edge so often. You listen; you never criticise. Well, not too often. But I know when you give me the maiden-aunt-with-a-bad-smell look that I've overstepped the mark. Then I try to put things right. We work well together."

She squeezed my hand. I blinked back my tears.

"We're getting maudlin," Eirwen said. "Time to go."

I tidied away the debris of our visit and Eirwen readjusted her own clothing and her sleeping daughter's. How, I wondered, could I have missed her insecurities? Because she chose to hide them from me, perhaps?

"And things are good with Denny?"

"He loves us unconditionally. He's Pippa's father. It's enough."

For whom? I thought sadly, desolate for both Denny and Eirwen.

"Were you trying for a baby?" I asked, despite knowing the answer, still hopeful of a positive.

"No. I'd had a bout of sickness, you know, throwing up, the trots, et cetera. Think I lost more pills than I took, and hey presto, Pippa." She held her child close and then stood to leave. "C'mon, M. Your mam will be evil if we're not back in time for food."

In the grey December light, we scanned the allotments, taking in the bare, broken earth, exposed and expectant, waiting for the winter's frosts to work their magic.

"We've had some good times here, M. Thanks for sharing it all with me."

I touched her arm. "Don't thank me. My life would have been empty without you. You've dragged me into some tangles yet I've had so much fun. Certainly, I would not have attended the Isle of Wight Festival. Then, how very different might both our lives have been?"

Eirwen considered this a moment. "Thank you," she said, closing her eyes and taking a steadying breath. "C'mon, M, dinner beckons. A nursing mother needs regular substantial meals. No time to dawdle or maudle. Is there such a word? Never mind."

And we were away, silly girls giggling again.

Chapter 44

All the way back to Newport I relived the glow I'd felt over the past thirty-six hours.

Lunch had been a relaxed affair. My mother *was* letting her hair down. She hadn't bolted her food so as to be washing dishes before we'd even finished our meal. Oh no, she was keen to participate in the pass-the-Pippa game, eagerly awaiting her turn with the prized parcel.

Anecdotes and memories were turned over and aired like allotment onions drying in the autumn sunshine. Tea and talk flowed as the film roll of our lives spilled around us. Then Eirwen changed the direction of our conversation and our thoughts.

"Right, spill the beans, M. How did you land a permanency at the recording studio?"

Silence descended as three pairs of eyes swivelled to meet mine. Evidently, Pippa saw this as a true centre-stage moment and screeched, burped and broke wind with effortless ease. We all laughed but Eirwen wouldn't be distracted.

"Have you managed to make yourself indispensable or just learnt where the bodies are buried? Or perhaps you've slept with the boss?"

My mother almost choked on her tea while my father howled with laughter.

"Ha, ha. You've obviously not met my boss." I paused a moment. "Seems I have a modicum of skill in the talent-spotting arena."

"Trailing around with rock musicians finally paid off then," Eirwen said, spooning another helping of gooseberry crumble into her dish.

"Brendan the bastard and his merry band of men," I retorted.

"Mari. Think of Pippa," my mother said.

"Yes," chortled my father. "We'll know who to blame if her first words are expletives."

"Well, I don't know about you," said Eirwen, between mouthfuls of dessert, "but I'm chuffed. Six months ago, she'd have been blubbing about Brendan." She ran a finger around her dish and licked it.

"Manners, Wen," my father interjected. "Swearing we tolerate when the occasion demands. But bad manners? Never."

"Do you want to hear about my job or not?"

They nodded.

"Well, to stay on at the studio I needed to be more than a spare part, then I discovered the tapes."

"Tapes?" Three voices in unison.

"Watergate all over again," Eirwen said with a grin.

I silenced her with a look. "Demo tapes."

Tapes arrived from all over the country, hand-delivered on occasion, by kids and adults alike. And although many crossed the threshold, few progressed beyond reception. Vague promises and assurances were made but submissions were largely consigned to a box pending evaluation. Such desperate measures should not be ignored, I maintained, but those at the top had seen it all before. They preferred recommendations.

"So I asked permission to go through the tapes – in my own time, of course," I continued.

"And?"

"I selected the best three and played them at work, you know, as background music. Eventually, people started commenting and asking questions. And as a result of the studio's intervention, one of the bands has been offered a recording contract with Apple. I have a role."

My words were greeted by cheers from the adults and a gleeful shriek from Pippa.

***

Back in Newport, I appreciated for the first time how attractive the houses were that lined the quiet road where I lived. Then I almost collided with the vehicle parked outside my gate, sure that I'd seen a figure withdraw from the window.

As the darkness deepened, house lights sprang up the length of the street and the welcoming glow of a lamp appeared in my living room.

Damn him, I thought, studying the black Volvo estate that occupied my space. Brendan Bradshaw. Never one for flashy rock and roll cars, Brendan opted for functional. "It gets people and kit about, Mari" he'd commented when I questioned his unwavering loyalty to Volvo.

I felt quite enfeebled by the idea of Brendan being in my house. My feet were leaden as I approached the gate whereas my senses were off the scale: the diamond-patterned terracotta pathway seemed to gleam in the jewel-like light cast by the stained glass of the front door, and the scent of the cypress hedge bordering the path was suddenly sharp as the distant sound of carolling children rang in my ears.

Brendan's low-profile hat and glasses lay on the hall table along with his car keys. I just about managed not to bury my face in his cotton bush hat, to inhale and savour the smell of him.

In the living room a welcoming fire burned. But the inviting aroma of coffee beckoned from the kitchen.

Brendan was looking out at the garden with his back to me. This is how it should be, I thought. He'll turn and greet me with a smile and a kiss. We'll drink coffee and talk… and then we'll make love in front of the fire.

But Brendan never said, or did, things lightly. He'd said it was over and it was. So why was he here? And he'd obviously been here for some time.

How dare he come here and unsettle me, I thought, trying to divert my thoughts from how good he looked in those jeans as he lounged long and lean against the doorframe.

Stop this, I thought, the palms of my hands on my flaming cheeks.

"Coffee?" His voice ignited every nerve along my spine, yet he hadn't moved. Then I realised he'd been watching me in the glass doors.

"You've got a nerve. And how the hell did you get in?" I retorted, angry with myself, my want, my desire for this man who no longer loved me.

He turned around and his gaze ran over me. Weak-kneed I moved to the table, glad of a barrier between us. I tried to look his way but found it too painful. He put a mug on the table near me.

"I kept a key. I was worried, Mari," he said. I flinched. His use of my name felt like an intimacy, almost as though he'd touched me. "Mrs Morris said you'd left the house early yesterday morning."

"Mrs Morris? You've been talking to my neighbour about me?"

"You were so…" He faltered. "Unhappy when you moved here. I asked her to ring me if she noticed anything…" Again, he paused. "Different."

I wanted to hurl the coffee mug at him and jump up and down in a Brothers Grimm, Rumpelstiltskin fashion. But this was my home. It would be my mess. And I wouldn't give him the satisfaction.

"I'm fine," I threw at him.

"I'll leave this with you." He placed the key on the table and pushed it towards me with the index and second finger of his right hand… Such long slender fingers. The sudden urge to slide my hand over his became overwhelming. I became light-headed with the effort of not adhering myself to him.

"I went home for the weekend. Eirwen and Pippa were there," I said in a rush, my hands folded out of the way. "I didn't realise that I was being clocked in and out of my own home. But I thank you for your concern. Now please leave."

He moved towards me and I felt the air between us ripple and pulse. Why didn't it feel over? Why was I certain that my feelings were reciprocated? I glanced up as he extended a hand towards me. I wasn't wrong. A look of naked longing glazed his eyes.

I lurched to my feet, spilling my untouched coffee, as a torrent of words poured from me. My deceit regarding the pill, how I probably couldn't have children, how I didn't want any really. I only wanted him.

There it was again. That unfathomable look. Was it fear or sadness? Then he turned away and headed for the door. His parting words reverberated down the hallway like a train.

"Forget me, Mari. Get on with your life."

And he was gone.

I reached the living room window in time to see him ease the car away from the kerbside. Still shaking, I dragged the curtains across the big bay window and turned towards the baby grand piano.

I sat at the keyboard and recalled my twenty-fifth birthday when the piano arrived gift-wrapped. I remembered how we'd shared the stool, pushing and shoving as we attempted to outplay each other.

In the early madness of my grief after our break-up, Eirwen had prevented me from destroying my piano. She'd followed me to the garden storehouse at The Elms, allowed me to select a large sledgehammer and to return with it to the smaller music room. Brendan had already moved out and was sending me details of houses for sale in and around the Newport area. I wanted to tear him limb from limb.

Eirwen stood and watched while I struggled to raise the wavering, weighty hammer above my head.

"It'll make a difference to how you feel, will it?" she asked, seemingly unconcerned.

"It might." I glared at the piano, which seemed to cringe at the heat of my anger.

"But who will it hurt? Brendan, or you?"

I paused and rested the handle of the hammer on my shoulder and gave the question some thought.

Brendan had his own piano. It had once belonged to the doctor whose house Brendan's mother had cleaned. With the owner's blessing he'd been allowed to play the piano as a child and went on to buy the instrument from the family on the doctor's death. Brendan spoke of the piano as his oldest friend.

For a brief moment, I contemplated smashing his piano into tiny pieces and grinding the gleaming fragments beneath my feet. At once my anger subsided. I couldn't do it. I couldn't hurt Brendan. And in destroying my own piano, I would merely feed my own pain. This icy water thought doused the flames of my fury and I lowered the hammer to the floor. Then Eirwen took me in her arms and rocked me like the child I'd become.

But I was better now, wasn't I? Yes, I was. I had secured a job. I wasn't drinking. I would survive. But would I ever fully recover?

I placed my fingers lightly on the cool keys to play the song I was trying not to hum, an Eagles ballad entitled "Wasted Time". Not that it was. Not for a second. No, it was because some of the lines resonated with me. For all the obvious reasons.

I played a C chord with my left hand and followed with individual C, G and E notes with my right hand, and Don Henley's soulful yet soaring vocals filled my mind. And I wondered how the man who was written into my soul had managed to write me out of his life.

Chapter 45

As ever, January 1979 was post-festive-season grim, and Britain was knee-deep in what became known as "The Winter of Discontent". Dustbins were overflowing, streets were piled high with rubbish and hospitals turned away patients. Then, with the disruption of food and fuel supplies and the likelihood of an undug grave or two, an election date was set. Eirwen and I were quite excited by the real possibility of Britain's first female prime minister.

Then… I wasn't with Eirwen when it happened.

It. Difficult to put into words, the death of a child. A baby put to bed for an afternoon nap, never to wake. A statistic. A cot-death. A nightmare.

A distraught Denny rang me that terrible day.

"Mari… Mari…" His broken-glass voice trailed off, the syllables of my name sounded as though they'd been torn from his throat.

"Oh, my God, Denny. What's wrong?"

Fear ripped through me like an electric shock when he failed to respond.

"Denny, please tell me."

"Pippa… Pippa's dead…" Denny's wracked words were a punch to the gut. "Wen needs you, Mari."

"I'm on my way."

I don't remember the journey. Almost two hundred miles of motorway and none of it registered. The enormity of Eirwen and Denny's pain and loss pressed down on me as nightmare images flashed across my mind. The throaty VW engine thrummed in my ears. But other cars? I was unaware of any. Instinct got me to Richmond.

Denny opened the door to me some hours later, his handsome face the same shade of grey as his T-shirt. His hands were shaking as he made to hug me. A brief smile of welcome, or possibly relief, skittered across his face. He appeared physically and emotionally diminished by the events of that afternoon. Certainly not the bluff blond bear of a man I knew.

"Denny. Denny…" I mumbled into his chest.

"Thanks for coming," he managed to say. Everyday words belying a nightmare scenario.

The normally noisy house was eerily silent yet lit up like a Christmas tree. A pall of misery hung about the place, blanketing sounds, catching in your throat, picking at your eyes.

I felt quite dizzy as I crossed the hall. I tried to calm myself, searching for something to say. But my mind was empty and dull and disbelieving. And what could I have said? There were no words.

Denny pushed open the living room door and announced my arrival in strangled tones I barely recognised.

"Wen, Wen." He went to touch Eirwen yet faltered at the last moment. Then he gesticulated in my direction in an exaggerated fashion, reminiscent of a silent movie star. "Wen. Mari's here."

I moved towards her, not knowing what to do with my hands.

"Wen, I… Wen, I'm so…"

She silenced me with a look, and I stood there inadequate and inarticulate, wanting to hold her but fearful of doing so. Her inertia was intimidating, accusing. How dare we move, speak, breathe? I knew in an instant that she would have exchanged either of us for Pippa. But was she aware, I wondered, that we, and others, would gladly have agreed to the transfer had it been possible?

Eirwen was perched on one of the large leather sofas that dominated the room. Simply furnished and usually illuminated by soft lamplight, the space was harsh and cold under the glare of the overhead beam.

At first glance, Eirwen appeared unscathed, as beautiful as ever in marked contrast to Denny, who wore his pain like some grotesque Halloween mask. But closer inspection revealed her skin to be porcelain pale, and her sky-blue eyes as empty as a shark's.

She sat poised, and perfect, a toy-shop doll awaiting the stroke of midnight to bring her to life. But Eirwen craved the magic of miracles, not fairy tales, and remained untouchable, unassailable, somewhere far away and beyond our reach.

Then Eirwen's mother bustled in, carrying a pristine white bedsheet.

"Don't fret, Mari," she said and began to refold the sheet along its length.

Increasingly confused, I watched her deft movements that resulted in a long, six-inch-wide band of material. Her matter-of-fact voice and usual efficient demeanour belied her ostensibly bizarre actions.

"I need to bind her breasts to dry up her milk. Could you give me a hand?" And she began to remove Eirwen's top.

I nodded, noting the two circular patches spreading across the fabric of Eirwen's T-shirt, and the sickly sweet odour of stale milk: an unwelcome reminder by a body programmed to provide for a child now gone.

Relieved that Eirwen was capable of movement, albeit assisted, I helped with the T-shirt, allowing Megan to wrap the sheet tightly around her daughter's swollen, leaking breasts and secure the ends with safety pins.

"The doctor's left some drug or other but this is the best way." Megan picked up the prescription that lay on the coffee table and pocketed it, along with the strip of sleeping tablets. She then pulled a clean top over Eirwen's head.

I was struggling to think of something to say when Megan drew me back. Her voice filled the choking silence and created unwanted images in my head: Denny trying to revive Pippa; the doctor arriving but unable to do anything except confirm her demise; Eirwen cradling her dead child until the policeman took Pippa from her; Eirwen running barefoot after him and the undertaker as they drove away with her baby. I wanted to vomit, but Eirwen didn't flinch.

I looked across at Megan as she gently lifted a white-tipped strand of hair from Eirwen's face. I stared at first in disbelief, and then in realisation.

"She's not cried yet," she murmured, barely audible. Poor Megan, wise in the ways of grief, a wisdom born of long, bitter experience. Her eyes were full of unshed tears and fear. Not bomb-proof after all, and suddenly I was afraid of the collapse of the stoic edifice that was Megan Watkins.

The sound of footsteps heralded the arrival of Denny, whose laboured movements had had a disastrous effect on the tray of hot drinks he was carrying.

"Let me help with that," I said as various shades of brown liquid merged and swirled around the tray.

"Fuck it." He relinquished his hold on the tray and collapsed onto the sofa alongside Eirwen. He emanated such anger I was sure his next move would be to kick the tray into the air. Instead, he exhaled loudly and reached for Eirwen, who recoiled as though he were wielding a weapon.

"Hold her, Denny." Megan grasped Eirwen's shoulders to prevent her from backing away from Denny's embrace.

The tortured tangle that ensued defies description. Eirwen, previously fragile and immobile, possessed the strength of many as she screamed and fought off her husband, who, urged on by his mother-in-law, maintained his hold while sobbing like a confused child.

I was silently screaming along with Eirwen, distant and useless on the wrong side of an invisible barrier of appropriate behaviour while longing to tear Megan and Denny away from my friend.

The furore ended as quickly as it had begun, almost as though someone had pulled the plug that had temporarily powered Eirwen's movements. Then she shuddered and shook, as huge tears tracked down her perfect face.

Eirwen's tears signalled a respite, a release of pressure on the flimsy dam holding back an immense lake of emotions. And suddenly we were able to talk and did so until dawn, whispering and laughing, marvelling at the impact of so short a life.

***

The week that followed was a frenzy of activity. The front door revolved as a constant stream of visitors vied for the attention of the grieving parents. Friends, neighbours, family, colleagues, health workers and undertakers arrived in quick succession to an unheard beat, to stay an allotted time, with the gifts of flowers, cards or advice.

However, speaking directly to Eirwen was not an option. She didn't respond to her fellow residents, let alone visitors. She avoided everyone, roaming the house night and day like a wraith wrapped in an old robe of Denny's, her diminishing frame lost in its copious folds.

Despite Brendan's many visits to the house, I only saw him towards the end of that first week. I was busy in the kitchen at the time, attempting to cobble together some semblance of a meal from the remnants of the previous week's groceries. It was a pointless exercise, anyway, as we all lacked any sort of appetite and ate like automatons only when the need for sustenance arose. The cook and part-time help had been early casualties of Denny's anger, dismissed for being too solicitous.

I looked up from the stove as Brendan came into the kitchen, and for the first time felt nothing on seeing him. On sensing my disinterest, he quickly crossed the room and hugged me.

My brain, addled through lack of sleep and an extensive catalogue of strained emotions, registered gratitude. I was thankful for the comfort of another human being who wasn't lachrymose and uttering the same old platitudes.

My witch's brew belched threateningly from the stove, drawing us apart. I lowered the heat and dared to taste my concoction. Brendan raised a quizzical eyebrow as he peered into the depths of the cauldron-sized saucepan.

"Well?" he queried. A range of conflicting flavours assaulted my taste buds. I pulled a face.

"It only lacks 'eye of toad and wing of bat'." I reached for the chilli powder. "But this'll have to do."

"Looks interesting." He eyed the lentils, baked beans and lumps of chicken and beef that surfaced and dived while I attempted to stir in the excessive amount of chilli powder now staining the muddy surface. All of a sudden, the chilli hit our throats and we were both coughing. Brendan leaned away from the pan but was still drawn to watching the swirling contents. "Such a pity I've already eaten." A smile twitched the corners of his mouth. He was forced to duck out of reach of the tea cloth I flicked at him.

"No one would notice if I served up horse manure. Wen's only ever been a cadger of fags but is currently emitting smoke from every orifice," I quipped despite my despair. I smiled wanly at Brendan, suddenly aware of how good he smelt. Personal hygiene, among much else, had been relegated to the perfunctory for the rest of us.

Brendan moved closer to me and gently lifted a tendril of hair from my face. The tropical conditions in the kitchen had turned the shorter lengths into loosely coiled springs.

"I love how your hair goes all Shirley Temple in the damp."

His statement seemed like a cue for a different kind of embrace to his earlier one. And the look on his face suggested that he felt this too, making me hopeful of something being right in the midst of all that was so wrong. But Brendan stepped back, turned away from me, and walked out of the room.

The wooden spoon I held clunked against the side of the saucepan as tears coursed down my face. Guiltily, I swept them away. How could I cry over a lost love when my friends grieved for their child?

***

Brendan's presence reawakened senses I'd almost forgotten I possessed. The clean smell of him had cut a swathe through the fug the rest of us had created. The air within the house was thick with misery and neglect. It tasted second-hand, stale and stagnant.

I opened the windows in the kitchen and then headed up the stairs to shower, vowing to clean tomorrow, to buy some fresh food, to attempt a return to some semblance of normality.

However, such plans seemed futile as I glimpsed Eirwen pacing in front of the large window that dominated her and Denny's bedroom. Like an old photograph, Eirwen was various shades of black, grey and white, her flat monochrome appearance accentuated by the kingfisher blue walls of the room and the candyfloss pink of the cherry blossom coming into flower in the garden below.

Denny was hunched on the bed, his eyes flicking to and fro in unison with Eirwen's pendulum motion as she drew on the cigarette she held. Barely pausing between each drag, Eirwen continued to pace, and a long column of ash fell unseen to the floor.

I looked away, hurrying on. It hurt so much to see her so. How long could she continue like this? I shuddered, shutting out any estimates. Perhaps she'd be better after the funeral. Nausea swept over me at the thought. This wasn't an ailment, something you "got over". This was something you got through, passing from one painful stage to the next. Eventually, your hurt would scab over, leaving a life-long scar to be periodically picked at. But it would always be there, a ghostly presence that pooped every party.

The water pounded against my scalp, as hot as I could bear, uncoiling my hair, scouring my skin. A temporary catharsis, but nonetheless a welcome one; to feel positive, hopeful even, however fleetingly.

Now, I thought, *we must attempt to draw Eirwen out of the dark place she currently occupies*. But she had shut us all out and put up an impenetrable barrier. She was as barbed and closed as the thorn hedge bordering Dad's allotment.

Once dressed, I attempted to blow-dry my hair as straight as was possible. So much for Brendan Bradshaw's preferences. Then, freshly clad and feeling more human, I crept down the corridor past the now-closed door to Eirwen's bedroom. Perhaps she was sleeping. I almost prayed this was the case when it struck me that to reinstate normality, we needed to behave normally. Well, as normal as anyone or anything gets. Stop creeping about and whispering for a start. This house that had once resonated with life and laughter now echoed like an empty tomb.

I ceased my thief-in-the-night tiptoeing and clattered down the stairs. I'd put the radio on and fill all the empty air. I'd… but I was stopped in my tracks by a sound that raised goose bumps on my skin.

It was reminiscent of a young child's laughter – bubbly, merry, bright. I dashed down the stairs following the sound, identifying it as music as I neared the source. Unsurprisingly, I found Brendan sitting astride a low table bathed in the fading light from the French doors.

He faced me with closed eyes, his now much shorter and greying hair shifting with his movements as he played an acoustic guitar. His music told a tale; it spoke of children and resonated with joy. But it made me cry.

Quickly, I wiped my eyes, amazed all over again by his skill as a musician and composer, and by how much I still loved and wanted him. In my life... in me.

My reverie was halted by the sound of muffled sobs. Megan, partially hidden from view by the high back of the winged chair to my left, shuddered and covered her face with her hands and I quickly moved towards her.

"It's meant to be happy." Brendan returned the guitar to its place on the wall rack.

"It is. It's beautiful. Pippa's song. She lives and breathes in your music."

He winced but managed a smile for me and then squeezed my upper arm as I stood ineffectively alongside Megan.

"We need to eat, and I happen to know there's something brewing in the kitchen, Megan." He winked at me as he hoisted Megan to her feet.

"You're right, *bach*." She patted her eyes, straightened her back and sighed, trying so very hard not to break down as we made for the kitchen.

Chapter 46

Eirwen insisted on taking Pippa back home.

"But we live in Richmond. She'll be so far away." Denny's voice crackled with pain.

"She died here. She'll be safe in Wales." Eirwen wrapped her arms about herself and left the room.

His expression one of total bewilderment, Denny followed her. No one should have to bury a child.

That Eirwen wanted Pippa to be interred in the chapel grounds at Gwaun was no surprise once she'd asserted that Wales was to be Pippa's final resting place. Nevertheless, I pondered on Eirwen's decision, unsettled and disturbed by the possible implications.

Further details regarding Pippa's funeral proved just as distressing.

"No cars," Eirwen said.

"But…" The funeral director looked at Denny, who looked at Phil, who shook and dropped his head.

"We'll walk. Denny will carry Pippa," Eirwen said.

Denny nodded in agreement and then buried his face in his hands.

Despite Eirwen's demands, she appeared on the morning of the funeral dressed in jeans and a T-shirt with flip-flops on her feet as though she'd planned a day at the seaside.

"I can't watch them put her in the ground," she said, leaning with her back against the doorframe, her gaze glued to the tiny white coffin on her mother's parlour table. She ignored Denny in his borrowed suit, his expression as ragged as the white shirt cuff across his hand that gripped the small box.

"Let's go, M." Eirwen headed to the front door.

I looked from Denny, who swallowed his pain and closed his eyes, to her mother, who nodded her consent. Her father, alarmingly grey and gaunt, raised sad eyes to mine. "Watch her, Mari."

"I'll ring," I said and followed Eirwen out to my car.

"Where to, Wen?" I turned the ignition key, mentally planning the quickest route to the coast given her choice of clothing.

"I want you to play your piano," she said, throwing me completely.

"My piano in Newport?"

"Yeah. Fabulous sound with that piano. Play me some happy tunes, M." Then she closed her eyes and rested her head against the car window.

***

Eirwen wouldn't go home to Richmond, or back to her parents. We pottered about my house but mostly we sat at the piano… day and night. I was grateful that my neighbour, Mrs Morris, was hard of hearing. By the end of the week, we were running out of happy tunes. I knew we were in trouble when Eirwen requested "Hushabye Mountain".

Throughout the day, Eirwen shadowed my every move, as though afraid of having to think of what to do next. Yet it was her proximity at night when we finally went to bed that I found the most disquieting.

During the course of our childhood, we'd often shared a bed. As girls we'd *cwtched* together out of necessity in our narrow, single beds. But now, with Eirwen only sleeping very fitfully, the nights were punctuated with much clutching and crying to the extent that my double bed seemed confined and claustrophobic – a place of torment rather than repose.

One of the few nights that she slept, actually slept, I lay tense and motionless, grateful for her temporary oblivion but also very afraid of waking her. Eventually, reassured by her peacefulness and the regularity of her breathing, I began to relax and drift off. Suddenly, she sat bolt upright.

"Wait." She reached out into the darkness, with open eager arms. "Please wait…"

"It's alright, Wen." I enveloped her in my shaking limbs, roused yet again from the edge of sleep. "*Popeth yn iawn, cariad*," I said.

She didn't fight but buckled against me, all hard edges. She exhaled, her breath hot on my neck, and began to cry. "She's safe, M. God showed me. I saw her hand. His voice said it was hers. But I knew that," she said through her tears.

Still jittery, I reached for the bedside lamp switch, fumbling in the dark as I felt down the side of the cupboard for the cable.

God's arrival at this stage in Eirwen's life was disturbing. She'd been cheerfully and irreverently an atheist for most of her life. Even as a little girl, she had dismissed God much as she had Father Christmas. "It's not possible, M." She'd patted my arm as she confirmed the claims of older local children regarding Santa. "It just can't be done."

So I was heartened that she took some comfort from this timely visitation. But my hopes were dashed when her face was suddenly illuminated in the lamplight. A fevered look had replaced the stony stare of her eyes. A hungry look, I thought, suddenly fearful, her words echoing around my head. *Wait, please wait.*

Still, as the days wore on, I found myself dropping swiftly and deeply asleep, often oblivious of Eirwen's movements, only to wake in a panic, suddenly aware of her absence and the cold, creaseless expanse of bed alongside me. But I became complacent, generally finding her shrouded in a blanket on a kitchen chair stationed near the French doors. She'd turn and smile faintly then speculate on the species of the first, very early bird at the feeders.

When I awoke some weeks after Pippa's death to find her gone, I didn't rush, expecting to find her in the kitchen. The empty chair and folded rug set my pulse racing. I darted from room to room in search of her, only to find a stark note beside the phone in the hall. *My dad's dead.*

Guilt gnawed at me as I packed her few possessions into a bag. I'd been asleep when she'd phoned home only to learn of her father's death. I'd slept on while she'd ordered a taxi and left my house. Useless.

***

Phillip Watkins died three weeks after his granddaughter. His family and friends were beyond shock. Denny, who was still with my parents, was joined by other relatives of Eirwen's there for her dad's funeral. She was insistent that Denny should not be with her.

"I can't breathe for him watching me," she railed, her skin paper-thin, almost translucent.

"We're all worried about you, Wen. What do you expect?" I placed a placatory hand on her arm. She shook me off. She felt cold then. I should have known.

"I just need some air. Keep Denny with you. Come down the pub at ten o'clock and we'll get pissed. Give Dad a good send off."

"We'll have a job with a ten o'clock start." I tried to match her manner.

"Oh, they'll have a lock-in for Dad. They always do for special occasions – you know, births, marriages, deaths. We can stay all night." She winked, and I saw a glimmer of my old Wen. Then she took my face in her hands and kissed me full on the lips, a light momentarily appearing in her sky-blue eyes.

"I love you," she said and was gone, blonde hair flying.

My Wen. I should have known.

***

We sat in the Miner's Arms – me, Denny and the others waiting for Eirwen. Then, at twenty past ten, when Megan Watkins came through the pub door with the bulk of her brood trailing behind her and no sign of Eirwen, I knew.

Megan's anxious eyes searched the crowd and then met mine.

"Where is she?" she demanded, her hands digging into me as if to prise the right answer out of me.

"Oh God, Megan, she said she'd come down with you."

Panic and tears filled her eyes. "I thought she was having a lie down. That's what she said. Where can she be?"

"The allotment." I shook off Megan's grasp and pushed my way out of the pub. I knew where she was.

***

Eirwen likened being in the den with being in your mam's womb. She reckoned the thorn hedge and the stream that it bordered shushed in unison, providing the appropriate background sound.

"Like your mother's blood and heartbeat."

"You scare me sometimes," I replied. To me, our willow hideaway was just one of our many special places. But it would be where we'd find Eirwen when she needed space – in the willow den in the foetal position, fast asleep.

***

I ran up the hill from the pub, my mind a blank, my chest complaining at the cold night air I gulped in hungry breaths. But on nearing the chapel and the gaping allotment gates, I began to pray in earnest. *Please be sleeping, just sleeping.*

The hillside was darkly shadowed in the stark moonlight as I instinctively made my way down to the den, the regular thud of my feet on the path reverberating through and around me as I pounded on.

In the distance a lonely owl called and a sudden a breeze blew up, rattling tree branches and ill-fitting shed doors, and raising goosebumps on my flesh. Then the burbling stream pinpointed my proximity to the den and I could just make out Eirwen through the open weave of its still, leafless branches.

"Wen! Wen!" I pushed aside an empty vodka bottle and ducked in through the opening.

Eirwen lay curled towards the entrance, her pale face partially obscured by the white silk of her hair. With shaking fingers, I felt for a pulse. Was there one? I couldn't be sure. The beautiful hair and face were hers, but Eirwen seemed to have gone. And so had her pain. Her face was tranquil in the moonlight.

I tried to wrap her in the coat she'd removed to lie on, the smell of alcohol burning my throat as I tried to draw her to me, to warm her, to reach her.

"You can't leave me," I wailed, my face buried in her hair as sporadic torch beams and desperate voices raked the night air. Suddenly wild, I shook her repeatedly and slapped her face.

"You're not to die. Do you hear me, Wen?" I held her shoulders and violently pitched her back and forth when I heard something. Was it a cough?

Then Denny's anguished cries filled the air. "Eirwen! Wen…" And he crumpled onto his hands and knees at the den's entrance.

"Denny, get her out and onto her feet. Shake her. I think she's alive." Yet it seemed pointless… She was so slight and lifeless in his crushing embrace.

"Shake her. Now!" I screamed, goading him, punching him, slapping him. "Again. Again," I urged as he sobbed and choked. It was brutal, barbaric. Minutes crawled and flashed by as time sped up and slowed down. My behaviour was as much about my own preservation as Eirwen's. I wasn't sure I could go on without her.

Then, with the distant nee-nah of an ambulance and a clutch of frantic people clattering down the path, Eirwen stiffened and jerked, took an enormous gulp of air and vomited over Denny.

"Christ Almighty. She's alive!" Denny shouted. "Mari, she's alive."

I just prayed we could keep her so. Then the approaching horde descended on us and took control, allowing me to step away from the mayhem, the madness. Stunned into silence, shock blurring all that followed, I was aware of nothing but one thought running on a loop around my head. *Eirwen's safe. Eirwen's safe. Eirwen's safe.*

I stumbled away from the frenetic activity, quite disorientated, when my father suddenly appeared out of the darkness. I lurched into his open arms and began to shake. Dad held me close and spoke to me in soothing whispers. Words of comfort and solace. Words of hope.

Chapter 47

Unable to sleep, I left my parents' house for the Royal Gwent Hospital. I thought my journey would be a wasted one, only to be allowed access to the ward on Megan's appearance. Megan looked ghastly but was fairly optimistic about Eirwen making a full recovery with no lasting liver damage. At which point my lower jaw dropped.

"Liver damage?"

"That's what a paracetamol overdose can do. She's had the gastro-intestinal decontaminator activated charcoal, and she vomited, which hopefully rid her of much of what they believe was one large intake of the drug. And mercifully, tests show her plasma paracetamol levels are low so they didn't give her the new antidote. In the next few days, she'll undergo further tests to check for any issues with her liver."

Despite all the positives, I felt my heart plummet, and given Megan's expression her thoughts were just as bleak.

"Have you been here the whole time?" I asked, trying not to consider a possible prognosis.

"Yes. I've only just persuaded Denny to leave. He's in a right state. I rang Terry to take him back to our house."

"Go and have something to eat and drink," I said.

"Thank you, Mari. I will." Off she went, sensible woman.

I watched Eirwen and turned over what Megan had said about liver damage. I tried to focus on my friend making a full recovery. I clung to the idea that Eirwen was going to be alright. But fear sat lead-like on my chest. So I closed my eyes and pictured Eirwen well and strong, hoping to will such an outcome into being.

Eirwen's silent inertia challenged my conviction. I looked away and thought about my job. I'd taken a fortnight's holiday after Pippa's death, which had become unpaid leave. How long would that be allowed to continue? Especially in light of Eirwen's actions. But I couldn't contemplate a return to work until Eirwen had been stabilised, only too aware that this implied mentally as well as physically.

My eyes began to close so I walked around the room and read every notice, Eirwen's chart and the labels on equipment. Then I stared out of the window at the transporter bridge on the far side of town, strangely reassuring and larger than life in the light of a full moon. Eventually, I gave in, slumped onto a chair and went to sleep. Half an hour or so later, I woke on Megan's return. Ever the pragmatist, Megan had devised and negotiated the implementation of a rota for those wanting to sit with Eirwen.

As soon as I got home, I rang my boss, who told me not to worry, which was a huge relief. Then I went food shopping. Eirwen and I had been living hand-to-mouth over the last few weeks. Later, I opened my post to find a letter from Brendan's solicitor.

Apparently, Mr Bradshaw was offering financial support while I supported my friend after the loss of her child. It was satisfying to inform Brendan's advocate that I needed no such help, thank you very much. But I was touched.

My next stint at the hospital was at nine that night. At home, once I'd eaten, I managed to get some sleep. So, I was reasonably restored and prepared for the hours ahead with fruit, water and a book. However, the anguished cries that greeted me on my arrival at the hospital made a mockery of my hopes and plans for Eirwen.

"I want Pippa. Where's Pippa?" Her cries ricocheted along the corridor.

By the time I reached her room, Denny and a nurse were attempting to console and control a now distraught Eirwen.

"M. M. She's gone. What happened? What did I do?" she wailed wretchedly, as the realisation of her loss ripped through her once again.

I repeatedly tried to reassure her that Pippa's death wasn't because of her – something she had or had not done – but she found no solace in my words.

I spent the remainder of the night on a chair alongside the bed, where Eirwen lay as close to me as possible, holding on to my arms as though fearful of being torn away from me. We slept fitfully, uncomfortable yet comforted by each other's presence. Despite Megan arriving to relieve me, I stayed, as much because Eirwen was reluctant to relinquish her hold on me as any desire to on my part. And the night passed.

The following days were busy with test results and more checks, and eventually a doctor declared Eirwen fit for discharge. Yet what we took home was an empty husk, one which only vaguely resembled Eirwen.

Chapter 48

For the next three and a half weeks, I was back at work, seeing Eirwen at her parents' house for an hour or so most nights. But I needn't have bothered. She responded to everyone around her like an automaton. Even Rhian and Thomas, whom she seldom saw as they both lived abroad, failed to engage her.

Nevertheless, her mother and siblings did what they'd always done in dire circumstances and carried on as though everything was fine and dandy. They cooked for her, told her jokes, took her out, ordered her about, and although Eirwen complied, she remained remote and impassive. And I felt to blame. She didn't want to be with us; she wanted to be with her baby. Once unsupervised I didn't doubt that's what she'd endeavour to do.

Then, halfway through the fourth week when Denny returned from Richmond to cover his stint on the care rota, there came the breakthrough that none of us had thought possible.

Denny had been reluctant to leave Eirwen on her return to Gwaun, but she wouldn't have him in the house, let alone anywhere near her. She'd curled up on the floor crying until he left. Unsurprisingly, there was much trepidation surrounding his imminent return.

When I'd given Mrs Morris my work's number, I never actually imagined her having to use it, but Eirwen sitting on my doorstep was reason enough. Mrs Morris reassured me Eirwen was safe and that she would be having chicken broth for dinner so there was no need to rush home. But I did anyway.

First off, I was surprised by Eirwen's appearance, which had markedly improved in the forty-eight hours since I'd last seen her. There seemed to be a fire burning behind her eyes, a rage that lit her skin, and I fleetingly wondered what Mrs Morris had put in the broth.

About to leave, I again thanked my neighbour for her kindness, and Eirwen hugged her with genuine warmth. The change in my friend's behaviour was difficult to explain. I should have been ecstatic, but Eirwen's sudden edginess was as disconcerting as her earlier apathy had been.

We left Mrs Morris's and Eirwen raced to my front door like a stray cat determined to gain entry. As soon as I unlocked the door, she pushed her way in and rushed down the hallway to the kitchen, where she began to pace around the table, agitatedly rubbing her hands together in a sort of washing motion.

"Why do men think that sex is the answer for everything?"

Totally baffled, I played for time. "Bit of a sweeping statement, Wen. What's brought this on?" Then it dawned on me... Denny. He'd been with her two nights.

Still pacing, and without naming him, she continued. "I felt angry as soon as I saw him. He irritates the hell out of me."

"So we have Denny to thank for your return."

"What do you mean?"

"We've hardly had a peep out of you since you've been home."

"It's only been a week."

"Three and a half weeks, Wen."

"I've been in a bit of a fog," she replied, almost apologetically. She was calmer but her confusion was evident.

"How did you get here?"

"I ran down the hill to the bus stop and Bert Jenkins stopped and offered me a lift."

"I'll ring your house," I said, deliberately not mentioning Denny.

***

"I was just about to telephone you," Megan said. "Denny's on his way to your house. He was about to contact the police when I got home from work. He, Thomas and Rhian combed the valley on foot looking for her. Keep me informed, Mari."

"I'll ring later," I said and replaced the receiver.

"He's coming here," Eirwen said, suddenly alongside me and visibly shaking. I nodded, noting how her nostrils flared as she clenched her teeth together, anger flashing in her eyes again. No crying, just a white-hot fury. She resumed her pacing.

"We're talking about your husband, Wen, not the Bogeyman."

"I can't be around him. As soon as he turned up at Mam's, I felt something ignite in me, something close to hatred."

"How can you say that? He's a kind man, and he loves you. He's not to blame any more than anyone else is. Given time, things between you will get better."

At this, Eirwen descended on me and all but pressed her face to mine, hands gripping my upper arms, her eyes wild.

"No, they won't," she railed, shaking me. "Last night he tried to convince me we should make love, have another baby. He has no idea. Nor have you." She released me and backed away, her breathing laboured when the doorbell rang: a cheery, chippy sound signalling the beginning of quite a different chapter in our lives.

Eirwen raced me down the hall, and in her haste to open it, almost ripped the front door from its hinges.

"Have I not made it patently clear that I don't want you anywhere near me?" she demanded, leaning menacingly towards her husband.

If she'd hit him in the face with a frying pan, Denny couldn't have looked more pained.

"Wen, let's not discuss this on the street." I tried to lever her hand from the doorframe. She swung away from me and stormed towards the kitchen, rattling the glass in the door as she relinquished her hold on it.

"You're welcome to come in, Denny," I said. Not the best choice of words in the aftermath of Eirwen's greeting.

Given his silence, pallor and stone-like stillness, I wondered if Eirwen had acquired Medusa's skill.

"I…" He gulped. "I need to sort this out." But he didn't move.

"I'm sorry," I said ineffectually, wanting to comfort him but fearing the fallout. Then he quietly stepped into the house and strode to the kitchen.

Dressed in a plain white shirt and pale blue jeans, Eirwen, illuminated by the light streaming through the French doors, faced us like an avenging angel, her blonde head aglow.

"Come home, Wen," Denny pleaded.

"I am home." Her reply surprised me as much as Denny.

"Let's go home to Richmond."

"You don't get it. Home is wherever Mari is."

Denny's head jerked back as though he'd been struck, a blow I also felt. "You're my wife," he said, pitifully.

"Your wife died on a hillside weeks ago."

"But, Wen…"

"I'm not going to pretend anymore."

Oh God, what was coming next? Yet I couldn't claim complete ignorance – Eirwen had dropped enough hints of late – I just didn't want it spelt out for me. My instinct was to leave but I felt rooted to the spot. Perhaps it was time to face the truth.

Denny made a move towards Eirwen, but she quickly backed away.

"What do you mean?" he asked, not expecting his simple question to unleash a torrent of such breathtaking magnitude.

"Isn't it obvious? I'm attracted to women, not men. It's why I tried to split Mari and Brendan up, and why I took up with you to be near her. Hadn't foreseen a baby though, or that Pippa would make everything bearable. But now she's gone, I can't go back to playacting, even if it means losing Mari altogether."

Then her gaze swivelled to mine. It had been strange until that moment being talked about as though I wasn't there. Fleetingly, time seemed to pause as I processed what Eirwen had said, what she'd declared. And my heart went out to her. Years of suppression and pretence… of yearning.

I reached out and took Eirwen's hand. "You're my friend. I'll always love you. I'll never desire you, though. More's the pity."

"I know." Eirwen took hold of me and we began to laugh.

We were drawn apart by the sound of Denny dragging a chair from the table and slumping down onto it.

"Shit. Shit. Shit," he said, repeatedly hitting his head on the table until Eirwen intervened.

"Hey." She stooped down alongside him, her anger gone.

"What a mess." He was hunched over the table's edge, the look on his face enough to rip a hole in the hardest of hearts.

"Denny." Eirwen grasped his shoulder. "You're a lovely man and one day you'll find the woman you deserve."

"I thought I had." A sad smile flickered across Denny's face, at which Eirwen stood up and moved away.

After an awkward silence, Denny also got to his feet and squared his shoulders, his gaze lingering on Eirwen before he looked my way.

"I'll head off." He nodded at us both as though we were passing acquaintances.

"Right-oh." Eirwen matched her husband's manner.

"Don't go like this, Denny." I rushed forward to grab his arm.

"I've no reason to stay." He looked from me to Eirwen, still hopeful of a crumb of compassion. I glared at her, and she offered tea. Tea, for goodness' sake.

"No thanks. I'll be in touch." He was about to leave, when the doorbell rang.

I dashed down the hall while considering an inordinate number of ruses to prevent Denny from leaving the house.

I was saved further deliberation by the fortuitous arrival of Eirwen's younger brother, Thomas. Thrilled that Denny would now have an escort back to Gwaun, I all but carried Thomas down the hallway.

"Worst party I've been to in a while," said Thomas chirpily, taking in the solemn faces as he handed Eirwen a holdall of clothing.

When Denny went to the bathroom, I said to Tom, "Make him stay on at your mam's. He shouldn't travel back to Richmond tonight." At this, Eirwen huffed in annoyance.

"Had a bit of a tiff, eh?"

"A lot more than a bit," Eirwen replied.

"Thought it was a touch frosty between you two," Thomas said with a grin, thinking things were back to normal. Tiffs were everyday occurrences.

"Go home, Tom," Eirwen said in exasperation.

"Keep an eye on him," I said to Thomas, just seconds before Denny appeared at the top of the stairs.

***

We had an omelette for tea. Eirwen wolfed hers, which was encouraging as she'd had little appetite for weeks. The atmosphere between us, though, was slightly strained. I'd felt her relief when she unburdened herself, but now I didn't know how to behave around her. I think she felt the same. Yet we made no attempt to discuss the matter, which was ridiculous.

Once we'd dealt with the dishes, Eirwen headed upstairs, obviously too exhausted to disagree with my suggestion that she took my bed and I the inflatable mattress in the back bedroom. It was unlikely that we'd share a bed any time soon.

With Eirwen safely out of the way, I rang Megan.

"How is she?" she asked without preamble. "Tom said she was okay. Just a bit offhand."

"She's gone to bed exhausted. But she's better than I've seen her for weeks." Since Pippa's death, I should have said.

"So did the row clear the air?"

"In a manner of speaking."

"Could you elaborate, and maybe explain why we need to watch Denny?"

"Eirwen will tell you when she's ready."

"Mm. You're almost as clam-shut as Denny. By the way, he's staying the night, so you can stop worrying on that score. Goodnight, Mari."

I wished her the same and hung up. Then, before I lost my nerve, I rang The Elms.

"Mari. How are you, lamb?" I could hear the delight in Mrs Booker's voice and fleetingly pined for her company and cooking. "I was so sorry to hear about your friend. And poor Mr Clarke. It's been a terrible time."

"It has," I said wearily. Then I heard Brendan in the background.

"Excuse me a moment, Mari," Mrs Booker said. And then...

"Mari?" Every hair on the back of my neck lifted as Brendan whispered into my ear. "Mari," he repeated at my lack of response.

"Denny's had bad news. I felt you should know. He's planning on making his way back to Richmond from Megan's tomorrow."

"Eirwen's divorcing him."

"Probably."

"So what's the bad news?"

"You'll have to ask him about that."

"Are you alright?"

"Eirwen's much better, so I am too."

"Good to hear. And thank you."

"Denny's a friend and I care about him, so save your gratitude."

Not trusting myself to say more, I put down the phone and made my way upstairs.

***

I woke well before my alarm. With so many things on my mind, I gave up on the idea of trying to get back to sleep. Besides, the trampoline-like quality of my mattress was enough to put paid to further rest. It was time I got another bed.

Shrugging on my dressing gown, I headed downstairs.

With time on my hands before I could ring into work, I decided to put into practice my mother's advice regarding pancake making. Apparently, prepared pancake batter should rest for at least half an hour prior to cooking.

Then, with the mixture prepared, I had quite a start when I turned around to find Eirwen leaning against the doorframe, watching me.

"What's the matter, Wen?" I asked, feeling slightly uncomfortable under her intense gaze.

"You know we're going to have to talk about this." She did not move from her spot.

"Waiting for pancake batter to rest?" I said, with a half-hearted grin.

"You know exactly what I'm referring to."

"I've nothing to add to what I've already said." Was there no end to my cowardice and ostrich-like behaviour?

"It's another presence in the house. An unwelcome ghost, a pesky poltergeist. We have to exorcise it, or it'll ruin everything. We don't want unspoken truths and lies littering our lives. I'm not prepared to live like that anymore."

"Why now? Can't it wait until…?"

"No. If we wait for the right moment, we'll never talk about it."

"You're right," I admitted.

"Besides, we're alone now, which we need to be if we're to properly deal with this." She suddenly moved away from the doorframe. Un-nerved, I backed away.

"Don't look so frightened. I'm not going to eat you. Not yet anyway."

I backed further away and she started to laugh. I was evidently los-ing my sense of humour to have missed such an obvious gibe.

"Had you never thought that I preferred women?" She avoided the lexicon of labels available to her. Then she pulled out a chair and sat down at the table, opposite where I stood with my back pressed against the cooker. I relaxed slightly.

"Why would I, with you giving it your all as a full-blooded heter-osexual?"

"Yeah, well, I was trying to shag myself normal."

"That's awful," I said, wounded for her younger self and her need to be what she wasn't. "What or who is normal, anyway?"

"I'm not the person to ask. I was convinced that you were like me. You'd shown little interest in boys and I hoped that my behaviour would eventually elicit some sort of response from you. Shows what I know."

"I wish there was something I could say that would help," I said, willing to say or do anything to protect our friendship. *Or was I?*

"You're not like me? And you didn't feel anything when we were in bed together in the hotel after I was sick?" Eirwen got up from the table.

"That was years ago."

"But you still remember," she countered, smiling.

How difficult could it be? I contemplated, as my beautiful friend carefully approached me. *This might well be the answer to all our problems.*

"How long have you known you were gay?"

Eirwen stopped in her tracks. Had I chosen the wrong word?

"I remember always thinking I was different, but it was only when I learnt about sex that I realised why... or in what way."

"I think everyone feels different, or odd, or whatever, at some point in their lives. And in answer to your questions: one, I'm not gay, and two, that moment at the hotel, I continued to avoid recognising what you'd been trying to tell me despite being aware, for the first time, of *your* desire rather than of feeling any myself."

"Shame." Eirwen stood awkwardly in front of me, as though waiting for a reprimand. I quickly reached out and drew her to me, realising that I could only ever embrace her as a friend. Eirwen rested her head on my shoulder and let out a sigh that seemed to acknowledge my feelings.

"Are we going to have pancakes any time soon?" Eirwen asked when we eventually stepped apart.

"Go and get dressed and I'll get flipping," I replied, feeling as though a weight had been lifted from my shoulders.

***

"Incredible. Almost as good as your mother's." Eirwen hovered at my elbow as I confidently turned over what would be her third pancake.

I looked at her questioningly, searching her face for some trace of animosity or dissatisfaction, some remnant of disappointment. But the look she gave me was unclouded and packed with familiar warmth and humour. There was about her, I felt, an untroubled acceptance of how things could only ever be between us. And I believe she was as glad of the fact as I was.

"I'll let you have the next one." She smiled and held out her plate as I lifted the pancake from the pan. Then she pecked my cheek and

I grinned, grateful that we could still be friends and that I might yet have a pancake, when the doorbell suddenly cut in. I left Eirwen slathering her pancake with butter, sugar and lemon juice and made my way down the hall.

Early start to the day, I thought, taking in the tall, blurred figure just visible through the glass. Not Thomas then, as he lacked his siblings' height. Trefor or Terry, perhaps? Either one was bound to want a pancake.

"Fancy a pancake?" I blithely said on opening the door, only to be almost felled by my least expected visitor… Brendan, whose dishevelled weariness dissolved into laughter at my offer.

"Hard to say no to that," he said, with a wide, mischievous grin.

All of a jitter, I pushed back my hair, clutched at my dressing gown, speechless and blushing like a schoolgirl.

"Are you going to invite me in or bring the pancake out here?"

"Very funny." I scurried towards the kitchen.

"Called for the cavalry, did you, M?" Eirwen said, suddenly icy as her gaze flicked between me and Brendan.

I opened my mouth to respond but nothing came out.

"I was hoping to cadge a lift to your mother's house," Brendan said equably despite Eirwen's stony stare. Then he turned to me and smiled.

"I'll get dressed," I said hurriedly, my nervousness intensifying with every second spent in Brendan's company.

"No need to rush. We've time for a pancake."

"There's a queue for the pancakes and you're at the back of it," Eirwen commented, her tone humourless.

***

It was an awkward thirty-minute drive back to Gwaun. Brendan was whistling nonchalantly but the tension along his jaw was visible when I caught a glimpse of him in the rear-view mirror. Meanwhile, Eirwen sighed and huffed beside me like a kettle coming to the boil. I couldn't think of a thing to say to diffuse the atmosphere. Then…

"Where did you spend the night?" I asked, knowing that Brendan had travelled down by train.

"In a hedge by the look of him," Eirwen cut in acerbically.

"Not all of us wear our concern as lightly as your good self," came his swift retort, at which I had to put a restraining hand on Eirwen, who looked as though she might vault the car seat and rip Brendan's head off. We spent the remainder of the journey in a simmering silence.

Despite Eirwen's subsequent sour mood, I did not regret contacting Brendan to accompany Denny home to Richmond. Another plus was Eirwen being available to her family, her mother and sister, in particular. Meanwhile, I hastily adjourned to my parents' house, hopeful of a question-free interlude. Fat chance. My mother could interrogate for the FBI.

Chapter 49

That night we were late back to my house. Eirwen continuing to stay with me was an unspoken agreement that not even her family could persuade her to renege on. Once home we went straight to our respective beds. Thankfully, I enjoyed a deep, dreamless sleep, by far my best for some time, even with a bobbing bed.

Eirwen was not as fortunate. Consequently, she was tired and tetchy the next morning, yet unwilling to go back to bed, so I bundled her into the living room for a mid-morning nap.

Glad of a respite from a cornucopia of strained emotions, I settled at the kitchen table with a cup of tea. Nevertheless, I continued to turn over random past events as I searched for missed clues and then pondered the purpose of doing so. After all, we were alright now. Well, I hoped so.

***

For the first time, Steph Laine came to visit me. Previously we'd always met up in Bristol, but with news of the recent calamitous events finally reaching her, she tracked me down.

We were too much alike to be great friends. There was no real spark between us yet we each enjoyed the reassuring ordinariness of the other, the calming balm of our dull and predictable encounters. But the cornerstone of our friendship was our mutual love of music.

However, Steph had the edge on me as a pianist, playing across genres all over the world. Not that I envied her plane-hopping lifestyle – permanently on tour, to my mind. She once told me that since she'd finally got over missing home at university, she had yet to find a reason or need to establish a permanent base in any one place.

"Steph," I gasped, genuinely glad to see her.

I quickly ushered her in and down to the kitchen, hopeful of not waking Eirwen. We'd only just sat at the table when Steph said, "I'm sorry but I can't stay long. I've a rehearsal this afternoon for a concert tonight at Bristol Cathedral."

"Ever life in the fast lane, eh, Steph?"

"Well, it's a surefire way of avoiding such emotional traumas as you've recently endured," she said, and I suddenly began to sob uncontrollably. Steph got up and stood alongside me, a reassuring hand on my shoulder. When I stopped crying, she handed me a tissue.

"Sorry," I said, once I'd blown my nose.

"You can never cry too much. It sets you up for a better moment or two."

"Bit longer than that, I hope," I said with a grin. "Fingers crossed, eh?"

Steph waved two sets of crossed fingers at me, a gesture reminiscent of Eirwen.

"Tea? Sandwich?" I asked, shaking off the image.

"Could I be cheeky and grab a banana and some milk?"

"Of course." I headed to the cupboard for a glass while Steph helped herself to the solitary, rather tired-looking banana from the fruit bowl.

"I'm with my parents for a week then I'm back to Boston for a stint. Ring me when you can or, if you get a chance, come over to Bristol. We can spend some time together. Here's my parents' number." She handed me a scribbled note.

She quickly finished her snack and headed to the bathroom while I started to write a grocery list. Fruit wasn't the only provender lacking in my metaphorical larder.

If I hadn't been so engrossed in menu planning, food shopping and ways in which to wear Eirwen out so as she'd sleep at night, I might have clocked Steph's protracted absence.

"Is that your friend in the living room?" she asked on her return.

"Yes. Her name's Eirwen."

"Which means?"

"White or blessed snow."

"Of course."

"Eirwen's at her most endearing when asleep," I said with more than a hint of wasted irony.

"It's heartbreaking to think she lost her baby." Steph swept away a sudden tear. Then, without warning, she snatched up her bag and jacket from the chair and headed down the hall with just a brief stop to glance in at Eirwen. She waited for me at the front door and grabbed my hand.

"Ring me," she said, in an urgent, most-unlike-Steph manner.

"Of course, I will," I said, a little taken aback.

***

With just enough bread for toast and eggs for scrambling, I was selecting the necessary bits and pieces to make lunch when Eirwen appeared. She smiled at me in a faraway fashion, which was most disconcerting.

"That was nice of you," she said.

"What do you mean?" I asked, wondering if I'd read her mind with regard to lunch.

"Waking me with a poem."

"I haven't recited any poetry in years. Scrambled eggs alright with you?" I replied. This was turning into a strange sort of a day.

"Mm." She sat down at the table, a confused frown crossing her face.

"It was probably a dream, Wen. Now let's have lunch before the eggs spoil," I said, unprepared to speculate and far too hungry to delay our meal.

Eirwen nodded enthusiastically.

***

"It'll be easier if I come to you," Steph suggested when I rang her a few days later. But I wasn't convinced, having already arranged for my parents to Eirwen-sit for a few hours. Besides, how would Eirwen react to an unknown visitor? She seemed okay, and yet she wasn't. Or was I the problem? Perhaps we both needed a change. The fresh face of an outsider might be the answer. Depending on the question, of course.

"Who the hell is Steph?"

"I've told you about her. We met at university."

"Oh yeah. When's she coming? I'll make sure I'm out."

"Don't be ridiculous."

"You can't watch me forever. I need to get a job. To do something. Something meaningful."

"Like what?" I asked, surprised at the turn in the conversation yet heartened by Eirwen's sudden motivation.

"I could volunteer with the Samaritans. Or speak with bereaved parents." Eirwen's eyes misted as she drew in a shuddering breath.

"There are lots of things you could do." I smiled despite my unease.

***

"I would complain about the number of eggs we're eating lately if I didn't love your quiche so much," Eirwen said, heartily tucking into her lunch.

"I don't think I've tasted better," said Steph, for which she received a "who asked for your opinion?" glare from Eirwen.

Given Eirwen's unwelcoming manner, I doubted that Steph would ever grace my doorstep, let alone table, again. Every comment or opinion she offered elicited sniping, huffing and puffing, and/or grimacing and gurning from Eirwen – certainly uncomfortable for me as the hostess but seemingly not so for my guest.

I was in awe of Steph's diplomatic and skilful parrying of Eirwen's many slights. Bigger and braver people had buckled under such an onslaught. And I was as aggrieved with myself as Eirwen. I felt I should have intervened but was wary of doing so.

However, once Steph had left, I questioned Eirwen on her harshness.

"She didn't take the hint though, did she? I thought she'd never go."

"Why should she? She was invited."

"Why *did* you invite her?" Eirwen asked irritably.

"Because I've had little opportunity to see her regularly in the past."

"You'd prefer to be with her?"

"Don't be ridiculous, Wen. I'm doing a job I love because of Steph. She's always been good to me."

"And I never have?" Eirwen said wildly and burst into tears.

I jumped to my feet and hugged her, not attempting to stop her tears. As Steph had implied, sometimes you just need to cry.

***

The following day I suggested a walk to the nearby Belle Vue Park. Eirwen was taken with the idea, and I was hopeful of a pleasant morning. But I hadn't considered that parks are largely frequented by retirees and mothers with small children and babies.

As this was Eirwen's first foray into a public place since Pippa's death, I should not have been surprised at her flinching on sighting a pram or pushchair, a mother cradling a baby. Nor that I would feel her pain.

We rushed across the hillside park, barely aware of its beautiful Victorian pavilion, shaded water cascade, bandstand, lofty trees and bright flowerbeds as we, not having exchanged a single word, headed homewards. It was a relief to close the door on the world outside.

"I'm sorry, M." Eirwen slumped onto the sofa in her jacket.

"Don't apologise. It was a mistake to go there and my fault that we did." I sat down beside her.

"I don't know if I'll ever again feel anything but pain and anger," she said, her beautiful face riven with sorrow.

"It will take time to heal." I slipped an arm around her shoulders.

She turned haunted, disbelieving eyes to me. "I'm looking at the world from inside a long dark tunnel. I can see what's out there in the light, but it's all so far away. Apart from babies and prams. They rush in at me."

"Dear God, Wen." I pulled her to me, frantically searching for the right thing to say. Both at a loss for words, we sat for some minutes holding each other.

***

That evening, Megan Watkins rang, as she or Rhian did most nights. However, on this occasion Eirwen answered the phone. Immobile on the landing, I tried not to listen but it was difficult not to with the stairwell amplifying the one-sided conversation.

"I'm fine, Mam."

"Yes, we went out for a walk."

"I'm planning on walking to the local shops tomorrow."

"No. On my own."

"I'll be fine."

"No, you can't speak to her. Stop worrying about me. I'm here now and I have to prove I deserve to be. I want Pippa to be proud of me. Night, Mam."

I waited, trying not to blub, until Eirwen returned to the living room. Then I crossed to the bathroom and sobbed into a towel.

The following morning during breakfast, Eirwen said, "I expect you heard me telling Mam that she couldn't speak to you."

I nodded.

"It's time she stopped checking up on me."

I wanted to speak, to say any number of things in Megan's defence, but Eirwen's manner precluded such action.

"And you know I'm going to the shops?"

Again, I nodded, quelling a request to accompany her. Eirwen was evidently ready to break loose from our well-meant moorings, and we had to let her.

***

From the shadows of the living room, I watched anxiously as Eirwen walked away from the house, wishing she'd taken an umbrella – rain was forecast. How long was she likely to be gone? Should I go and meet her in an hour? I rushed to open the front door but she'd already disappeared from sight.

What should I do? I thought, dithering on the doorstep. *I should let her be*, and I closed the door on the leaden sky and sluggish breeze. I settled on some therapeutic gardening.

Soon engrossed, I potted on my kidney beans, dead-headed the pansies and clipped back two shrubs, and the time sped by despite some heavy drizzle. I was locking up the shed and about to return to the house when Eirwen briefly appeared on the patio.

"Come in, you fool," she shouted, gesticulating wildly.

Good grief. What's happened now? I thought disbelievingly as Eirwen beamed at me through the rain-streaked French doors. I wiped the worst of the dirt from my hands with an old cloth and quickly returned to the house.

It would seem Eirwen was no longer sporting the anger-driven persona Denny had ignited – welcome though it had been at the time. She now looked as though she'd been given a shot of something… something cathartic, fundamental. She appeared to be lit from within. And this after a two-hour round trip to the string of shops along Stow Hill?

"M, M. I've got a job. I start Monday. You can go back to work." She caught hold of me and danced me around the room. It wasn't hard to join in, to ride the wave of her enthusiasm, to feel her joy as we clattered about cavorting and laughing.

"The bakery?" I echoed her reply to my question then turned to wash my grimy hands at the sink, hoping I hadn't sounded as disappointed as I felt.

"I'll be on the counter in the shop. Mr Harris, the baker, reckons I have the personality for sales." She grinned.

To say nothing of the face and figure, I thought, contemplating the workwear, certain my own face was a muddle of misgiving and doubt despite my attempt to return her smile.

"I'm on a week's trial and if it doesn't work out, I can leave. I know it's not what either of us envisaged, but what's more meaningful than bread?"

I burst out laughing, at which Eirwen drew me into another noisy caper around the kitchen.

***

Eirwen was as high as a kite that weekend. Even a rather lacklustre visit by Sylvia and Ruth failed to dampen her enthusiasm. Ruth had rung to ask if Eirwen was ready to see them before warning me that Sylvia was out of sorts yet determined to speak to her.

"Is she ill?" I asked, concerned.

"I wish I knew" was Ruth's disconcerting reply. "Something's obviously up with her. What exactly, I can't say."

"Have you asked her?"

"I don't pussyfoot around anyone, Mari. But Sylvia is establishment to the core. Stiff upper lip and all that nonsense. Can't get a word out of her."

We needn't have worried. Sylvia, schooled in the art of brief, polite and pointless conversation, ruffled no one's feathers. And Eirwen, more upbeat than she'd been in months, was proving impervious to anything otherwise.

But I was only too aware that Sylvia, normally quite pale, now had a yellowish tinge about her skin and, more worryingly, the whites of her eyes. I kept glancing at Ruth, who'd merely raise her eyebrows and shoulders a tad or give a slight shake of her head. If Ruth, the grand inquisitor, had failed to elicit an explanation, what chance did I stand?

It was only on the point of departure as she advanced on Eirwen that Sylvia said anything of significance. She looked as though she might grasp Eirwen's hand, her own hovering briefly in the air, awkward and hesitant. It was upsetting to note that Sylvia's fluid, effortless grace seemed to have deserted her. We waited silently as she gathered herself to speak.

"I commend you," she finally said, her accent lacking its usual knife-edge clarity. "To have endured such trials without the aid of stimulants or medication defies belief."

"She's not wrong." Ruth hugged Eirwen and me in swift succession as Sylvia opened the door to leave.

"Please keep in touch." I glanced meaningfully at Sylvia, standing alongside Ruth's car.

"Will do," said Ruth and headed down the path.

"Well, that's a first for me," Eirwen said when I joined her in the living room.

I looked at her expectantly.

"Sylvia stone-cold sober," she said matter-of-factly.

"Of course," I said, my voice a Eureka-moment high. "That's what's wrong with her."

***

I should not have been surprised that Eirwen enjoyed working at the bakery. After all, she'd loved *Tad-cu*'s shop. And with Eirwen happily and gainfully employed, I felt able to return to work. We gratefully fell into the everyday humdrum rhythm of our lives, plodding on from one day to the next, not talking of our old lives nor of our lost loved ones. We were living in an emotional vacuum, of a sort, and glad of the fact.

Steph came and went regularly enough for me to contemplate the purchase of a bed for the third bedroom. Sylvia checked into the Priory. Desert Heat didn't go on tour that autumn.

"Do you think that's because of Sylvia?" Eirwen asked when I mentioned the latter.

"I would think so."

"What else could it be?"

"Perhaps they're reappraising their music given some of the current trends."

"Really? I know the Sex Pistols have split up and punk rock has had its day. And that beautiful singer Kate Bush has released a couple of great albums."

About to enlighten her about electropop, hip-hop and two-tone, I began with, "That was last year, Wen," and her face fell. I could have bitten my tongue off. It was difficult not to inadvertently remind her of the hole in her calendar, never mind her life.

Six weeks later, Pink Floyd released *The Wall*, reminding me that if a band was good enough, trends didn't matter. Only the quality of the music did.

I was dreading Christmas but thankfully our families intervened with invitations to return to our respective homes. Not that it changed anything. It was still a Christmas without Pippa and Phil.

"How was it?" I tentatively asked Eirwen when we reconvened at my house the day after Boxing Day.

"Much as past Christmases, apart from the two elephants in every room. Bert Jenkins and his missus popped in to reassure us that the first major celebrations after a death are always the hardest. It gets easier after that apparently. So, roll on." She struggled to finish her trite little speech and, bereft of words myself, I drew her to me in the slim hope of providing some comfort.

***

"Let's have a New Year's Eve party," said Eirwen, on the Friday night after Christmas. We were watching the Kate Bush Christmas Special on the television at the time and still fasting after an enforced over-dose of festive fare at our respective childhood homes.

"Why?"

"We should be hungry again by then," Eirwen unexpectedly offered.

"Maybe," I replied. But who could we actually invite? Besides, parties usually involved alcohol and neither of us needed to reintroduce liquor into our lives.

"What a good idea," Steph said enthusiastically.

"What's good about it?" Eirwen asked, caustic, her expression and body language questioning not just Steph's right to comment but her actual presence at the discussion.

Steph fleetingly flinched before steeling herself to meet Eirwen's piercing gaze. "It would be a way of getting to know the neighbours. If we only invite those we know within walking distance of here, it'll keep everything simple."

"Well, you've convinced me," I enthused and gave Eirwen a bit of a glare. She pulled a face at me.

We decided to give it a go. Eirwen and I were to cover the catering and Steph the non-alcoholic beverages. It was made plain to our guests that anyone requiring anything stronger should bring their own. With just two days to prepare it was pretty frantic, especially as Eirwen was working on the Saturday. On the plus side, it meant I had little time to worry.

My fears were groundless. We had a wonderful night. The guests included Mr Harris from the bakery along with his extended family and the neighbours we were on chatting terms with, plus a few of those curious enough to attend for any gossip doing the rounds.

The only moment of real concern was the proposed opening of a Watney's Party Seven can with a hammer and nails. Fortunately, a beer-dowsing disaster was averted when Mr Harris junior turned up with another Party Seven and, more importantly, the appropriate opener.

We needn't have worried about food either, as Mr Harris senior arrived with trays of freshly baked sausage rolls, pasties and an assortment of sweet pastries. Along with our sandwiches, quiche, cheese and pineapple on sticks, crisps, Twiglets and peanuts, there were sufficient calories for a sizeable crowd.

The biggest surprise was hard-of-hearing Mrs Morris banging out innumerable musical hall classics on the piano: "Roll out the Barrel", "A Bicycle Made for Two" and "I've Got a Lovely Bunch of Coconuts" to name but a few.

The Harris men proved equally as entertaining with their interpretation of the linked-arm dance from the film *Zorba the Greek* while a couple of our neighbours opted for Russian Cossack moves. A raucous round or two of charades and the Hokey Cokey followed.

The party finally drew to a close with a conga down the street and the revelation (by a neighbour) that we were referred to as the Coven.

Despite the night's sobriety, we found this highly amusing, and from that point on referred to ourselves as the Three Coveneers.

"I fancy running," Eirwen said when we eventually closed the door on the last of the guests. Steph and I looked at her in weary bemusement. Then Eirwen reopened the door.

"Are you serious? It's gone one," I said.

"I ran in the park lunchtime yesterday," Eirwen said. "It was so exhilarating. I felt about six years old, and free of everything. From now on I intend to run a lot."

She then left the house with me and Steph scrambling to follow her.

Chapter 50

Eirwen literally began the new decade running, as she had resolved. I was never sure if she was running away from or towards someone or someplace. Either way, she was now properly equipped with tracksuits, running shoes and water bottles. She ran locally on a daily basis, venturing further afield on a weekend, when she often participated in charity events.

The party had proved a turning point in more ways than one but the most fortuitous outcome was my discovering that our neighbour three doors down had relatives who were members of the local running club. It was a huge relief to have Eirwen taken under their collective wings and ferried to and from races and events.

Thankfully, I did not have to match Eirwen's sudden commitment to running, a prospect that horrified me. Running was an in-an-emergency-only mode of movement, I maintained, despite Eirwen's assertions of its many benefits. Yet her ongoing need to be continually doing something or other, almost as though she was ticking off activities on a bucket list, was disturbing to say the least.

There weren't enough hours in the day or days in a week for her. If she wasn't running, she was swimming at the local pool. She'd also tried kayaking and was talking about giving surfing a go. Meanwhile, her running events continued to grow, with people visiting the bakery not just to buy bread or pastries, but to enlist her help with fundraising. She was never without a sponsorship form.

"You'll self-combust if you don't slow down," I said on the point of leaving for work as she was returning from the first run of the day.

"Nag, nag, nag. You're as bad as a husband." Eirwen quickly removed her sweaty hairband and rubbed it across my face.

Later that night we watched the news, horrified to learn that an oil platform used as a floating hotel had collapsed into the sea with well over a hundred men feared dead.

"There," said Eirwen, as though continuing our morning conversation. "You have to make the most of your time as you don't know when it's all going to end."

She had a point.

***

When a subsequent invitation to London to spend the day with Ruth and Sylvia arrived, we didn't hesitate to accept. The dash to the Thames from Paddinton was certainly worth the effort - lunch at the Savoy, no less, Sylvia's treat. Eirwen and I were no strangers to luxury but our rendezvous location took some beating, to say nothing of the fare on offer, especially now that we were responsible for our own catering.

I was still trying to improve upon and expand my culinary skills, but Eirwen viewed cooking as a waste of time and habitually served up baked beans, fish and chips, bacon and egg and the like.

With the meeting and greeting out of the way, Eirwen and I were keen to get into the restaurant. It had been an early start to the day and we were now famished. Then Eirwen's attention was suddenly focused on Sylvia.

"Where's your bag?" she asked, as though enquiring about something of importance rather than a fashion accessory.

"You're the first to discern how I have been diminished." Sylvia raised the neat but petite handbag over her arm.

"You'll never get your glass in there," Eirwen continued, despite Ruth's warning glare.

"My glass has been forcibly retired to a cupboard at Ruth's. Largely a symbolic gesture, I may add."

"You're on the wagon, then?"

"Unfortunately, yes. I hope not to require assistance to remain in situ, but you're at liberty to strike me if I do demur."

"Will do." Eirwen grinned as broadly as the rest of us.

***

The cluttered comfort of Ruth's home was a balm after our busy day. Much like its owner, there was a cosseting ease about the place. Once we were settled on the shawl- and cushion-strewn sofa and armchairs, Ruth said, "I'll make tea and toast for now. We'll have supper later," and she disappeared into the kitchen.

"I've never possessed Ruth's ability to both issue orders while also getting on with the necessary," Sylvia said ten minutes or so into the easy silence we'd been enjoying.

Neither of us responded. I for one was taking in the soothing sounds of Ruth's activity in the kitchen whereas Eirwen had fallen asleep on the sofa. Then Ruth reappeared with a tray of steaming mugs and toast.

"Let's adjourn to the kitchen. Sleeping Beauty evidently needs to rest," Sylvia said. She seemed thinner and more brittle of late but was now, thankfully, as on the button as ever.

We settled in the kitchen at the open gate-legged table, a much larger and more ornate version of the one at my parents' house that Eirwen and I used to hide beneath as children. My parents, however, would not have approved of the array of crystals dangling from the curtain pole nor of the joss stick puttering smoke signals from its spot on the window sill below.

"How is she?" Ruth didn't need to specify whom.

"Preoccupied. Always looking ahead to the next event," I said without a great deal of satisfaction.

"With the past too painful to contemplate, there's wisdom in such action," Sylvia said. I smiled at her gratefully. It took Sylvia to state the chuffing obvious.

When the soothing silence was shattered by a clatter from the hall-way followed by a sudden shriek, Ruth and I rushed into the living room.

"For God's sake, Jim," Eirwen exclaimed, rosy-cheeked and flus-tered on her eruption from sleep.

"I'm duty bound to wake a sleeping beauty." Jim stood as regally as his height and girth allowed, quite unapologetic.

"He licked my face." Eirwen grimaced and rubbed at her cheek with a tissue. "You must have heard I bat for the opposition," she added.

"Ah, but you've yet to tango with me." Jim wiggled his hips.

"Behave, you old goat," Eirwen said with a grin.

"I'll have you know I've turned many a head," he countered.

"Largely in disgust," Ruth chipped in as we returned to the kitchen, laughing.

"Terminally unruly," Sylvia commented, still seated at the table and pointing a pair of cigarette-bearing fingers at Jim as he entered the kitchen behind Eirwen.

"Guilty, as charged," Jim asserted unashamedly.

"Isn't it time you gave up the wicked weed, Sylvia? You evidently have the willpower to do so," Eirwen boldly commented.

"One travail at a time, darling." Sylvia returned her cigarette holder to her lips.

Later, we all mucked in and put together the best bacon, eggs and chips I've ever tasted. Even Sylvia rose to the occasion and buttered the bread. Baz turned up when we'd finished eating and promptly set about making his own bacon and egg sandwich.

"He's very domesticated," Sylvia said proudly.

"Just as well one of you is," Eirwen quipped.

"My capabilities are legendary," Sylvia replied, totally unruffled, at which Eirwen shook her head. "Take my ineffectuality," Sylvia contin-ued. "My pretension, my arrogance, not to mention my alcohol de-pendency."

"Stop that," said Jim. "Sounds like you're nailing yourself to the wall."

"Well put, old man," said Baz.

It was Jim's turn to shake his head.

"You're all of that and so much more, Sylvia," Ruth interjected. "You've a heart of gold, a will of steel and an intellectual wit that's solid platinum. You are, in fact, a legend."

At this we all hammered the table and cheered.

"I applaud your generosity," Sylvia said, while surreptitiously squeezing Ruth's hand.

***

"We'd best be off if you plan to get that train." Baz got to his feet and Eirwen and I erupted from the table like a pair of school kids at the last bell of term, hurriedly gathering belongings before making for the door.

"What about the mess we're leaving you?" I said to Ruth. Her kitchen resembled a bomb site.

"I'll assist in the clean-up operation," said Sylvia.

"Steady on, old girl," Baz said, as though Sylvia had volunteered for a suicide mission.

"No time for this nonsense," said Ruth, and she chivvied us out of the door.

Eirwen and I quickly got into the back of the car and waved enthusiastically to our friends on the doorstep until the Jaguar XJ6 gave a throaty purr and Baz geared up for Paddington.

Chapter 51

Three weeks later with Eirwen at work, I was busy planning for our trip to Ashbourne. We'd been invited to accompany "the old girls", as Eirwen had recently taken to calling Ruth and Sylvia (she'd cop it when they found out) to Derbyshire. We were to stay with an aristocratic relative of Sylvia's which, no doubt, would prove interesting in one way or another.

"Ooh, the Peak District," Eirwen had said during our last trip to London, when the proposed visit was raised.

"A ridiculous label," Sylvia had commented disdainfully. "The landscape is littered with hills and valleys, gorges and lakes, wild moorland and gritstone escarpments, but not a single peak."

Nevertheless, we were thrilled to have been included, irrespective of the area's misleading name.

"That theme park is near there." Eirwen was determined to visit Alton Towers. She'd been nagging me to do so since its opening at the beginning of the month. She was evidently still as enamoured with roller coasters, dodgems and the like as I was repulsed. My blood ran cold just contemplating what was merely a glorified fun fair. Then the doorbell rang.

"Hello," he said.

He might as well have been the Betterware salesman, such was my desire to slam the door in his face. I definitely did not want whatever he was pedalling.

"Any chance of me coming in?" Brendan asked hesitantly, clearly unsettled by my silent glower.

I can't do this, I thought, and walked away from the still-open door. A major Freudian slip, obviously, as he took up my unspoken invitation and followed me through to the kitchen.

We stood at opposite ends of the room. He, near the table, and me, anchored to the handle of the French doors as if about to exit my own home. He broke the awkward silence by pulling out the chair and sitting down at the table. I relaxed my grip on the door handle.

In the decade since I'd met the man quietly observing me, much had changed in my life, to say nothing of the wider world. The music business, however, remained as capricious and potentially destructive as it had ever been. And I loved that I was still a part of it without any help from my former lover.

Brendan gestured to the chair across the length of the table from him. Fleetingly, I toyed with the idea of telling him to clear off, but good manners got the better of me. Besides, I was curious as to why he was here.

I relinquished my hold on the door handle and sat down opposite him. I took time to arrange myself in an upright position on the chair, as though good posture would armour me against whatever he had to say. Then I slid my gaze to meet his and almost gasped at the intensity of his stare.

"You look well," he said, breaking the lengthy silence. I've never known how to respond to that particular remark, as much a criticism as a compliment, in my opinion.

"To what do I owe the honour?" I asked curtly.

He lowered his eyes and sighed.

"I had thought we could have a chat," he said irritably. I briefly considered throwing the fruit bowl at him.

"Ooh, like grown-ups. I'll start. How's your mother?"

It was gratifying to see him struggling with his annoyance.

"She's fine and often asks about you."

"She's a lovely lady. Please pass on my good wishes."

He nodded. "How are your parents?"

"They're fine and, despite my best efforts, continue to speak well of you." A jury would have noted his lowered gaze and fidgeting. "Denny's an ongoing worry, though," I continued. "Ruth and Sylvia say he's coping, but is he?"

"He is," he said more evenly, grateful that I'd stopped throwing daggers his way. "He just hopes Eirwen can be happy."

"We're all hoping for that."

He flashed me a sympathetic smile. And the rush returned. To smell him, taste him. Feel him.

He seemed to sense this and gathered himself together, avoiding my hungry stare.

"I know I've got a nerve just turning up, but there are a few things I need to speak to you about."

I wanted him to leave as much as I wanted him to stay. I should have told him to go… but I didn't.

Brendan then took out his wallet and removed a small clear plastic holder which he pushed down the table towards me.

The girl in the black-and-white photograph could have been me, as I was then, that night in August 1970. Could have been, but not quite. Her eyes were light, probably blue. Mine are brown. Her face was longer than mine. But in essence we were alike; we could have been sisters. Then I heard the hunger, the longing in his voice as it came winging down the years to whisper her name in my ear. *What was it?*

"Chrissie." I looked across at Brendan.

He nodded.

"The 'someone' I reminded you of," I said, my anger building again. I didn't need to know this. Not now. "Break your heart, did she? Shame." I flicked the holder down the table at him.

"She did more than that. She died."

"Oh, so I was just a stand-in for a ghost," I said heatedly, glad to see that he flinched.

"I know how this must seem. You looked like her and played like her. In the early morning light you could have been her."

"But I wasn't." The words weighed heavily on me.

"Believe me." He leaned forward and extended a hand down the table towards me, only to quickly withdraw. "From the moment you began your *Mabinogion* monologue, I was hooked. And the hungry look in your eyes was particularly hard to resist."

He grinned at the memory and I couldn't help but return his smile. Nevertheless…

"What has this to do with anything?"

Then he began the story that went further back than I'd imagined.

Chrissie and Brendan had attended different grammar schools but the same county school orchestra. She played the cello and he the piano. But, as I had just learnt, Chrissie also played the piano. With Brendan unable to read music, Chrissie helped him to learn the pieces selected for concerts. Tragically, aged sixteen, they both developed leukaemia. Brendan survived but Chrissie died just after her seventeenth birthday.

"I don't understand why you never told me any of this."

"I found it so hard after Chrissie died. In hospital they used my first name, William. So when I was well again, I saved up and changed my name by deed poll. I cut that part out of my life and buried it. It's why I was never tempted by drugs and drink and other excesses. I felt I owed Chrissie a good clean life."

"The hard drugs of your teens – they were part of your treatment."

"They don't come much harder," he said flippantly.

In an instant my anger and frustration dissipated, and my heart went out to the boy and girl I'd never known. For their hopes and dreams so cruelly cut short, for the lives forever marred. The events of those years explained so much about Brendan.

"You haven't guessed how this relates to you?" he asked.

I shook my head.

Suddenly, he looked his age. "The cancer treatment left me sterile. I couldn't give you the child you craved."

"But, Maureen…" I said, my words flailing about like a whip.

"I told you the boy wasn't mine."

"I'm sorry."

"Don't apologise. There's so much I should have told you."

"From what I've learnt about Maureen, I don't understand why you were with her at all."

"Maureen was everything Chrissie hadn't been, which suited me at the time. We were happy for a while. Then four years into our marriage, she was pregnant."

"You hadn't told her either?"

"No, but I was planning to. I'd talked to my mother about adopting."

"Pity you didn't talk to Maureen first," I said, almost feeling sorry for his wife.

"Maureen is a survivor. She doesn't need anyone's sympathy. She'd been having an affair with Marshall's father for some time. And there'd been others, apparently."

I was more perplexed than ever. "So why didn't you divorce her?"

"It was a way of paying for her silence, and of protecting myself from others like her."

My anger flared again.

"Did you think so little of me? Is that why you walked out on me?"

"You know that isn't so."

"Do I? That's how it seems to me."

He shook his head and gripped the table.

"I knew you'd never deceive me, nor leave me, no matter how much you wanted a child. I thought that if I finished with you, you were young enough to get over the split, meet someone new, and have the bairn you craved. All of that will happen when you're ready."

He searched my face for some sign of acknowledgement of this, but I considered myself just as likely to sprout wings and fly.

"Why are you telling me this now?"

"I should have explained from the start, but ultimately I can't regret the outcome of my actions."

I looked at him blankly, not wanting to contemplate what he meant.

"Can you not see all that you've become and achieved without me? And it's just the beginning. You never lost your fire, Mari." He smiled, an all-enveloping hug of a smile. A goodbye smile. Then he pushed away from the table and walked out towards the door.

Stunned, yet finally satisfied, I remained seated as he left, wanting to watch him go and fighting it. I had too much else to do. Eirwen would soon be home; there was food to cook and share. We had to prepare for our weekend away with Ruth and Sylvia. I had a life to live.

Glossary

ach â fi – an expression of distaste

Ar Lan y Môr – By the sea

bara brith – speckled bread

cariad – love

cwtch – cuddle

diolch yn fawr – thank you very much

iawn – very, alright

I Bob Un Sydd Ffyddlon - To All Who Are Faithful

mam-gu – grandmother (South Walian)

nain – grandmother (North Walian)

popeth yn iawn – everything's alright

rhagorol – excellent

tad-cu – grandfather (SW)

taid – grandfather (NW)

uffern dân – hellfire

wedi blino – tired

Y Mabinogi – The Mabinogion (a collection of Welsh folktales)

Author Profile

Julia Florrie is a retired teacher. She loves being outdoors, with gardening, walking, swimming and, until quite recently, skiing taking up much of her time. She also enjoys reading, cooking and music, and with a kitchen large to accommodate dancing she's able to enjoy the latter two simultaneously. As a keen needlewoman, she is currently upcycling rarely worn items so as to "make do and mend" as her mother and grandmother did before her. She also likes flower arranging, and has created bouquets and arrangements for three family weddings and floral tributes for two funerals.

Eight years ago she became a grandmother, an ongoing riot as far as she's concerned... they make her laugh so much! And of course she loves to write, and despite time running short, it's a hard habit to kick.

What Did You Think of Nicely Out of Tune?

A big thank you for purchasing this book. It means a lot that you chose this book specifically from such a wide range on offer. I do hope you enjoyed it.

Book reviews are incredibly important for an author. All feedback helps them improve their writing for future projects and for developing this edition. If you are able to spare a few minutes to post a review on Amazon, that would be much appreciated.

Publisher Information

Rowanvale Books provides publishing services to independent authors, writers and poets all over the globe. We deliver a personal, honest and efficient service that allows authors to see their work published, while remaining in control of the process and retaining their creativity. By making publishing services available to authors in a cost-effective and ethical way, we at Rowanvale Books hope to ensure that the local, national and international community benefits from a steady stream of good quality literature.

For more information about us, our authors or our publications, please get in touch.

www.rowanvalebooks.com
info@rowanvalebooks.com

www.ingramcontent.com/pod-product-compliance
Lightning Source LLC
Chambersburg PA
CBHW020942260626
47169CB00006B/1771